SHOPPING LIST 3

A HellBound Books Publishing LLC Book
Houston TX

HellBound Books Publishing

**A HellBound Books LLC
Publication**
Copyright © 2018 by HellBound Books Publishing LLC
All Rights Reserved

Cover and art design
by
HellBound Books Publishing LLC

www.hellboundbookspublishing.com

Printed in the United States of America

Foreword

You can have no idea, fellow aficionado of horror, slithering monsters, and all things dark and wonderful, just how thrilled I am to be writing the foreword to the third in this exemplary anthology series – yes, that's *third*, as in *three!*

Once again, we have brought to you within the covers of one big, fat volume, a whole wealth of the very best horror authors writing today – some seasoned, and some so brand new to the scene that they still have their literary umbilicus attached!

And, of course, each one of your authors has laid bare their soul in the form of their shopping list – be it their everyday provisions, or something altogether more sinister…as a species, we are never more opened up than when we are doing the hunter/gatherer thing – it's pretty much what we were designed for, after all.

Naturally, we at HellBound Books hope that you enjoy this terrifying collection on tales – of that much we are more than confident – but may we also wish upon you many a sleepless night as the nightmares that unfold amongst these very pages come back to haunt you, and set your imaginations alight with the horrors they impart.

Still, they *are* only stories, right? Flights of fancy, snippets of fevered imaginations laid out by our authors using no more than those well-worn, twenty-six letters of the English alphabet…

…or are they grim portents of what lurks out there in the dark, murky shadows, to which these twenty-one authors have some intimate, insider knowledge?

Sleep well, Dear Reader, and have the sweetest of dreams.

James H Longmore
HellBound Books Publishing, December 2018

HellBound Books Publishing

Contents

SHOPPING LIST 3

Richard Farren Barber's Shopping List

Carne asada
Key limes
Onions
Cilantro
Tortillas
Tomatillos
Avocados
Bottle of gin
Bread
Milk
Cheese
Coffee
Coffee creamer
Chips
Vegetable oil
Lunchmeat
Mustard

Black Light
Richard Farren Barber

It was a Wednesday, which meant the envelope was in the kitchen, fastened to the board with the familiar red push pin. Sometimes there was no message inside, just the fifty pound notes, but Sophie didn't have to reach the board to know that today the instructions were there: the giveaway was the collection of bottles and cleaning rags on the table.

"Must have been a big one," she muttered to herself. She placed her key on the worktop and stripped off her coat. She checked behind her, just to be certain she had closed the door, before starting across the kitchen.

The room was bigger than her flat; no exaggeration. In the middle was an island with a six-burner cooker and a chrome extraction hood that had to be a bugger to keep clean, but that was a problem for the other cleaner; Sophie could sweep through the kitchen without having to worry about the breadcrumbs or the splashes of grease on the hob.

She looked at the supplies first. Three bottles of industrial bleach, bin liners, cloths, and black rubber gloves that she pulled on after she put the money in her purse and reached out to pluck the note from under the push pin.

Sometimes Grant provided a list, but this time there were only two words on the piece of paper: Master Bathroom. His handwriting was small and precise, and Sophie held the paper in her hand and tried to imagine him standing there writing to her. She imagined his bright eyes and the droplets of sweat on his forehead. He would hold the pen tight between his fingers, in control—she knew this from the way each letter was perfectly formed. Maybe he would be breathing faster than usual. As he was writing he would be thinking of her; the rubber gloves warming her hands, reading what he had written.

She folded the note and placed it in the pocket of her jeans. She would take it home and add it to the others she had saved over the last seven months: this last note would make nine. Each note hidden behind an air brick at the bottom of her bedroom wall, where no one would ever find them.

Sophie scooped the bottles and the cleaning cloths into her arms and walked out of the kitchen and down the corridor to Grant's bathroom. The walls were decorated with paintings and although she was no expert, to her they looked to be originals. If they were, then they were even more valuable than the house; after her first visit she had spent a few hours with Google to discover that one was a Van Gogh valued at £3million. She couldn't imagine having £3million, let alone having enough money that you could spend £3million on a painting that sat in a corridor. She suspected the other paintings were equally valuable, but after researching the Van Gogh she had been struck by a sense that she shouldn't pry any further; Grant wouldn't like it.

The master bathroom was on the first floor of the house; up an ornate oak staircase that twisted above a marble foyer. The door to the bathroom was closed, just as Sophie had expected, and she had to empty the contents of her arms onto the floor before she could push it open.

Inside, the smell of fresh blood was almost overwhelming, but she remembered not to breathe for the first ten seconds.

She removed the black light from her pocket and placed it on the floor. Grant had bought it for her—a present wrapped in pink crepe paper and left on the counter beneath the message board a few months back. The light was for the end of her shift, to reveal any traces of blood that were otherwise invisible.

Before she stepped onto the white tiled floor she bent down and unlaced her trainers. She removed her shoes and then sat down and pulled off her socks and balled them together and stuffed them into the heel of one of her trainers. She pulled off her jeans and then her fleece and her T shirt and left her clothes in a small pile outside the door. The pile looked like she had melted away, leaving only her clothes as evidence that she had ever existed.

She walked into the bathroom. The cold of the tiles pressed flat against her naked feet and she drew in a shocked breath which dragged the stink deep into her lungs. She surveyed the work; cataloguing the scene like an expert, just as Grant had taught her.

To her right was the shower cubicle; easily large enough for two. The inside of the glass was smeared with blood and although the moisture had distorted the patterns, she could still make out a flurry of handprints; clear near the top but becoming more blurred and frenzied as they faded away, so that by the time they reached the bottom there was only a confused swirl of blood.

Sophie's professional eye swept across the rest of the bathroom. Even in the poor light she could see a trail of footprints between the shower and the large freestanding bath at the back. The footprints were mostly water, maybe a little sweat and urine as well, if there was any blood mixed in it was impossible to see with the naked eye, but she would clear it up anyway, just to be certain.

Inside the bath was a black bin liner, knotted at the top.

"You've had a busy night, Grant," she said, and then regretted speaking, because the flat echo of her voice caused the hairs on the back of her neck to rise.

She looked around the room to be sure she hadn't missed anything, and then started to haul in the bottles from the corridor. The shower would be the toughest job, so she started on that first, squirting cleanser onto the glass and wiping it down with a cloth. She opened one of the bin liners and dumped the first cloth into it almost immediately. Once the blood had dried it was a bugger to clean and from experience, she knew that after a minute or two she was simply pushing the blood around. She picked up a second cloth and that soon joined the first in the bag.

The glass walls of the cubicle trapped the sound of her own breathing and reflected it back to her. She tried to ignore the sound, but when that wasn't possible, she started to hum a song under her breath to drown it out.

She hated the shower. Once she had almost suggested to Grant that he lay off it for a while, but she didn't have the courage to say anything because he would only point out that she was getting paid to do a job—well paid—and that was all that should concern her. Although Sophie would never claim to understand Grant, she suspected that if she had suggested avoiding the shower he might use it more regularly just to prove who was in charge.

Maybe she was wrong, though. Maybe he was more considerate than that. Maybe if she told him how much she hated cleaning the shower he might alter his behaviour. The last one had been in the cellar; all grey sand and old bricks, and although she hadn't liked being down in the bowels of the earth with the meagre light from a 40 watt bulb, she had preferred that to the bathroom with its slick tiled surfaces and blood splatter.

She was sweating after only ten minutes of work. When she stood up to take a rest, her knees were mottled from the shower floor and her skin blushed red. She picked her bra away from her skin but when she let it go it clung just as tightly to her chest.

She looked across to the black bag in the bath and tried not to estimate how heavy it would be. The thought came once again: Whoever had been in the bathroom with Grant the previous night had been big.

But of course, he wasn't really called Grant, was he? That was how he had introduced himself to her, and when they had met, Sophie had shaken his soft hand and enquired: "Is that your first name or your last?" only for him to smile at her. So he was Grant—one name, like Rhianna or Madonna—except Sophie had found a letter addressed to David Hansen when she had been cleaning the bedroom one Wednesday and had bundled all the bloody sheets into a collection of bin liners ready to burn them.

So David was Grant. Or Grant was David. Sophie didn't know, and she understood well enough that she wasn't supposed to know. She had burned the letter and then taken the ash and crushed that into a black, sooty pulp. Even then she had been worried she had not done enough to hide the evidence that she had learned his name.

She bent back down to the inside of the shower stall and wiped the sweat from her brow. A few minutes later she threw another bloody rag into the open mouth of the bin liner.

When she had first started the job, she had tried counting backwards from a thousand to distract herself. It worked up to a point, but occasionally she would lose track and come awake and realise that she was crouching in her underwear wiping someone's blood and skin off a glass wall or a decorative tile. In some ways that sudden awareness was harder to cope with than the constant knowledge that someone had been standing in the room just a few hours earlier; standing and screaming and pleading for mercy that was never going to come.

Sophie checked over her shoulder to the open door. She could only see a small slice of the corridor that showed the cream carpet and magnolia walls and three of the oak banister rails.

Nothing there, and yet she felt there had been. Almost a sixth sense. As if just before she had turned around someone had been standing in the hallway, watching her while she worked.

She shuddered and sat for a moment with her red-raw hands pressed against her thighs.

"Grant?" she called. Her voice echoed within the shower. The house was silent. She strained to hear, but the only sounds were her own breathing and the swish of the air conditioning unit in the far corner of the bathroom.

She paused for a moment longer before returning to her work. Sometimes the house gave her the creeps. It was the stillness of the place, as if it was a show house. She couldn't imagine Grant relaxing on the white leather settee as he watched the cinema-screen television. She couldn't imagine him lost in the huge kitchen, seated at the breakfast counter and drinking coffee while he read the newspapers. It was his house, and yet she didn't think he actually lived there. All she could imagine, because it was the only evidence she ever saw in the place, was people dying.

She shuddered again and then, because she could actually see all the small hairs on her forearm raised up, she started to sing softly. "Inchworm, inchworm, measuring the marigolds..." Something she remembered from primary school when it had been end of term and none of the teachers wanted to do anything except watch television.

She dumped another cloth into the bin liner and had to open the next pack before she could continue. In the silence between each breath she was sure she heard movement elsewhere in the house. She froze, the packet of cleaning cloths held between her hands.

"Grant? Mr Grant? Are you there?"

The air conditioning unit thumped, as if it had finally managed to eject a huge blockage, and Sophie screamed. Just a slight sound; an escape that she stopped as soon as it passed her lips, but it was still there.

The scream echoed inside the bathroom and then faded away. She imagined her scream trapped with the many others in the room and shuddered.

Sophie put down the pack of cloths and reached out to haul herself to her feet. The metal edge of the shower stall cut into her palm and drew a red line across the skin. The glass still held a pale tint to it and the puddles of water collected in the plastic tray underneath her were definitely pink.

The room was darker than she remembered. There were shadows in the far corner that had not been there before.

From the hallway came the very deliberate sound of creaking wood. As if someone had shifted their weight and the floorboards had groaned in response.

She paused, dismissed it as her imagination. The sound repeated.

"I did everything you asked, Mr Grant," she said. She was sure that he would hear the waver in her voice and know that she was afraid, and Sophie cursed herself for revealing such weakness.

"I never told anyone."

She pressed her lips together, waiting for his response. She inspected the thin sliver of hallway, expecting to see him ease into view.

He knows, she thought. *He knows about David Hansen. He knows that I know.*

She lifted herself, like an athlete rising on the starting blocks. She straightened her back and took a baby step away from the shower. She swept her eyes around the room. At the back, beyond the freestanding bath, was a large window. She tried to remember what was outside and considered crashing through the glass onto the flat roof of the garage as she fled. Not that it would do any good. Grant would follow her. He could not permit her to live.

She had to convince him to trust her.

She took a step toward the door and reached out. She realised she was holding her breath and as her fingers touched the hard wood she flinched as if it burned. Across the hallway she could see the crystal chandelier that hung over the entrance foyer. She could see the carpet and the banister and the edge of the wall of the room opposite. There was no one in sight.

Sophie stepped into the hallway. Her heart raced. Her breathing came in short rasps. Sunlight flooded into the foyer, sharp as glass.

The pile of her clothes was undisturbed. She considered pausing to get dressed but imagined the moment of blindness as she pulled her top over her head or stood on one leg to pull on her trousers; she couldn't afford to be that vulnerable.

Her first step into the corridor elicited a noise when her foot pressed down on a loose floorboard. The creak was the same sound she had heard when she had been inside the bathroom. This was where he had been; close enough to peer through the door. She imagined him standing there, listening to her breathing, listening to the hiss as she sprayed cleanser over the glass and then the almost silent sound of the cloth as she cleaned away the blood.

It wasn't worth it, she understood that now. Too late, but she understood it. She'd thought she'd lucked onto something special with this job; one day a week for more money she could earn the other four days. All she had to do was clean and keep her mouth closed. And she'd done that; for seven months she'd done exactly that.

She realised she was still holding the cloth and laughed. That would be a great weapon. When Grant came for her she would be able to swat him away with a blue J cloth and a spray of Mr Muscle.

She looked both ways along the corridor and wondered where he was hiding. Was he standing behind the door of one of the bedrooms with a knife clutched in his fist? She looked down, past her grubby toes. The carpet was cream. "You don't want to do this, Grant," she called out. "My blood would ruin the carpet, and who would you find to clean up after you?"

She waited for his reply, holding her breath and standing on the balls of her feet.

"I did everything you asked, didn't I?" She was conscious of the sound of her voice. He needed to hear her as an equal, a partner in crime. Not a servant who could be dismissed.

"Grant?"

There was no answer. Sophie wondered whether she was imagining all of this. Maybe the house was empty, and David Hansen was sitting in his office on the other side of the city, oblivious to what was happening.

Maybe she had allowed herself to get spooked. Perhaps the sounds she had heard were simply the house settling.

And maybe all the blood I clean up each week comes from a shaving cut, Sophie thought to herself.

She took a step forward and peered over the banister. Downstairs the coloured glass in the door sketched patterns of light on the marble floor. The door itself was locked. She tried to visualise her escape route: down the grand staircase and along the corridor. Past the Van Gogh and out through the kitchen. Her car was parked on a circle of gravel to the side of the house. She imagined slamming the door behind her and punching down the lock before she stabbed her key into the ignition; and all the while Grant would be chasing her.

From downstairs she heard the plink of water dripping from the tap into the ceramic basin. Pipes gurgled. The air conditioner thumped; as if someone was trapped inside, battering the sheet metal sides to be let out.

Sophie took one step toward the head of the staircase and gently shifted her weight between her feet, expecting the floorboard beneath her to groan in betrayal once again. She held her arms outstretched like a high-wire act, the blue cloth fluttering from her fingers at the edge of her vision.

"Focus," she whispered to herself. She cast a quick look over her shoulder at the empty corridor and then stared at the top of the stairs hard enough for her eyes to ache with the effort. Each breath she took was a short, harsh rasp.

The noise came from behind her. Soft and yet clear so there was no chance she could mistake hearing it. A rustling sound.

The bathroom?

Sophie hesitated. Could Grant have tricked her? Could he have slipped into the bathroom behind her? It seemed impossible and yet as she stood, stranded, in the middle of the hall, she heard the noise again and there was no mistaking where it came from.

She took a step back toward the bathroom and glanced inside, twitching to keep sight of the top of the stairs and all the closed doors that ran along each side of the corridor. It was impossible to watch everywhere at the same time and her nerves spiked at each sound.

She stood in the doorway. The bathroom was as she had left it: smeared bloodstains on the glass of the shower cubicle where she had not yet finished cleaning.

The selection of cleaning cloths and bottles of bleach huddled together on the floor. The long walk across the tiles, past the toilet and the hand basin, to the freestanding bath with the knotted bin-liner.

She cast around for a weapon; anything more effective than the cloth she was holding. On the side of the sink was a toothbrush and toothpaste in a glass beaker. There was a razor which Sophie considered and then dismissed unless she thought she was going to shave Grant to death. There was a glass with a shallow measure of liquid in the bottom, which Sophie assumed to be the remains of an ice cube from Grant's drink the previous night. There were no knives, no guns, nothing that immediately screamed at her that it could be used as a weapon. She stepped into the room, swooped down to snatch up a bottle of bleach and struggled to open the child-proof cap of the container.

The sound repeated: a plastic rustling coming from the direction of the window.

Sophie pressed the heel of her hand down on the cap of the bottle and felt it click. She unscrewed it and the stink of bleach bloomed through the room, pricking at her eyes.

She walked the length of the bathroom. She had crossed a Rubicon, and she was able to pinpoint exactly when. It was the moment when she had picked up the bottle of bleach: when she had armed herself against Grant. Up to that point she might have been able to argue with him, but after that she couldn't feign ignorance.

The rustling sound came from the black bin liner.

"It's alive," Sophie whispered.

"Yes."

Grant's voice sounded close. Sophie screamed and then whirled on her heels. The scent of bleach grew sharp and she heard liquid splash over the tiles.

He stood in the doorway. He wore a grey suit, red tie. He appeared just as she remembered from the time when they had met seven months earlier and she had accepted the job. There was a flash of sunlight down by his side as the sun reflected against the knife he carried.

Behind her, in the bath, the bag rustled again.

"A present," Grant said. "For you."

Sophie assumed that her look of surprise was almost comical. *For me?*

"I haven't told anyone, I swear," she said.

"I know. This is your reward."

He did not move from the doorway and Sophie tried to judge what would happen if she threw the bleach at him and ran. She would fail, of course. The bleach would fly harmlessly away, and Grant would catch her in a couple of strides.

"Why?" she asked.

Grant shrugged. "The opportunity presented itself to me and I took advantage. He was tougher than I had anticipated. The blood…" he said and motioned his hand in the direction of the shower stall. "But then, you know about the blood. You know all about the blood."

"But why me? Why now?"

"You said it yourself: you haven't told anyone."

Sophie watched him closely. Maybe he was telling the truth; there probably was no one he could trust with his secret. *Our secret,* she thought.

She was aware of the differences between them: anyone looking in would find a skinny woman with grey, baggy underwear an unusual partner for the man with his clipped fingernails and plucked eyebrows. They could never be equals, the idea was absurd. But partners...

He stepped closer, still beyond arm's reach. She was conscious of the knife he held by his side and the bottle of bleach that weighed heavy in her hand. Another inequality. She wondered how he would react if she asked him to lay down his weapon.

Behind her, the body in the bag rustled.

"He won't last much longer," he said.

Sophie turned her back on Grant. Even so, she could feel his presence in the room. He moved silently and she only knew for certain that he was behind her when his fingertips touched her bare arm. The hairs on her arm reacted immediately, rising in response. Once more her breath came in short, sharp, blasts. She didn't turn toward him, it was the only power she could wield and she sensed that it was effective.

She placed the bottle of bleach on the edge of the bath and used both hands to untie the neck of the bag. Close to her ear, she heard Grant's ragged breathing. She felt his warm breath on the nape of her neck.

"Quickly," he whispered.

When she pulled open the bag the stink of blood rose up. She heard Grant draw in a deep breath, sucking the scent down into his lungs.

The flat edge of the blade pressed hard against her naked thigh.

The thing inside the bag could not be called a person. Sophie chose not to look at the mass of blood and muscle and organs only loosely held together. She closed her eyes for a second, but in the dark there was no escape. Her mind churned up images of the bloody shower stall and arterial arcs of dull rust sprayed onto the crumbling bricks of the cellar. She already understood who she was.

She turned and snatched the bottle of bleach. Threw the liquid into Grant's face.

He screamed, and underneath the high-pitched sound of his pain she heard the metallic clink when the knife fell from his grip as he brought his hands up to his eyes.

She pressed her hands into the middle of his chest and pushed him back. He stuttered and fell, and his keening took on a different tone; shifted from pain to rage. And maybe just a hint of fear. But not terror. Not yet.

Sophie hesitated for a moment as he writhed on the tiled floor of the bathroom. His hand spasmed against the floor in search of the knife and so she picked it up. The handle was still warm from his palm. The blade, when she tested it against her tongue, cool.

She smiled, and then leant over to make the first cut. It would be messy, her first time, she did not have the finesse of an expert such as Grant. But she would learn.

Mark Thomas's Shopping List

-light gauge bluegrass banjo strings
-case of Crest Super Lager
-one spray of cut flowers (peonies)
-10 Kilogram bag of Quicklime
-shovel
-new shoes

A Boy and His Turtle
Mark Thomas

In his human existence, Luc had been a celebrated artisan, famous for creating the elaborate wood-block templates used to illustrate the gigantic bibles in Castle Bruniquel. Luc had developed his own technique of removing material from slabs of Ironwood with sturdy tapered needles, so that the bold outlines of his printed images were shaded with a delicacy that could not be duplicated until the invention of copper plate etching.

But, as it so often happens, Luc's talent was both a blessing and a curse.

Luc met his beautiful wife when the inquisitor Berneil, who was charged with distributing funds for the Bruniquel Bible project, inspected the local paper-maker's shop. Luc happened to be there at the time, in the throes of experimentation, pressing elaborate mulberry-stained "A"s, embraced by God's amphibious creatures—salamanders, frogs and turtles—onto the sun-bleached sheets. Berneil's young sister, Catherine, had accompanied the theocrat and she gasped with pleasure upon seeing Luc's beautiful designs.

Luc's marriage to Catherine was reluctantly approved by the inquisitor because of the devotional importance of the printing project. Association with the Bruniquel Bible elevated the woodcarver's status just enough to make the union palatable.

Unfortunately, Luc's part of the project was completed after three years, his salary was discontinued and the beautiful collection of seventy-one Ironwood blocks was seized in the name of God by his brother-in-law, Berneil.

Luc no longer felt welcome within the monstrous vaulted cathedral attached to castle Bruniquel and started to attend mass in a little chapel closer to his home.

Luc desperately needed another printing commission, not because of immediate financial need, but to prop up his fragile self-worth, to convince himself that his beautiful young wife wasn't experiencing misgivings about their marriage.

Luc was habitually parsimonious, even going so far as to catch Chub in the little stream that flowed behind the house for his lunches, baking his own bread, and bartering a set of carved finials with a neighbouring farmer for a steady supply of frangible fall cheeses. But the church had been parsimonious as well, and the residue from his wages wouldn't last indefinitely.

Ideally, any new commission should be religious in nature because Catherine was astonishingly pious, but each passing day rendered Luc more pliable in his imaginary negotiations with future employers.

As luck would have it, after one particularly angry and puzzling Sunday sermon, Luc was introduced to a wealthy new parishioner, one of the first silk merchants to inhabit Southern France and someone who needed a printer. The man, Laparesse, wondered if Luc would consider carving another series of his famous Ironwood blocks, to press designs onto bolts of plain, ashy woven silk.

Luc was excited at the prospect of starting another extended commission, but he was wary as well. Something about the merchant's manner, his smile that wasn't really a smile, made Luc defensive and he avoided discussing any particulars of the proposal in front of Catherine. When Luc met Laparesse the following day at his loomery, the merchant offered a fantastic sum of money, triple what Luc had received to illuminate the Bruniquel Bibles, to decorate the hems of a dozen silk robes with naked female figures.

Luc nervously accepted the job.

It would be imperative to discourage Catherine from overseeing this project. She had become used to supervising his efforts, along with her brother, when Luc was employed in God's work, but it would be dangerous for her to witness an endeavor that nibbled at the edges of sin. Luc explained to his young wife that he was merely printing invisible "mordants" onto the cloth, chemicals that inhibited the absorption of dyes, so there were no positive images that could be immediately seen and appreciated. He hinted that the drawings themselves were merely repeating geometric patterns and also pointed out that urine and other unpleasant fixatives would be sloshed around during the dyeing process.

Catherine happily declared her intentions of staying away from the primitive factory.

So far, so good.

But Luc's fortune quickly unraveled in three distinct stages. First of all, the artisan was severely limited in his knowledge of the unclothed female form, so the naked figures he carved into his first few experimental blocks bore a striking resemblance to his beautiful young wife.

Secondly, when Luc started attending religious services at the small chapel near his home, he had unwittingly joined a heretical sect known as the Cathars. How could he know? All church masses were recited in Latin, and Luc never understood more than a tiny fraction of the words uttered by the priests. When Luc talked to other parishioners about ideas like the transmigration of souls or the efficacy of deathbed repentances, he had no idea that they were radical departures from established heterodoxy. Luc simply assumed that every mass in the county had received the blessing of his brother-in-law, the inquisitor. After all, why would Berneil allow the services to take place, why he would allow his young sister to attend them if they threatened the eternal safety of her soul?

And thirdly, in early September, 1243 C.E., the silk merchant Laparesse showed Berneil one of the silk robes Luc had successfully decorated. The gesture was a calculated insult, because Laparesse's wealth insulated him from the inquisitor's power as a moral arbiter. Berneil was outwardly calm in his approbation, but roiled within, partly because his impotence was being openly mocked but mostly because he had immediately recognized his young sister's naked form.

So, in mid-September, 1243 C.E., Luc Bucheron, celebrated illustrator of the Bruniquel Bibles, was enthusiastically drowned by his brother-in-law in a marshy creek near the river Tarn, a mile or two from the wood carver's home. The Inquisitor must have struck Luc from behind, or he wouldn't have been able to overpower the strong young artisan in that humiliating way. And the outcome was far from certain, despite Berneil's cowardly assault. The initial blow severely injured Luc, but he still managed to thrash bravely for several minutes while Berneil's soft fingers slipped and fumbled at his throat.

Just before he lost consciousness, Luc burbled a curse and his personal essence, his very *soul* transmigrated into the body of the nearest spiritually empty container, a Common Spanish Pond Turtle.

Luc had spent that fateful morning angling for Chub, the fat little fish that constituted the major part of his summer diet. At least that was one vestigial memory. In reality, he may have crawled into the reeds in an effort to hide from the inquisitor and his army of religious thugs. It wasn't long before specific details relating to his own murder and subsequent reincarnation faded both in color and importance.

Occasionally, Turtle-Luc tried to re-construct the series of events leading inevitably to his death, but he suspected that his memories were subtle modifications of reality, like his elaborate wooden blocks tended to be variations on a single theme. Luc was positive that there had been a distinct cooling in his relations with the inquisitor almost immediately after he started to work on the silk printing project. And the woodcarver had also been warned by several fellow parishioners *not* to discuss certain theological subjects with his powerful relation. But Luc didn't see the intersection of those two dangers and foolishly believed that Catherine would shield him from her brother's disapproval.

Luc never imagined that the last thing he would see as a human was Berneil's face, purple with rage, eyes bulging, spittle flying from mouth, upper lip curled to expose a ribbon of black gum tissue above yellowing incisors.

Ironically, one of Luc's unorthodox beliefs about the "soul" had been proven true at the moment of his death, when his personal essence slipped out of one physical container and into another. The portable nature of the soul had always seemed like a valid proposition to Luc. It was accepted that the soul vacated the body upon death, so it also seemed natural that the essence would miss being housed in a living vessel and would actively seek a new biological home rather than immediately ascend through the sterile atmosphere to heaven.

And Luc was right! *Quod Erat Demonstrandum.* The theory became truth when his own ineffable being seeped through his nostrils and immediately entered the nares of the first soulless creature it encountered: the little Spanish Pond Turtle.

Luc should have been revered as a saint, or a second Socrates, but that blockhead Berneil was so insanely focused on crushing the woodcarver's trachea that he couldn't see the proof floating at his elbow.

Luc's new turtle body bobbed up and down on a series of angry ripples and he had the surreal experience of watching the inquisitor, apoplectic with rage, throttle an oddly familiar corpse. When Berneil was finally sated he stood upright and breathed heavily. Then his boots sucked at the creek mud as he laboriously turned his body and trudged towards the bank. Berneil didn't even drag the empty cadaver onto shore for a proper burial; he left it tangled in the long, rope-like tendrils of the pond lilies.

In the distance, Castle Bruniquel's bell-tower filled the air with sonorous hammer blows.

Turtle-Luc twisted his tiny head to watch the Inquisitor squelch back toward the village, then he swam clumsily above his former body. The swollen, distended tongue didn't look as if it would fit back in the mouth opening even if an effort were made to retrieve it. The corpse-eyes were wide open yet sadly empty, like un-shuttered windows in a deserted house. Luc paddled away, relying solely on his forelegs to generate the motion. He was unable to manipulate the nictitating membranes blurring his vision or control the mix of air and water that flooded his throat. Finally, he exhaled and sank to the creek bottom, ready to drown a second time, eager to let the river silt entomb his new body.

But Luc didn't immediately die, as he thought he must. The natural impulses of his new turtle-being functioned more or less automatically, and a fleshy gland in his throat started to process oxygen from the dark water. A few hours later Luc found himself snapping at small minnows and aquatic worms that floated past his jaws.

Had Luc been able to understand the controversial sermons delivered in his little chapel, he would have better understood the principle of reincarnation; that, ideally, it rewards a life well-spent by allowing a transmigrated soul to move through a series of increasingly exalted creatures towards a blissful reunion with God. Unfortunately, the bitterness of Luc's departure seemed to trap him in a depressing cycle of Pond Turtle to Pond Turtle lateral shifts. It took almost six centuries of digging muddy burrows and desultory mating rituals for Luc to experience his only incremental change: his soul transmigrated into the body of an

Alligator Snapping Turtle hatchling, just as Luc was being eviscerated by the enormous parent.

Luc couldn't know it, but this reincarnation was the bizarre end result of a famous local murder case. The giant Alligator Snapping Turtle that mutilated Luc had been transported to France from the Spanish colony of Louisiana to be part of a ridiculous private zoo. A Tiger, three Wolves and a Mountain Gorilla had also been shipped to the estate, but they were sick and docile in their cages. The Alligator Snapping Turtle, which had been placed in an unfenced decorative pond, was extremely active. In fact, it chased a small child down a cinder path then dragged her into the water and stuffed her body beneath a water-logged Chestnut trunk.

The killer-turtle possessed a devious species of intelligence and quickly sensed the human outrage its (very reasonable) action had spawned. So, the animal dug underneath a distant perimeter fence to escape the compound, and waddled down an overflow ditch, with several baby turtles clinging to the moss on its shell spikes, until it reached Luke's creek, near the Tarn. The sociopathic turtle managed to annihilate Luc and several dozen other animals in that estuary before it was hunted down and killed by a mob of angry villagers.

Luc would have found the story interesting, because his soul remained sensitive to violence in the human world and he could still decipher scraps of bank side conversation. But the shock associated with his latest transformation left Luc unable to fully appreciate the enormity of events. He was only peripherally aware that the massive killer-turtle had been dragged onto shore with grappling hooks and its appendages cut off with shovels. Luc let his new unfamiliar body drift a few meters away from the creek mouth into the Tarn itself.

There, he was immediately sucked into the bilge hold of a wooden steamer named the *Eugenie*. That ship sailed slowly down the Tarn picking up several thousand pounds of moveable-type printing press letters from local artisans and expelling a comparable amount of ballast water with each load. Luc used his new sharp little claws to resist each pumping surge. He hunkered down in a corner of the hold and braced himself against the raised edges of some swollen planks. Eventually, he decided that the violent pumping had stopped for good and he relaxed and ate an eel's face. Luc had spent so many centuries confined to his creek mouth that any degree of change terrified him. He decided to make this bilge hold his new permanent home.

Luc shut down most of his sensory mechanisms and went into a turgid hibernation filled with terrible dreams.

But even that three-month period of stability was destined to end. Luc and the load of moveable type pieces were transported from the Tarn to the Garonne, through the port city of Bordeaux then across the Atlantic Ocean. Finally, the *Eugenie* made a slow transit down the St. Lawrence River and through the narrow wooden locks of the first Welland Canal.

The exhausted snapping turtle was sluiced from the *Eugenie*, along with a few gallons of filthy water and the rancid remains of several lampreys, as the ship dropped anchor behind the luxurious walls of the Springbank Hotel. Luc, stunned from the rigours of his journey, floated downstream like a piece of sodden ship's timber and wondered why he hadn't died.

A century and a half later, Luc still hadn't died.

In fact, he revived, and thrived, patrolling a quarter-mile stretch of water, eating ducklings, rats, muskrat, mink, Perch, baby beaver and crayfish. At first, survival had seemed tenuous, but Luc met and gutted challenges so frequently that he began to wonder if he were immortal. During that first spring in his new environment, Luc had encountered three large, insanely territorial snapping turtles who had waddled onto shore to lay their eggs. Luc had been sunning himself on a packed dirt path and the three giant females blocked his escape back into the water.

Without thinking, Luc stood up on his hind legs and strode like a malformed human toward his enemies. Luc grasped the edge of the nearest shell with his front claws, lifted sharply, and the turtle was flipped over onto its domed carapace. While the animal was helplessly lolling there Luc plopped down on all fours and buried his beak into the upper thigh of a hind leg. Luc clamped his powerful jaws as the animal emitted breathy screams of pain. Luc had to release his victim because the other two turtles made flanking moves to attack. But Luc immediately rose to his hind legs again and maneuvered artfully around each dangerous head and flipped these turtles onto their backs as well.

Now, Luc was able to latch onto his enemies' hind legs with his powerful jaws and squeeze and pull and shake until the appendages were disarticulated.

Missing their hind legs and dribbling gouts of bright red blood, the turtles succumbed to the shock of their injuries and let their large heads meekly fall backwards, on the dirt path. Luc plunged his beak into each vulnerable throat in turn and slashed and chewed and tore until the heads were completely separated from the bodies.

Other turtles eventually sensed a power vacuum and tried to sidle into Luc's territory, but he repelled each sortie with extraordinary violence. And all the while, Luc grew larger. Soon, river creatures actively avoided him, and Luc had no enemies in the animal world.

Strangely enough, Luc had lost all interest in mating when his distressed body had been dumped from the *Eugenie's* hold. Luc patiently waited for the desire to return, but it never did, and he settled into a simple routine of hibernation and engorgement. His distended body squeezed out of the openings of his carapace in a grotesque way, but he continued to be agile on land and in water and generally felt in good health.

Had anyone been able to capture Luc and measure him they would have found his shell to be forty-two inches from head to tail. In area, it was twice the size of an industrial garbage can lid. Luc's mass was an astonishing two hundred and eleven pounds.

A handful of other snapping turtles throughout history had achieved slightly larger sizes, but none of them contained the tortured soul of an Albigensian woodcarver.

Luc was sometimes subject to bouts of depression and paranoia, no doubt related to his previous existence as a human. For a brief period of time he had taken to sunning himself openly on fallen logs near the bank. But as he became more monumental in size, the canal workers seemed to take an unnatural interest in him, pointing and jabbering excitedly as their barges were drawn by. Luc suspected those people were plotting to kill and eat him, so he gave up that pleasure and spent most of his existence buried in black mud or floating underneath a thick screen of duckweed, even during the times when the canal paths appeared to be deserted.

***

Given sufficient time, the world can change in astounding ways. In a couple of million years, for example, a mouse can evolve into a bat or a lower primate can morph into something that is easily confused with a human. Of course, some changes occur much more quickly. It took just a little over a century for Luc's new canal home to become obsolete. Ships like the *Eugenie* were too small to be economically viable and larger vessels were diverted to wider cut channels with massive stone locks. For several decades, Luc's section of the river was largely abandoned.

But that quiet era was inevitably succeeded by a period of change. A series of local governments decided to convert Luc's territory from an inner-city wasteland to a ragged park with a network of fitness trails.

Strangely enough, Luc appreciated those latest intrusions into his world, particularly the beautiful Stewartia trees that were planted on the margins of the canal and several small containment ponds. Piles of toxic marine detritus were lifted out of the water by a barge crane and suddenly the water was filled with silver clouds of baitfish. The packed dirt path where donkeys and men had once labored to tow coal barges had been replaced by a broad, soft, cinder path that retained the sun's heat in a delightful way.

Inspired by these changes to his home, Turtle-Luc decided to improve himself as well.

It took Luc less than twenty years of diligent observation and practice to re-learn how to speak. That achievement would have been simply impossible in any of his previous iterations as a Spanish Pond Turtle. But his Snapping Turtle form gave him a massive, flexible mucous membrane in his mandible that could be curled into fantastic shapes. Combined with a large tongue and other fleshy appendages, he could form a sound chamber within his powerful jaws and expel bursts of air that were whistling approximations of human words. He often crouched in one of the shallow overflow ponds right next to the jogging trail, and held his giant jaws stiffly open, rolled his enormous tongue, and mimicked the noises made by people walking or jogging along the sluiceway.

Occasionally, he thought he recognized faces from his distant past, when he was a human in Bruniquel. Once in particular, he thought he heard the voice of his beautiful young wife Catharine and his eye membranes clouded ominously.

Mostly, people just passed Luc by, completely unaware that he was intently studying their vocal mannerisms. But one day, a human visitor to the park was engaged in an irrational argument with himself. The man had halting speech rhythms to begin with, and he also had to allow space for an imaginary companion to intercede. But one of these conversational pauses was filled with the hissing echoes of words that had just been uttered. The man stopped walking and slowly spun in a circle to locate the phantasm that was mocking him. Eventually his eyes lowered, and he noticed Luc's shovel-sized head and piercing red eyes floating in an island of blackened leaves just a few inches from the margins of the trail. Luckily, that human, the only being to notice and appreciate Luc's unusual talent, was a homeless gentleman nicknamed "Toothless Jimmy" who was both lonely and theatrically mad. No one would have believed his story about a talking turtle, and anyway, he was far more interested in initiating a conversation with the monstrous Chelonian than lobbying to have him killed.

Initially, Luc was inclined to hate the strange-smelling human and he had fantasies of latching onto the man's skinny ankles and ripping his feet from their spindly appendages. But Jimmy's guileless persistence won Luc over, and they regularly met on that stretch of the jogging trail to converse. It would be difficult to characterize their interaction as "friendship" because both parties were extremely self-centred, but it contained the unfertilized egg of that relationship.

Two or three times a week after that first awkward meeting, from mid-March to late October, man and turtle would sit on a low-slung branch of a Stewartia tree and talk about the things that were important to them. Jimmy would complain about the high cost of *Ensure* meal replacements and the condescending tone of the nurses in the emergency ward of the local hospital. Luc would confide that he had a festering hatred for humans and that he sometimes longed to lurch out of the overflow pond and attack joggers on the fitness trail. Jimmy mentioned that if he collected aluminum beer cans for ten hours on recycling day he could earn as much as thirty-seven dollars and sleep at the Springbank shelter rather than the emergency hostel. Luc groaned that eight hundred years of imprisonment within his carapace had created a festering sense of grievance, a self-righteous violence that could only barely be contained. Jimmy explained that he once tried to hoard his Methadone, but doctors had found him out and cut him from the program. Luc mentioned that the only thing restraining him from going on a killing spree was worry that if he ever *did* give in to his dark urges, the act might be witnessed and then he would be pried out of the muck and strangled by angry villagers.

The two companions tended to talk at cross purposes because neither had any extended practice at being empathetic. But one day, Jimmy seemed to suddenly realize that he was sharing a branch with an exceptionally dangerous creature. The scrawny human looked over his shoulder at the darkening trail at their backs, then shifted his eyes forward to see the empty faltering trail in front of them and felt precariously alone.

Jimmy needn't have worried. Luc had stopped considering him potential prey ten days after their first meeting, but the only facial expressions a snapping turtle can muster are various degrees of malevolence, so the shift in attitude wouldn't have been apparent even if Jimmy had possessed the social skill to decode it.

"Maybe you're looking at things the wrong way," Jimmy suggested, nervously. "Maybe you need to hunt at night when you're less likely to be seen." He wanted the giant turtle to move his thoughts away from the here and now.

"No one uses the trail at night," Luc clicked and whistled.

Jimmy jerked his head away from the canal and the fitness trail to a little-used road that ran alongside the park for a short distance then snaked up the valley. "Well, how about this. That road leads somewhere," the human said. "There will be secluded, shady places where you can lie in wait." He struggled to look at it from the turtle's perspective. "A little reconnaissance should let you select a place with the proper mix of foot traffic and solitude."

Luc became immediately anxious. He associated any form of travel with pain and constriction. The thought of wandering even a few meters away from his own established territory made the membranes in his throat constrict. "I don't think I could do it," he sadly admitted.

"I'll help you," Jimmy said, eager to curry favour. He got off the branch and extended a hand to the turtle. The Stewartia barely shivered when the human's weight was removed.

Luc hopped off the limb as well, and this time the wood creaked and flexed upward a couple of inches.

Luc placed his clawed forefoot in Jimmy's hand. The turtle walked comfortably upright on his powerful hind legs, swinging his pelvis from side to side and sweeping the ground with his serrated tail.

"Your skin is surprisingly soft," Jimmy said and rubbed the loose, leathery material back and forth over the hard bumps hidden in the palm structure.

Luc's beak was open, and the corners of his mouth curled up in the permanent half-smile that wasn't a smile. He expelled air noisily and his eyes, washed by transparent membranes, seemed to stare unblinkingly at Jimmy's cheeks. The two beings walked across a narrow margin of saw grass to stand in front of a guard rail.

"Would you like some help climbing over?" Jimmy asked. Without answering, Luc let go of the man's hand and scrabbled quickly over the curved metal barrier, his movements ringing in the air like blows from a blacksmith's hammer. Jimmy was impressed. He raised an arthritic leg and clambered to the other side of the rail as well. Then they re-joined hands and started to walk along the gravel shoulder of the road. Above them, there was the soft hum of traffic and gentle pulse of headlights flashing between houses.

The human was a creature of habit almost as much as the giant Turtle. Jimmy usually wandered around a three-block area on the East side of the old canal. That's where the church parking lot was, and the indigent shelter, and the bagel place and the old Springbank hotel that charged a monthly rate that was almost always just out of reach. He was guiding his menacing companion to a part of the city that was relatively unfamiliar which lessened the sense of betrayal.

The claws extending from Luc's foot pads were almost as long as human fingers and they dug into the soft gravel with increasing excitement as they climbed up the curving road. The giant turtle had expected an invisible force to press him against the ground and demons to slice his shell into fragments if he ever left the creek bank.

But the escape was incredibly easy; all it took was the willingness to scramble over a metal barrier. Turtle-Luc hissed happily.

Suddenly, headlights raked across their backs as a small-bodied electric car rounded the switchback at high speed. There was no time to react, the driver of the car didn't even have time to stomp on the brakes he just decelerated slightly before slamming noisily into Luc's shell. The giant Turtle lurched forwards, dragging Jimmy with him, and they fell face-first in the untrimmed grass on the road shoulder, a dozen feet in front of the vehicle. There was a creak, not unlike the sound of an over-sized Alligator Snapping Turtle climbing off a Stewartia branch, when the driver opened his door. Then the sound of footsteps.

"Oh my God, oh my God!" a human voice said.

Smooth leather soles scraped on pavement, approaching the front of the car. "I'm driving the Prius," the stranger said. He was talking to someone on his cell phone, but to Luc and Jimmy who were lying dazed in the grass it was just another disembodied voice somewhat unconnected to their own activities. *That* part of the experience was more or less normal.

"You know I can't call nine-one-one from my phone!" the voice said angrily. "You have to do it from one of the disposable hand-sets!" The steps were very close now. "I didn't hit them that hard, I just want to make sure they're still alive, then I'll get out of here." There was a pause, then: "I think they were out trick or treating." Another pause. "The kid was dressed up as a Ninja turtle or something."

The stranger knelt beside the two darkening lumps at the road side, intending to place two fingers on the child's throat to make sure there was a pulse. As the driver delicately touched a fold of loose, flexible skin Luc suddenly pushed himself up on his powerful hind legs. The man gasped and tilted his upper body backwards. The monstrous turtle twisted around, and his serrated tail swept a shower of fine gravel into the nearby grass. Luc cocked his head for an instant, looked directly into the man's shocked eyes, then slashed the face with powerful claws.

"Uh," the stranger said, and fell backwards.

Luc climbed on the man's upper body, pinning his shoulders to the gravel. Luc waited until the man tentatively opened one eye then sank his giant beak into a white patch of exposed throat. "Uh," the man said again, only quieter.

The cell phone had clattered onto the pavement but the voice coming from it seemed louder than ever. "Bernie! What the hell is going on there?"

Jimmy didn't fully regain consciousness until he heard the bell-like clang of a large object being dragged roughly over the guard rail. Then there were a series of ripping and scraping noises followed by a loud splash. Jimmy knew instinctively that the giant turtle had dragged something into the canal waters and would probably wedge whatever it was under the network of beaver-felled trees and branches that cluttered the deep drop off.

Jimmy carefully got to his feet and shifted his weight gingerly to test for broken bones. His chest was sore, but he was fairly certain that he wasn't critically injured. He picked up the cell phone and held it to his ear. "Bernie! Bernie!" the voice shouted. Jimmy breathed out heavily and pressed his thumbs on the screen until the light disappeared and the device turned into a dead thing. He walked to the open driver's side door and flipped the phone onto the passenger seat. The car was still running, but Jimmy didn't realize it at first because the electric motor was so quiet.

Jimmy looked around carefully and reconstructed the last few minutes of his life before he had been struck by the little car. *Where was the driver?* he asked himself. Where was Luc? After a few minutes, Jimmy's fragmented mind wandered towards the inevitable conclusion. He noticed the rapidly coagulating splatter of gore near the road shoulder and realized that Luc had killed the driver and dragged him into the black canal water, venting his tremendous resentment against humans as he had often threatened to do.

Strangely enough, Jimmy was relieved when he reached that conclusion. After all, if Jimmy hadn't subtly directed Luc's attention up the hill, he may well have furnished his own corpse to sate the giant Turtle's anger.

He carefully climbed into the driver's seat.

Jimmy hadn't operated a car for years, and the winking screens and dials were baffling. Then he noticed a pile of change and small bills stuffed into one of the cup holders. Jimmy looked suspiciously from side to side, licked a thumb and counted the money. Thirty-seven dollars. He stuffed it into the one pocket that didn't have a hole.

Eventually, Jimmy felt confident enough to move the gearshift into "drive." The car lurched forward like a golf cart and he steered it in a tight circle back toward the canal. Jimmy didn't trust himself to move in reverse. He made it past the guardrail then bumped down a gentle slope and wound up on the jogging trail. The little car fit neatly on the cinder path. Jimmy took his foot off the accelerator and the Prius slowed to a crawl as he steered in the same direction as the current, past the Stewartia branch where he occasionally sat and talked with a giant disaffected turtle.

He wouldn't have been able to explain why, but Jimmy *knew* he had to hide the Prius in the canal. Tight-lipped with determination, he twisted the steering wheel to the right so that the little car's front wheels dipped down onto those round stones that lined the ancient waterway. It was extraordinarily brave because Jimmy couldn't swim and if the car had rolled a few feet further he might have been trapped inside the vehicle as it submerged. Jimmy waggled the gearshift and hoped it was in the neutral position.

The vehicle teetered between land and water as Jimmy carefully opened the driver's door and stepped back onto the path.

The man placed a weathered, blue-veined hand against the door frame and gave a tentative push. To his great surprise, the little car tipped forward and dark currents grabbed a tire and tugged at it playfully. Jimmy moved to the very back of the car and pushed again, but he needn't have bothered, the canal had already decided to absorb it. A back eddy caught the vehicle and spun it in a circle toward the center of the river. Even though the driver's door was open the vehicle continued to float like an odd-shaped boat for many minutes as it washed downstream. Jimmy watched its slow descent until the roof finally disappeared under the grey reflection of the sky.

Jimmy walked back up to the scene of the accident, determined to sluice the blood off the road to hide evidence of Luc's atrocity. It had nothing to do with a personal sense of guilt, it was just typical of the way Jimmy fixated on self-imposed tasks. Once he had decided to wash the gravel, he wouldn't be able to focus on anything else until the chore was accomplished. Unfortunately, he didn't have anything to use as a pail. He looked around for a bit of plastic garbage that could be dipped into the canal, but there wasn't anything suitable.

Then, to Jimmy's great relief, it started to rain. There was a slow pattering of drops at first, but within a couple of minutes the sky itself seemed to move towards him, like a metal curtain being drawn, and the ground was scoured by a torrential storm. Jimmy watched the water pour down the roadway, digging runnels in the gravel shoulder, pour under the guardrail turning the saw grass into a swamp, splash over the cinder jogging path in tiny waves, and spill into the canal.

The next day, Jimmy and Luc sat on the low-slung branch of the Stewartia tree. The exfoliating bark was especially beautiful, showing a pattern of green, grey and gold patches. Luc fixed his unblinking eyes on Jimmy's face and opened his powerful beak into the half smile that wasn't a smile. "Thank you," he whistled.

The two stared at one another, their spasm of friendship hampered by genus, phylum and madness. Jimmy coughed delicately and buttoned his coat up underneath the loose skin of his neck. The accident had hurt him more than he realized, and he felt the first faint stirrings of a chest cold. It was November first. He would have to start sleeping in the indigent shelter again soon, unless he could find enough money to reserve a monthly room at the old Springbank.

Luc's tail was a red, serrated wedge of muscle, and it twitched happily, noisily scouring bhjuththe Stewartia branch. He felt vibrant and alive. He sensed that it was almost time to dig into the pond bank just below the frost line and sleep, but he wanted to delay that for as long as possible. His lower jaw rested on fold after fold of green and black neck scales that sagged over the inadequate shell opening. "Thank you," he hissed again, as the sun touched the tree line.

"Well," Jimmy said, looking at the darkening trail, "I think it's about time."

Turtle-Luc lumbered down from the Stewartia branch, then extended his razor-clawed fore foot and gently pulled the human to a standing position. They both stood quietly for a moment, shifting their weight as if they were visitors to an unfamiliar planet.

Then they silently joined hands and walked toward the roadway.

Jeremy Thompson's Shopping List

-Beer (IPAs)
-Milk
-Water
-Paper towels
-Olive oil
-Candy
-Tortilla chips
-Tortillas
-Mozarella
-Mexican cheese
-Chili beans
-Ground beef
-Chicken
-Tomato sauce
-Chili seasoning
-White onions
-Mole
-Bacon
-Eggs
-Apple Cinnamon Cheerios
-Butter

An Opening
Jeremy Thompson

Stumbling up the driveway—with every wobbling step a triumph, for which he grinned in whiskey-snug dementia—Gilman Just was a sight to behold. Eight days prior, he'd *finally* mustered up the courage to purchase his dream tattoo: ebon bat wings sprouting from his lower eyelids, their well-replicated bones and membranes stretching from his earlobes to his chin.

Knife slits made his spike-studded leather vest seem to breathe. So powerfully had the night's music moved him, he'd torn clumps of hair from his scalp. A broken nose dribbled blood 'twixt his lips, which he sometimes spat to the ground, sometimes swallowed. Blood of another type coated his boots, shed by a parking lot scumfuck who'd never emerge from his coma. The bastard shouldn't have said what he said.

The night sky was striated, exhibiting unearthly hues of yellow, green and indigo. "The fuck?" Gilman wondered, realizing that those striations emanated from the condemned building that his girlfriend and he currently squatted in: a duplex's charcoaled corpse, with holes in the roof for starlight to slip through. Dismissing the sight as an acid flashback, Gilman wondered, *Is Becky still up? I've got a cock for that angel, a tongue for her...*

Half-erect, he stumbled through the door of the fire-gutted residence. The shadows were heavy, swallowing the meager illumination spilled by the stubs of black candles, drowning within their own wax.

"Becks, I've got something to give ya!" he hollered. "Come and get it!" Receiving no reply, he added, "Wake up, darlin'…I'm horny!"

Spilling from a crevice, a closet's remains, a figure fell to the floor and crawled into the candlelight. Greasy black hair overhung her back, which was to Gilman. A seeping wound blemished her Goth attire. "Becks, is that you? What's wrong, baby?"

Her throat hitched, unraveling a strangled sob.

"Say something. You're not on the nod again, are ya?" Shared needles were the emblems defining their courtship, but that was years ago, high school idiocy. Too many mutual friends had descended into grave soil. Jackalish, time had expanded the void at the heart of things. "Hey, what's that smell? Did you shit yourself? Is someone barbecuin' garbage? What the fuck?"

Beneath a dress of black lace, flesh hills formed and collapsed. Afraid to step any nearer, Gilman murmured, "I can't see your face."

Reluctantly taking those steps, he breached the island of candlelight to gently grasp Becky's shoulder.

Though she was the only person he'd ever loved, his every instinct demanded that he flee immediately.

One perfect memory—them cuddling in inebriated ecstasy amidst a sea of concertgoers, as a pallid-faced rock and roll frontman chucked raw steaks to frothing fans, darkly intoning—returned to him, then shattered. "Please, Becky...look at me."

Startled by a sudden sonance, it took Gilman a moment to recognize it as human speech: a hellish parody of his beloved's voice. "They came...down through the ceiling. Each had...*dozens of eyes*," Becky hiss-wheezed. "The goddamn light!" she then shrieked. "Gilly...is that you? I musta been blinded."

As his post-fight adrenaline abated, and numbness supplanted each and every one of his accumulated aches, Gilman groped for phraseology to set the world right. "What happened?" he eventually asked, meeker than seemed possible. "You're not makin' any sense to me, baby."

Don't touch her! a voice in his head demanded, a stern tone he'd never before heard. Defying it, Gilman crouched next to his girlfriend. Thrusting his fingers through sweat-slimy locks, he grasped her jaw. *It feels...scaly*, he thought, turning her countenance toward him. *What's that word horror flicks use? Fuckin' squamous.*

Shrieking, Gilman abruptly leapt backward, thinking, *That can't be real. Not that...that...whatever it was.* He stared at his feet to avoid confirmation, reminded of salting snails as a child to observe their slow-bubbling implosions. *This is just a nightmare, goddammit. I passed out somewhere...at some point. It's my imagination, nothing more. Too many Cronenberg and Carpenter movies as a kid.*

"Gilman..."

"You're not Becky."

"You coulda stopped them, Gilman."

"You're lying," he whispered.

"Creatures I've never seen before, Gilman. No one here to protect me."

"Becky." Raising his eyes, defeated, he felt his every spectral ancestor turn away in disgust. *All your dreams are pathetic*, declared his dying ego.

On her hands and knees, Becky faced him—her neck bent unnaturally, her lips and nostrils now absent. Below two tear-streaming eyes, her mouth had enlarged to account for most of her face. Wide enough to swallow bowling balls, that suppurating tunnel wailed Gilman's name.

"Wake up!" he cried, punching himself in the temple to dissolve a nonexistent nightmare. "Wake up, ya dumb bastard!"

"Gilman…stop that."

"I…I don't wanna," he countered, self-inflicting a blow that blurred his vision. In a brief, gorgeous haze, Becky seemed herself, the same as always. But when clarity returned, so did her blasphemous maw. The sight of it was so disturbing that, had Gilman been gripping a firearm, he'd have squeezed its trigger until Becky's entire visage was obliterated.

As his girlfriend unsteadily stood up, keeping her warped face upraised, a realization struck Gilman: the tunnel was widening. Into that ebon void, Becky's eyes disappeared. As the tunnel traveled down her neck and torso, the black dress she'd been wearing fell to tatters, while Becky's proportions swelled ovaloid. Soon, all that remained of her was a flesh-and-bone tunnel mouth—featureless, save for random hair clumps.

The passage's depths seemed illimitable, its destination point galaxies distant. Impossibly respiring, it wafted out decay stenches.

"Gilman." His name arrived hideous, devoid of humanity, like an a cappella record with its RPM sped up. Echoed as a prolonged moan, it went, "Gilllmmmaaannn."

Suddenly, an arrival: a head the size of a school bus emerging from the passage. *Is that thing from hell or from Mars?* Gilman wondered, even as terror-spurred regurgitation sent brown chunks down his leather.

Fishlike flesh—suppuration-wet, iridescent—covered the monster. Its strangely configured skull radiated gloomlight through its face. Of its shoulder-length hair, a rapier-thin segment descended from a forehead full of thrumming antennae, past its chin, bisecting a pallid countenance wherein deep-set, burning eyes like hell cherries glared above an anemonefish's mouth. From that rubbery, toothless maw, a basso profundo sonance emerged.

With impossible elasticity, what remained of Becky widened enough for the behemoth's shoulders to pass earthward. There were four of them in total, attached to a quartet of humanoid arms that encircled the monster—two where arms usually dwell, plus another mid-chest, and another mid-back—right above its quadruped legs. Its muscles exceeded in girth those of the most roided out bodybuilders. Dark hair enshrouded its torso. Awkwardly, the creature crouched, having emerged entirely, the vaulted ceiling not being tall enough for it to stand upright.

Retreating from the new arrival, Gilman froze in his tracks when the thing pointed at Becky and roared throatily. Seconds later, its sibling emerged from that same flesh-and-bone passage, followed by another…and another.

The condemned residence being too meager to contain them, the four giants smashed through its plaster and steel to greet the night. Wolflike, they howled, under a gibbous moon that now shone cherry-red.

After sparing one last glance for his desecrated soul mate—knowing that all the promises they'd made to each other had been rendered irrelevant—Gilman followed Becky's unnatural spawn into the eerily striated nightscape. Already, the four monsters were bludgeoning menfolk to death and abducting women for sexual congress. Crumpled corpses bestrew crimsoning lawns. Bodiless heads perched atop hedges.

Taller than buildings, Becky's children howled a chorus that connected with Gilman on a level most primal. He found himself grinning dangerously, darkly amused. Remembering the parking lot scumfuck from earlier, and the way that his skull met the blacktop with such a satisfying *CRACK*, he smiled even wider.

Mid-street, a broken man crawled, blood masking his features. "Please…call the police," he mewled, mush-faced. When Gilman began to howl, approaching the crawler, that pulped facial mass shaped itself quizzical. "No…what are you…wait…" were the man's final words, as Gilman lifted his boot.

From both ends of the street, shrieking sirens proclaimed fresh arrivals: squad cars, ambulances, and fire engines offering hollow reassurances. Gunshots sounded, as did cries of terror once it became apparent that Becky's howling progeny were immune to the slugs. Buried in residential wreckage, half-dead families wailed, agonized.

The unholy quartet departed the neighborhood, howling for societal annihilation, each with a woman slung over their shoulder. *Soon they'll be parents, too*, Gilman surmised.

Down came his boot, satisfyingly.

Steve Stark's Shopping List

4 packs of Aspirin - I get these headaches
8kgs of Fresh mincemeat
24 Eggs
4kgs of Chicken thighs
2x 2kg Ribeye Steak
5 Tins of Hewitt's Headcheese
6 pints of Milk
1 Pack of Summerisle red apples
6 litres of Bleach
3m Duct tape - For taping something
2 packs Sponge scourers
24x AirWick plug-in refills
2x Shake N' Vac
2 litres Malibu white rum
2 Litres coconut cream
2 Pineapples-Yes, I like Pina Coladas

Angel of Mercy
Steve Stark

The dirt track was better, and even though he'd smirked when he said it, implying innuendo, Phil from the office had been right about that. Running on earth definitely felt better than concrete, its softer impact much kinder on the joints. But Angela found the uneven and unfamiliar terrain made things a little tougher in its own way, especially when fleeing for your life. One misstep, one slip and it could all be over. She was already cut and bruised, her Lycra vest and shorts torn from having forced her way through brambles and dense growth. At least she couldn't hear the voices anymore. Not like before when they were practically breathing down her neck. It seemed a good time to risk breaking into the open.

Thin branches snapped, and coils of thorns were shed as Angela exploded from the crowded woodland back onto the dirt path without breaking stride. Her heartbeat in her ears, her breathing louder than the world itself, she powered on, up and down the inclines, over and across ditches and bumps. Before long she sighted the cattle gate, the one she'd climbed to gain access to the grounds. It sat there atop a final incline, a big steel grimace, as though someone had slapped a muzzle on the mouth of the forest. She was less than eighty meters from it, and only twenty more from her car and escape, when she heard them again: their rabid chatter, their frantic strides.

They'd gone around the other way to cut her off. The whole track ran in a circle and they were already coming back, knives ready. Angela wasted no time attempting for the gate, the glimmer of their crimson robes flickering through the green told her they were nearer to it than she was, and she dashed into the bushes on the other side. It was well covered in there, a thick carpet of waist high ferns mingled with nettles, shaded by tall oak trees. But Angela didn't wait and try to hide like all those bimbos in slasher flicks. She kept right on going, driving deeper and deeper into the woods.

The view ahead was a web of spindly deformed branches, infested with snakes of thorns that entwined with each other and spread out along the undergrowth, beneath a cover of dead leaves like traps waiting to be sprung. Angela started one way, jogging low and bear crawling whenever the thickening growth demanded it, until her path dead-ended with a large moss-covered rock.

From her squat angle it seemed enormous, some great forgotten monolith, then as she rose against it for the climb, she saw that it was slightly shorter than herself; an easy vault with a good run up, but not so easy without the space for one. Her first attempt fell short and she slipped back, taking a chunk of the moss to the forest floor with her. When she stood again, she noticed an unnatural blue glinting through this fresh tear and as she probed it, her fingertips recognized the feel of metal. Without really meaning to her hand glided under the carpet of moss, effortlessly lifting more of it away, and she instinctively began to peel further, to tear, to shred. Her efforts, growing frantic with each handful, steadily revealed more and more of the obstacle until finally she realized what it was.

The car had clearly been there too long to still work, but its doors were unlocked allowing Angela to clamber through and out the other side where her path was blocked by another car in a similar state, and another and another. There were over a dozen in all, each in varying stages of being devoured by the forest, and even though they'd been left unlocked they still had personal items on their dashboards, in their glove-boxes. All those Ipods, hats and designer sunglasses indicated that these cars had not been abandoned willingly and though that left only one disturbing possibility as to the owners' fates, it gave Angela hope that she might at least find a mobile phone amongst it all.

"Shit," she hissed, after the search proved fruitless. The closest she got was an old charger, so old it wasn't even a USB fitting.

So what? she reasoned, dropping the thing as stark reality dawned on her. *How would anyone find you here anyway? Even if they could, you reckon they'd get here fast enough to help? And what help could anyone really be against all those crazies?*

Angela knew she needed a plan, a strategy of her own, not relying on anything else to get her through, and she started looking around for her next route. The path by which the cars had come to be there was unclear. Several trees had been felled by the elements and growth had sprung up around them in a twisting network of vines, climbers and thorns. This was an old dumping ground, she thought, and most likely not the only one in the sprawling 3000 acre reserve. She imagined that her car had likely already been moved by the hoods to the most recent dump site and decided not to risk attempting for it again. If she was getting away it was going to be on her feet or not at all.

The nearest tree appeared an easy climb and one that might offer a view of any potential routes out of the forest. Angela halfway scaled it in a few seconds and to her ten o'clock she sighted a clearing in the distance; one that looked like it went on for some way, perhaps all the way to the path on the other side. She dropped down quickly, and commando crawled through twenty meters of dense brush, then pulled herself over and across the rotten bark of a long dead tree before the growth permitted her to crawl again. Then it was another forty meter stretch of thorns stabbing at her knees and palms before she could stand, and another forty or so of pushing, ducking and bounding before she arrived at that welcome interval.

The clearing. It was so much easier to run in there and even at her standard pace Angela felt sure she could cover the distance to the path within minutes. She ran flat out, hurdling obstacles with ease, but fatigue was creeping in now and she could feel it too. Her mouth had gone sandpaper dry, her muscles burned from lactic acid. She caught herself wishing if only she'd arrived later, or worked out with less intensity, and had to stop that train of thought before it left the station. Angela knew she couldn't afford to waste so much as a second on such pointless fantasies, not with just her life, but possibly her very soul at stake, if she believed what they were saying.

Forget that. She believed her eyes well enough, believed in the blue flame which had engulfed that girl, scorched her to nothing in under a second. No fire burnt like that. No fire on earth. It belonged to some other place. The place where that Thing came from. That Thing with its glaring yellow eyes. And Angela had cried out, like a stupid girl. And they'd seen her, so many of them. At least fifty, all armed.

Mid-stride something caught Angela's ankle. With sudden mechanical speed it yanked backwards and up, dragging her away from the ground. Instantly she felt that lurch in her stomach, that disorientating feeling of lightness you get in an elevator, and knew something had her, something strong, powerful. Thankfully her own momentum was such that she managed to slip from its grasp, fall forward and crash head first into the wet dirt, arms spread out in front. She spun over sharply and wiped the mud from her eyes, ready to face whatever had assaulted her, aiming to give it some back. But once her vision cleared, she could see nothing behind that might have caused the fall. There was only the growth and the faint breeze whistling through it, tousling the leaves and branches as if the forest was giving a shrug of innocence.

For several moments Angela stared out, focusing in on all that passive activity with extreme scrutiny, searching for even the slightest hint of danger, of the hoods, of that Thing they'd brought here. There was a faint creak and rustle overhead, then up above, in the treetops she spotted it: A homemade net that had scooped no more than the dead leaves and dirt which had kept it hidden from her sight on the ground. The net swayed in the tree, spilling some of its catch, and not far from it, Angela noticed the massive dead-fall log which had powered its ascent, realizing then that she was in even more trouble than she'd first thought.

She would have to watch her step now too.

Getting up again wasn't as easy as she anticipated. Her ankle had twisted in the fall and was beginning to swell against her tightly laced Nikes, their inner rim pinching her skin there. She wasted no time thinking about it and hobbled on, more cautious, more wary and tiring. To her far right she could already hear them again and when she narrowed her eyes she could glimpse flickering streaks of red through the gaps in the trees, moving parallel to her direction.

Angela knew she would have to pick up the pace or they might cut her off before she could get to the other side, back onto the track. Breaking into a jog she felt the full extent of the pain in her ankle. A dead throb, as sickening as a punch in the gut. Her tired muscles were finally beginning to rebel as well, cramping up, and she cursed under her breath, berating herself for such weakness. This wasn't the time for it. This wasn't training. This wasn't a race for fun. This was a race for her life. Now more than ever she needed her body to work, and if it was unwilling to do so then she would drag it through every agonized stride. In spite of the pain, the leg would lock out, it would bear her weight, it would propel her on. It simply had no option and neither did its counterpart.

The mud that caked her body was ice cold, but it occurred to her that it served as camouflage and she was glad for it then. They might not see her, while she could easily make them. Even on the fringe of her field of vision those flashes of red stood out against the forest's greens and browns. Although she soon noticed to her despair that the frequency of those reds was steadily increasing. There were more of them and they were getting closer.

The Executioner would be somewhere among them, that towering, vicious creep. Angela weighed him as the biggest physical threat, but what of the other kind? The kind presented by the Leader? It was his voice that'd first caught Angela's attention, causing her to drop out of her run to see what was going on. The words weren't at all clear, seeming little more than lunatic gibberish. But whatever it meant she could tell the rest of them were into it, all bowing their heads up and down like greedy birds picking up breadcrumbs, while that girl on the altar had lain so still.

Angela knew her from regional news and the nightclub scene. She was a local glamor model, Paige *something*. Big doe eyes, vacant grin of perfect teeth which stayed fixed even when the Leader's hairy hands tore off her robe, stripping her bare. Paige didn't have a rep for being the brightest, but to react like that, as in to not react at all Angela guessed she had to be drugged.

The reveal clearly excited the Leader. From there his ranting became even more fevered, his gesticulations almost spasmodic, and with a chant spreading through the crowd one of the hoods had stepped forward, the one Angela would later dub: The Executioner. At the far side of the altar he'd approached Paige, allowing them all to see what he was doing, what he was going to do, giving Angela pause to wonder if she'd stumbled upon a bizarre porn shoot. But then she saw the knife, that curved, nasty looking thing, flashing in the light. The Leader raved nonsensically while its razor tip hung poised over Paige's soft, spray-tanned navel and for a fraction of a second Angela thought she read fear behind that girl's frozen smile.

"In Death she will give Birth," the Leader said, the only thing Angela had understood, and on his silent command the Executioner plunged the knife, sawing her open from gut to gullet like a butchered hog. It took a while, the big man having to put some muscle in to cut through the sternum, but Paige didn't scream, or even flinch, not once. However, that glimmer of frozen terror Angela had detected was plain for all to see by the time the blade reached her chin.

His bloody work done, the Executioner stepped back and paused, finger caressing the dripping tip of the knife as he waited, *For what*? Angela had wondered. Then it'd happened, beginning with sounds, wet, sloppy, bubbling, belching sounds, and on the slab Paige's inert body had started to jerk, to wriggle as if there were still embers of life in it.

The smell arrived next, choking Angela even from that distance. It was like barbecue and rotten eggs. Then from the still steaming wound she'd seen them emerge, those long, long, spindly, slimy fingers with their thick black crescent shaped talons. Like spider's legs they'd come creeping up to grip the flaps of flesh, and with seemingly small effort they'd pressed the opening wider, in the process cracking Paige's bones into splinters. Like an overfilled bath, buckets of blood and offal were spilled sloppily onto the ground as a great glistening mass began to haul itself up and out. It was like the most revolting version of the rabbit in the hat trick. The creature itself twice the size of the corpse it was emerging from had to be coming from somewhere else, somewhere far deeper than the wound in that slim little girl.

Angela was primed to run right then, to get out of there as fast as she could, as fast as she should've the moment she saw what they did to Paige. But as the

Thing shakily arched up on its glistening, slimy limbs, it'd looked right at her. Its eyes like dazzling headlights somehow rooted her to the spot and in an instant she felt them under her skin, in her very soul, as though invisible fingers were peeling back layers of her memory, picking at scabs of past traumas, fondling her filthiest thoughts, her most hateful fantasies.

The Leader was ecstatic at the Thing's appearance. He'd chanted more gibberish but didn't get to finish because that was when Angela had finally cried out. It was an uncontrollable, primal scream at the psychic violation and it forced those invisible fingers into retreat like they'd just been singed by fire, the same fire which suddenly erupted from the base of the altar, engulfing both Paige and the Thing birthing from her.

A bloodcurdling almost infantile squeal rang out from within the flames and just as the hoods all turned and saw Angela, she'd bolted faster than she ever had in her entire life. The run had been so easy then, not like now, now when she could only hobble at her lowest jogging pace.

Fatigue clung to her like wet clothes, weighing her down and the cramp was worsening, especially in her calves. At the site of an uprooted tree she finally had to stop to stretch it out, to catch her breath. She told herself it would only be a moment, though that moment became a minute in the blink of an eye.

The cramp receded stubbornly, leaving a constant ache as a parting gift, the way a bee leaves its sting. Carefully Angela lifted her leg, propping a heel against the tree, her ankle throbbing worse at the change in angle. She forced herself to ignore it, to focus on her environment and as she retied her laces she was struck by the quiet here, the inactivity. The most glaring absence were the hoods, their mad cries, their excited chatter, and her first thought was that they must have quietened in order to sneak up on her.

But there was no footfall either, not the slightest scuff or shuffle.

Listening hard, Angela noticed that the constant static of woodland, the twitter of birds, the chirp of insects, was also entirely absent. There wasn't even a breeze working through the treetops, only the purest silence. As that silence stretched on it seemed almost as though she'd stumbled upon an oasis, a sanctuary, and she soon began to reconsider her thoughts on hiding. Perhaps that might work she reasoned. After an hour or so they'd assume she got out and they would have to widen their search, spreading themselves thinner. She could wait even longer and slip away under the cover of darkness. There was always the risk of more traps, sure, but by then she could probably just work back the way she came, the route she already knew.

The more she thought about it the more convinced Angela became that it was the right way to go and she was all set to slump down into the groove of that tree when behind her there suddenly came a crash, so loud she thought another tree was falling. A glance over her shoulder revealed that it wasn't that, it was one of the hoods breaking through into the clearing. He was fast, and he was agile. The two seconds she wasted looking at him haunted her every step as she ran. She'd seen how easily and freely he moved, how every obstacle became another tool with which he could propel himself forward. Emerging rocks became platforms to leap from, hanging branches were grips to swing from. Nothing got in his way, everything was his to use. He gained fast and Angela realized that she couldn't outrun him, not with her ankle. She would have to out- maneuver him instead.

As the hood closed in, Angela took a sharp turn left and dove through another web of thorns, feeling the air from his hand swipe at the back of her head as she went. Her face was cut badly going through, but she simply clenched her eyes and pressed on, weaving in and out of the crowded trees before diving into a heavy patch of understorey where she began to crawl on her elbows.

He tried to follow, but due to his greater size he had much more trouble getting through. Angela could hear him breaking and snapping things, his breathing becoming more labored. He began to grunt and curse in frustration at every branch and bramble that snagged his robe, while under the shade of the waist high plant life she crawled on, smoothly, still heading toward her goal. The mud that coated her skin served her well here and the sound of her pursuer's movements soon faded behind her.

Eventually she arrived at a break in the undergrowth where she had to stretch out, crawl on her palms and press along with the balls of her feet to keep from being seen. Her finger caressed something sharp then, something metallic, and she quickly retracted it before peering up cautiously to inspect the object.

It was an old animal trap, rusty. No, only rust colored so to blend in. Its steel jaws lay set like an open shark mouth waiting for something to chomp down on. Angela thought to disable it, to spring the trap so that she could safely pass and found the perfect tool in a broken twig.

Then she had a better idea.

***

A swift swipe, an arcing gleam and a blanket of ivy fell like a dropped curtain, allowing Cass O'Neal to step through into the clearing, leaves crunching under his boots. Seeing the distinct and gnarly trees he soon recognised this place as an old hunting ground and was surprised to find that even all these years later the green they'd disturbed had not yet reclaimed it. What had grown in their wake was sparse and fine with only a few saplings to mar an otherwise clear view spanning hundreds of metres in some directions. But where was the bitch? She wasn't that fast. He'd almost caught her once already and although he'd lost sight of her for a few seconds, she couldn't have gone far. She had to be hiding he thought, smiling thinly and as he proceeded, he began to wildly hack away at what had grown there, hoping to make connection with flesh and bone soon.

O'Neal had a way with a blade. Proof of that could be found with the mutilated mannequins piled on his basement floor like a scene from a death camp. In spite of the monetary cost, O'Neal got a buzz from each one he destroyed, but there was always something a little hollow about the act, a little pointless. The dummy didn't care if he hurt it. The dummy didn't even know he'd hurt it, and the hurt was the tasty part, the thing that made all the effort worthwhile. To O'Neal, violence without pain was about as pointless as rape without coming.

Nine years he'd been with the Order and though his extensive tattoos suggested otherwise, the Order's beliefs, the religious aspect of it all had always been beside the point for him. That is until today. For once they'd actually succeeded in summoning something and witnessing that power had affected him, given him reason to *believe*, to *serve*. When he saw the Pilgrim crawling out of that girl he'd resolved right on the spot that he would truly devote himself to this. The killings weren't just for fun anymore. They were for a cause. They were to appease.

'Ours are hungry Masters,' the Deacon had said, words that only now held true meaning for O'Neal.

A decade of Catholic school had failed to instill any religious values or morals in him. Just a few vague concepts and simplified stories had stuck in his mind, like the thin scraps left behind when you peel wallpaper down. One thing that'd always lingered though was the idea of Hell. There'd been days, not many, where the thought of that place had crept up on him and after a certain point, he'd come to think that if he was going anywhere after he died it was probably there. It was a surprisingly easy thing to accept, mainly because he didn't truly believe it, only in those brief moments when he was at his lowest, sitting alone in his vast empty house, or brooding in a cramped cell.

But if Hell was where that Thing had come from then O'Neal thought he'd better start building bridges there, making connections fast, because he knew for certain now that was where he was headed and like when he'd gone to prison the first time, he imagined he'd need all the friends he could get.

This witness, this runner would be a good offering to start with. He'd make it painful too, flay her slow over the altar as punishment for the trespass. They'd appreciate that he thought and just as the notion crossed his mind, he caught sight of her, almost as if the universe was telling him: YES. DO IT!

At the very edge of the clearing she was stood still, her back to him, chest heaving like she was catching her breath, or maybe sobbing, and like an enraged bull he began barreling down the most direct route to her. No longer leaping and hurdling obstacles, he trampled plants, bushes and crushed fallen branch underfoot.

The clumsy, brutal noise telegraphed his approach, but the woman didn't move, not until O'Neal was within a couple of meters. In her grasp he glimpsed something then, asked "What have we got there?" and as way of answer she spun and hurled the animal trap.

***

The hood's arms came up to shield his head and the knife tumbled from his hand to drown in the sea of leaves and dirt. He closed his eyes and planted his heels, but he was traveling too fast to stop so abruptly and continued skidding in the mud toward the flying jaws. They sailed under his raised arms, flesh met steel and the trap clamped shut around his lean waist, cold teeth sinking into his thorax and lungs. The impact sent a shock wave through him that made his body convulse once violently, causing him to trip and shed the hood from his head as he crashed to a halt on his knees not two feet from where Angela stood. She saw then that he was just a man, not some monster as she'd imagined, and as he struggled for breath, she circled him, like a cat stalking wounded prey. Her eyes glaring with a blank, animal hostility were the only clear feature on her muddied face.

The hood's eyes were bulging with agony and he coughed blood, but with his target so near he somehow managed to reach out, to lurch forward still, forcing her to lean away. On reflex she delivered a straight heel kick to the man's midsection, driving the trap further into him, and he tumbled backward into the brush where his corpse disappeared from view, swallowed by the growth. A disturbance seemed to spread from that spot throughout the forest canopy, like giant invisible fingers were combing through it, but it was only the breeze. A light rain of leaves fell from above like confetti and Angela tilted her head back to receive it, the accompanying white noise resembling the distant match-day cheers that so often drifted from the local stadium to the yard of her childhood home. She closed her eyes and raised shaky arms in victory, feeling immense satisfaction as she replayed the scene in her mind, how perfectly the trap was set, how precise her throw.

Then she vomited.

Within moments an army of midge flies and ants had amassed on the half digested cocktail of wheat grain and soya and Angela dropped to her knees, not from exhaustion, but to search for the hood's knife. With both hands she delved deep into the soft forest floor, making circular sweeping motions like Danielsan waxing on and off in the Karate Kid. She scoured the area either side of the hood's tracks for what seemed like minutes then suddenly gave up. Enough time had been wasted. Better to maintain the lead than lose ground looking for a slight advantage.

When she re-emerged onto the dirt path Angela found that she'd gotten some few hundred meters ahead of her pursuers. They were shocked to see her, she could tell that much in the instant she squandered with a glance at them and in that same instant she bitterly regretted her failure to recover that hood's knife.

"Get her," she heard one cry. "Bring her to the altar. Feed her to the Pilgrim."

At the mention of *The Pilgrim,* Angela's body flooded with adrenaline. It blocked out the pain, blocked out the noise all around her, the screams and shouts and footfall at her back and suddenly she was sprinting again, full pelt. Two of the bladed weapons whistled through the air at her. One stuck into the bark of a tree just as she passed it, missing her by inches. The other flew hopelessly on, shearing leaves and thin branches, disappearing into the dark of the forest.

At a narrow turn in the path another hood pounced from the bushes in front of her, arms wide and laughing horribly. Before Angela could react, he smothered her, snatching her up in a bear hug, pinning her arms to her sides and arching his back to keep her pedaling legs from getting leverage on the ground. The other hoods were still rushing toward them and he turned with her in his clinch so that she had to face them as they came.

"Shh, don't fight it," said the hood, in that same desperate way Sammy Riley had whispered it after the school prom. "Just let it happen."

His forearms bit hard into her biceps and ribs, making her fingertips numb. He was strong, far too strong for Angela to break his hold, even with the mud for lubrication, and after several seconds of fruitless, exhausting struggle she finally gave up and went limp to conserve her precious energy for a chance that might never arrive. She could only watch then as they surged nearer, daggers drawn and raised. So many of them, too many of them.

"That's it. Good girl," her captor panted. He was excited, she could tell from the dull stabbing at her buttocks.

"Easy, easy. Shh."

Angela stayed silent. She wasn't going to scream again, no matter what happened she wasn't going to give them that. Her jaw clenched to block the cry rising in her chest and she closed her eyes tightly, the way she used to when she'd watched horror movies as a child; as if closing them tight enough would somehow shut the monsters out, keep them from getting to her. She drew a deep breath and on the exhale his arms constricted further, preventing her from drawing the next one. Panic set in when she tried. Her eyes flicked open to see her vision go dim at the edges and her head lolled as if she'd suddenly lost the bones from her neck.

"Here. We...Come," the hood gasped and the strain in his voice suggested he'd actually reached climax right then and there. His grip loosened a fraction as a shudder rattled through him allowing Angela to suck just one breath. It was enough to prolong her staying conscious, enough to press the closing shadow back to the fringe of her vision and enough to briefly revive her oxygen deprived muscles. The hood felt her body stiffen in his arms for a moment before going limp again, then with a sudden surge of animal ferocity she thrust her head backwards, twice, into the soft tissue of his face.

THUD

THUD

Reeling from the pain he released her to cover his stinging nose, his fingers not recognizing this new shape she'd made of it. When he withdrew his hands, he saw the blood on their palms, so much of it, so wet, so thin. Then through his fingers a lump of wood flashed into view.

CRACK.

The blow knocked the man out on his feet, the jagged wood carving three vertical lines up his face, from chin to brow with Angela following through on the swing as if she was at the driving range. He fell like a tree and in his wake, Angela saw more hoods coming from the direction he had. Trapped on both sides she turned toward the other mob closing at her back, her grip tightening on the broken branch, so tight it gave her splinters.

"Meat for the Master," one of them said.

With everything she had Angela flung the branch at the head of the nearest hood, who tumbled and took out another runner while she retreated into the thick. Unlike them she knew the route, having already beaten the path for herself, and as she gathered speed along it the red flashes in her peripheral began to fall away, the voices at her back fading with them. She decided to head west, back to where the whole thing had started, the altar, and hopefully find an exit beyond. It would be the last route they'd expect her to take.

Angela was pretty certain any traps along this path had already been sprung, or discovered, when she came through the first time and she allowed herself to proceed with less caution and more speed. It made all the crawling a hell of a lot easier and at the car graveyard she made up even more time by swinging clean through the already open doors of each vehicle like a Parkour gymnast. In less than five minutes she arrived at the altar and though she'd guessed as much she was nonetheless relieved to find no hoods waiting, no *"Pilgrim"* in sight either. She pelted on through, aiming for a steep bank on the other side of the altar. Telephone wires streaked the sky beyond that bank, indicating some connection to main roads, to civilization, giving her hope she might see more from the top, housing perhaps, passing cars she could flag down. But before she could get there something snagged her foot, sending her careening head first into the shallow sea of mud and leaves.

Angela quickly turned over to see what it was, finding no enemy or obstacle in sight. This brought on a distinct sense of Deja vu, but there was no sign of any traps either. Blaming herself then, her own failing balance, she started to pick herself up when suddenly a charred, skeletal hand came bursting through the forest floor. Blindly it grabbed for her again and she quickly scurried back on her palms and buttocks as those black claws raked the dirt inches from her feet.

Angela couldn't tear her eyes from the Thing as it hauled itself from the muck, its silently screaming head appearing next, forest debris peeling from it to reveal eyes like dusty light bulbs. She'd seen them before. Another arm, more charred and withered than the first, locked out with a crunch and pressed upon the ground, prying the rest of the body from the soil as Angela's back met the granite of the altar. She slid up it to stand and the Thing lurched forward onto all fours, the jutting bones of its great long spine clacking rapidly like a falling row of dominoes as another faint sound seeped into the air, something vaguely resembling speech.

It sounded like: "*Why*"

With what seemed a tremendous effort the Thing suddenly arched up to gaze at Angela, those light bulbs flickering dimly with murderous intent. What remained of its lips stretched back to bare teeth like ivory needles and as it held that predatory stare it salivated a beard of green goop which dripped with every heavy gasp. Angela froze against the altar, caught in that limbo between fight and flight for what seemed more than ten seconds, but was in actuality little more than one. Choice made, her leg and hip loaded a kick with a subtle shift of her weight, but before she could throw it, the creature suddenly collapsed onto its side, utterly spent.

"*Hurts,*" it whimpered.

There was no mistaking the malignant visage which had earlier leered into her mind, but the Thing's wretched face now spoke only of agony, frailty, and its burnt corpse was telling the same story. Angela observed its painful struggle for breath, its wasted chest expanding unevenly, its distended, hollow gut pulsing above hips so bony and sharp that they'd penetrated the very skin which covered them. Wounds such as these were all over the creature, at the elbow and knee joints, the clavicle, the jaw and they were gradually spiderwebbing out across its hide like cracking ice.

Those eyes, so bulbous and bulging, glared intensely as Angela's gaze returned to them. She couldn't feel those invisible fingers, but she got the sense it might be trying to use them again, so she snapped a swift kick into its thigh, putting a dent in the brittle bone. The creature rasped in pain, its grimace fully showcasing that fearsome set of teeth, a ring of needles, the type of mouth befitting some nightmare from the bottom of the sea. Disturbed yet undaunted Angela shot a look that said, *There's more where that came from*, and proceeded to stare it down.

The texture of its eyes was repulsive, dry but gelatinous, two hard-boiled eggs left out in the sun with bits of leaves and dirt clinging to their surface. Bugs were crawling all over them too. Angela blinked first out of empathy and wondered why it didn't do the same to shed them. Then she realized the creature had no means to; they were completely lidless.

"What is it?" she whispered, thinking out loud. Then to the creature: "What are you?"

"*I am*," it said, as if that were a complete answer. "*I was. And you people ripped me from my home...my family...dragged me...here into this unformed shell...into all this pain...All this*—" The speech died abruptly there, the apparent stress bringing on a violent, hacking cough which sent a cupful of that green fluid gushing from the creature's slack mouth. The stink of the stuff caused Angela to gag and cover her nose while the Thing's breathing returned to its previous Cheyne-Stokes rhythm.

Angela shook her head. "I didn't have anything to do with that."

The creature appeared relieved by the answer. The malice in its eyes melted away and the rank fluid bubbled gently as it spoke. "*Then you can help me.*"

Angela was taken aback. For whatever reason her first instinct TO RUN didn't prompt any more action than a switch in her stance and her second instinct, to respond, 'Why should I?' never reached her mouth. In spite of the horrific aspects of its appearance, those teeth, the claws, the eyes, no longer was she in fear of the Thing. Its pathetic presence now evoked only pity and repulsion, like a street beggar or a charity advert. She stepped towards it, still slightly wary and its sad stump of a tail slithered and twitched impotently in the dirt as she came.

Regardless of all the other questions bubbling in her mind the one that came out first was "Help you how?"

"*Kill me,*" said the Thing.

"Then you'll go back? Back where you came from?"

"*Then I'll die.*"

Although she had no real sane reason to care, Angela found herself asking: "Can't you go back?"

"*Only higher demons and mortals can be granted that right. I am neither.*"

It didn't make much sense to Angela, but she gave a slight nod as if it did. Her next question was stifled by a sudden burst of chatter in the distance, three voices at least, and although she couldn't pick out the words their tone rang excited, conspiratorial, *Hood*-like. Sound carried in that clearing preventing her from gauging their direction, their proximity, and she stood alert as a wild Deer, primed to take flight at the slightest hint of approach.

"*Please,*" begged the demon, fearing her departure. "*Help.*"

After a few beats the voices faded again and Angela lingered. Carefully she crouched beside the demon, her eyes still roaming the vicinity for sign of danger.

"How do I do it?" she whispered, expecting some elaborate method, a silver bullet or something. She'd never killed anything before, much less a demon.

"*Any way you wish*," said the demon. "*This flesh is weak.*"

Angela studied the creature. It would be easy enough to throttle that scrawny neck, but she didn't want to get that close, nor did she want to touch it, at all. Instead she looked for the nearest tool to hand, spotting a few rocks at the foot of the bank and as she made for them her mind cast back to when she was four and found that wounded Sparrow in the garden. The bird had been fluttering wildly, unable to take flight, its little head beating out a rhythm against the plastic sheeting of her Wendy house, falling over after each collision like a dancing drunk. She remembered the feel of its tiny heartbeat against her fingers, how fragile and light its body was. It was the first and last time she ever held a bird.

"Daddy, Daddy."

She'd taken the Sparrow to her father who was working in the front yard. He had to switch off the lawnmower to hear her and when he saw what the situation was, he wore a look she'd never seen on his face before, kind of regretful, disappointed, almost defeated. She'd realized why when he explained what he'd have to do.

"No, Daddy, take him to the vet," she'd cried.

"I can't," her father had sighed, while gently peeling her soft, chubby digits from the bird. "I'm sorry."

She'd followed him to the side of the house, crying hysterically all the way. Mum hadn't been there to pull her away, so Dad had to shut her out of the garage. When she realized how futile her pleas were, Angela had ceased making them and could only listen, part curious, part expecting her father to open the door and say, "It's okay, honey, I've fixed him," like when he'd fixed the wheel on her trike.

But all she heard was the brick hit the concrete floor.

Little Angie didn't speak to her father for days after that. She'd never thought about it since, hadn't even remembered it until now, carrying a head sized chunk of rock in both hands, knowing what she had to do with it. She understood how her Father felt then, what that look was all about. He was sad that she would be exposed to death so early and in such a manner, having actually touched the life beforehand. He was disappointed that he wouldn't be able to keep her world perfect anymore, that he couldn't fix it for her. At four years old she'd had to face the fact that things die and that sometimes death is better. Sometimes death is a merciful release.

The rock was heavy and sharp, its rough edges scratching Angela's bare arms, stabbing her stomach as she waddled over, towards the altar. There on its back in the mud, the demon lay waiting, staring up at the sky, wondering about the *other place*, what the bastards up there might have to say about all this. He didn't consider it for long though, none of them had ever said anything of interest as far as he was concerned, and soon turned his attention to the trees, to a great buzzard coming to rest on a high branch some twenty feet up. The branch bowed under the bird's weight and continued to wobble while it surveyed the scene, head rapidly tilting and twitching this way and that, a rodent's tail dangling from its beak like a string of spaghetti. It returned to the air just as Angela's silhouette loomed into view, for a split second the position giving her the appearance of bearing wings.

The sight raised the slightest ironic smile on the demon's skeletal face, and it spread when he noticed the burden in her arms. *"Thank you,"* he said as she lifted the thing higher, right up over her head.

There was a flash of red and Angela disappeared from the demon's sight. For a joyous half moment, he thought the impact he'd heard was his own skull collapsing under the rock. But it wasn't. He was still alive. His eyes slid to his left and saw Angela lying beside him as one of the Order mounted her and struck her about the face twice. On the second blow she slumped and fell unconscious.

Panting desperately, Angela's attacker removed his hood and sat back on his haunches. He turned to the demon, eyes wide with concern.

"Are you unharmed, Master?"

The demon said nothing, his state spoke for itself, and the hood shuffled closer, impatient for an answer.

"Are you unharmed?"

"Rast," said the demon, a word that meant nothing to the hood, but quite a lot where the demon came from. He seemingly had a lot more to follow, but that was smothered by a string of gloopy coughs.

"Master," gasped the hood. Desperate to help, he lifted his beloved Master's head onto his lap and began to stroke his flaking skull. The demon felt disturbed, even violated by this tenderness, but was too frail to resist the embrace. He saw to his disgust that the man's eyes were shining with tears and attempted to ridicule him for it before choking again.

"What is it?" asked the hood, leaning down. "I'm here for you."

The act of speaking appeared to bring utter agony to the demon and all in vain, his words drowning in the goo blocking his throat. The hood leaned closer, imploring him not to force it, to rest instead and as he turned this into a cooing mantra the demon noticed only the way it made the man's Adam's apple move.

"Rest my lord, don't spe—"

The last syllable resonated in the demon's mouth, for it had sunk its needle teeth clean into the hood's throat. The hood twitched and wriggled like a worm on a hook, blood gushing in stops and starts from his mouth and from the wound. Normally here the demon would wrench its neck to tear the flesh, but it lacked the strength. Not that it mattered. The flesh between those jaws was as butter to a razor and it took very little effort to simply bring them back together.

CHOMP

The hood fell away, and the demon spat the salty flesh from his mouth, looking to Angela, praying to Lucifer she wasn't dead. "*Arise,*" he implored, in his other voice, and is if on command her eyes flicked open. She sat up quickly but stood with less ease and hobbled groggily to where the demon lay. He seemed to be smiling slightly, somewhat triumphantly at his own work: the dead man to his side.

"You still want my help?" said Angela.

"*I do,*" said the demon, the desperation, the need in his voice reminding Angela of the way her cousin Lydia had said the words on her wedding day.

"Okay," she said, already bending to retrieve the rock. She hadn't the strength to raise it high anymore, so instead she held it at waist height over the creature's head and, when ready, simply allowed it to drop.

There was a hollow cracking sound, like a coconut breaking and the demon's body jolted once, then moved no more. Angela imagined that was how the Sparrow had gone too. She didn't dwell on it any further and staggered on toward the muddy bank.

From the bottom looking up she guessed it had to be at least a hundred feet, the incline around forty degrees, a Crossfitter's wet nightmare. Fit as she was Angela had no delusions about her own ability and knew full well the climb would've been a struggle if she'd come to it fresh. The state she was in it was going to be Hell, she thought, and that phrase jarred a vague memory from the vault as she stepped up the bank. It was of the road to her parent's house, the route she ran every day from school while Marilyn Manson screamed through her Walkman.

With an odd, drunk smile Angela mumbled the lyric *'I wanna live, I wanna love, but it's a long hard road out of Hell,'* and then it occurred to her that she might be going delirious. *'Keep it together, girl.'*

Loose earth slipped out from under her feet with every step, threatening to topple her balance and she flopped into a crawl as the angle increased. The steeper it became the less it seemed that she was gaining, as though the hill itself were growing at a rate that kept her crawling in place. She knew that wasn't the case but felt the need for proof and soon found makeshift markers in the form of the grass tufts dotting the sparse ground. They served a dual purpose, as whenever possible she would grip a handful of it for leverage while whispering thanks for the sacrifice of each blessed blade that broke and died so that she might live.

No more than halfway, and white hot pain came streaking up the back of her legs and around her core, the sensation there not so much burning as stabbing, clawing, like something was tearing its way out of her. For Angela, who'd completed countless grueling runs, who'd bested serving marines and pro crossfitters in the previous year's *Maniac Marathon,* this was an entirely new sensation and one that let her know she was pushing way beyond any limit she'd previously dared approach. Her blood was boiling, but her skin was cold, goosefleshing allover. It wasn't much longer before her muscles shuddered like a failing machine, their reserves totally depleted and as she attempted to drive them on her head suddenly went light, as though someone had peeled the top off and very quickly scooped out her brain. Darkness swarmed like a billion ants and she had to pause for breath, every lungful gradually pressing them back out of her view. They were still scuttling in her peripheral when she resumed the climb and though a lengthier pause might have driven them from sight completely Angela had no choice but to keep going, to flee from the angry voices now gathering below, the ones which seemed to be getting louder.

Closer.

Closer.

Something snagged Angela's heel, but she managed to pull away from it as she crossed the military crest of the hill. The sharp decrease of the incline there saw her upright again, swinging her injured leg as though it was dragging an invisible ball and chain. As awkward as her technique had become it felt like gliding in comparison to her previous uphill slog and when she took the downward slope she did so in great strides and bounds that made her feel like she was walking on the moon.

The road lay waiting below, a winding barren A-road, but a road all the same, one that would eventually lead to houses, to civilization, and sanctuary. Before that stood a barbed wire fence which Angela was preparing to vault when a red blur to her right forced her to veer left at the last instant, spoiling the approach, and she grazed her hip as she went over. The snag on the wire turned her slightly, so that when her feet planted on the roadside she wound up facing the direction from where she'd came and the hood who'd been but a blur only a moment before. To her relief she saw that he was out cold and tangled up in the fence. Still he had to have been fast and he had to have been close. Angela reckoned a few more strides and he would've had her if not for the apparent fall. But there was something far more troubling about his presence there, as it shattered her frail hope that they might shy away from the open, from such exposure, that she might be safe once out of the woods.

As further proof of how wrong her theory had been Angela craned her neck upward to witness a mass of hoods descending toward her, rushing and weaving and tumbling like some terrible red tsunami flooding down the hill. So terrifying was the sight that Angela began to run from it before she'd even turned and when she did turn it was just in time to see the gleaming blue metal hood of the oncoming car.

WHOOMP

Angela's legs flew out from under her and she experienced that sudden weightlessness, the kind that makes you feel almost unreal, immaterial, as if you don't really exist in the physical world at all. The next sensation was the exact opposite of that, the giant hand of reality hitting her at thirty miles an hour like she was just a fly in its house. Gravity stepped in then, providing the knockout blow that left her sprawled on the tarmac, looking like a toy doll flung off the stairs.

"Oh my God."

The driver was a woman. Angela could hear her startled shrieks, muffled only slightly by the thick glass. She could hear her baby's piercing cry too, the glass not doing much against that. She wanted to get up, to warn them, but she couldn't speak. All the air had escaped her body, leaving her lungs in the throes of spasm. At the click of the car door opening Angela managed to press herself up onto all fours, her bloodied palms slipping against the grit. Finally air returned to her lungs and she hissed through her teeth in pain, spraying sticky coppery tasting spit onto the ground. But it wasn't spit. It was blood. And it wasn't from a cut in her mouth. That was just where it was coming out.

"Oh my God," the woman said, her voice clearer, and the car door shut again with a panicked slam.

Angela's bloody hand reached up and slapped down on the bonnet. She used it to steady herself as she rose, feeling the vibrations from the idling engine running through her palm, and she peered through the cracked windscreen at the terrified face behind the wheel. She couldn't see the baby beside it, the carrier seat faced the other way, only its arms and legs were visible, kicking out frantically in distress.

"Get out of the way!" the mother screamed, and the effort showed on her face as she pressed the accelerator.

The car nudged forward, pushing Angela off, but she managed to keep her balance and used the momentum to start running again. She hadn't got but two steps when she heard the sound of fists hammering the car, then breaking glass and the baby screaming louder as the engine died suddenly.

"Meat for the Masters," someone said and the mother's pleas were drowned in a celebratory cheer, then cut short as suddenly as the engine had been.

There was nothing Angela could do, she knew that. She could only hope to get away, to be able to report what she'd been through, what she'd seen so that others could put a stop to it. As much as that made sense the logic did little to comfort her, and even less to silence the baby's scream. Angela's main focus became outrunning that bloodcurdling sound, lest it tempt her to turn back for some suicidal rescue attempt, and she hurried toward a blind bend in the road with no idea how close the hoods were at her back, or what awaited her around the corner. The answer to the latter came without warning in the form of a speeding white van, the front end, with its angled headlights like evil eyes and wide muddied grill like a slathering mouth, appearing to her blurred vision as a giant monster skull screaming toward her. She had no time to react and even if she had her exhausted reflexes were hardly up to the task.

This is it, she thought.

The driver's reflexes were in slightly better shape and he was able to swerve so that the side-mirror just clipped Angela's shoulder when it went by. The force of the collision turned her as the van itself turned, its back end drifting out to overtake the front, tyres screaming across the tarmac and leaving black arcs in their wake. The van ploughed clean into the army of hoods, cutting down all in its path, flesh and bone battering the side panel in a rapid off-beat rhythm. Bodies piled up against the vehicle's side like so much cut grass in a mower, and quickly reached a tipping point which caused it to flip and roll over them. It was still spinning and bouncing, crushing anything it fell upon, a door flapping like a broken wing, severing anything it met, when a fire sparked under the bonnet. Another bump and the van exploded, the mushrooming flame igniting several of the hoods' robes, sending them streaking in all directions, squealing like pigs.

Angela hobbled on around that blind bend. She thought the devastation might be enough to deter them at last and when she focused on the road ahead, on the car bearing down it she felt a swell of relief so powerful it shook her knees and brought tears to her eyes.

But as she hurried to meet that car she could still hear their voices, their lustful threats, their screams of anguish. She could smell the charred flesh and hair.

And she could feel the heat from the flames even before the burning one touched her.

Jeremy Wagner's Shopping List

-Heineken (1 case)
-Milk (1 Gallon)
-Eggs
-Deli Ham (1 pound)
-Tombstone Pizza (Canadian Bacon)
-Paper towels
-Astroglide
-Guitar strings
-Printer paper
-Count Chocula
-6-oz. filet mignon (2 total)
-Pepsi
-Spool of razorwire (1 total)
-Rubber tubing
-Hack saw
-Gas
-Gloves
-Cuffs
-Hatchet
-Gladys

Dead Half

Jeremy Wagner

Lester Clay woke up in his bed and was greeted by a mixture of pain and paralysis. His head hurt, his right eye throbbed, and the left side of his body felt like it was asleep. It was a late Saturday morning in July. Sunlight poured through the dusty blinds in Lester's bedroom and bathed his face and tattooed body in summer sun as he rested on his back, naked.

"Fuckin' Christ." He tried to use his arm to block the sunshine, but it wouldn't budge. Dead weight. Maybe his arm was asleep? He raised his SS and Swastika-inked forearm and laid it over his eyes and moaned. His head felt like a melon ready to split. Why'd it hurt so much? Must've been the brews at Collin's Tap and the fifth of Jack Daniels he downed when he got home last night.

Last night...

Lester's cloudy mind went back to last night. Back to the pain. Back to the humiliation.

Those fucking niggers...

Lester Clay was proud to be a full-blown racist. He and the guys he rolled with were all hatemongers; full of intolerance, anti-Semitic, anti-color—all on a white-power trip. He was bred on hatred, raised in an Aryan household by his father and two older brothers—all of whom were doing time in the state pen. His mom might have made a difference in his upbringing but she didn't stick around to try. She left the Clay men behind, gone when Lester was a year-and-a-half old.

Lester lived alone in his father's house while his old man and brothers all did life stints for raping and killing two Mexican girls. The house was run-down, in need of repair. Located on an older, grittier side of Springton, Illinois, the town locals dubbed, "White Trash Central."

Springton was located in the southern part of the state and was said to have two major exports: corn and assholes. Springton was also a college and party town. The college—Hawthorne University—was a definite bottom-of-the-barrel, party-college with a 70% dropout rate.

Collin's Tap was a local dive on the edge of the Hawthorne University campus. Failing college students, bikers, and some locals frequented the bar. Lester Clay and two of his skinhead friends decided to stop there last night just for kicks and for trouble.

Lester Clay was proud of his formidable reputation. He was twenty-six and stood six-feet tall and every inch was lean muscle. His arms, neck, and head were covered with neo-Nazi and racist tattoos.

Lester's two friends—Fuzz and Gino—were nearly the same height and build as Lester. When the three men went out, they all dressed the same; black, steel-toed

Doc Marten's boots, Levi's blue-jeans rolled up at the cuffs, white, tucked-in t-shirts, black suspenders, and black bomber jackets made up their entire outfits. They looked like triplets.

It was at Collin's Tap last night that Lester and his two sidekicks ran into a couple of college students from Uganda. The two students were in their early twenties, tall and thin ebony men dressed in colorful robes, hats, and sandals. The men entered the bar, taking in the loud music, the rowdy voices, and dozens of sports-filled televisions in the smoke-filled establishment.

In Collin's Tap, the Ugandan men stuck out like they were from Mars.

Fuzz had been the first to see the foreigners enter the bar. He elbowed Lester and Gino as they sat at a small table sharing a pitcher of beer. "Looks like Martin Luther Coon just stepped in."

Lester and Gino looked up from their beer mugs and saw the Ugandan men. Lester's loud and deep voice penetrated the din. "Hey Kuntakinte! The Soul Club is over on 5th Street. You're on the wrong side of town."

A few people chuckled, including Fuzz and Gino. The strangers stared at Lester for a moment without expression, and then approached the bar.

"Time for a little ethnic cleansing." Lester drained his sixth mug of Bud. He stood up from the table and walked toward the bar while Fuzz and Gino stayed in their seats, looking on with anxious smiles.

Lester came up behind the foreigners—who were nearly a foot taller than himself—and slapped them hard on their backs as they stood at the bar talking. Their glasses of booze spilled on their robes.

"You boys lost?" Lester grinned. The men turned around and frowned as they looked down at him.

"Damn, you niggers are tall. Don't suppose you play basketball, do you?"

The foreigners looked at each other for a moment, and then stared back at Lester, as if trying to figure out who he was and what his intentions were. One of the men spoke, his voice tinged with accent. "We're students at Hawthorne University. From Uganda. We don't play basketball."

"Wow. Uganda, huh?" Lester wasn't impressed. "I don't suppose you boys are familiar with the word *nigger,* are ya?"

The men glared at Lester. The quiet one took a step toward Lester before his companion stopped him.

"Yeah, c'mon and do it." Lester balled his hands into fists. "I double-dog dare ya, Kunta."

The talkative one looked Lester up and down. "You call me M'loke and you call my friend, Joba. Now treat us with respect and leave us be."

"Maybe I don't want to let you be."

Lester noticed that M'Loke and Joba were looking at his chest and not his face. Lester looked down and realized they were looking at his t-shirt. The shirt was white and had a design in black ink depicting three pointy-hooded clansmen with words written across the top: *The Original Boyz in the Hood.*

Lester laughed. "Hey, you like my shirt? It's a hoot, ain't it?"

M'loke and Joba glowered at Lester for a moment, and then M'loke smiled and turned to Joba, and whispered in his ear. The men both erupted in laughter as if they shared the funniest joke in the world.

Lester started fuming. Was some fucking joke on him? He was inebriated and rowdy and the laughter was excuse enough to make Lester pick a fight. "You niggers fuckin' laughing at me? I'll kick your asses back to Africa."

M'loke and Joba continued laughing. Big bright and white smiles filled their faces as they looked down on Lester. There was something malevolent in their expressions...as if they had suddenly transformed their faces into devil masks. Lester blinked, and their diabolic countenance disappeared.

Lester had enough. "Fuck you." He kicked M'loke in the crotch. Their laughter stopped, and the entire bar went quiet—aside from the sound of classic rock blaring from the jukebox. Lester stared at M'loke with astonishment. The African man didn't even blink when Lester kicked him. The steel-toed Doc Marten had hit hard, but it didn't even seem to faze M'loke at all. In fact, M'loke started laughing again as did Joba.

"Fuzz! Gino!" Lester waved. "Knuckles, now!"

Fuzz and Gino came up and stood behind Lester as he faced M'loke and Joba. People began clearing out of the way as the face-off ensued.

"My foot didn't seem to do the trick. Musta left your balls in Africa." Lester looked M'loke in the eyes. M'loke was still laughing. "I'll knock that grin off your black face."

Lester swung his right fist as hard as he could at M'loke's face. M'loke's left hand came up in a blur of speed, and blocked Lester's punch. Then M'loke grabbed Lester's bald head with his large right hand and pinned him to the bar. Fuzz and Gino jumped on M'loke and tried to wrestle him to the ground, but with no luck. M'loke couldn't be moved. Joba stepped in and grabbed Fuzz and Gino by their necks and threw them like a pair of kittens into a wall where they fell together in a bruised heap.

Lester couldn't believe the uncanny strength that Joba and M'loke possessed. M'loke drove Lester's head into the bar and it felt as if a hydraulic press was pushing his skull forward. Lester thought his head would explode. He struggled and fought as hard as he could, but M'loke had him pinned in permanently in place—and with only one hand.

"I'm gonna fucking kill you, you goddamn nigger motherfucker!" Lester's fury and pain were rising. "Get this fucker off me! Fuzz! Gino!"

No one stepped forward to help Lester. The patrons in the bar kept their distance, and Lester's friends were still on the floor, struggling to get on their feet.

Lester could see M'loke's face out of the corner of his eye. M'loke leaned down as he held tight to Lester's pinned head, his face now an inch away from Lester's left ear. Lester could feel and smell M'loke's breath; warm and wet like Nile water, and stinking like the dead fish therein.

"There be all kinds of people in this world..." M'loke whispered in a demonic tone as he held Lester. "...and everybody full of different things. But one thing is always the same, every man has two sides: good and bad. I'a kill your bad side."

Lester suddenly felt an intense, burning, and nearly unbearable pain in the left side of his body. It was as if a giant stinger had penetrated the side of his stomach and ejaculated venom throughout his left half. Lester released a piercing scream that quickly died to a weak whimper as he was released from M'loke's grip. Lester slid down to the floor and curled into a ball amid puddles of beer, cigarette butts, and peanut shells.

The jukebox was silent, and Collin's Tap was still and quiet. M'loke and Joba took one last look at Lester and his friends before exiting the bar.

As soon as the Ugandan men left, Collin's Tap filled with murmurs, then talking and drink orders resumed while Charlie Daniels began pouring out of the jukebox, telling a tale about a swamp and things out there that made strong men die of fright.

Lester, Fuzz, and Gino picked themselves up. All of them were hurting. A bouncer in a black Collin's Tap t-shirt walked up and folded his large arms. "Okay, time for you guys to leave."

"Why, Jerry? You saw what happened. We were jumped." Lester rubbed his head and caressed the left side of his stomach. "If you would've been doing your job those niggers would've left in an ambulance."

"I'm not going to argue with you, Lester." Jerry shook his head. "I've already covered for you with the cops when you broke that guy's jaw last month because he was from Pakistan."

"Fucking sand-nigger."

"Yeah, well, I can't have you guys in here anymore. We've always had a rowdy reputation, but you skinheads take shit too far." Jerry pointed a finger at Lester. "Frank Collins has owned this place for forty years and he's seen all kinds, and he gets all kinds and all colors from the university. Racism is bad business. You guys cause too many problems and the cops are watching this place. In fact, they've already been called."

"We've been coming here forever, man!" Lester tried defending his right to stay put. "My old man grew up with Frank Collins and this has been a hang-out for all of us."

"Sorry, Les, but that's the rules now. We can't have you busting heads because you don't like someone's color, religion, or where they came from. This ain't Trump's bar."

"Fuck this shithole. I don't need to come to a place that serves subhuman immigrants." Lester almost screeched as he put a hand on his wound. The distant sound of police sirens could now be heard through the barroom noise. Lester turned to Fuzz and Gino. "Let's roll outta here."

The three men dashed into Gino's pickup truck and peeled out of the parking lot and into the night. It was beginning to rain. Thunder and lightning filled the sky. Fuzz sat in the middle while Lester sat next to the passenger-side door. They all let out intermittent moans of pain as they traveled down the road.

"Goddamn crazy Africans got us good." Gino grimaced as he drove. "The one who grabbed us must've been on something to have thrown us like he did. Skinny as a bean-pole and strong as a friggin' bull."

"Probably on PCP or crack," Fuzz offered.

Lester was silent. His left side was on fire. His gut churned, and he felt a block of persistent, burning pain lodged between his pelvis and the bottom of his left ribcage. The block of pain shot out razored tendrils that went down to his left ankle and all the way up his neck and to his left temple. He carefully rubbed the tip of his right index finger through the hole in his blood-soaked t-shirt and touched the wound. "Fuck me." Pain flared higher from his touch.

"Hurting good, huh?" Fuzz turned toward Lester.

"Nothing that a little Jack Daniels won't fix." Lester winced as he lightly poked the puncture in his side. Was there something in there? He could feel something beneath the skin, like a hard bump. A little more pain and exploration made Lester realize that there was indeed an object inside of him. He leaned back in his seat and began undoing his belt.

"Whatchya doin'?" Fuzz watched Lester remove his black-leather belt with its KKK buckle. "You're not gonna get naked are ya?"

"Shut your cum-catcher." Lester removed his belt. "Give me a little room here."

Lester un-tucked his bloodstained t-shirt and placed the belt between his teeth and bit down hard. Then with his right index finger and thumb, he pinched the object beneath his skin and squeezed it until it popped out of the wound.

"What the fuck, Les?" Gino nearly went off the road as Lester let out a cry of gritting pain.

"You dyin or what?" Fuzz's eyes grew huge.

Lester let the belt drop from his mouth as the object in his wound broke through. His eyes watered, and he breathed hard, feeling as if he had just squeezed and busted the grand-daddy of all zits. He looked down at his left side and saw something poking out of the blood-oozing hole in his abdomen. He hesitated for a moment and then reached over again with his right index finger and thumb and pulled the object out of his side.

"What the fuck is that?" Gino and Fuzz spoke at the same time as they looked at the object Lester was holding out in front of him.

"Not sure." Lester's eyes blinked tears of pain as he studied the thing in his fingers. He thought it looked like some kind of needle or pin. It was about three-inches long, made out of black wood, with a razor-sharp tip and a miniature, hand-carved, grinning skull on the other end between Lester's pinching digits. "Some kind of needle. Fuckin' nigger-needle."

"Yeah, well a nigger with a needle means AIDS." Gino's voice sounded alarmed as he drove.

"Yeah, Les. You need to get to a doctor before you wind up with capital HIV." Fuzz moved a few inches away from Lester. "Or that Ebola shit!"

"Fuck both of you." Lester was irritated, but relieved now that the needle was out of him. "I'm not gonna get Ebola or AIDS or any of that queer shit. I'll clean myself up and that will be the end of it."

Gino and Fuzz looked at with other with uncertainty. "You sure you don't want me to take you by the hospital?" Gino asked.

"Just take me home, goddamnit." Lester tried not to yell. "Jack Daniels is calling."

Gino and Fuzz didn't say anything. They all drove on into the stormy night while Lester rolled down his window and threw M'Loke's nasty needle out into the dark.

Now it was the morning after. Lester Clay lay in his soiled bed and pushed away last night's bad memories. He needed his attention on other things—like the pain and paralysis taking over half his body.

Maybe if he just popped some Advil all would be better. What he wouldn't do for the throbbing in his head and eyes. He wanted to get his blood circulating. He hoped it would reawaken his left side.

Again, his left arm wouldn't budge. Lester tried, but couldn't raise the dead weight of his left arm or left leg. He wasn't so sure if his left limbs were truly asleep. There wasn't any of the typical sensations of pins and needles or any dull feeling of numbness. No, actually, there wasn't any feeling at all. No muscles obeyed his mental commands. What the fuck was up with that? Lester pinched his left forearm as hard as he could with his right thumb and index finger, but there was nothing. Not a flicker of pressure in the skin or nerves of his left arm. It was like pinching a corpse.

Cindy better get her ass over here before work. She can take a look at me.

Cindy was Cindy Morgan, Lester's steady for the last year. She was also a Springton native and lived within the limits of White Trash Central. She was a little smarter than Lester, he knew that, but she shared most of his racist and political views. That's what attracted them to each other. Like Lester, Cindy was also from a long line of hatemongers.

Lester would've called Cindy, but his phone had been disconnected for several weeks. He didn't have a job and his need to pay for groceries and the electric bill trumped his need for a mobile phone. "Fuck it." Lester spoke to his messy bedroom. "Don't need no phone. The bitch'll be here."

Using his right arm and leg, Lester rolled over, twisted, and threw his limp left arm and leg over so that he was now sitting up. Summoning all of his strength, Lester managed to stand, putting all of his weight on his right leg, and made for the attached bathroom with an awkward, naked hop as his lifeless left leg and arm flopped.

Lester made it into the dimly-lit bathroom and rested his lively right-side against the dusty, soap-scum covered sink. "Fuck." Lester felt dizzy. He gasped for air. "This sucks." After catching his breath, Lester reached into the mirrored, rusty metal medicine-cabinet above the sink and pulled out a bottle of Advil. With his right hand and right thumb, Lester popped off the safety top and sucked three tablets into his mouth.

Lester wobbled on his right leg and dropped the Advil bottle into the sink. "Shit!" He steadied himself and then cautiously reached for a grimy drinking glass on the bathroom countertop. He grasped the glass in his right hand and turned on the faucet with his chin. Once the glass was half full, he sucked the water in and choked down the Advil. He set the glass down and turned off the water.

Did I have a fucking stroke last night? What the fuck?

Just as he was about to go back into his bedroom, Lester took a quick look at himself in the medicine-cabinet mirror and didn't like what he saw. He could see himself from the chest up in the mirror. The left half of his face, neck, and chest was an extremely pasty-white color, in stark contrast to the normal skin tone on the right side of his body. Looking down, Lester saw that the pasty-white flesh continued below his chest, left arm, down his abdomen, left testicle, left leg, and foot. It was as if the right side of his body had been perfectly masked off, while the left half of his body had been perfectly sprayed with some kind of dull, off-white paint. He was split right down the middle by two different pigments of flesh. Even the few hairs around his left nipple and his pubic hair—which were normally jet-black—were white.

What the fuck is happening?

Lester imagined his backside was probably divided between two skin colors right down his spine, but he was confident that his pimple-dotted ass probably looked normal as it never had a ray of sun touch it in all twenty-six years of his life.

No matter how bad he looked and no matter whatever was ailing Lester, it didn't bother him too much. The men of the Clay clan would never admit to being sick and they certainly would never see a doctor unless they were down to their last five ounces of blood and about to expire. Lester was no different, and he wasn't too worried about his current condition—yet. His late grandmother called him ignorant, prideful, and too stupid to pull himself out of a bear-trap. Boy, was she right.

Lester looked himself over one more time, shrugged his working shoulder, and hopped back to his bedroom. The heat in the room was rising as the summertime sun did its work. The few feet he hopped to his bed left him exhausted, light-headed, and hot. He began to sway and then fell forward onto his septic mattress and passed out.

"Hey, asshole. Wake up!"

The voice of a woman cut into Lester's consciousness, waking him. His eyes fluttered, and he wasn't sure where he was for a moment.

"C'mon, Les. Get your ass up."

Lester knew the voice. It was Cindy, his steady girl. Her voice sounded strange to him as it was accompanied by a constant buzzing sound.

"Hey." Lester rolled over and looked up at her. His eyes focused on her face, which was dotted with flies which circled her head and lit upon her blemished cheeks and forehead. She was wearing her blue and white waitress uniform for her day shift at Roxanne's Diner. She had her green contacts in, and her dirty-blonde hair was tied back into a French-braid.

"Hey, yourself." Cindy waved her hand through the air to dissipate the numerous flies buzzing throughout the bedroom. "What the hell is going on around here?"

"Dunno. Just sleeping in is all."

"Yeah, you must've had a hell of a night. I didn't get one call from you." Cindy wrinkled her nose. "P-U. It fucking stinks in here, Les. All these goddamn flies and the heat is making your room into an oven."

Lester couldn't smell anything, but he felt the heat. "Open the window for me, would ya?"

"Is your fucking arm broke?"

"It might be. I actually feel really numb. Half my body isn't working."

"Yeah, well that's probably thanks to Jack Daniels or Jagermeister." Cindy opened a window and began shooing the flies out. A light breeze blew into the bedroom. "That's better."

"You on your way to Roxanne's?" Lester welcomed the breeze that cooled him.

"Actually, I'm on my lunch-break." Cindy pulled out a cigarette and lit it. "You've been sleeping the day away."

"So it's like, after twelve or something?" Lester moaned as a wave of dizziness went through him.

"Something like that." Cindy released a long exhale of smoke. "Day's half over, dummy."

"Quit calling me names, bitch. Now how 'bout a kiss?"

"How 'bout a bath, stinky?"

"Awww, c'mon."

Cindy rolled her eyes. "All right." She took the smoke from her mouth, leaned over and was about to kiss Lester. Then Cindy stopped suddenly and stood up. She stared down at Lester for a moment and narrowed her eyes. "My god, what's wrong with you?"

"What are you talking about?"

"You're like half George Hamilton and half Pillsbury Dough-Boy."

"What the fuck are you talking about?"

"Half of your body is darker and the other half is white as fresh milk." Cindy looked Lester up and down as he lay on top of his mattress, naked. "And I don't want to even look at what's going on south of the border."

"I'm fine." Lester felt himself getting irritated with her. "Why don't you get off my back?"

"No, I'm serious." Cindy flicked ashes out the open window. "You're like divided in half by two different colors. Like one side is sick and the other is healthy or something. And you reek to high heaven. Gawd, it's like a rat died under your fucking pillow. You smell rotten."

"Bitch, I feel fine and I can't smell anything." Lester tried to sit up. "Your nose is probably fucked from all that slop they sling over at the diner."

"My nose is just fine, asshole. You got some problems. What happened to you last night?"

"Just had boys-night-out with Fuzz and Gino."

"Yeah, I heard about your 'boys-night-out' from Amanda."

Lester closed his eyes and groaned. Amanda was Gino's old lady and Cindy's best friend. As much of a tough-guy Gino was, he couldn't hold his own under Amanda's interrogations. Whatever the issue under question was, Gino always cracked and spilled his guts, no matter how innocent or guilty he might be. And when it involved Lester, it was always bad. By the time Gino opened his mouth, the old-girl-network of Cindy, Amanda, and all their other girlfriends already knew what dirt the boys had gotten into and they already knew what punishments were to be dealt out.

"Okay then. What version of last night did you hear?"

"I heard you got into a tussle with some niggers over at Collin's Tap."

"Yeah, so?"

"I heard they threw you, Fuzz, and Gino around pretty good. Heard you got stabbed or something. Any truth to this?"

Lester thought to himself for a moment. He couldn't believe what a pussy Gino was. Gino could have at least lied to Amanda and said that they beat the living dog shit out of those Ugandans. That would have sounded better. "Uh yeah, something like that happened."

"Something like what? I wanna hear it from you."

"Look, I don't want to talk about it right now. I feel like shit."

"What about being stabbed? Is that true?"

Lester let out a long sigh. "Yeah. Nig poked me with a fucking pin or something. Nailed me in my left side. It's nothing."

"*Nothing?* Sure looks like something to me. Explains all this ill-health you're in." Cindy leaned over Lester's nude body and inspected him. "Shit, is that where he stuck you?" Cindy pointed at a crusty, black hole a few inches below Lester's left ribcage.

Lester glanced at the small crater which was oozing a thick, yellow and green fluid from it. "Yeah, that's where he got me all right."

"What was it? A knife? A shank? Gino said it was a needle."

"Goddamnit! I don't fucking remember, okay? And Gino and his bitch need to keep their mouths shut."

Cindy was quiet for moment. She shook her head. "Well, it looks nasty. You look nasty. I sure as hell hope you don't have some disease."

"Shut-up already."

"I'll be right back." Cindy walked into Lester's bathroom and rummaged through his bathroom doors and cabinets. She returned with her hands full.

"What are you doin'?"

"I'm cleaning that wound." Cindy kept her smoke between her teeth as she removed the tops off a bottle of rubbing-alcohol and a bottle of hydrogen-peroxide.

"Be careful."

"After this, it's enema-time." Cindy laughed.

"Fuck off." Lester watched Cindy dab some cotton balls with alcohol and cleaned the oozing stab-hole. Cindy then dabbed more cotton balls with hydrogen-peroxide and Lester watched as the suppurating crater bubbled as the peroxide swam inside it.

"Does that hurt?" Cindy asked as she mopped up septic matter from the wound.

"I can't feel a fuckin' thing. My whole left side is dead."

"Maybe you have some pinched nerves or something. I sure as hell hope that your numbness doesn't have anything to do with that nigger-wound you got there. If you're not better by tonight, I'm gonna take you to the hospital."

"Fuck that." Lester tried to sit up. "I'm gonna be fine and I'm not going to any doctor."

"Lay down, dummy." Cindy pressed Lester's chest and forced him back down on his back. She opened up an adhesive bandage and covered the puncture in Lester's side. She patted the bandage. "There. All better for now."

"Thanks, bitch."

"You're such a romantic." Cindy looked at her wrist-watch. "Gotta run. I'll be off work at around 6:30 or so."

"Kiss?" Lester puckered his pink and white lips.

"Yikes. Not today." Cindy blew him a kiss. "That'll have to tide you over, honey."

"Whatever." Lester wished he could actually smell himself. "Do me a favor would ya?"

"Sure. What?"

"Bring me home a lake trout dinner and fries from Roxanne's, okay?"

"Sure, hon." Cindy started to leave the bedroom. She stopped and turned. "Do me a favor, too."

"What's that?" Lester asked as he stared up at the cracked and water-stained drywall of his ceiling. He wasn't sure, but his left ear felt like it was plugged up.

"Let this room air out and please, please take a long bath or a shower."

"Get bent."

"Love you, too," Cindy said and then was gone as the front door of the Clay house shut behind her.

"Beddr be bek thooner than lether, bith." What the fuck did he just say? Lester felt fear as the words left his mouth. He had meant to say, *Better be back sooner than later, bitch*, but the words got all jumbled.

Maybe I did have a stroke. A massive one...

But Lester knew that it was worse than that.

Lester drifted into troubled sleep shortly after Cindy left. He had terrible images of M'loke, his face huge and grinning with a mouthful of large, pointy teeth bearing down at him. The giant M'loke chased Lester into a wheat-field surrounded by a dozen KKK clansmen decked out in white hoods and robes. They were all calling Lester a nigger and were laughing at him. "No! No! I'm no fucking nigger!" Lester screamed in his nightmare. The Klansmen all removed their hoods, revealing themselves as M'loke. All of the M'loke's laughed and bared their pointy cannibal teeth.

All together, the multiple Klan M'loke's spoke like a choir. "In Uganda, our witchcraft is oldest of all. Since the Paleolithic. We sacrifice people and children for wealth spells. We eat people like you. And we hex people like you who menace our peoples."

Then, the giant M'loke, nearly fifty-feet tall, picked up Lester with an enormous hand, and in his other hand, he held the witchcraft needle of black wood, with its sharp tip and hand-carved grinning skull, but now it was the size of a javelin. M'loke stuck Lester through his chest and the giant needle skewered Lester's entire body. The Kong-sized M'loke stuck the needle into the field as the Klan-M'lokes danced around Lester as he writhed, pinned like a bug in a field of screams.

Lester was wailing as he awoke in his bedroom. If his heart was beating, he didn't know as he couldn't feel any life in his left chest. He sat up, panting and trying to see. In the late afternoon light, he tried to focus his eyes, but had trouble seeing clearly. With his left eye closed, he could see fine, but when the left eye was open, everything was blurry. It was as if his left eye had been fitted with a hazy, distorted lens.

Lester let out a yelp of startled surprise as he saw the left side of his body was black and buzzing. There was a blanket of black flies—poop-flies his old man used to call them—covering and crawling on every inch of skin from Lester's left foot to his left earlobe. Not one fly was on his right side.

"Fuckers!" Lester tried to use all of his limbs to get up. Only his right arm and leg were cooperating, and they flailed as his left-side limbs were motionless. Using his right arm and leg, Lester managed to roll over and get on his stomach. Flies buzzed angrily as they fled the unstable flesh and swarmed above Lester.

Gotta get in the shower, Lester thought to himself. He was revolted by the mass of flies that had been blanketing him while he was sleeping. *Get these nasty fuckers away from me.*

Lester implemented his right arm and leg and pushed himself up from his mattress and onto his ass. As before, but with much more difficulty, he was able to get onto his good leg and make his way to the bathroom. He fell a couple times, and while he was entering the bathroom, his left foot somehow got caught on a corner of the metal threshold in the doorway. Without looking down,

Lester jerked his body, and moved forward as his left foot was freed. As he moved forward, Lester's right ear picked up a wet, ripping sound, but he didn't give it much thought.

With slow, and deliberate care, Lester sat himself down on the edge of the filthy bathtub, turned on the hot water, and then ran the shower. He stood up and braced himself on the counter of the sink as steam filled the bathroom. In the fogging mirror, he gazed at himself and could see the left half of his body was even more discolored and nasty looking than it had been earlier. His skin was now a dark gray and covered with white and blue spots. The left-side of his mouth looked cadaverous as his left-side lips were drawn back, nearly gone, revealing receding and bloody left-side gum-lines filled with yellow and black teeth. His left cheekbone and jawbones stuck out beneath the spotted and shallow facial flesh, while his left eye appeared to be sunken into its socket with the pupil and iris now a glassy white color. Steam covered the mirror, eliminating Lester's reflection. He was thankful for that.

This isn't happening. NOT HAPPENING.

In the shower, Lester was able to hold himself up on a stainless-steel bar that his dad had installed years ago into the wall of the shower. Lester's dad had bad knees and had put the bar in so that he wouldn't fall down while washing himself. Lester was washing himself, actually more like rinsing himself since he couldn't scrub himself with soap because his right arm had to hold the bar and his weight had to remain on his right leg in order to keep his useless left-half up.

Did that nigger give me AIDS? Maybe it WAS Ebola. Maybe it WAS witchcraft.

Lester tried to ignore his thoughts. He took little comfort in the hot water...water he could only feel running down the right-side of his body.

Maybe I better get to a doctor. And then I'll find that nigger and hang his black ass.

Lester looked down and was shocked to see that the inked swastikas, burning crosses, and the other racist tattoos on the left-half of his body were running down his body in black and blue streams, as if they were being washed right out of his pores. Panic owned him as the hot shower-water was churning the flesh of Lester's left arm, chest, and extremities into gray oatmeal.

Lester was going to scream, but he choked and spit up a mouthful of blood and some meaty debris that had come from somewhere deep inside him. He spat out a red glob into the bathtub and gagged. Frantic to get out of the shower, Lester twisted around violently and used his right leg to launch him. He lunged and hopped out of the bathtub, tearing the plastic and moldy shower-curtain down as he did so. He crashed into the bathroom counter, sending toiletries and bottles of cheap cologne to the floor.

Lester muttered to himself hysterically as he fought to untangle himself from the shower curtain. Blobs of cottage-cheese flesh sloughed off of Lester and spattered onto the floor. As soon as Lester was free of the curtain, he tried to run, but his right foot slipped on a slick pile of dead-tissue and he fell backwards. Unable to gain any balance, Lester crashed, the back of his head catching the edge of the bathroom's urine and pubic-hair encrusted bowl as he went down. He was instantly knocked unconscious.

***

The shower was still running, completely cold now as Lester stirred. He felt as if his mind was short-circuiting. His thoughts, his surroundings, and whatever physical feeling he had left came to him in flashing chunks of information. This info wasn't completely connected. It was like he was viewing slides. There would be pictures and then momentary blackness, then more pictures, then blackness again.

Lester found himself on his back. His right ear picked up the shower running. Blackness. He was able to lift his head and realized he couldn't see out of his left eye. He also knew that the left half of his body was rotting as countless, wriggling, white and plump maggots now burrowed into the butter-soft tissues and organs of his left-half gave their purpose away.

My mind...mind is rotten.

Somehow, Lester summoned the will to stand up one last time and see what he'd become. He gazed into the bathroom mirror and found himself standing tall—a semi-animated, semi-undead scourge. He'd gone from hate slinger to carrion merchant in twenty-four hours.

Lester's reflection revealed his head; half of it looked normal and healthy, with the right eye sparkling and full of life, while the left-half of his head was in advanced decay. Cracked and mottled yellow flesh wrapped around the left half of his skull. Wispy and sparse white hair had sprung up and hung rooted like dead weeds from his fetid scalp.

He tried to make a sound but only drooled like some rabid dog. His right eye widened, but he bore no expression on his half-skeletal face. It reminded him of the super villain, Two-Face, from the Batman comic.

His left ear was missing, and his left eyeball was nearly gone. The malignant eyehole boiled over with fly larvae and the dirty yellow eyeball within wept sebaceous, maggot-filled, secretions. The unsavory egress ran from the ocular hole in a slimy rivulet. Lester tried to focus, and the cankered and blighted globule twitched in its moldered socket and rotated about before stopping to give the mirror a marcescent stare.

Lester became unhinged and struggled to keep lunacy away. His taxed brain tried to comprehend how the stagnant, wasted spheroid could move—much less see—from inside his hideous head.

He blinked and saw he was noseless, with the shrunken septum and nasal bone out in the open. Lester blinked again with weary loathing, he noted hairy and jointed legs of some arachnid hung outside the dark cavity. At the sight of that, he opened his mouth to scream, and as he did, a swarm erupted...his mouth had become a haven for flies. They buzzed in and out of it like a multitude of tiny planes at an airplane hangar. His mouth hung open and displayed carious teeth, protracted and discolored, all visible and imbedded in jawbone devoid of gum tissue. The exposed mandible hyper-extended on leathery strips of muscle and dry-aged skin. His left cheek was nothing but mere sinews that snapped apart and revealed more of his rotting teeth and his jawbone. When he opened his mouth in mute protest, a black and withered tongue lolled from the sordid cavern, moist with noxious drool from deceased salivary glands he couldn't get his mind around.

Lester tried keeping his shit together. He held himself up with his muscular right arm on the sink. He looked away from the mirror and scanned the left side of his body with his good eye. His left arm hung as a rotten limb with an ossuary claw swung limp next to his bloated and deleterious left-side gut. He groaned and twisted to look away, his threadbare bottom jaw ratched and flopped open wider. The movement of his body tore open his insubstantial abdominal flesh and released an unpleasant throng of decomposed entrails. The lower abdomen and its swaying bag of guts opened into a wide gash and eviscerated him, releasing pounds of feculent viscera that splashed to the floor. It didn't seem to stop. Lester, a poster-child for putrescence, watched in pure horror as the tainted innards, bright green with rot and slick, slopped out of him.

At that, Lester collapsed to the floor. It took nearly an hour and a half, but he managed to crawl the few yards that lay between the toilet and his bed. On his way to the bedroom, Lester caught a glimpse of the big toe of his left foot stuck to the threshold of the bathroom doorway.

Lester crawled on with only one purpose, one goal that his rotting brain tried desperately to hold on to.

The bedroom was darkening as the sun was beginning to set. Lester had a mental flash of Cindy before flashing to clarity again. Another flash of Cindy with a trout dinner with fries. She should've been off of work by now.

She'll...she'll wish she stayed at the diner when she...sees what's left of me.

Lester found it hard to think. He also knew it would be hard, if not impossible, to even talk now. He'd never be able to say anything to Cindy when he saw her.

Forget...the bitch.

He had to stay focused on his new objective. Somewhere in the tainted mess of his brain, Lester had a new idea he needed to see through. He crawled to his bedside and reached under his bed with his right hand and found what he had been looking for. His objective. In his right hand, Lester gripped the rubber combat-grip of a stainless-steel, Smith & Wesson .44 magnum revolver.

It took all the mental effort and physical strength he had to pull back the hammer. The pictures in his brain were becoming more and more infrequent. He began seeing images of M'loke. The Ugandan man was laughing at him and spoke to him. *Look at who you are.* M'loke's voice saturated Lester's septic mind. M'loke images intertwined with images of all the hate crimes and racist atrocities Lester had committed in his life. Lester could almost detect a hot, burnt-flesh stench from M'loke's breath. *I told you. Every man has two sides: good and bad. I'a a kill your bad side.*

For a moment Lester felt a minute pang of remorse for all of his intolerance as he placed the four-inch barrel to his right temple. He would repent for his evil and racist ways if he thought it would do any good, but he knew it was too late. M'loke and his terrible witch needle had done a fine job at turning him into half of a rotting corpse—but he'd be damned if he'd try and survive and somehow live his life half-embalmed.

As he lay on his back upon the dirty floor of his bedroom, he placed the revolver to his right temple, and in a blink, Lester's living side joined the dead half in a loud explosion of blood, bone, and brains.

James Watts' Shopping List

1. Video games
2. Movies
3. Collectibles
4. Tacos
5. Pizza
6. Milk
7. Books
8. Dr. Pepper
9. Bottled Water
10. Orange Juice
11. Apple Juice
12. Cheese
13. Ice Cream
14. Fruits
15. Chocolate drink.

Deranged Innocence
James Watts

Not long before the school day ended, the sun had shown its face and scared away the rain. Jason Hicks left his school, moving past the bus stop kids, the car riders, and the little groups of kids who, like him, walked to and from school, either by choice or by circumstance, and crossed over to Lee street, with its *Leave-it-to-Beaver* houses and its perfectly manicured lawns. His house was on Burch Avenue, and Lee Street was the quickest route on foot. That and there were no mean dogs on Lee Street, well except for Mrs. Smith's Chihuahua, Rodney, but ankle biters like Rodney didn't scare him any.

He was about halfway down Lee when he saw Terry Callahan standing next to the street lamp across from Linda Bennett's house. Terry was a grade behind him in school, but two years his elder, having flunked the fifth grade twice, as well as on his way to flunking a third time, and was the one person that knew how to bury himself right up under Jason's skin.

Terry saw Jason and waved, then dropped his backpack to the sidewalk and waddled toward him. Terry was fat, smelled like fried bologna most of the time, and his wardrobe seemed to consist of nothing but grease stained baggy jeans and tee shirts from every comic book ever created. Today he was sporting a green *Dr. Strange* tee with a fading, crumbling decal and no sleeves. His hair, which was firebrick red, was always greasy and in need of cutting, and today, it was in no better shape than usual.

"Hey, Jason! Wait up, man!"

Jason stopped and waited for Terry. When the older boy did catch up, his chest was heaving breaths in and out so hard that Jason expected to see him exhale his lungs. "Ho…hold on. Got…got to…got to catch my breath. You tryin' to kill me, walkin' so damn fast."

Jason, who had not even noticed that he had been walking fast, just looked at Terry and shrugged. "If you weren't so…*big boned,*" Jason said, using the term Terry so often used to indicate his weight. "And in better shape, you wouldn't be about to barf up your insides right now."

"Ah, man. I wait here for like ten minutes to tell a guy my biggest good news ever and he cuts on me. What kind of shit is that?"

"Lighten up, Callahan. I'm just messing with you."

"You could be nice to a guy every once and again, that's all I'm saying."

"So what's your biggest good news?" Jason asked, not really interested but quite aware that if he didn't ask, Terry would not stop pestering him until he did.

"Hold on," Terry said, trundling over to where he had dropped his backpack. He picked it up, slung it over one bulbous shoulder, and came back over to where Jason was waiting. "Okay. What would you say if I told you I know a way you could get your Walkman back from Ricky Shands, *and* impress little miss proper..." Terry, smiling like a mad clown on acid, gave a nod towards Linda Bennett's house. "...at the same time?"

"And how do you plan to do that?" Jason asked with authentic curiosity. Ricky Shands, local school bully, and Linda's current beau, with a couple of his close buddies (Jerry Tucker and Matt Harman), had cornered Jason behind the Gym on the first day of school after Christmas Break, and had forced him to hand over his Walkman, Jason's favorite *Iron Maiden* cassette still inside. Ricky had actually *forced* him to give it to them. Jason had complied rather than take a beating, either way, they would have taken it, and he had known this, so he had chosen option one and saved himself a world of misery. His heart hurt to see it go, as it had been a Christmas gift and the best one under the tree, but he had handed it over. He wanted it back, more than anything.

"What makes you think Ricky even still has it? It's been like five months, dude, it's probably busted by now or traded to one of those other dicks he hangs with."

"I saw him with it. And I know it's yours because your initials are carved on the back of it."

"Ricky's a lot bigger than me, Terry, and he'd kick your fat ass all over town. It's a lost cause." Jason was walking away from Terry as he spoke.

"C'mon, dude, I know a perfect way," Terry persisted as he fell in alongside Jason, panting heavily, struggling to keep up, and trying to get a word in between breaths. "They won't even know it was us."

Jason slowed his walk and looked at Terry with a questioning glance.

The bigger boy, relieved by the slower pace, continued with his pitch. "The Garrison house over on Douglas." He spat, fighting to catch his breath.

"What about it?" Jason asked, ignoring the way Terry was wheezing and hitching breaths like a chain smoker attempting to run the triathlon.

They had reached the end of Lee Street and Jason stopped to check for traffic. At this time of day, you could usually expect to see one of the older kids come speeding by in one of their souped up rides, oblivious to anything but the loud blasting of their stereos or their glass pack mufflers.

"That's where they hang out after school. In the backyard, smoking cigs and jerking each other off for all I know, but dude, they are always there alone. Jerry and Matt usually hang with him and sometimes that weird kid from the seventh grade, Johnny something, shit; I don't know his name. Dude freaks me out."

Johnny Dawson was his name and Jason knew a little about him. He was tall and lanky with greasy hair and a face full of pimples that he would pop while sitting in class, wiping the pus on his jeans. The kid was weird, no argument there. He had transferred in about three months ago, and the word around school was that he was kicked out of his old school because he had been caught stroking off Barry the Bulldog, the school's mascot. Jason didn't know if that was true, some form of gossip always seemed to trail in behind the new kids, but he did not doubt it either. Just last week Johnny had got into some trouble over bringing a dildo to school to harass the girls in his class with, screaming how he was going to stick it in their butts. Though Johnny had found his obscene antics hilarious, Miss Malcolm, the history teacher, and Principal Davis did not. He received a three-week suspension for that stunt.

"Why would they hang out with that guy? That's just creepy."

"Tell me about it," Terry agreed. "But they do. And sometimes Linda and a few of her friends hang out with them, too. Those dumb bitches think they so cool smoking cigs. So what do you say, Jay, you in or out?"

Checking the traffic once more, in a hurry to get home, not entirely sure he wanted to go along with whatever it was that Terry was cooking up in his disillusioned mind, Jason said, "I don't know, it sounds… Dude, if we do anything to those guys, we're likely to get burned."

Terry stared at him for a moment, frustration, and irritation plastered across his face as big as a billboard advertisement and shifting from foot-to-foot impatiently. It reminded Jason of the way his little sister Amy looked when she was waiting her turn at the upstairs bathroom in the mornings before school. "They won't know it was us," Terry went on. "No way they'll know. Them boys will be too *scared* to notice anything but how fast they can get home."

"Look. I got to get home before my mom calls out the National Guard to look for me, but I'll think about it. Is that cool?"

"Yea, I guess so," Terry said, a little disappointed. "But you think about it, Jay, and let me know in the morning. I swear, dude, this will have those boys shitting their pants."

"I'll think it over. See ya, Callahan," Jason crossed the street, leaving Terry to sulk on the corner of Lee and Burch.

Lying in his bed later that evening, serenaded by the crickets and the toads in the little patch of woods behind his house, Jason breathed deeply of the night air passing through his open window. On cool nights such as this, he loved to sleep with his window open, to snuggle in nature's caress, on top of his covers and bare-chested. It was ecstasy to sleep this way, not quite baring it all, but close enough, and it felt right somehow. As if he were some primal thing that ran free in the night, wind against his face, bloated silver dollar moon at his back. It was natural; he supposed that was the best word he knew to describe it, and that was fine by him.

As he lay there, Terry Callahan's idea to get even with Ricky Shands rolling over in his mind, Jason wondered just how good it would feel, how *natural* it would feel, to go through with it. Though Terry had not explained in any detail what sort of plan he had, outside of the fact that it would scare or embarrass the older boys, the thought of it was enough to make him ache for it. Either way it went, he did not care if he got his Walkman back or impressed Linda Bennet. He just wanted to see Ricky Shands on his knees crying like a little bitch. That would be oh so funny, and even worth the ass kicking he was sure to endure afterward. School let out for the summer in a couple of weeks, giving any bruises Jason would receive plenty of time to fade away before he had to face any of his classmates.

For this once in a lifetime opportunity, Jason would pay any price.

***

Two days before the last day of school, Jason's troubles with Ricky Shands and his dumb-as-rocks entourage escalated. A little over a week before, his friend, Terry, had mentioned a plan to get even with the small gang of bullies but had not gone into any details of his plan since. Terry had only hinted at how boss it was going to be and that he would explain before school let out for summer. Yet, still not a word. This had the powerhouse that was Jason's imagination sending several different scenarios pinballing through his mind. Many of which included Ricky knelt at Jason's feet blubbering like an infant and begging for forgiveness. Jason had imagined everything from the classic haunted house scare to a colony of plague-ridden cannibal transients feeding off prostitutes and children. This, in turn, would lead to his unfortunate run-in with Ricky and crew.

Summer break was only a matter of fourteen school hours away and his classmates, excited and blabbering over what they were going to do over their three-month hiatus' from classrooms and teachers, irritated the hell out of Jason. Luckily, it was only a few minutes before the end of the day bell and Jason could finally get away from these spazoids.

Jason divided his class into groups, which was not a particularly difficult task as they all huddled together in little packs like wild animals gathering in their own territories. On the far left of the room up front of the class was the good ol' boy redneck group, mainly discussing fishing down by the river or mud riding. The back, left corner of the room contained the thug and gangster rap types. Their plans simply consisted of smoking blunts at Atkins Park and sipping on a forty or a pint of this or a fifth of that. Which meant some dad's liquor cabinet was going to come up short. Jason wondered where they would get their weed now that Marcus Feldman went to prison. The police busted him in a raid on his small mobile home over on Atkins Park road a little over a month ago.

In the back center was a combination of Goth kids, with their black clothes and black spiked hair, and the metalheads, which coincidentally shared similar plans to the young thugs in training. In front of them was the A and B honor roll preps, bragging about their vacations on the lake at the family lake houses. On Jason's far right were the A and B honor roll geeks and nerds, whose plans included everything from playing *Dungeons and Dragons* in someone's basement to Larping. After a month of hearing all of this seemingly non-stop, Jason was tired of it. Summer did not hold the same excitement for Jason as it did for everyone else, but he more than welcomed it to start just to get away from his classmates.

Just ring already! Jason thought. *C'mon!*

Having lowered his head to rest on his folded arms in an attempt at muting the cackling hyenas encircling him and finding an odd interest in the ancient graffiti carved into the top of his desk, Jason made the decision to ask Terry what exactly it was he had in mind. He was tired of waiting on the tubby flunky to come to him and spill the deal. He would do it today after the bell. Terry had seventh period P.E. and would leave straight from the gym. Jason would go around the back of the school and catch him as he was coming out of the locker room. Then he could at least sate his curiosity. Maybe.

"Mr. Hicks."

Jason raised his head to see Mr. Erikson standing behind his desk, arms crossed over his chest, a piece of chalk still wedged between the fingers of his right hand. And he did not look all that happy.

"Sir?" This was just going to be more crap. Around Maple Grove High, Howard Erikson had the reputation for carrying a certified degree in prickology. Jason mused that this would make Mr. Erikson a certified prickologist. This last caused a small smile to form on Jason's face. Yet another mistake.

"Do you find the tone of my voice amusing? Or perhaps there is some humor in getting caught sleeping in class." Erickson unfolded his arms and set the piece of chalk back into the chalk tray beneath the blackboard before moving around his desk to sit on the edge of it.

"Regardless of it being the end of another rewarding school year with all of you intellectual giants, I still require my students to stay awake during class," Erikson said with a hint of sarcasm. Furthermore, with all the rather poor scores some of you have, you, Mr. Hicks, are walking the line rather close, you all need to consider working a little—"

The end of the day bell rang in all its delightful glory and Jason was up and out of class with Mr. Erikson calling after him. This did not worry Jason in the least. Mr. Erikson could suck it. The school year was over, well for the most part. Tomorrow he would only be in class long enough to get his report card and hang out in homeroom for Mrs. Taylor's annual end of the year pizza party. Mrs. Taylor was always doing things like that for her students and Jason was actually sad that this would be the last year he had her for any of his classes.

Forcing his way through the throng of other kids eager to be out of class and going home, Jason moved through the hall heading to the exit leading to the gymnasium, the sound of locker doors slamming, excited laughter and the raucous crowing of the jocks fading as he went. Jason reached the end of the hall, pushed open the heavy wooden double doors hard enough for them to give a loud cracking sound as they swung outward against their stop and hurried along the covered walkway leading to the gymnasium.

A large group of kids was coming out the front of the gym as Jason reached it and he quickly veered to the left along a small gravel path leading around to the side of the building. This was where the locker room exit was and would be the exit Terry used to leave the gym. He always used this one when school let out.

Good old predictable Terry, Jason thought.

Rounding the corner Jason happened upon a scene he would rather have avoided, cursing his luck as he stopped so suddenly that the tips of his toes curled painfully in the front of his shoes. On this side of the gymnasium, there were a few gazebos and several picnic benches, some covered, some not, and a handful of vending machines added along the side of the gym. The area was mainly for the honor roll kids to use as a study hall on clear, weather cooperative days. Some of the teachers would sometimes hold class here, too, a treat for their students. Today its use was for a more warped purpose. One Jason regretted stumbling upon and wished he'd just went straight home instead of coming this way to begin with.

Thanks, Terry, thanks a lot.

About ten feet from the gym exit Jason saw Terry was on his hands and knees, one hand clasped to a wooden bench, as if in the process of pulling himself to his feet. He was breathing rapidly, his black tee with "Fuzz Scum Rulz" stenciled across the chest stretching to constrictive proportions with each one. Terry's hair, mussed and sweat soaked, was not long enough to hide the large, menacing bruise forming on his cheek. Semi-circled around him were Ricky Shands, Jerry Tucker, Matt Harmon, and Johnny Dawson. Johnny, giggling like Puck on an acid trip, lifted a dirt-encrusted finger in Jason's direction.

"Best kick rocks, Hicks," Ricky said as he sent another kick into Terry's hefty backside. Terry grunted in pain, but held onto the bench next to him, gripping it even tighter. "Unless you want to help us kick this tubby fuck around. Oh, but you wouldn't do that, would you? Callahan is a friend of yours. Ain't that right?"

The smirk on Ricky's face was a bitter perversion of benevolence.

"That's right," Matt said. "All buddy-buddy."

"Couple of fag boys is what they are," Jerry added, spitting a blackish wad of tobacco in Terry's hair. Terry winced, and a tear ran down his bruised cheek.

"They be doin' it in da butt," Johnny said, barely able to contain another of his insane giggling fits.

"What ya say, Hicks? You goin' to get out of here or do we beat your ass too?" Ricky knelt down next to Terry and gave his shoulder a squeeze.

Jason's eyes met Terry's, seeing in them a look that puzzled him. Instead of fear and humiliation, what lurked behind the larger boy's eyes was something close to a dark rage, seething pure hatred. Then Ricky was saying something else and Jason forgot about Terry's lunatic glare, focusing on the bully.

"Are you even hearing me, you little grease stain?" Ricky was asking him.

"I heard you," Jason heard himself saying, oddly exhilarated by his friend's anguish.

"Then why you still standing there?" Ricky asked. "Get the hell out of here!"

"No," Jason said.

"What?" Ricky let go of Terry's shoulder, stood up, and motioned for his backwater buddies. "So you askin' for a little hurt too, then?" Ricky stepped closer to Jason.

"Hick's tryin' to grow a pair," Matt Harmon said, grinning and moving in next to Ricky.

"That'll be the day," Jerry Tucker added, falling in beside Matt.

Johnny Dawson just stood behind them cackling like a hen.

That's right. Piss them off. That makes perfect sense.

"What you goin' to do?" Ricky asked. "You goin' to be Callahan's hero?"

Ricky reached out and shoved Jason backward.

Jason stumbled back a few steps but maintained his balance.

What are you doing? These guys are going to crack your skull. Is Terry worth all of that? Really?

"He's my friend," Jason said aloud. "And you guys are going a little far. You got what you wanted, right? So just, leave him alone. You proved you were all big and bad, so just leave Terry alone. I'm sure whatever he did to make you guys so mad he's sorry for."

Wow! You said that without choking up. Not even a crack or squeak in your voice. They're still going to hurt you. You stood up to them. That is not a part of their understanding and now they are going to hurt you bad.

Ricky was in Jason's face now, nostrils flaring; face reddening. Matt and Jerry flanked him on either side, looking just as angry as Ricky was, waiting on his lead for the pummeling to begin. Jason fell back into his imagination, his safety net, his way to dull the pain. A small concrete room of foreign origins filled his mind's eye. He was a tough old army captain strapped down to a rickety wooden chair and toughing out an interrogation by an unknown, masked group of enemies. He would tell them nothing but rank and serial number. He would rather die than sell out his friends and brothers-in-arms.

There was an unpleasant pressure on Jason's chest as Ricky wadded a portion of Jason's shirt into one balled fist, Ricky's bony knuckles digging painful dimples into the soft flesh underneath. Terry was screaming something incomprehensible in the background and Johnny Dawson was crowing like some wild thing in the woods. Jason tensed up and, closing his eyes, desperately held firm to his P.O.W. fantasy. It would be over soon, and he and Terry could go about their afternoon in relative peace.

Unless they put you both in the hospital.

But they wouldn't go that far. Would they?

"WHAT IN THE EVERLOVING HELL IS THIS!"

Jason knew that voice, although he had never heard such anger behind it. The pressure on his chest subsided as Ricky's hand moved away and Jason opened his eyes, risking turning his head toward the newcomer's voice. Mr. Erikson stood a few feet behind him, hands on hips, face candy apple red with fury. If anyone had to intervene on his part, Jason figured it would have been one of the coaches. The last person he expected to see was Howard Erikson.

"Nothing goin' on here, Mr. E," Ricky said, stepping away from Jason, his cohorts doing likewise.

"Congratulations, Mr. Shands, you have learned enough of the alphabet to know which letter my last name begins with," Mr. Erikson said, his cynicism lashing out like a well-sharpened blade. "However, scholastic prowess aside, don't try to BS me. What were you four planning on doing to Mr. Hicks? The same as you did to Mr. Callahan, I imagine. Maybe worse, eh?"

"We wasn't goin' to do nothin' but intimidate them a little," Matt said, stuffing his hands into the front pockets of his jeans and taking a seat at the nearest picnic table. "That's it."

"Intimidate? Wow, now this is impressive. Experimenting with big words is a step forward for you, Mr. Harmon. I imagine that ugly bruise on Terry's face is a part of this non-violent intimidation you speak of."

Terry had used the bench to pull himself up with and was sitting at a weird angle, probably due to the kick Ricky had administered to his backside and had pulled his hair back away from his face. A large dark, purplish bruise had formed on his right cheek, the same bruise Jason had noticed earlier, only much worse than he had originally thought it to be. The swelling was painful to look at and Terry was narrowing his right eye. Mr. Erikson was looking past Ricky and crew to where Terry was sitting, who was wincing at the slightest of movements, and shook his head disapprovingly.

At that moment two of Maple Grove High's coaches, Coach Miller and Coach Vines, emerged from the gym, stopping abruptly, stunned by the scene before them, their conversation about what college football team was going to do what the following year fading away. Coach Miller broke the silence.

"What's going on here, Howard?" Coach Miller asked.

"What does it look like, Phillip?" Erikson replied. "Ricky and the Peanut Gallery were beating up on a couple of the younger boys until I broke it up."

"What do you boys have to say for yourselves?" Vines asked. He was moving closer to Ricky as he spoke. "The four of you are in it deep this time."

"Not our fault, coach," Jerry Tucker said. "Callahan took us seriously and got overexcited. Tripped over his own feet, the klutz, and hit his head on the bench. Honest, coach, we was just messin' with him."

"I cannot imagine that to be the case," Mr. Erikson said. "It's another lame excuse to get out of trouble."

"Wait a minute, Howard," Miller said, joining Coach Vines beside Ricky and Matt. "Is that true, Ricky, what Jerry said?"

Ricky's eyes gleamed with confidence. As if he already knew, he was going to get by with what they had done to Terry. And it was likely he was right. With the exception of Johnny Dawson, they all had parents with
128

big ties to Maple Grove's elite. Ricky's father was on the town council, owned a couple of real estate companies in Birmingham, and was a regular contributor to the elementary and high schools as well as several churches in the area. Jerry Tucker's father was on the school board, and his mother on the town council, as well as owning a popular bakery in Jasper. Matt Harmon's parents were old money, having grown up swimming in inheritance money from a late great uncle that had owned a large retail chain in the sixties. So, when the three of them got into any trouble, heads generally turned the other way.

"Yes, sir," Ricky responded.

Coach Vines turned his attention to Terry. "That right, son? Is that how it went?"

"It's not, coach," Jason said. "Tell them, Terry. These guys are always pushing us around."

"Hold on a minute, Jay," Coach Miller said. He had been calling Jason Jay since the fourth grade. "Let Terry tell it for himself. Well, Terry, is that the way it happened?"

Mr. Erikson had kept silent during the exchange, his arms crossed over his chest. Now it seemed he could not keep quiet any longer. Howard Erikson was a shrewd man, and he obviously knew how to spot when someone was about to be thrown under the bus. "Phillip? Doug? You cannot possibly be buying into this nonsense. Those boys are about as innocent as Jack the Ripper!"

Coach Miller shot Mr. Erikson an irritated glare. "Everyone is allowed the benefit of the doubt, Howard. That includes Ricky and his friends."

Jason thought Coach Miller's tone sounded a bit threatening. It sounded like a warning for Mr. Erikson to back off.

Yeah. No stirring of the pot, not in this town. Not when it could mean your jobs and tenures.

"Now, Phillip—" Mr. Erikson started, but Coach Miller cut him off rather sharply.

"We're going to hear what Terry has to say on this," Coach Miller said. "Then decide on what course of action to take."

"Well, Terry?" Coach Vines pushed.

Mr. Erikson put a reassuring hand on Jason's shoulder, but when Jason looked up at him, he had a deep frown on his face. Coaches, Miller, and Vines were facing Terry, their expressions hidden from him, but Jason figured them aimed at swaying Terry. It was tough work being spineless, especially when the words of a fifteen-year-old boy could cost you your job.

"It's okay, Terry," Mr. Erikson said. "Tell them what happened. Never be afraid of the truth, son."

Coach Miller gave Mr. Erikson another of those sharp looks before returning his attention to Terry. Terry looked from coach to coach to Ricky, his face full of doubt. Coach Miller wanted Terry to lie about what had happened. Jason was more than positive about that. He wanted this to all go away. And it would go away, yet more of Ricky Shands' violence toward younger, weaker kids to end up swept under the rug and never spoken of again.

"Y-y-yes, coach," Terry stuttered. "It happened just like Jerry said. I do get a little clumsy sometimes and we were all messin' around and I tripped."

Terry turned his head away from everyone and stared at his shoes. However, Jason caught a glimpse of the shamed expression on his face as he did so. Jason glanced up at Mr. Erikson, whose hand was still resting on his shoulder. Mr. Erikson was shaking his head.

Jason could not determine if it was out of disgust or frustration.

"See, Howard," Coach Miller said. "It was just boys being boys and they had a little accident. No foul play here."

"So it would appear," Mr. Erikson said, taking his hand from Jason's shoulder. The tone of his voice seemed deeper than his usual cynicism. It held the edge of anger, bordering on fury.

Coach Vines walked over to Terry. "C'mon, big man, let's see about getting you cleaned up and a little first aide on that cheek."

Terry stood up and followed Coach Vines into the gym without saying word, nor looking back. Coach Miller gave Mr. Erikson a look that said he knew this was a load of bullshit, but there was not a thing he could do about it. Then he turned to Ricky.

"Why don't you four come and give me hand? I have a load of sod needs to be unloaded at the agribusiness building before Mr. Thomas locks up for the day."

"Sure thing, coach," they all said, with the exception of Johnny Dawson who just smiled and nodded his head.

As Coach Miller was passing Mr. Erikson with Ricky and crew in tow, he stopped, put a hand on Mr. Erikson's shoulder, and whispered, "Cut the shit, Howard, and get with the program," before moving on.

Mr. Erikson waited until they had rounded the corner of the gym and then turned and looked at Jason. He was still frowning. "Whatever you do, Mr. Hicks," he said. "*Do not* take what happened here to heart. What happened here is an example of gross negligence at its finest. It's not the same everywhere, or with everyone. Always strive to do the right thing and you can do no wrong."

Who are you trying to convince? Jason thought. *Me or yourself?*

Jason nodded.

"Now I want to ask you to do me a favor."

Jason nodded again, and said, "What kind of favor?"

"I want you to wait here for Mr. Callahan and make sure he goes straight home. I want you to make sure his mother or father get him to the hospital and have that bruise seen after. Can you do that for me?"

"Yes, sir," Jason replied.

"Good, then," Mr. Erikson said, giving Jason a pat on the shoulder. "I have to go try and get a word in with Principal Davis before he leaves. You just make sure Mr. Callahan gets home."

"Yes, sir."

Mr. Erikson gave Jason an uneasy smile and then left him to wait on Terry. Jason walked over to the bench where his friend had sat just minutes earlier and sat down, propped his elbows on his knees, and rested his face in the palm of his hands.

They are not going to let this slide. You know that, don't you? They got by with it, sure, but you interfered, and they don't take kindly to anyone that goes against them.

"As if that is something new," Jason murmured.

***

It was half an hour before Terry emerged from the gym. There was a large bandage on his cheek and his hair looked like he had washed it. Terry walked with a slight limp as he approached Jason and winced with every step.

"Ready to go?" Jason asked.

"As ready as I'm gonna be," Terry replied.

The two boys left the school and headed north along Maple Street before cutting through the parking lot of the Maple Grove Church of God, and then through the patch of woods next to it, to come out on Lee Street. Much to Jason's protest, Terry snuck around the side of his house to get his bike. He told Jason he could not let his mother see his face right now, not until after he and Jason had returned from the Garrison House. Jason hesitantly agreed, and the two continued to Jason's house to pick up Jason's bike, with the promise Jason would say nothing to his mother about the incident outside of the gym, in fear Jason's mother would immediately phone Terry's mother and change his plan. So much for honoring Mr. Erikson's favor, it was pretty much off the table, now.

The Garrison House was on the southern part of town located in the Deer River Estates community, which was a short trip down Maple and then a sharp right onto Douglas. It would take about fifteen-to-twenty minutes if they rode their bikes, which they were, and would put them in the heart of their longtime tormentor's playground. After what had just happened, Jason questioned his sanity for following Terry's lead so blindly. Itching somewhere deep in his mind, was a need to know what the older boy had planned, and to scratch that itch he would have to dare to face off against Ricky Shands and the gang. Jason kept rolling different scenarios for that confrontation through his head as he peddled his bike along Maple, Terry just a few feet ahead of him, and not the first one of them played out in his favor.

Just turn around and go home. Go up to your room, read comics, and say to hell with Terry and his death wish.

If only it were that simple. Jason's curiosity, the forge fueled by the uninhibited conflagration burning from the depths of his mind's eye, would not allow him to miss an opportunity to get even with the ones responsible for the majority of his anguish throughout the years. Ricky, Jerry, Matt, even that dim bulb Johnny, they needed to be put in their place. They needed someone to show them they were not the Gods' of the Grove as they fashioned themselves to be. Someone needed to make them see how little and insignificant they were in the grand scheme of things. Why should not that someone be him? Why not Terry? The two of them were the ones most troubled by the older boys; the ones bullied the most, so why not them?

"Head's up, Jay!" Terry shouted back at him and brought his bike to a stop on the shoulder of the road. Jason coasted his bike to a stop next to Terry and dropped one foot to the ground.

Ahead of them was Founders Bridge, an ancient, narrow steel frame bridge crossing over Flat Creek, and one of the three bridges connecting to the southern half of Maple Grove. To Jason's knowledge, Founders Bridge, outside of Tillman Bridge, which crossed over Sanders Creek on Pine Line in the northern half of the Grove, was the oldest in town. It was also the most dangerous due to its narrow width and the steep slope of the road on the southern end. It was a miracle there were but a few accidents on record due to the decrepit old bridge. Jason still wondered why the town would not replace it, as it was obviously past its prime and a possible danger to anyone crossing it. His dad had told him it was because people considered it a landmark.

Then why not leave Founders Bridge where it is and redirect the road some and build a newer bridge?

Because when it came to the Grove, nothing ever made sense. That's why.

"I don't hear any cars," Terry said, glancing over at Jason. "Wait here, Jay. I'll let you know if it's clear."

Jason watched Terry pedal his bike across, the whole time expecting someone to come over the small hump on the other side and run his friend down, flattening Terry like a cartoon character in an old Warner Brothers cartoon. Much to Jason's relief, Terry made it across with no issues.

"It's all clear, Jay!" Terry shouted as he waved for Jason to cross. "Not a soul in sight!"

Taking a deep breath and praying Terry was on point about it being clear, Jason hurried across Founders Bridge, unheeded, and joined his friend on the other side. "I hate that bridge," he said, stopping his bike next to Terry.

"Everyone hates that bridge." Terry smiled. "C'mon, let's go."

Ten minutes later the two boys were riding into the Deer River Estates community, approaching the cul-de-sac with a fervor neither expected. Out of the rows of meticulously kept-up homes of a mixture of designs and styles, with neatly trimmed lawns and expensive rides in the driveways, the Garrison house was not very hard to spot. It was the only run-down, unkempt property in Deer River. Situated between two large brick homes with large, immaculate side yards, the Garrison's old property was at the end of the cul-de-sac and surrounded by an old wrought iron fence; the gate swinging open and shut with the shifting breeze, hinges needing oil squeaking loudly. The house was one of only three Victorian-era homes in Maple Grove, the other two belonging to the Sanders family and the Blackhalls, and had belonged to the late Milford Garrison, a coal tycoon that had suffered a gruesome death in the late seventies.

One of the stories told of his son, Gerald, a young man that people said was to have been standoffish, a loner that preferred seclusion, murdering his father. The old man was said to have been sleeping soundly as his son slit his throat and eviscerated him. Some rumors had it that Gerald was mildly retarded, born from an inbred relationship between Milford and his younger sister Barbara and that was why the boy had snapped. However, rumor and truth were rarely the same.

Jason and Terry stopped at the curb in front of the derelict old house, popping down their kickstands and climbing off their bikes. Jason walked up and grabbed hold of the gate, taking in the poor condition of what at one time was one of the grandest homes in the Grove, the sad disrepair of the house made worse by the neglect of the grounds around it. The pictures at the town library in a small section dedicated to Maple Grove's history showed the Garrison house in its prime with the grounds neatly trimmed and cut back with neat rows of waist-high hedge bushes following the fence line. Those same hedges were now mere skeletons smothered by untamed grass. The two cobblestone pathways, which oddly had only a few stray blades of grass poking through the cracks, led up to the kudzu shrouded cherub fountain where they split to either side and converged into one single path leading to the main house.

A set of four steps led to the large concrete porch, more kudzu wrapping around the six fluted columns supporting its roof. Jason hated kudzu vines, their invasiveness was a noose choking the life out of other plant life as they converged upon them, covering, and then killing them without mercy. Fortunately, there were only a few places left in the Grove where the intruder plant retained a small hold. It seemed the Garrison House was one of those places. The fact that it had not spread beyond the grounds was as odd as the walkways being free of the high grass to either side of them.

The house itself showed heavy weather damage, its once brilliant white paint job was dingy, mildewed, and the paint had chipped away in several places. Between the windows on the first and second floors, Jason counted eight that were broken. Had no one in the Garrison family even cared to keep the place up? Or were they all too ashamed of its past to care?

"We can hide our bikes over there," Terry said, interrupting Jason's assessment of the old house and startling him.

"Huh?"

"The old carriage house," Terry said. "Why so jumpy?"

"I'm not jumpy," Jason replied. "Just a little surprised at how bad this place has gotten. It's ruined."

"Yeah, it's a pile of crap these days. Let's go."

Jason and Terry pushed their bikes around to the driveway. The old carriage house was converted into a three-car garage years before and appeared to be in a similar state as the house, the roof on the far front-right corner sagging and leaned forward. Jason imagined it would not take much more abuse before it toppled over.

"Over there, Jay." Terry pointed toward a small gap between the carriage house and the fence.

A few minutes later and after the two boys had stuffed their bikes far enough into the gap as to be concealed from sight by the overgrowth of weeds there, they approached the Garrison House's front door with both caution and awe. Jason noted how much more intimidating it seemed this close-up. Glancing over at Terry, expecting to see an expression on his face similar to the one Jason figured would mirror how he felt, he saw no emotion on the older boy's face. It was almost as if no one was at home in Terry's head, a blank automaton ready for programming.

"Hey, man," Jason called to him. "You okay?"

"Yeah." Terry shook his head as if shrugging off disorientation. "I was just thinking a little. Want to go in? It's not locked."

"How do you know it isn't locked?" Jason asked.

"I have been inside a few times already. This door is never locked."

"How many times is a few," Jason asked, genuinely curious.

"Pretty much every day since I first told you about it. That's what those dill berries were so mad about. One of them saw me yesterday. I guess they really didn't like the idea of me on their turf."

"Wait! What?" Jason was more than a little pissed. Not only had Terry been creeping around the Garrison house for nearly two weeks without telling him, but also the older boys knew. They knew he had been here and were not very happy about it. They were willing to beat Terry to a pulp over it.

Just what the fuck was you thinking, Terry? Jason thought. *What was his damage?*

"That's just perfect," Jason huffed. "Ricky and the peanut gallery will be expecting to find us here now—or at least be looking for us to show up."

Terry smiled wide, an image that was somehow idiotic and terrifying at the same time. "It's cool, Jay," he said. "After their message today, I don't think they will be looking for me or you to be here. They probably think we are too chicken-shit to show our faces."

"You can't know—"

"—you are sweating this for nothing, man."

Jason's protests ended before he even had a chance to open his mouth as the distant rumble of a glass pack muffler halted any further argument. As much as he wanted to believe that it was one of the other locals cruising around, enjoying the sunshine with his girlfriend all scrunched up against him and listening to some country singer wailing about their wife leaving them, he knew better. With this being Ricky's spot, Jason doubted that it could be anyone else.

"Didn't figure they would show up today," Terry said as the rumble grew nearer, growing louder and even more intimidating.

"Why do I even listen to you?" Jason turned toward the road. "We're toast, man. Burned toast."

Terry smiled that weird smile again.

"Why are you smiling?" Jason asked. "Those guys are going to beat the snot out of us! They are going to drag us right around back and beat the living snot out of us!"

"Take a chill pill, Jay. C'mon." Terry reached out and grabbed the doorknob. "Stop being such a spazz. There's nothing to worry about." Terry pushed open the door and stepped into the Garrison House.

Jason stepped inside behind him and shut the door just as Ricky's 69 Chevelle entered the cul-de-sac.

***

The air inside the Garrison House was stifling and stale with a smell of mothballs and cat piss. As expected, cobwebs lurked in almost every corner and thick sheets of dust coated everything. No curtains covered the windows, allowing natural sunlight in to illuminate the house slightly. It was just another abandoned old house, if not for how strange it felt. For all the warmth outside, Jason expected it to be boiling hot inside. Instead, he was shivering a little. It felt how his house felt when his mom decided to turn the thermostat down to sixty. If not for the very real and present danger posed by Ricky and crew, Jason would bail on Terry and go home.

Another fine mess you've gotten yourself into, Jason thought as he eased toward the double staircase and away from the windows of the large foyer, cringing as he heard Ricky's Chevelle swing into the driveway and come to a stop. A few moments later, the car's engine went silent, the loud rumble dying, leaving in its wake a horde of barking dogs.

"How come the neighbors don't call the cops?" Jason asked. "Aren't they trespassing?"

"Nope," Terry replied. "Ricky's parents own the place. His mom's maiden name is Garrison."

"You dick. You could have told me this crap a hundred times already. So, we are the ones trespassing and any trouble will fall on us. My dad would kill me."

"Don't have a cow, Jay," Terry said. "They don't know we are here and they ain't gonna know."

"You literally just told me a few minutes ago they saw you yesterday. What is to keep them from coming in here looking for you?"

Again, Terry flashed his weird grin, made even more ghastly in the dim light by the stairs. "This place scares the shit out of them. The only one that even tried to come in was that Johnny dude, and he hauled balls after about five minutes. That is why they waited to catch me after school. As far as they ever go is the backyard."

Jason did not know what scared him more, Terry's creepy *Joker* grin or the fact that Johnny Dawson was too scared to enter the Garrison House. Johnny seemed too crazy to be afraid of anything, much less an old abandoned house. Jason could not understand what was so scary. He knew people made up stories about places

140

like this, stories aimed to scare others, especially little kids, but had never understood how made up words could cause such terror. Granted there was a dark, gory history here, but that was all over and in the past.

So what was the big deal?

"This way, Jay," Terry said, motioning for Jason to go with him.

Rowdy laughter erupted from the boys outside, followed by the sound of two car doors slamming shut. Jason hoped that Terry was right because if Ricky and crew came inside and found them it would be ugly.

"C'mon," Terry persisted.

Jason shrugged off his worry for the time being and followed Terry behind the stairs into a short, nearly pitch-dark hallway. All Jason could make out were the outlines of the objects around him, of whatever pictures and other items hung from the walls. Up ahead, sunlight from the other side crept through the crevices of a shut door. Jason halted, believing they were about to walk right into the very ones he wished desperately to avoid.

Somehow, Terry must have sensed that he had stopped moving and without a break in stride, said, "It's only a kitchen, Jay."

Jason did not reply. Instead, he crossed his heart and started walking. As the boys reached the shut door, and as Terry slowly pulled it open, Jason could have sworn someone whispered his name. The voice was papery and weak and sounded like a man's voice, but it was gone so quick and did not repeat that Jason marked it off as a part of his imagination and stepped into the kitchen behind his friend.

More cobwebs occupied the corners of the kitchen with even more layers of dust covering the antique appliances and furniture. The windows, a total of four, two above the deep porcelain sink, and two in the small breakfast nook, had blinds over them. The blinds were old seventies designs and each set had at least two missing blades, allowing a fraction of sunlight through. It was nowhere near as bright as the foyer, but not as dark as the short hall they had used to access the kitchen. Jason walked over to the sink, maneuvering around a dusty old kitchen table, which oddly enough, still held place settings for four people, and leaned forward to peer through a gap in the blinds. Over by the breakfast nook, four shadows passed by on the other side of the window.

The overgrowth in the backyard, with the exception of the patio where Ricky and his friends hung out, was worse than the front, five of the six outbuildings lost to the birthing jungle around them. The swimming pool just beyond the patio retained water, but not the inviting blue water of backyards across the Grove, but swamp green. Three patio sets took up space between the pool and the main house, their umbrellas warped, skeletal relics with pieces of rotted cloth hanging from them like loose, dead skin. Rust had overrun the tables and chairs and the patio set closest to the pool apparently served as a toilet for the avian residents of the Grove, the tables, and chairs looking as if painted in bird droppings.

A sudden loud rush of laughing fits caused Jason to flinch as Ricky and his friends entered the backyard. Stopping by the patio set nearest the house, Jerry and Matt plopped down into two of the chairs, big grins on their faces. Shit eating grins is what his dad would call them. Johnny Dawson, looking even more disturbed than usual, pulled a five-gallon bucket from somewhere out of Jason's line of sight, flipped it over, and took a seat. Reaching into his front pants pocket, Johnny pulled out a buck knife. A flick of the wrist and the knife was open. Johnny held it up to catch the sun then knelt forward, arms over his knees.

"Why don't you put that thing away before you cut yourself with it?" Matt said.

"Or I could just cut you!" Johnny snapped back, pointing the knife at Matt and doing a little slashing motion.

"Calm down, man," Jerry told Johnny. "Don't get your panties in such a bunch."

"That loony bird don't know what calm is." Matt pulled a crumpled pack of cigarettes from his front pocket, took one out, and handed the pack over to Jerry. "Crazy fucker."

Jason did not think Matt or Jerry noticed it, but the angle from which Jason was watching them, he could see it perfectly. Johnny's head jerked nervously every time one of the other boys spoke. Johnny was growing more unstable with each passing word. Surely, they knew Johnny was nuts and should leave well enough alone.

Matt and Jerry don't understand, or least not enough to take Johnny seriously, Jason thought and cut his stare over to Ricky, who was standing a few feet away from them, Jason's walkman clipped to his belt, and holding two bags of ice. He seemed to be enjoying the back-and-forth between his friends with some sick pleasure. *Ricky knew. He knew and could care less one way or the other if Johnny stabbed either Matt or Jerry. It was as if he wanted it to happen.*

Jason was not aware of what had caused this sudden discord between them, noting that Johnny's hyena giggle was absent along with his twisted humor. Just a moment before they were laughing like long lost friends, now they were ready to fight one another. Were they always like this?

"Crazy," Matt repeated, lighting his cigarette and shaking his head.

"Call me that one more time!" Johnny shouted as he snapped to his feet, the five-gallon bucket flying out behind him and ricocheting off the back of the house.

Inside the house, Jason flinched at the unpredicted movement.

Matt was on his feet with surprising quickness, the cigarette falling from his lips. "You feelin' froggy, loony tunes, you'd best be jumping!"

"Whoa, whoa, guys," Jerry said, jumping up to grab Matt's shoulder and pull him back. "What the hell?"

Jason tensed up as if he was outside with them. Johnny Dawson was shaking from anger and Jason had no doubt that he would stab Matt without a second thought. And as quick as Matt was, Johnny was quicker, Jason had witnessed this a few times at school.

"Hey, Tweedle Dipshit and Tweedle Dumbshit, cut the crap," Ricky finally intervened. "Johnny is just upset that we didn't get to finish kicking the hell out of Callahan. Let him simmer down."

"I want to get that fat boy good," Johnny mumbled, lowering the knife.

"I know you do, Johnny boy, but we have to be smart. Just relax a little, man, his time's coming." Ricky sounded like a police negotiator trying to talk someone out of jumping off a building. Jason was unaware his longtime tormentor had that ability. If Jason did not hate Ricky so much, he'd be and,impressed.

"And Hicks," Matt added as he leaned down to pick up his cigarette. "Hicks got it comin' to him for acting like he had a pair."

"Yeah, we got to knock that twerp down a few pegs," Jerry agreed.

"And we will, guys, just hang tight," Ricky said before turning to walk off.

Matt and Jerry sat back down, Matt's eyes fixed on Johnny.

Johnny retrieved his bucket and flipped it back over, his eyes fixed on Matt.

Their anger with one another remained, but neither would act on it any further, neither wishing to risk crossing the alpha male of their small pack. Ricky was, in many ways, as crazy as Johnny Dawson was, if not crazier, and getting on his bad side could land you in the hospital.

Jason cut his eyes in the direction Ricky had gone. A small, wooden shed with a tin roof that had somehow avoided the encroaching wave of weeds and vines that had claimed the other outbuildings sat against the fence line adjacent to the pool. Ricky pulled out his keys, unlocked the door, and went inside. Jason could hear muffled sounds coming from inside the shed, then a few minutes later Ricky emerged dragging behind him a red *Radio Flyer* wagon with a plastic ice cooler inside.

"Cool those hotheads off with this," Ricky said as he reached his friends. Opening the cooler, he reached inside and tossed what looked like a can of beer to Matt. "Fuckers are still cold from Saturday."

"Now that's more like it," Matt said, catching the beer, popping the tab, and taking a long swig.

Ricky tossed another beer to Jerry who nearly fumbled it. "I am sure as hell glad you are not a receiver, man. You catch like shit."

Jerry laughed, apparently unfazed by the insult, popped the tab, and took a swig of his beer.

Ricky pulled out another beer and offered it to Johnny who waved it off. Ricky just shrugged his shoulders, popped the tab, and emptied the can in one guzzle. He burped loudly and crushed his beer can before tossing it away. "That's how you drink a beer, girls."

"Look at them, Jay," Terry whispered into his ear. "Can't you see how easy it would be?"

Jason could not only feel Terry's breath, warm and fetid, against his neck but could also feel Terry up against him; the older boy's weight more than enough to pin him against the lip of the counter. Jason wiggled around, trying to push him off, but this only caused Terry to press harder, keeping Jason restrained.

"It's our turn, Jay. It's our turn to push them around. Show them what it feels like."

Through the gap in the blinds, Jason watched the four boys outside, the four responsible for so much misery to him and so many others and felt a brief but powerful urge to strike them down, to throttle them, to kick and stab them, to punish them. He closed his eyes and shook his head, desperate to purge those horrid visions of bloodshed and murder from his mind. The images were brutal and violent. He could see in detail him doing things to them, things with knives or power tools, things that were slow and painful. Jason wanted to scream for Terry to get off him so he could get his bike and go home. However, to scream out would alert Ricky and crew and bring them running inside. He believed they *would* come inside, no matter how many times Terry said they were too scared to.

"I need you to help me, Jay, help even things up. I can't do this myself."

Help you do what? Jason thought, trying again to push free of the older boy's bulk. *Just what are you thinking of doing?*

"Get off of me, Terry," Jason said, careful not to raise his voice loud enough for anyone from outside the house to hear him. Surprisingly, Terry backed away. Jason turned to face him and nearly pissed his pants.

That empty look was back in Terry's eyes and he was shifting from foot-to-foot. "Our time," he said.

"Where are the girls, Terry? You said Linda Bennett and her friends liked to hang out with Ricky. Where are they?"

Terry's lips twisted into a grisly smile. "Sorry, Jay, but you have such a huge crush on her that I knew you would come if you thought she was here. You are better off, anyway. Linda is such a skeezer, dude."

"Okay, man, I'm out," Jason said, his heart beating faster as fear stole through him. "You are really starting to sound a little bonkers."

Jason moved to go around Terry, heading for the kitchen door, and the bigger boy reached out, grabbed his shirt, and shoved him back against the sink with enough force to knock the wind from him. Struggling to catch his breath, Jason looked up through watery eyes in time to see Terry reach back and swing something at him, and then shadow blanketed his vision.

***

Jason walked alone, trapped in a starless night. The womb-like darkness surrounded him in all directions and his head ached, the left side of his face stinging intensely. The last thing he remembered was Terry shoving him back against the sink. And then...

Did Terry hit me? He did. I think he did. Why?

They were watching Ricky and his friends from inside the house. Terry had some kind of plan to embarrass them. To get back at them for all the years Ricky had bullied them around. Then Terry had started to act weird, holding him against the counter and saying strange things. But it wasn't so much what he had said that was so strange, as it was the way he said it, the edgy, sadistic tone of his voice as he spoke. Jason remembered being scared and trying to leave. That was when Terry had grabbed him and pushed him back hard enough to wind him.

Then he hit me. I looked up at him and Terry hit me. And now—

—now he was lost in this void, curtained in by utter blackness and wandering a directionless path. A new ache stirred within him, this ache born of a longing need to be free of this gloomy nightmare, to bask in the warmth of a summer sun. Jason wanted to cry, but no tears would come. He wished he had never followed Terry to the Garrison House. He wished he had never even been friends with Terry to begin with. Just look at what it has gotten him. Jason did not even know if he was alive or dead. He did not know where he was. He did not know if he could escape from it and go home. His mom and dad could be strict at times, but they loved him and treated him good and he loved them and he just wanted more than anything to see them. And Amy, as annoying as she was, tattling on him whenever she could, coming into his room without permission, or just being an all-out pest, she was not really that bad for a little sister. Jason wanted to give Amy a big hug right now and let her know he would be there to protect her from all the bogeymen of the world, to keep her safe from things like this.

That's a joke. How can I protect her when I couldn't even protect myself?

He could not give up, however. That is what all the bullies of the world expected you to do. They wanted you to be a helpless victim that would curl up and die rather than stand and fight. Quickening his pace, Jason was resolute to do just that. Ricky, Terry, it did not matter, he would make it out of this, he would fight back.

Vile images began flickering through his mind as he moved with each image being worse than the last. In one, Terry was standing behind Matt Harman, who seemed confined somehow. Matt was crying and was saying something Jason could not hear. Terry said something back, smiling cruelly, before holding a large Bowie knife up to Matt's throat. Then there was darkness followed by a sickening gurgling noise.

Another image broke through the murk, this one had Jerry Tucker tied down to an old wooden table. At least what remained of him. Splayed from neck to crotch, his body was jerking, his feet kicking wildly. Terry was bending over him and had one chubby arm elbow deep in Jerry's chest. He looked in Jason's direction, or at least it seemed that he was looking at him, and that vindictive smile reappeared. This image cut out as quickly as the last and Jason suddenly felt like throwing up.

What have you done, Terry?

More images attempted to force their way into his head and Jason pushed them away. He did not want to see any more. He was not sure he could mentally survive bearing witness to the macabre peepshow should he continue to let it in. But the realization of the situation was simple.

I have no choice.

Piercing light finally penetrated the darkness around him and Jason found himself looking at his Walkman. It was set in front of him, scratched and bloody. Raising his head slowly, Jason saw the bottoms of a pair of *Converse* sneakers. The kind Jerry Tucker was fond of wearing. Blood was dripping off them and pooling around the heels. The one-time bully had suffered a brutal evisceration. To the left of Jerry's corpse, tied to a dining chair with what looked like some kind of thick twine, sat Matt Harman. The front of his shirt was nothing more than a bloody rag. Matt's throat was sliced, causing his head to tilt back and spread the gash on his neck into a crimson grin.

Sitting at the opposite end of the table, with Jerry's dead eyes staring up at him was Ricky Shands, bound to his chair the same as Matt. Unlike Matt, however, Ricky was still alive.

"Hicks," Ricky said in a hushed voice upon realizing that Jason was awake. "Jason, man, whatever, you have to cut me loose. Callahan is fucking nuts."

Ignoring Ricky for the moment, Jason took note of the room. It was darker than when Terry had knocked him out, the sole source of light was about twenty or thirty candles strewn randomly around the kitchen. There was no light coming in through the windows so Jason figured night had arrived. His parents were probably going crazy right now wondering where he was.

I wish they were here. I am scared, and I can't stop trembling. And I feel like barfing.

"C'mon, man," Ricky persisted. "I am sorry for all the shit I did to you. You can't let that tubby psycho kill me. I don't want to die, man."

One thing that Jason would remember no matter how long he lived was Ricky Shands begging Jason to free him. It was not how Jason had imagined, not at all. There were no tears, no breakdown whatsoever. He was calm, or calmer than someone in his situation should be. In fact, Ricky was not showing the first signs of being afraid. All Jason could sense from him was anger.

"Where's Johnny?" Jason asked, noticing that Johnny Dawson was nowhere in sight.

"Fuck if I know," Ricky replied. "Crazy little screwball hauled ass."

"He got away?" Jason was hopeful.

"I don't know," Ricky said, seeming unsure.

"Maybe he will get the police. Or maybe tell someone and they will call the police."

Ricky laughed. "Do you really think that matters? By the time the bacon gets here your friend Callahan will have carved us up." Ricky looked Jason over. "Or at least me, anyway. He didn't even bother tying you up. You're free. You could run if you wanted."

This was true. Jason raised his hands to his face, awed by them. He was free. He could leave. For the first time since waking, tears welled in his eyes. He could just slip out the back door, grab his bike, go home, and end this horrendous day in the comfort of his bed.

But I'd have to call the police. I couldn't leave Terry running around killing people. He needed to be locked up somewhere. Somewhere far away.

"For Christ's sake," Ricky grumbled. "You gonna leak like a baby, now. Grow some balls, Hicks. We got to get out of here."

How can he be so calm? Jason wondered, lowering his hands to the table.

"He's still here." Ricky wiggled in his chair and pulled at his restraints. "You going to help me or not?"

"Y-Y-Yes," Jason stuttered. H-Hold on a minute." Saving Ricky was the morally right thing to do. Even with all the times he'd beaten Jason up or made fun him, generally in front of several other students, which was embarrassing and had made Jason feel like the biggest loser to ever walk the planet, Ricky didn't deserve death.

"Hurry up, then."

Jason eased out of his chair, nearly slipping on the blood-slicked floor. The urge to vomit rose again and Jason fought to hold it in. Mid-ways of the table he lost his tug-of-war with nausea. He was opposite the late Mark Harman when Jerry's corpse released gas so putrid Jason swore he could feel his nose hairs curl. Only a small amount of bile sprung forth, leaving Jason to dry heave for a couple of minutes. It had been several hours since lunch and there was nothing to throw up.

"Way to go, hoser," Ricky snapped. "Why not just shout for that nutball friend of yours to come running?"

"Sorry. I just...I just..."

"Fuck it, man. Just untie me so we can jet."

Jason armed spittle from his mouth, wiping his arm on his shirt, and then went over to Ricky. He studied the thick twine binding the older boy to the chair, unsure how to loosen it. Jason was terrible with knots; he got them in his shoelaces on a regular basis and always had a bitch of a time getting them out. And these knots appeared to be really hard, like the ones his dad would tie when securing something in the bed of his truck.

"Nah, man, just take your time."

"I don't know if I can untie these," Jason fretted.

Ricky groaned in frustration. "Then cut them." He dropped his eyes to the table and nodded.

Following Ricky's gaze, Jason's eyes widened at the site of the gore-slicked Bowie knife. His stomach began to twist and lurch again at the thought of touching that bloody blade.

"For the love of Christ, just grab the fucking thing and cut me loose!"

The sudden rise in the older boy's voice startled Jason. If he did not want Terry to hear what they were doing, why would he scream out like that? That seemed like a bad idea and the last thing you would want to do in a situation like this.

Ricky rolled his eyes, said, "Oh, man. Look, Hicks, just pretend you just got done cleaning a deer you and that lame ass old man of yours bagged. And that knife is what you used. Don't think of what... Well, don't even consider thinking about what it *was* used for."

"Okay," Jason said in a shaking voice as he reached for the Bowie with a trembling hand.

On his first attempt, the knife slipped away from him and fell to the floor, leaving Jason gawking at his blood-smeared palm, black as tar in the flicking candlelight. Balling his hands into fists and dropping them to his side, he resisted a new rush of tears. The fear inside of him was a juggernaut and he was but a lost boy caught in its rampant path, but he refused to yield. The reality was that he did not want to die either and that he *would* die if he did not hurry and cut Ricky free. If he didn't hurry, they would both die.

"Shit! You're as jelly handed as Jerry was. Fuck!"

Jason reached down and picked up the Bowie without replying. Raising the knife level with his eyes, the darkened reflection of insanity stared back at him.

"Slit his throat, cut out his eyes, or gut him like a dog," a gritty male voice whispered in Jason's ear. *"He would do it to you. He is as twisted as they come and has abused you so many times. Made you feel inferior. How many more tears will you shed over his actions against you before you do the right thing?"*

Again, Jason closed his eyes and shook his head. When he opened his eyes, all he saw was a dim reflection of him, streaked in scarlet. The odd voice did not repeat and Jason turned his attention to Ricky.

There was a new look on the older boy's face. One of pure terror.

From over his right shoulder came Terry's voice. "Do it, Jay. Fillet that asshole. You know if you cut him loose, he'll kill you. Think about it, Jay. Why would you even want to let that spaz live?"

When did Terry come in here? Jason wondered. *I didn't hear him come in. The kitchen door never opened.*

"Your mom, your dad, your sister," Terry continued. "Now that Ricky has seen what we did, do you think he will let that go? Even if the *we* was all *me,* don't you think he will still blame you for some of it? He'll hurt them, Jay. He'll do it to get at you. He'll do it because he is a twisted piece of shit.

Jason's grip on the knife tightened, the Bowie's smooth bone hilt becoming more familiar with each passing second. The knife was a gift from his father. He had just turned eleven and his father had been out of town on business. But when father did return, he had with him this knife. Purchased from some sporting goods store or roadside flea market somewhere in Texas, it was an I-am-sorry-I-missed-your-birthday again present.

Father? Jason was confused. He had never in his life referred to his dad as father. His dad had never worked out of town, either. A garbage man was what his dad was, in Birmingham. As for the Bowie, Jason had no clue that it existed before today.

"Do it, Jay," Terry urged. "Do it and we can go and find Johnny. That loose nut is hiding from us. But we'll find him."

"C'mon, Hicks," Ricky pleaded. "Don't listen to that tubby freak. He's nuts, man. Don't let him blow smoke up your ass. Knife the crazy bastard. Shit!"

"Father was a bully, you know?"

It was that weird voice again.

"He struck me quite often out of shame of having such an imperfect son, a defect. He'd said it was because I was conceived in sin and that I had brought him nothing but misfortune. One can only be beaten so many times before they must act in order to survive. I had to do what was right. I had to kill father. I had to keep him from killing me. You must do what is right, Jason. To survive."

Jason spun around, prepared to face Terry and the owner of the weird voice. But Terry stood alone with madness in his eyes. Whatever had consumed Terry's sanity was now hungry for Jason's and he knew the longer he stayed here, the more the evil possessing the Garrison House would devour his free will. The homicidal urges he has had since stepping inside, the unexplained voice, Terry's insanity, it was all because of this house or rather caused by something in this house.

"Do it, Jay. Do what's right."

"No," Jason said. "It's not right."

"Do it!" Terry demanded. "Do it!"

"No," Jason repeated, reaching behind him and laying the knife on the table.

"Worthless, boy," the weird voice hissed.

From behind him, Jason heard Ricky saying something, but it was muffled and he could not make it out. Then there came a grunt and a muffled scream. Not wanting to take his eyes off Terry, but feeling like he had no choice, Jason turned back to Ricky. Johnny Dawson was standing behind Ricky, one hand over Ricky's mouth, the other gripping the Bowie's hilt. Johnny had driven the big knife through the top of Ricky's skull.

"You had your chance," Johnny drawled.

"You should have just done what was right," Terry said, moving in close to Jason and putting a hand on his shoulder.

"Blew your chance," Johnny said, walking toward Jason, flipping open his buck knife as he moved.

"Give me what I want." The weird voice echoed throughout the kitchen.

"To be born again," Johnny and Terry said in unison.

"Blood of my blood shall I take 'til all the corpses of my lineage lie in my wake."

"Blood of your blood," Johnny mumbled and lurched at Jason.

Despite the horror of his situation, despite the way fear had taken hold and shook him all over, Jason managed to pull away from Terry and spin around him, nearly slipping in the process. A guttural scream escaped from Terry right before Johnny sunk the buck knife into his throat. Not looking back, Jason hit the kitchen door shoulder first, slamming it open so hard the doorknob punched through the sheetrock.

Without looking back, Jason sprinted down the short hall and to the foot of the stairs, taking no notice of the family portraits on the walls lit up by the sixty or more candles along the floor and small tables, specifically the one with the deformed young man in a blue suit holding a small boy in his lap. Behind him, Johnny screamed in rage. Jason did not stop running.

Rounding the stairs and beelining for the front door, Jason came to an abrupt stop. Blocking his path was a tall young man with long black hair, his head lowered. His clothes were seventies throwbacks: bellbottom jeans and a tie-dyed shirt with a big pot leaf on the front.

"Blood of my blood." The young man laughed and raised his head. *"Shall I take!"*

156

His face was severely deformed, one eye larger than the other, his nose off center, and his cheekbones were larger than normal, stretching his skin to the point, it looked ready to split open. Regardless of these physical defects, however, Jason could not help but notice the peculiar resemblance to himself.

Risking a peek over his shoulder, Jason saw Johnny lumbering toward him at a zombie-like pace, buck knife held out in front of him with Terry's blood still dripping from the blade. Returning his attention to the weird young man with the jackal grin and the out-of-date clothes and Jason made his decision. Life or death? Jason chose life. Breaking into a run, Jason maneuvered around the weird young man and dove through the front window, landing on the concrete porch then rolling off it. Stinging from a thousand cuts, he pulled himself up and froze. In the window he had used to make an escape, stood the weird young man with the warped version of Jason's face.

"Our bond will not allow you to run forever," he said, holding up Johnny Dawson's severed head. *"I can wait."*

As the candles in the house went out, one-by-one, the weird young man dropped Johnny's head and began to fade away until all that was left of him was his predatory smile. And eventually, even that died away.

***

Jason sat at the back of an ambulance wrapped in a blanket waiting for his parents to come and pick him up. He heard the EMT telling one of the police officers about him being in shock. Maybe he was, maybe he was not, but he was not scared anymore, only confused. Watching as the coroners brought out the bodies, sealed inside what he thought of as giant garbage bags; Jason played back the memory of the weird young man. If not for the deformities, it would have been like looking into a mirror. And what was this bond? There were so many questions that he was still afraid to ask.

One of the morticians slammed shut the back doors of a black non-descript panel van, startling Jason. It was one of the five vans brought out to pick up the murdered teens. A line of police officers stood near them, keeping nosey neighbors away as best they could.

Looking back at the house, Jason felt that he should be sick to his stomach just looking at it. Instead, he felt a sort of longing need to go back inside, to find the weird young man. Maybe later, after all of this calmed down, he would do just that.

"Blood of my blood," Jason said under his breath.

Kevin McHugh's Shopping List

Can Of Deodorant
Pie Cases
Bag Of Ice
Blonde Hair Dye
Bag of Frozen Pork Sausages
Box Of Frozen Hamburgers
Bottle Of Strawberry Milk
Multiple Bags Of Sweets
Bag of Frozen Yorkshire Puddings

First Do No Harm
Kevin McHugh

1 34. Attempted Kidnapping. No.

140. Murder. Still no good to him.

140. Again. He briefly pondered the rationale of looking for a single psychopath in a city that is seemingly teeming with hundreds of them on any given night.

"133" the radio squawks informing the officers in the surrounding area of a possibly dangerous person. Promising but no guarantee this is the kind of felon he is looking for. If it was a particularly aggressive rapist, then it might be worth him starting the engine and heading a couple of blocks over, but if it's simply a flasher or some other kind of low-level deviant then he would be wasting his time.

No. After spending nearly every night for the past three months hunting the streets armed only with his trusty CB radio tuned into the police band and his a Ruger LCR he wasn't going to squander a potential encounter with the man in the ambulance on some creep who couldn't control his compulsion to expose himself to single women stumbling home from the club or out of the subway.

"141" crackled out from the tiny speaker in his Dodge bringing a reluctant smile to his lips. He briefly wondered when he had become the kind of person that upon hearing of an accident he was filled with a sense of satisfaction and excitement. The answer to this, like so many other questions about the current state of his life, or lack there off, was three months ago.

He spun the wheel and slipped out of the stream of traffic he was in and joined the trickle of automobiles heading towards the suburbs and outskirts of the city.

The gentle hum of the windscreen wipers muffled the sound of the radio and began to lull his mind back to the memories of that night.

It had begun in the bar just around the corner from the Newsday offices. Celebrating the story that would make his career, or so he thought at the time. A local politician had been involved in the rape of an underage girl from one of the poorer parts of his constituency. Once he began investigating the story of Councilman Edward Glass, he'd been given the literal gift that kept on giving. Despite a visit from some of New York's finest and some minor damage to his car he had kept digging and found that the girl was not a one-off incident and that there was a sad supply line running between Glass and an as yet unknown criminal called Marcus Huffman.

Like all news stories, it was the centre of a media storm until the New York Times ran a piece about some other politician, further up the food chain, doing something slightly more deplorable. His article had gotten the attention of not only the senior editors at the Newsday offices but those at many of the other New York newspapers. Especially those with large circulations and salaries.

He left the office about three pm and had been celebrating, off and on, for a good six hours before friends, well-wishers and onlookers had begun returning to their own lives. His brief moment being the bright shining light at the centre of their universe was over. The funny thing about that night is how little he could actually remember. Maybe it was because the evening had been so unremarkable to anyone but himself, little more than set dressing to the drama which was to unfold.

He almost walked past the alley, but a rogue headlight reflected upon the surface of her watch with the refraction drawing his alcohol-fogged attention. He tried to brush it off and keep walking, but his reporter's instincts rose up, reigniting his dulled senses. He entered the filth and murk that inhabited the cracks in most of the city's blocks.

"Help…" a fragile whisper crawled out of the gloom. Followed by an equally pathetic "…please."

He closed his eyes. Squeezing them tight together both in a futile attempt to gain some measure of sobriety and to help his eyes adjust to the absence of light in the alley. When he opened them, he was greeted by what remained of Sharon Terrell. Her blonde hair matted to her face with blood and dirt. The tattered fragments of material that had once been her clothes clung to her bruised flesh, her naked form exposed to the world. The crime stripped her of any sense of modesty that she may have possessed. The following moments he remembers as little more than an itinerary of actions. He must have done this. He just had no recollection of doing it. The presence of another witness would have made his current obsession seem more palatable or at the very least less lonely.

What happened next was something he can remember with a crystal clarity to match any wedding day or child's birth. He sat upon the cold wet ground, dirty water soaking into his pants. He held Sharon's hand in his own, gently caressing her shredded fingers, attempting to comfort them both. He had thrown his jacket over her and placed several pieces of folded cardboard— scavenged from a nearby dumpster—under her head like a makeshift field hospital.

The sirens shrill cry shattered the tenuous silence he and Sharon had somehow fallen into. The alley's inky blackness was washed out by a tidal wave of red and blue flashing lights. The audio-visual assault broke across his sense and reminded him just how much he'd had to drink that night. Almost as if exposure to the ambulance had brought about the hangover, he had forgotten he was due to have.

"Mr. Varon," came a call from within the cavalcade of illumination at the entrance to the alley.

"Over here! Quick," he waved frantically at the formless voice.

"How long has she been like this?" It was neither a question nor a statement, more the voice making an observation to itself.

When the voice finally acquired a shape, it was possibly the most unremarkable man he had ever laid eyes upon; black hair cropped neat in a military buzz cut, heavy-set features devoid of scars, wrinkles or any distinguishing marks and a relentless bland and disinteresting nature conversely made him all the more noticeable.

"What happened?" The paramedic asked, checking for signs of a pulse.

"I... think she's been…" he struggled with the word as if saying it would compound the terrible crime he had been drawn into the aftermath of.

The paramedic said nothing in response, just nodded his understanding and continued to check Sharon over.

"I am going to need your help getting her onto the gurney." It was here he should have suspected something was wrong, should have known that paramedics, like all of those who work for the emergency services, travel in pairs.

"Sure."

"Sharon, can you hear me? You are going to be fine. Me and…" The paramedic waited. The wind blew down the alleyway and a siren could be heard somewhere in the distance. The three of them simply existed before the paramedic cleared his throat and brought him back to the present.

"Conrad," he stammered.

"Right, Conrad and I are going to get you up onto the gurney and into the ambulance. The care you need is beyond the meagre help our budget or my skills can offer. Okay?"

Sharon nodded but kept her gaze fixed on the moon. It was then he realized she had not looked at him once in the whole time the pair had been together.

"Conrad, we go on three. One. Two. Three," And with that, the two of them slid the frail remains of Sharon Terrell onto the gurney. Without saying another word, the paramedic snapped the stature up onto its wheels, before rolling it into the back of the waiting ambulance with a cold and practised efficacy.

The paramedic slammed the door shut and turning, held out his hand to him.

"Consider this the thanks she can't give you. Most people in your position would usually fall apart or turn this into some kind of late night circus. You should be proud of how you handled this." The paramedic then put one hand on his shoulder and leaned closer in a conspiratorial manner. "Listen. I need to get her to the hospital ASAP. Not just for her physical well being, but her emotional stability as well. The last thing she needs to see right now is more men, so can you wait here for the police and let them know what happened?"

The paramedic was back in the ambulance before he could even finish the reluctant nod of his head. The beast snarled into life, it's crimson lights adding to the demonic rumble of its engine. He watched as the chrome taillights disappeared around the corner and into the lost highways of a New York City night. He tried to take note of the license plate but, like most of that night's events, it had since disappeared into the miasma of his memory never to resurface.

The police arrived seven and a half minutes later along with an ambulance. They found the husk that had once been Sharon's body discarded in a disused industrial complex on the far side of town. On top of the sexual horrors that had been perpetrated upon her prior to getting in the back of the ambulance, every last drop of blood had been syphoned from her. The dried up remains and his version of events conflicted to such a degree that had he not been able to provide a cast iron alibi for the day of her disappearance he would be serving several consecutive life sentences.

The Dodge rolled through the rain-slicked streets, cawling towards the answers that had eluded him these past few months. In his darker more reflective moments he had wondered what he would do upon finding this man. Was he capable of matching the others depravity and cunning? In the physical altercation who would come out on top? The faded ghosts that made up his recollection of that night had become so entwined with his own wild imaginings that the difference between the two had become almost as elusive to him as the man in the ambulance. If their confrontation where to end in a physical altercation would he be capable of doing what he knew must be done? Could he destroy the demon that consumed his waking life, and if he did survive the ordeal and vanquish his foe, what then? Could he return to the life that had once defined him?

The headlights blasted his field of vision moments before the horn thundered through his ears and pulled him back to the present. He managed to pull the car back onto the right side of the street and himself into the present. A quick glance in the rearview mirror found the silhouette of the other driver giving him the one finger salute. For a moment he was surprised to find that such a brush with death had done little to his heart rate. He rubbed his hands across his face in a vain attempt to regain some composure and focus his mind on the road before him.

"This is Officer Barker responding to the 144 at Wiltshire. I should be on the scene in 14 minutes." Like a bucket of cold water, the sudden voice on the radio echoing around the inside of the car sharpened his mind. He had to get there before Officer Barker had the chance to scare his prey off. He could not see the ambulance rising from the rain splattered asphalt if the authorities were there with awkward questions or worse official records.

He put his foot down on the accelerator and watched as the needle arched through responsible and safe speeds then into dangerous before settling into illegal.

He himself was less than six minutes away according to the strange internal navigation system he had developed in his relentless nighttime pursuits.

The powerful engine roared and the vehicle surged forward. What little traction his worn tyres had was almost completely obliterated by the rain-soaked surface of the road. An unexpected pothole shook him and the well-thumbed manila folder on the passenger seat. A deluge of newspaper clippings and crime scene photos spilt into the footwell.

To the untrained eye, this looked like little more than a collection of discarded clippings fished out of a drawer and destined for a waste paper bin. To the trained eye, it was the treasured possessions of a madman, a nightmare narrative of his own imagining. Clippings from the New York Times reporting the strange death of a Hispanic shopkeeper clipped to a twenty-year-old article from the Weekly World News about a botched spate of alien abductions that resulted in discarded mummified cadavers being found in a low rent district of some lost midwestern township.

The shrill sound that split the night this time, came from his own horn as he rained his fists down upon it, trying to clear the human refuse that blocked the final stretch of road between him and Wiltshire.

"Move, mother fucker! Don't you have a bottle to fucking crawl into or an alley to piss in?" he ranted to no one in particular. He briefly considered the notion that the city itself was somehow involved in this and that the constant stream of night people and reckless drivers where it's way of protecting its own dark secret.

His trusty hip flask silenced that notion, the warm brown liquid coating his throat and granting him the courage he needed for the next stage of his journey.

A block from Wilshire he abandoned his vehicle between a dumpster and the burnt out remains of a Buick. He got out, slipped on his parka and pulled up his hood, armouring himself inside the plastic and faux fur against the rain. He could feel the heft of the revolver in his coat pocket counterbalanced by the three-quarters full hip flask slipped inside the other. An atrophied muscle memory sparked briefly into life and he found himself checking his pockets for a notepad and pen. A strange tinge of loss surged through him as the image of his editor looking up at him from the floor—holding back the torrent of blood trying to escape his nose, screaming at him about how he would never work in this town again, how he would make it his personal mission in life to make sure that no one ever published another byline with the name Conrad Varon—bombarded him.

He pushed that life aside. Unless he finished what he started then nothing he could write, no truth he could tell or secret he could uncover would make up for the forgotten dead he was damming to the muteness of history.

Gazing upon the silent and sunken facade of the buildings on the street he had to wonder who had called the police. Even a casual glance told him that this neighbourhood was the kind of place that ignorance was bliss and willful blindness was a survival mechanism. The alleys between the buildings were spaces where light died. Noises crept from the gloom but gave no indication if they were the danger he was seeking or some drunken reveler stumbling home after one too many at the nearest bar.

He looked towards the far end of the street, wondering how long he had before Officer Barker arrived. A distant siren stopped him dead in his tracks. His heart seemed to pause at the notion of a becoming a 137, 139 or even a 140. He cursed himself for not getting here quicker. For that fraction of a second he had spent considering his options. He should have driven here right away instead of waiting around to see if some more suitable crime was broadcast. As the siren faded away into the night, his heart slowly began to beat again. A false alarm. Officer Barker may have still been on his way but what had moments before been a potentially ruinous situation suddenly began to look like a blessing in disguise.

"Don't move. If you keep your mouth shut and do exactly as I tell you then you have a very good chance of walking home tonight in one piece," hissed a voice.

In one fluid movement, a hand shot into his pocket and helped itself to his poorly concealed revolver. Something equally blunt and heavy was driven into the small of his back.

"Look. I don't want any trouble. Just take what you want and go." This was all he needed. The gun the man behind him had just helped himself too was the only thing on him of any value. If it wasn't the only thing he actually needed that night, he would have been prepared to allow his mugger to take it and disappear back under whatever rock he had crawled out from.

"I can get you money…" he spat out in desperation.

"Don't fucking lie to me," snarled the voice from behind his back.

"I'm not. I don't have it on me, but I can get it. We can get it. Surely there must be an ATM around here?"

He took the lack of response as a cue to continue.

"Okay, so we go and get some cash. You take the money and give me the gun back. A simple transaction, no need to involve the police." His mouth was moving, and words were coming out but there was no way they were coming from any rational part of him. Somewhere beyond the unheard commands for his legs to work and the impulses flooding his mouth demanding that he scream for help—his obsession with the hunt would not let him go or give up. Tonight it would all come to an end. Of that he was certain, and this cretin was not going to stand in the way of the grand finale he had written in his imagination.

In the silence of the night, the sound of rubber splashing through rain-soaked asphalt drew him around to face his assailant. Only instead of coming face to face with some pawn bartered weapon and a desperate man, he saw a faded green raincoat fleeing into the empty night.

"Fuck!" He snapped before hurtling after the green ghost as it slipped between the raindrops trying to escape with its ill-gotten gains.

"Stop! Wait!! You're not in trouble. Please, I just need my gun back." He was out of breath already and his voice sounded like a tired whine. Even across the short distance, his lungs burned like he had smoked fifty a day for the past twenty years. On impulse, he grabbed the lid of a garbage can as he passed. Like a blind discus thrower, he made a hail Mary play and launched the abused steel lid towards the mugger.

He was certain it would neither stop him nor hurt him, but it might disorientate the man just long enough for him to catch up. It struck his left thigh, producing an unexpected wobble that brought the fleeing mugger down onto one knee.

This was his shot. If he didn't act now, then his gun was as good as gone. The muscles in his calves only had enough energy for one final action. The chase was over. He launched himself into a flying tackle, driving his shoulder—the bulk of his weight behind it—into the mass of wet green polyester. Both men crashed to the ground in a muddle of bodies, water and whatever grime inhabited that particular stretch of New York city streets.

He heard a dull popping noise from somewhere in the tangled mass of bone and cartilage the two had become. Elbows, knees and fists struck indiscriminately in the melee. Blood began to flow freely and pool beneath the two of them, neither sure whose it was or where it was coming from.

He managed to manoeuvre in such a manner that his own weight and momentum pinned the mugger beneath him. He could now see the boy inside the hood clearly, his malnourished face a mask of rage, like a wild animal clawing and scratching to be free of its cage.

"Get off me, you fucking creep. I will gut you like a fucking fish, just you watch bitch."

"Just shut up!"

"Keep your hands to yourself. And keep that the fuck away from me…" the boy spat as he tried in vain to raise a knee and strike him in the groin.

He pulled the younger man up and slammed him back down. The pockmarked paving stones unyielding behind him.

"SHUT! THE! FUCK! UP! AND! LISTEN!" he roared through gritted teeth.

The punch landed just above the left-hand side of his rib cage. He looked down into the eyes of the boy below him. The mugger had stopped struggling and looked just as shocked as him. He released his prisoner. Although the boy made no attempt to move, he kept him pinned in place with his knees.

Reaching around he found the blade sticking out his side. It hung limp, desperately clinging to the tattered track of flesh it had ploughed into his skin.

"Come on, man, get your ass up!" hissed a new voice from somewhere just beyond his field of vision.

"What did you do?"

"Saved your fucking ass, is what I did! Now get the fuck up before someone shows up and calls the cops."

With a little help from his former captive, he slumped over and into the gutter with the rest of the discarded refuse. He briefly thought about the potential infections that could be pouring into his bloodstream through the chewed knife wound.

His ears were the first thing to begin shutting down. For some reason, he always thought it would be his sight that would fade first but he could still see and smell the stream of detritus flowing past him, long after the sound of running feet faded into nothingness.

The wound had yet to hurt. It was little more than a patch of cold spreading across his body, consuming any trace of vitality and warmth it encountered.

His vision filled with a strange kaleidoscope of light. The cold yellow of the street lamps reflecting in the dirty water and the sterile white of the moon—full and bright above him—formed the first pattern, only for the shapes and colours to move and reform when a third colour was introduced.

A dull red strobed into the broken shards of light dancing before his eyes. What little breath he had, caught in his throat. Not him. Not now. Not like this. He pulled what little energy his slowly collapsing body could muster and channeled it all into his ears. Slow, methodical footfalls echoed out as they splashed in the puddles. He desperately held on for the announcement of Officer Barker having finally arrived on the scene. The man he had once feared would be his ruination was now his best hope for salvation.

The sound of the footsteps thundered through his head for a moment, further blurring the broken prism his vision had become. The black shadow swooped in and devoured all the light, leaving him cold and alone. He could still hear the rain falling, assaulting whatever was standing before him and the unforgiving concrete all around.

There was a sigh.

"I always thought It had some strange power to make any witnesses forget. Like a spell, it could cast to make the memory of what happened fade like a bad dream come the next day. You though, you are the first person to not let go. To actively seek It out. So I guess that means either It doesn't quite work like I thought it did, or that you are somehow special or you are just too stupid or stubborn. I guess at this stage it doesn't really matter."

He was gently pushed onto his front and he felt no pain or discomfort only the sensation of being moved.

"I won't lie. This bit is going to hurt."

Every nerve in his body exploded back into life in an instant, a spark of pain dancing across them. A scream shattered the silence of the night and his body spasmed upwards only to be push gently, yet firmly, back into the gutter.

"I can't have you dying on me now. It wouldn't like that, and I will be honest, the old 'First do no harm' still means something to me." The voice was jaunty and friendly but he was certain it was him.

"I suppose I had better keep this." He heard the sound of something heavy, most likely the knife, being dropped into a plastic bag. "The police normally don't take that much of an interest once the family has been shut up, but… well… after you, I trust nothing now. Don't want some enterprising young officer looking to make a name for himself joining up the same dot's as you did."

A sharp popping noise was next—a needle being pulled free of a cork—like a modern-day Excalibur.

"To be frank, I just can't be bothered with the hassle and It wouldn't like it. You were an amusement, I think. That's the only reason I figure you were allowed to keep going as long as you were. Listen to me talking like I know anything about It. I'm just it's... keeper... I think would be the closest comparison."

Something pierced the torn edge where the knife had snapped out. A new cold feeling flooded into his bloodstream, this one clean, like a white void eating through his arteries. A fleeting tickling feeling brushed across his skin, the fluid moving under his muscles and over his joints.

"I don't normally talk this much. Maybe I'm nervous or maybe I just feel you are entitled to answers," the voice paused for a moment before continuing. "I'm not drunk or high or crazy if that is what you are thinking. I can't move you anyway until the lidocaine kicks in."

The pushing and pulling sensation returned. He could feel his clothes being pulled up his back to expose the wound properly. Two edges of his flesh were pinched together before the sound of a staple gun filled the air. The first clasp bit into his flesh. A further three snaps split the silence before the field operation once again stopped. He was left with little more than the dull sensation of the staples biting into his flesh and the two edges desperately trying to separate again.

"I would consider myself lucky if I were you. Would you really want to be found dead in a place like this? That house over there is a crack den and I can count at least three brothels from where I am sitting." Over the casual banter, he could hear the sound of a bag being closed and the snap of rubber gloves being removed.

"I could probably go get a coffee, come back and you would still be lying where I left you…" There was a deliberate pause and while he couldn't see the paramedic, he imagined a smug grin etched on his face.

"…Kidding. I can't run the risk of you bleeding out. As I said, the Hippocratic oath is a hard habit to break. Right, let's get you into It."

"Murderer," he coughed. Dark crimson bubbles broke forth from deep in his throat and showered over him. A single drop wound its way down the left-hand side of his face, flowing towards his ear before suddenly stopping its journey short and dropping delicately into the scummy water of the gutter.

"Shit. Your friend with the knife must have hit something important." The jovial mood of the paramedic had changed to one of fear, his words tinged with a mixture of panic and resignation. The next sound he heard was a gurney being pulled from the back of the ambulance and slid into place beside him.

"I need you to stay with me and let me know if anything changes. Can you do that?"

"Murd…" he began before his mouth filled with the dull iron taste of more blood. He could feel it coating his teeth and crusting upon his top lip.

The paramedic took his feet first, raising them slightly and placed them almost reverently down upon the stretcher. He was left lying at an angle, his body temperature beginning to drop and a cloud of numbness spreading outwards from the heart of his wound. He made no effort to communicate the fluctuation in his temperature. He wasn't going to give the paramedic either the assistance or satisfaction. If he had had the energy he would have smiled.

"This may sting a little. I am afraid that there is no other choice, really. Needs must as they say." The paramedic had reverted back to his faux jovial attempt at bedside manner.

"One. Two. Three," the man heaved with an exaggerated sigh.

It felt as if someone had put their fingers into the wound, going even deeper than the knife, and grabbing hold of bone and muscle before pushing outward. His mind and body suddenly awoke, the fog and numbness replaced by a searing pain. He had no choice but to let out a guttural roar towards the heavens. A furious torrent of blood exploded from his mouth. He must have looked like a Daliesque fountain. If he could have heard anything over the sound of his own screaming, then he may have picked up the faint pinging noise as a couple of the staples broke free. They pulled chunks of flesh free, before flying through the air and dropping down into some dark recess on the road's surface.

When he was finally in place upon the stretcher, the man raised it into place and began to trundle it forward. The paramedic leaned over him and confessed, "I have never murdered anyone. Ever."

The paramedic raised his head up, gave a quick look around for some unseen big brother figure, and carried on towards the waiting ambulance.

"I need a day off just to catch up on sleep. Once I am done here the paperwork alone will take another couple of hours…" The chatter and the stretcher stopped.

Nothingness filled the night air. A void of silence had descended over New York City. All life had simply faded into the blackness, except for the dull red glow of the flashing lights reflecting upon the chrome, creating the effect of a morbid silent disco.

The Paramedic took a deep breath and opened the back door of the ambulance. He clipped the stretcher into place and pushed it into the back of the machine. It received its passenger as It had done so many times over the years. There was no malice or darkness within Its desires, of that the paramedic was almost certain. The paramedic took one final gaze down upon the broken man strapped to the gurney. He either did not notice or could not feel the thick black tendril-like cables slowly creeping across his skin. They searched out the wound or some other way of burrowing down and into the flesh. Its hunger was almost palpable at this point. The flashing lights had begun to throb like the beating of a heart. The gloom in the back of the ambulance moved, pressing down upon him and smothering any hope he may have harboured.

The paramedic thought about saying something. Anything—a parting word that would give this poor soul some comfort. He had been doing this long enough to know that there were no words for such a thing, as it did not exist. All he could do was look away and think about what he would do when his shift ended if it ever truly would. He slammed the door to the ambulance shut trapping the horror of what was about to happen inside. It began to feed.

Brian MacGowan's Shopping List

* Lettuce Hearts
* Heartburn Relief
* 9-Ball For Dummies
* Pool Cue
* Chalk
* Sgt Pepper's Lonely Hearts Club Band

Gotta Have Heart
Brian MacGowan

I was down at the pub shooting pool and had just sunk my last ball, scoring myself $500. I raised my arms like a prizefighter yelling, "Yeah! That's the way it's done!" Walking around the table I grabbed up the cash and just waved it in the guy's face. "Thank you for your contribution."

Next thing I knew someone shoved a beer into my hand. *Hey, I'm not going to give up a free drink.* I downed half the glass without even stopping to breathe. I was on fire that night. Raising my arms once again, like Rocky Balboa, I announced, "Ladies and gentlemen, is there anyone else who wants to give me their hard-earned money?" I spun looking at the faces around me. *The wimps, no one wanted to play me.*

The guy I beat looked at me like I just kicked his dog.

"Hey, come on, Jimmy. That's my rent. My old lady's going to kill me if I don't come home with it."

The guy was pleading with me because he was foolish enough to put his rent into the pot. I just shrugged. "So you're a dead man." I shoved the wad into my shirt pocket.

"Double or nothing. I'll play you…" He moved to the end of the table and started racking the balls. "Double or nothing."

I looked at him, he was sweating like he was crashing down from a high. I pulled the cash out and placed it on the table. "Okay, I'll play you. One game, double or nothing."

"Thanks, Jimmy, you're a champ." He finished racking the balls. "Do you want to break first?"

"Aren't you forgetting something." I looked down at the table pointing to my dough.

He just stood there biting his upper lip and then he pointed a shaking finger at the wager. "I, uh…" He rubbed his hands together. "I…I'm broke. But, but you know that I'm good for it." He ran his hands through his hair, wiping sweat from his forehead. "Oh god, Jimmy, please."

I looked at the poor sap, I knew he wasn't good for it. I smirked at him. "Sorry, pal." I picked up the money and looked at it. "I'll tell you what I'm going to do." I unfolded the wad and thumbed through it. "I'm not totally heartless, so here…" I pulled off a sawbuck and flipped it to him.

The guy looked at the ten and just lost it. "You fucking bastard! Someday I fucking hope that you're the one who will be fucking begging. You fucking piece of fucking shit."

Ha! As if that will ever happen. I turned and finished off my beer while I looked around for another sucker.

This was Frank's Pub and on a Friday night it could get rowdy. Keeping an eye on everything was Frank, the big man himself. He was in his usual place, standing behind the bar pulling brews, mixing drinks and shortchanging those too drunk to know the difference. He'd wipe down the bar with a cloth that stank like the devil puked on it. The servers worked the floor hustling drinks, slapping down wandering hands or shoving their tits in the faces of the drunks, hoping for bigger tips. Also behind the bar was Martha, Frank's twelve gauge shotgun. We all knew that the fun and games were over when Martha made an appearance.

At this time of the night there was always the constant clacking of pool balls, TV's blasting sports, their sound drowned out by the whoops and hollers of who the fuck knows why. Sports jocks, well past their glory days, had shoved tables together, getting shit-faced because they won, or lost. Business guys hung out at the bar while they tried to drink away their crappy day. Fat old men were sitting by the can, shooting the shit, sucking warm brew as they eyed the parade of tits and asses go past them.

Most of the people here were regulars, but one guy caught my eye. I had never seen him before. All night long, there he was just occupying one of the corner booths. He was dressed sharp; all in black, like some Don Mafioso. He had been talking with some other Dons who would come and go. Normally, crime guys like this huddle together, with lots of muscle close by playing bouncer. Not these guys, they were by themselves like they didn't give a fuck who saw or heard them. But now, this Godfather Don was sitting by himself, nursing a whiskey.

My balls were feeling enormous, so I walked up to his table. He ignored me like I was a nobody. *Hey, I just won five hundred bucks!* He must have heard the cheers.

I was getting tired of standing there, so I slammed my pool stick across the table in front of him.

He didn't even flinch. All he did was stare at the cue stick and then put his glass down. Finally, he looked up at me. His eyes were…I don't know. It was like looking into an empty grave. I probably should have just backed off, but my balls wouldn't let me.

Giving him my best tough guy stance, I said, "I've been watching you. You look like a pool player. Wanna give it a go?"

He just looked at me as if I was a gnat. He half smiled at me, turned back to his drink and then said, "I think not."

Bullshit! He was a player. "Come on." I pulled the wad out of my pocket and dropped it on the table in front of him. "I'll give you two to one odds." Fire was running through my veins, so I wasn't worried. There was no way that I was going to lose.

The guy just looked down and kinda laughed, "I don't play for petty cash," he said in a snooty tone.

Yeah, right. That suit he was wearing was expensive. He needs cash and lots of it. I wanted to play him now more than ever. "What d'ya want, then?"

He picked up his glass. He didn't even look at me, he just spoke over the top of his drink. "What do you have that I might want?"

What the hell type of question was that? I'm thinking, I have cash, who doesn't want that? I was trying to goad him into playing. So I just gave him a whatever shrug and said, "I never lose, because I have heart." And that was no lie, I put my heart into every game that I play. Without heart, you're nothing.

"Your heart, you say?" That seemed to spark him up. I swear his eyes changed and he gave me this…smile. It was just creepy. He smoothed down his tie, then turned to me. "That, I will take."

I stood there trying to figure out what the hell he was saying. "What? What do you mean?" I was confused. I had no idea what he wanted.

Then he pointed to my chest and said, "Your heart. We'll play for your heart."

Whoa there, buddy. "My heart?" I sneered at him. "You mean like a lover? Because I'm not into that." I admit, he was good-looking, but I don't do guys.

The Don finished his drink then stood up. He held out his hand. "Let me introduce myself, I am Damien Onyx. And you are?" He voice was low and as smooth as the expensive booze that he was drinking.

I took his hand, it felt cold. "Jimmy. Jimmy DeFalco." He had a firm, confident grip. I squeezed his hand harder.

He increased the pressure on my hand. "Well, Mr. DeFalco, it's simple." Then he spoke to me like I was a kid. "I want your heart. The one beating inside of your chest."

I just laughed, "Yeah, sure." I looked around to see who else heard this. "But what do I get when I beat you?"

He gave me this one eyebrow lift look. "Well, if you should happen to win, and that is not very likely, you get to keep your heart." His expression changed to pure seriousness. "I would think that would be incentive enough. But, if you want something more *tangible*." He reached into his pocket, then pulled out this enormous money clip. He just casually looked at it. "You can have this. Which is more than you will ever see hustling pool."

That bastard must have had at least 10 G's there. I slapped him on the shoulder. "Deal!"

He gestured toward the table like some high and mighty big shot. I walked up like I was the king of the block. I was going to enjoy taking him for all he was worth. My brain was already spending all of that cash.

When we got to the tables, I threw one arm over his shoulder. He cringed under me, but I didn't care; I was going to be rich. Turning to the crowd I announced, "My good friend Damien here, is going to challenge me for my heart." I put my hand on my chest. "But I get his dough!" I couldn't help but smile. I grabbed up a beer and chugged it down, slamming the empty glass onto the table.

Damien came up to the table, running his hand over the rail as if he was brushing dirt off of it. "Since I have been challenged, I choose eight-ball. The best of fifteen racks."

I tried to hide a smile. What a sucker, I could run racks all night long. The crowd around the table cheered. This was going to be easy.

He reached into his pocket again pulling out his money clip; he held it out for everyone to see. "I believe it is customary to put the wager on the table before the game begins." The crowd gasped when they saw how much dough was up for grabs.

Damien just looked at me like he was expecting me to do something. I spun around pretending to pull my heart out of my chest. Then, smiling, I smacked my hand down on the edge of the table beside the money. The crowd laughed.

Apparently, my new best friend wasn't impressed. Damien came up to me and put his left hand on my back. "Let me help." He put his other hand on my chest, then unfastened the top three buttons.

This was getting a little freaky for me. He obviously got his rocks off feeling guy's chests, but for ten large I was willing to put up with it.

He then slid his right hand under my shirt, his fingers digging into my skin.

"What the fuck, man!" I tried to pull back, but his left hand held me firmly in place. I then felt him pushing his fingers into my skin.

Holy fuck! My chest felt like it was about to explode. I was in so much pain I could hardly breathe. Eventually, all I could do was throw my head back and let out a "Gahhhhhh!" I looked down and the guy's hand was inside of my chest. Everyone in the pub was freaking out. Some people ran for the door, a bunch of them puked their guts out, others just stared. I could feel his cold hand on my heart, he was squeezing it, playing with it like he was choosing a tomato. I thought that the pain couldn't get any worse; then he gave a quick twist of his hand. *Motherfucker!* I felt and heard a sickly ripping sound. He then slowly pulled his hand out of my chest. I started hyperventilating; there in his hand was my beating heart.

I looked down; blood was oozing from my chest. *How the fuck was I not dead?*

With a wet slurp, he put my heart on the edge of the table beside the money. I could see and feel my heart beating rapidly.

Damien just looked at me, casually licking blood from his fingers. "Are we going to play? Or do you forfeit?"

I just stood there, dumbfounded, trying to figure out what was happening. A cold sweat broke out over my body. All I could do was stare around the room. Everyone seemed to be frozen in place...like those dead people in Pompeii. No one was moving, or blinking. Even the pictures on the TV's were in freeze frame.

Out of the corner of my mind, all muffled, I heard Damien sigh. "Oh for the love of all things unholy." His cold fingers were on my forehead; something moved through my mind, and then it was gone. My thinking was clear again. I looked around the pub, still, nobody was moving. I saw my heart sitting on the edge of the table. Studying my heart, I was fascinated by its beating. I looked up at Damien. "Am I…dead?"

"No, but wagers must be placed on the table," Damien said as he went to the wall rack of pool cues. He picked up a cue, sighting down its length. "Once again, as the challenged player, I decide who breaks first." He turned to me and gave a short bow. "When you are ready, you may break."

I'll tell you, all of those people not moving, it was freaky. It was like they were living statues. "What about them?" I said pointing around the room.

He just shrugged it off like it was an everyday thing. "They'll be fine. Most likely traumatized, but still alive. When we are finished with our game they will be restored. But, for now, we don't need the commotion that they would cause."

I really didn't want to touch anyone, some of them were crowding the table. I wiggled my way around a couple of them to get to the end of the table.

Looking annoyed, Damien went around the table touching the people who were in our way. They just crumbled to dust. Poof, they were gone. Damien looked at me, one eyebrow raised and a slight smile. "Oh dear. These ones, *won't* be so fine."

"What do you mean they won't be fine? You can restore them? Right?"

"I know of only one being that made a person out of dust." With a wicked smile, Damien leaned in close. "And that's not me."

I glanced down at the piles of dust thinking, *"Did I know these people? Where's Tina? What about Mark?"*

With a nervous hand, I picked up the cue ball and placed it in my favorite position, about midway to the left of center, just slightly behind the line. Out of the corner of my eye, I could see my heart beating. Taking a deep breath, slowly letting it out, I watched my heart slow down. Closing my eyes, I took a cleansing breath to center myself. Opening my eyes, I pulled back on the cue, and then rapidly sent it forward, squarely striking the cue ball. The ball flew down the table making a clean break, pocketing two balls. Making my way around the table, I pocketed more balls. Within minutes the table was cleared. I racked another set of balls, then ran the table again and again.

At first, I was careful to avoid the dust piles of people. It just felt wrong to step in them, like I was violating them. By my fourth rack, it was tough shit for them. I was having a great run; making shots that I never made before. Their ashes just became part of the regular dirt on the floor. I was smoking those balls and that was all that mattered.

While I was running the racks, Damien just sat there quietly watching me, like he didn't have a care in the world. At one point, probably out of boredom, he wandered around the room looking at the frozen people. He broke a hand off one guy. He just chuckled to himself saying, "Now, he's going to be in for a surprise."

Damien walked over to the bar. Frank had pulled out Martha, her trigger fully pulled back. The shot had already left the barrel, it hung in mid-air while the pub was frozen in time. Damien went behind the bar, pulled out a fresh glass and poured himself a whiskey. He looked at Frank while he sipped his drink. He let out an evil, "Ha! Ha! Ha!" If death could laugh, that's what it sounded like.

Damien picked up Frank like he was a mannequin, brought him around the bar then placed him directly in the line of the shotgun blast.

Aw shit, Frank, you're going to shoot yourself. I sighed. There was not much that I could do to help him right now. Besides, I had far more important matters of my own.

On my thirteenth rack, Damien was still moving around the room. He stopped by a tough looking biker dude. The guy had been running for the door, but he was looking back at where we were. Damien looked at the guy's face. He got mad, then growled, "You!"

He scared the crap out of me; I almost miscued. I stepped back from the table, as I applied more chalk to my cue.

I glanced over. Damien tapped the guy on the forehead, bringing him back to life. Well, at least his head, the rest of him was still frozen. For a tough biker, he looked like he was scared shitless. His face was sweating; his eyes were bulging out of his head. Damien got real close to the guy's face and said, "I told you, that if I ever saw you again, I would have your balls." Calmly, Damien unbuckled the biker's pants then dropped them and his boxers to the floor. He then reached down to the guy's crotch, grabbed him and then slowly squeezed. I could see the pain on the guy's face, his mouth was opened but he couldn't say anything. Damien stopped. "I have changed my mind. I have no need for your balls." Relief showed on the biker's face. "And neither do you." Damien gave a quick twist of his

188

wrist. The wet popping sound of the guy's nuts made my stomach churn. I could feel my own balls retreat.

Damien turned to me. "I do apologize for that unpleasant business. It interrupted your run." He waved at the table. "Please continue."

Looking toward the edge of the table, I tried to calm my wildly beating heart. *Deep breaths, deep breaths. You've got this.* After rebuilding my confidence with some easy shots, there were just three balls were left on the table. I went for a bank shot, one that I had made many, many times before. Like a cocky bastard, I fired the cue ball down the table.

Oh, Fuck!

I collapsed on the table, my run over. All I could hope for is that he had a lesser run than me.

Damien gathered up the balls for his first rack, "It appears, Jimmy, that your run has ended."

My heart was beating feverishly; I could feel it palpitating. I was surprised that it stayed on the table.

All that I could do was sit there, stupefied, as Damien ran rack after rack. The clacking of the pool balls in sync with the beating of my heart.

After a while, I couldn't sit there any longer. I had to do something. I moved about the room looking for my girlfriend, Tina. I couldn't find her, I closed my eyes. *Shit, I bet she was one of the dust people.*

"Hey, I have to take a whizz. Can we do a time out?" I shouted to Damien.

Damien stood back from the table. He grabbed his glass of whiskey, swirling it around. "As you wish."

While I was pissing, I was looking around. I could see that someone was kneeling in one of the stalls. *Ha! Probably puking their guts out.* For shits and giggles, after I zipped up, I opened the door to see if I knew who it was. Yup, I knew exactly who it was. There was my best friend, Mark, sitting on the crapper, pants to his ankles, head thrown back and eyes closed. Kneeling on the floor in front of him was some chick, deep diving into his crotch.

"Way to go, Mark!" I laughed. "Who's the skank?"

I took a look at the girl. "What the fuck, Tina!"

My girl was going down on my best friend.

I just lost it. I was yelling at both of them while I kicked the fucking shit out of the joint. *Frank is going to be so pissed when he sees this place.* But Frank is not going to care when Damien unfreezes everyone. His face is going to be scattered all over the pub when that buckshot hits him.

I slammed the stall door shut. The latch broke letting the door swing inward whacking Tina in the ass, forcing her forward onto Mark. *I hope the bitch chokes.*

I stormed out of the can. *There is no way the day could get any worse.*

Damien was finishing off his drink. He raised an eyebrow. "Something the matter?"

"Let's just get this over and done with," I growled.

"Very well. By the way, thirteenth rack, Jimmy," Damien announced.

This break was his most powerful. The sound was like thunder. The balls quickly scattering, pocketing almost half of them.

I slumped down in a chair. My shoulders dropped, and I broke out into a sweat again. *I'm going to fucking lose.* Reality was starting to beat its way into my head. *He was joking about my heart, right?*

He quickly ran the table as if he couldn't wait for the end. "Last ball, Jimmy." He confidently dropped it into a side pocket.

Oh, Christ no! I stood up. "Double or nothing." I blurted.

"Excuse me?" Damien couldn't pull his gaze away from my heart.

"I'll play you, double or nothing."

Damien looked at me. Then his eyes narrowed, he had a wicked smile on his face. "Double or nothing you say. What do you have two of, that I may want?"

I shook my head in confusion. "I...I...I..." *He had already ripped my heart out of my chest, what else is there?*

He stepped toward me, shoved his hands down my pants and grabbed my nuts. "How about these, Jimmy? How about we we play for your balls?" He started to pull on them. "Remember, all wagers are to be placed on the table."

I shook my head. "No, no, no. Not that."

Damien stopped. He pulled his hand from my pants then wiped it on my shirt. "As you wish."

He walked over to the where the wagers were laid on the edge of the table. Damien picked up his money clip. "Tell you what, Jimmy, I did so enjoy the game. You may be heartless..." He paused and snickered at his own joke. "But I am not. We'll split the pot." He tossed the wad of cash toward me. "You can have that, but the heart *is mine.*"

What the fuck would he do with someone's heart?

He picked up my heart, squeezing it, stroking it. "Do you feel that, Jimmy?"

I felt his hand on my heart, I nodded, "Please, please don't." I clutched at my chest where my heart should be. He kept squeezing and relaxing his hand, changing my heart rate. My eyes started to flutter, my mind was becoming foggy.

"How about this, Jimmy?" Damien licked my heart. I felt his tongue running over the surface and down into the open aorta.

My eyes rolled back, I crashed to the floor, convulsing. *Jesus, please make it stop.* Damien continued manipulating and licking my heart. My breathing became ragged. He then stopped. *Oh, thank God.* My heart slowing as it came into a somewhat normal rhythm. My convulsions subsided, sweat poured from my body.

Opening my eyes, Damien was standing over me. He was still holding my heart, but at least he wasn't playing with it anymore.

This started out as a simple game of pool. How was I to know it would turn into a life or death situation. I just wanted out of there. I shouldn't have challenged him. I should have just backed off when I had the chance.

Fumbling for the money clip, holding it out, I gasped, "Please, please," *Oh God it hurt.* "Please. Take it back." Dropping the clip to my side, I swallowed hard. "What do you want?" I was struggling to speak. "Name it."

Damien bent down on his haunches like some sort of beast. He held out my rapidly beating heart for me to see. I closed my eyes; I could still feel his hands holding it, subtly manipulating it, caressing it.

"I've already told you. I want your heart." He didn't even look at me, all he could do was look at my heart, like…like it was a piece of fruit. Then he licked his lips and said, "And I'm hungry."

What the fuck! He's hungry? Fuck! Fuck! Fuck!

He opened his mouth, fangs protruded from his upper teeth. *No, no, no. This cannot be happening.* He bit down on my heart like it was an apple. Ripping a chunk of it away. *Gah!* My jaw locked tight as pain shot through me. Spasms racked my body, my lungs gasped for air. I struggled to look at Damien. Blood, my blood, was running from the corners of his mouth. He was chewing thoughtfully like he was some type of gourmet chef.

"I must say, Jimmy," he held my heart out again, looking at it appreciatively, "this is delightfully tasty. You wouldn't happen to have any siblings?"

He took another bite. My life force was draining. My vision gone. My hearing fading, but I could still hear him chewing, swallowing.

"Good-bye, Mr. DeFalco. It was a pleasure meeting you."

Mark Deloy's Shopping List

Beer
Headache powder
Coffee
Half and Half
Limes
Chocolate bars

Island Food
Mark Deloy

"Here," Anna said and thrust a hot dog to Thomas.

"Thanks. I was starving."

"Yeah, me too. Can you see the island yet?"

"Not yet. Oh wait, there it is," Thomas said, pointing.

Kimcheck Island was three miles across at its longest part. It had one restaurant, one grocery store and a few antique shops. Their aunt Cleo had owned one of those shops until she sold it and retired after her husband died. Now she did crossword puzzles, played pinochle, and fussed over her flower gardens. Thomas and Anna were the only ones riding the ferry today, which wasn't unusual. Aside from food and supply deliveries the island didn't get many visitors. There were a few summer people who owned vacation cabins and stayed all summer, but it was almost August. They would have already been here over a month now, *and probably bored out of their heads*, Thomas thought.

The ferry pulled into its slip with a thud. Thomas and Anna walked down the gang plank and stepped onto the weathered dock. The sun had bleached the wood almost white and the boards creaked under their feet.

"I hate walking on this thing," Anna complained, looking down at her feet to see where to place her next step on the weathered boards.

"It'll probably be here for years after we're gone," Thomas said, jumping up and down once.

"Hey, quit it."

"What? It's fine. Come on, Cleo said she rented bikes for us at The Shack."

The Shack was a tiny general store at the end of the dock. They sold bait, sunglasses, life vests, and cold drinks. They also rented Jet Skis and bicycles. It was always the first place they stopped whenever they came to the island.

"Ewww, gross. That's disgusting," Anna said, sidestepping closer to the deck's railing.

Thomas looked down at what she was grossed out by. It was a pelican, nearly dead. It was lying on its side. Its mouth was opening and closing slowly, and its eyes were wide and black. It seemed to be staring at them, pleading for help. Part of its belly had been torn out and its blood soaked into the dry deck planks. The white feathers around the gaping hole were matted and clotted.

"What do you think happened to it," Thomas said mostly to himself.

"That looks like a bite mark from another animal. Come on. It might have rabies or something."

Thomas felt like he should put the poor bird out of its misery, but he had no way to do it. He thought he might buy a knife if they had one for sale at the Shack. They walked inside. The store was deserted.

"Hello?" Anna said and rang the bell on the counter. "Hello, anyone here?"

There was no answer.

"I wonder where everyone is." Thomas said and rang the bell again. He looked around and saw most of the shelves were bare. There were a few bags of chips and a couple of candy bars still on the shelf.

"Hey kids," came a gruff voice behind them.

A man Thomas didn't recognize came out of the back room. He had his hands full. In his right hand was the biggest sandwich Thomas had ever seen. In his left hand he held a roasted game hen with several bites taken out of it. Thomas couldn't help but think about the pelican outside. The man was overweight already but didn't seem to care. His shirt was covered with other food stains and his mouth looked greasy. A round, hairy belly overlapped his jeans and hung out of the bottom of his "The Shack" t-shirt.

"Uh, we'd like to rent two bikes and get a few things," Thomas said, opening the cooler and grabbing one of the last Cokes. He spotted several knock off Swiss Army knives in a basket on the counter. "How much for the knife?"

"Ten dollars. Hey, are you kids hungry?" the clerk asked as he took a huge bite from his sandwich, then took one from the small chicken.

Thomas passed on the knife, thinking that was too much for a knock off.

"No, I'm not. I ate on the ferry. Anna, you want something to eat?"

"Nah, not right now," she said.

"I for one have been really hungry lately," the clerk said. "Must be the salt air. I've been pigging out all morning. You want anything else? The bike will be another ten dollars for all day."

"Okay. My Aunt Cleo Walker said she rented the bikes for us already?"

"Oh, you're Miss Cleo's nephew and niece. She said you'd be coming to visit. I've got your reservations for the bikes right here. She also said to put whatever you wanted on her tab, so you're all set. Anything else?"

"Anna, you need anything else?"

"Nope, I'm good."

Thomas noticed she was staring at the clerk. He nudged her, breaking her gaze.

"You ready," he said. The clerk didn't even seem to notice Anna looking at him. He went right on eating, then washed two alternating mouthfuls of meat, cheese and bread down with half a Pepsi.

They retrieved their rented bikes from the rack on the side of the building. Cleo's house was on the other side of the island. The bikes would make it a fairly quick trip.

Thomas peddled back over to the dock. The bird was dead. Thomas watched as a fly landed on the pelican's beak, then crawl inside its mouth, looking for the first place to lay its maggoty eggs.

"Come on, Thomas. Leave that thing alone," Anna said, peddling away quickly.

"I'm coming. Hey, wait up!"

They peddled along Main Street, which was really the only street on the island. The sidewalks were deserted. There were a few stores open, but many more had closed signs in their windows and on their doors.

"Is it a holiday or something?" Anna said. "Where is everyone?"

"I don't know. Casey's Hobby shop should be open. Its Saturday, his busiest day."

They'd always made it a point to stop at Casey's at least once whenever they visited the island. The place was filled with model cars, comic books, gaming cards like Magic the Gathering and Dungeons and Dragons books. Thomas jumped off his bike and walked it up over the curb in front of the small shop. There was a closed sign on the door but there was also a note.

Closed due to illness it said.

Thomas cupped his hands to the window and looked inside. Anna did the same thing beside him. The store was dark, but there was a light on in the back room. Casey had a fish eye mirror mounted in one corner so he could keep an eye on kids who might have sticky fingers around the magic Cards. Thomas saw a flash of movement in it and got on his tip-toes to see a little better.

Reflected in the corner beneath the rows of game cards was Casey. He was crouched down and eating something greedily, taking large bites out of whatever it was. It was too dark to see much. Whatever it was, it looked like it had hair or fur on it. As Casey took another bite, his food twitched, then jerked convulsively.

Thomas pushed back from the window quickly, making an erk..erking sound in his throat.

"What's the matter?" Anna asked.

"No…nothing. We need to go. Cleo is waiting on us I'll bet."

"Thomas? What did you see?"

"Casey was in there. I saw him in the mirror. He looked like he was busy doing something in the back," Thomas said, peddling away, hoping Anna would follow him." Come on!"

"What the Hell," Anna said and picked up her bike.

They rode up Aunt Cleo's driveway twenty minutes later. Thomas parked his bike in the garage and he and

Anna mounted the front steps to the screened in porch. On the window sills were Conch shells, Horseshoe crab shells, sand dollars and a few potted plants. Anna knocked on the door and Cleo immediately opened it as if she'd been waiting for them. She grabbed them both and hugged them.

"You're both getting so big," she said. This was the same thing she'd said to them every summer since they started visiting four years ago. Come on inside. Are you hungry? You must be. I'm making chili for supper, but I've got cheese and crackers, deviled eggs, and some ham on the counter. I'm afraid I've eaten all the bread, or we could have had sandwiches while we waited to eat."

"I think we're good until supper," Thomas said. "That's a lot of food."

"I stocked up for your visit. The store in town was out of a lot of stuff for some reason, but they'll be getting a truck tomorrow on the ferry. Come on, sit down and tell me all about your school year. You don't mind if I eat while you talk? I swear I think I have a tapeworm or something today. I've been eating since I got up."

Cleo had always been a thin women like Thomas and Anna's mother. Thomas noticed Cleo now had a little pouchie belly. It bulged against her shirt. She took three pieces of ham and pushed them into her mouth with two fingers then greedily chewed them up. Saliva slid out of her mouth and dribbled onto her shirt. She didn't even notice.

Anna shot Thomas a look but didn't say anything.

"So what's new with the both of you?" Cleo said as she opened a sleeve of crackers and popped three into her mouth, then proceeded to talk with her mouth full.

"How was school? Your mother said you were both on the honor roll this year."

"Uh, yeah," Anna said. "I had a little trouble with Algebra, but dad helped me."

"That's terrific, dear," Cleo said. She got up and went to the fridge and stared inside for a second before taking the plastic wrap off the tray of devilled eggs. She grabbed two of them, smushed them together and shoved them in her mouth. Thomas didn't think she'd even finished eating the crackers yet.

"Aunt Cleo. Have you been feeling okay?" Thomas asked.

"Sure never better," she said around egg yolks and whites. A piece of yolk fell out of her mouth, but she caught it and tossed it into the air and caught it in her mouth. "Will you be a dear, Thomas, and ride over to Mrs. Kimble's and see if she has any hamburger meat? They were out of it at the store this morning and we'll need it for the chili. She had a baby. Oh you haven't seen him yet. Cute little boy, so sweet. His name is Harley, like the motorcycle. Can you imagine?"

Thomas rode down the street to Mrs. Kimble's house and rang the bell. There was no answer, so he knocked. He saw her minivan in the driveway, so she should be there. He knocked again and the door opened. It hadn't been latched all the way.

"Mrs. Kimble!" he called out and stepped inside. "Your door was open. It's Thomas, Cleo's nephew! She was wondering if she could borrow some—"

Thomas stopped in his tracks. Every cabinet door in the kitchen was open and so was the refrigerator. Empty boxes of food, wrappers, food storage containers, empty cans of vegetables littered the kitchen floor.

"Mrs. Kimble, are you okay?"

There was no answer. Thomas walked through the kitchen, stepping over the empty boxes, bags and containers. He made his way down the back hallway, looking into the first bedroom, then the second. When he reached the third, he stopped and starred, unable to comprehend what he was seeing. Mrs. Kimble was crouched on the floor, much in the same way Casey was crouched in the corner of his store. Mrs. Kimble was holding her baby.

Little Harley hung limply in her hands. He was so tiny, obviously a newborn. Mrs. Kimble was struggling to remove the infant's diaper with her teeth, like unwrapping a candy bar. Chunks of white plastic and cloth from the diaper lay at her feet, along with a lot of blood. The baby's chest was torn open. Its tiny ribs poked out like glistening white fingers. As Thomas watched in horror, Mrs. Kimble reached inside Harley's chest and tweezed his tiny heart with two fingers. Then she tore it free and popped the swollen red organ into her mouth as if it was a ripe plumb. She chewed noisily as she turned and looked at Thomas.

Her entire face was awash in crimson. Chunks of flesh mixed with blood congealed on her lips and cheeks. She smiled and gave Thomas a miserable look.

"I was hungry, so hungry and there was no more food in the house. I told myself just a bite. Just a bite to tide me over until I could go shopping."

Thomas turned his head and vomited onto the hallway carpet then turned and ran, tripping over a grease clotted Tupperwear container and falling to the linoleum.

"How much do you weigh, boy?" Mrs. Kimble said following him. Harley's body dangled from one hand like a doll. "I'll bet you have a hundred pounds of meat on you."

"Nooo, noooo!" Thomas screamed and was able to make it to his feet. He slammed into the front door and turned the knob. He flung it open and burst outside, trying not to vomit anything else up. He landed hard on the front lawn and scrambled to get to his feet. He needed to get Anna and get out of here. Right now. That was when he realized he'd just left her with his aunt. His very hungry aunt. Thomas ran back next door and tried to seem calm as he entered the house. It smelled like his aunt had already started cooking.

"Did you get the meat?" his aunt called from the kitchen. "We need to get this Chili going. It'll take a while to cook, and I'm soooo hungry."

"She was all out," Thomas said, trying to control his urge to vomit.

Think about something else, he thought. *Think about something else.*

Thomas walked into the kitchen. His aunt was standing at the stove. Something was sizzling in a large fry pan, sending up an aroma of cooking meat.

"That's alright. We'll make do," She said.

Anna was sitting at the kitchen table tied to a chair, unconscious. There was a bloody butcher block cutting board in front of her, along with a huge cleaver. More blood pooled around the base of Anna's chair. As Thomas came around the table he saw where the blood was coming from. Aunt Cleo had used a zip tie around Anna's bicep to keep the bleeding at a minimum.

"Oh God, Oh God," Was all Thomas could say.

"I know, dear. I'm hungry too. It won't be long, I promise. Let me get the meat off this pesky bone and then we can start the chili."

Thomas bolted. He didn't know what else to do.

He crashed out the front door and stumbled off the porch then kept running. He crawled behind a shed in a neighbor's yard and pulled out his cell phone and dialed his father's number. It rang once and went to voicemail.

"Shit! Get off your phone, Dad!" Thomas screamed and hung up. Dad was always on the phone talking with friends and business partners. Didn't he know this was the twenty-first century and no one actually talked on their phones anymore? Next he tried his mom.

"Hey, honey, can I call you back? I'm in the middle of a meeting."

"No, don't hang up. Cleo's gone crazy along with the rest of this island. She ate Anna's arm! Send the police!"

"Is this another one of your zombie apocalypse practical jokes, Thomas? Because I don't have time—"

"Mom! Listen to me! Cleo is eating your fucking daughter right now!"

There was silence on the other end.

"Mom!"

"I don't think this is funny, young man. If you can't find a better way to spend your vacation than to play a prank on your mother then—"

Thomas hung up.

He looked back at Cleo's house. She hadn't come running outside to chase him with her huge cleaver yet.

No, because she's too preoccupied with eating your sister, he thought.

"Psst."

Thomas looked around. There was a girl about his age under a nearby porch. She was waving at him, then waved him over.

Great, a cannibal girl under the porch was now giving him a come hither gesture probably so she could chew his face off.

"Come here!" She whispered harshly. "I'm not infected."

That got Thomas moving. He craved information almost as much as he did a baseball bat right now.

He scrambled over and crawled under the porch.

"What do you mean infected?" he said as soon as he was under.

"I came back on the ferry yesterday from visiting my dad on the mainland and people had started eating each other. I barely got away from my mom this morning."

"What the fuck is going on?" Thomas said. "My aunt has gone crazy. She was frying up my sister's arm."

"I think it's the water. I haven't drank anything but bottled water since I got back. I usually don't. I've always thought the island's water tasted nasty."

"When did it start?" Thomas asked, trying to remember if he'd drank any water since they got off the ferry.

"I think it's been building up for a few days. People just started getting really hungry. At least that's how it started with my mom. She ate everything in the house. And I mean everything. Even those marshmallow Peeps no one likes that were still on the top of our fridge since Easter. Then she went to the grocery store in town last night at midnight. I told her it was closed, but she went anyway. When she got back she came in my room with a knife and said I would have to sacrifice something so we could eat tonight. I barely got away." She held out her arm. She'd wrapped a shirt around it, but the blood had soaked through.

"Are you okay?"

"I will be once we get off this island."

"How? The ferry doesn't come back until tomorrow."

"I can drive a boat," she said. "We just need to get to the marina."

"Okay, good idea. I'm Thomas, by the way."

"Lea," she said.

"Should we try to take bikes?"

"Shhh, listen," Lea said.

There was rustling in a nearby hedge and then two little kids emerged from the bushes. They had strips of red cloth tied around their heads, Rambo style. One of them had a knife, the other held a slingshot. Tied to one of the boy's belt were three dead squirrels.

Thomas waited for them to pass.

"Were they hunting?"

"Yeah, food is running out. They're starting to get desperate I guess."

"How are we gonna make it all the way to the marina without someone seeing us and turning us into Sunday dinner?"

Lea pulled keys out of her pocket.

"You have a car?" Thomas said excitedly.

"Yeah, it's my mom's Jeep, but since it's not something she can eat, she won't mind if we borrow it. Come on. It's in the garage."

They scurried across back lawns until they reached Lea's house. The garage was standing open and the Jeep was sitting inside.

"Is she still in there?" Thomas asked, trying to see inside the dark windows.

"I don't know. I think so." Lea said.

They ran for the garage and squatted down next to the big front tire.

"Oh shit, look!" Lea said and pointed down the street.

An overweight man was doing his best to hobble down the street. His pants were ripped and bloody. He kept looking behind him as he shuffled across the street and tried the door on an old Dodge truck parked in front of the hardware store. The door was locked and he pounded his fists against the hood in frustration.

"We should help him," Thomas said. "Try to get him to come over here."

"No way. He's too far away. It'll only attract attention. We can try to pick him up on the way by."

But as they watched the man put his head down against the hood out of fatigue and frustration, an old woman emerged from an alley across the street. Her back was hunched and she looked close to eighty. She was wearing a blood splattered flowered house dress and only one slipper. She held a large axe in both hands. The large man didn't see or hear her. He still had his head down.

"We've got to help," Thomas said and started to stand up to get the guy's attention.

Lea pulled him back down.

"You're only going to get us killed," she said.

It didn't matter anyway. The old woman sprinted the distance between her and the man. He looked up right before the axe came down on his head. There was a soft crunching sound as the blade slammed through his skull and into his brain. He stood straight up for a second, then collapsed to the pavement in a heap, his head gushing blood. The old woman looked down at him and cocked her head, as if she was trying to pick out what part to eat first. Then she dropped the axe, sat down next to the dead man and cradled his head in her lap. She looked like a little kid getting ready to chow down on a ripe melon. She reached down with both hands and used her skinny fingers to pry open the initial gash she had made. There was a sickening ripping sound as the opening widened. She began pulling out brain matter and popping it into her mouth as if she was enjoying a bowl of popcorn while watching a movie. She had a huge bloody grin on her face. Thomas turned away, struggling not to be sick again.

"Come on," Lea said.

Thomas could tell she was trying to be brave, but tears stood out in her eyes.

They got into the Jeep and Lea started the engine. Thomas kept an eye on the door to the house, praying it didn't open. Lea put the Jeep into gear and they sped down the street past the old woman and her meal. She never even looked up.

"We've got to go get my sister," Thomas said.

"We should go get help first."

Thomas hated to admit it, but Lea was right. If they went back for Anna they could get caught and wouldn't be able to help anyone.

"Alright, but we have to hurry."

They pulled into the marina parking lot.

"Now what? Thomas said. "How do we get boat keys?"

"We've already got them," Lea said and dangled the Jeep keys. "We have a boat and Mom keeps the boat keys and the car keys together. Come on."

They made their way down to Lea's boat, keeping an eye out for anyone, but the dock was deserted. Thomas wondered where everyone was. An image flashed through his mind of all the hungry residents having a Bar-B-Q, cooking up everyone who wasn't infected.

They reached the boat and boarded it. Lea's stomach growled audibly.

"Sorry, I haven't really eaten anything since yesterday."

"It's okay. We can get some food once we get to the mainland."

They pulled away from the dock and were out in open water in a few minutes, cruising along at a steady pace.

Lea was staring out at the ocean. Thomas figured she was lost in thought.

"You okay? Lea?"

Lea turned around. There was something about her eyes that told Thomas everything was not alright. She cut the engine off.

"I really thought it was the water," Lea said. "But I'm really starting to get hungry. Maybe it's in the air. I really don't know, and don't care anymore. Did you bring anything to eat? I have to eat, Thomas."

"Lea...Lea listen to me," Thomas said, holding out his hands. "We'll be on the mainland in just a few minutes. I'll buy you a nice juicy steak. There's an Outback really close to shore. Or seafood. We could get you a huge King Crab meal."

He was backing away, which wasn't easy on the small boat. Trying to put distance between them.

"So hungry. It's like an itch right here," she said and put both hands on her stomach.

"I know and we're going to get you some food, but we have to make it to shore. That's where the food is. There's no food here."

"Sure there is." Lea pulled the keys out of the ignition and tossed them over her shoulder into the water.

"Nooo!" Thomas screamed.

Lea lunged at him but she was slow and Thomas dodged her easily. He pushed out, trying to just get her away from him, but she tripped over a coil of rope and went overboard. She splashed and struggled.

"I can't swim. Thomas help!"

He thought about it for a second. He thought maybe he get her back up in the boat and then knock her out until help came. He rushed over and reached out to her. She smiled, reached out, grabbed his outstretched hand and clamped her teeth down on his index finger. He felt her bite through the second joint. She jerked her head violently, snarling like a dog and pulled the digit free of his hand. Thomas pulled and fell back into the boat, his hand gushing blood.

"Fuck, stupid…stupid," he chided himself. He picked up the anchor and without thinking lifted it and threw it overboard at Lea. It hit her squarely in her forehead, splitting her head open. Her eyes rolled back, and she went limp. She floated for a few seconds and then she began to sink into the bloody water.

Thomas fell back onto the seat and closed his eyes. This couldn't be happening.

He managed to get his shirt off and wrap it around his hand. He tried to put pressure on it, but it hurt like a bitch. He almost passed out from either blood loss, or pain.

"Now what?" he said to himself.

His only hope was for someone to come along and see him and hope they weren't infected with whatever this was turning people into eating machines.

He tried to keep watch for the first few hours, but he was in a lot of pain and he also hadn't eaten or drank anything since the hot dog he'd eaten on the ferry. His stomach felt queasy from the boat's constant rocking and his blood loss. Everything seemed hopeless. At least his hand had stopped bleeding. He finally slumped down on the floor of the boat and went to sleep.

***

"Hey boy! Hey, wake up!"

Thomas opened his eyes. He wasn't sure where he was at first. A scruffy looking man he recognized as the ferry boat captain was looking down at him.

"You okay, son?"

"Yes, I think so," he said, then his hand began to throb as he tried to get up. He saw the sun was low in the sky. Had he slept right through the night? He supposed he had.

"What happened to your hand?"

"Long story," Thomas said. "Can you give me a ride to the mainland?"

"Sure. I have to drop a couple of passengers off on the island, but then we'll head home and get you to a doctor."

"The island? No! We can't go there. There's some kind of outbreak going on. We have to go back to…"

"Okay, okay. Come on. Let's get you on board and we'll head back." the captain said, helping him up.

Thomas sat on one of the wooden benches which lined the ferry's deck. There were a few passengers milling about. One woman caught his eye. She was wearing a short skirt. Thomas's eyes locked onto the woman's calf muscle. All of a sudden he could picture how good that muscle would taste. Swelled with blood, sweet and thick in his mouth. Maybe put some hot sauce on it.

He shook his head violently. What was he thinking?

A young boy around five or six chased his older sister along the railing and Thomas stared at the boy's neck. The soft, smooth skin there would probably crackle like pork rinds in an open fire. He licked his lips and rose from his seat.

The captain said it would be twenty minutes until they reached the harbor. That would be plenty of time for a quick meal.

Jason Gehlert's Shopping List

Jimsonweed
Eggs
Roasted Peppers
Energizer hearing aid batteries
Mountain Dew Kickstart (mango lime)
Individual box of Mike and Ike's
A bag of cherry cola Oreos
Hearing aid
Bottles of water
Lemon bars
Another bag of Oreos
Crackerjacks
Kombucha juice

Beaver's Claw
Jason Gehlert

"Shelter is sparse, stores ransacked... [static]...attacks have tripled in the last few weeks. The virus is now airborne... [static]... decimates the body...[static]... internal bleeding, rotting flesh, curled...[static]... everyone please heed this warning...[static]...find shelter if you can...[static]...rogue groups...[static]...safety is a priority. Beaver's Claw is the closest sanctuary city. [static]. There is a cure. A population of...[static]... they are immune."

"Dash, do you have the list?" His father turned off the radio and signed the question. Barry glanced over at his son.

Nodding his head, Dash maintained a focused stare out the passenger side window. His fingers unfurled the well-worn piece of paper. The pencil's words smeared against the blue lines. His left hand signed 'milk', 'juice', 'water', and 'love.'

His teenage years were formative, if not filled with many challenges. The eighteen year old marital arts student experienced grueling obstacles as a young man with Down syndrome. A series of heart ailments during infancy nearly derailed his promising life. Arduous scheduling of physical therapy rebuilt muscles stronger and tighter, preventing further erosion of elasticity. Dash found solace in countless comic books and superhero movies, with the Marvel universe being his favorite. His persistence and adherence to structure aided in his development both physically and mentally. Dash's uncanny ability to remain unscathed from the virus left others to wonder about his true nature. Although his health remained immune, his troubles understanding the situation frustrated him. His father, a man in his early sixties and possessing unworldly patience for his son, managed to dodge the virus utilizing wits and careful obedience to strict rules to overcome adversity. Dale's sign language remained a key form of communication between the two men. Dash's immediate family died early on from the initial outbreak.

"Mommy," his words were soft and loving. He raised the shopping list.

Sniffling back tears, his dad's stoic response was routine conversation between them. "She always loved making those lists with you." His eyes scanned down the list and saw the word love printed on the bottom in his wife's pristine handwriting. "You still remember her, don't you son?" Barry knew the real truth of how his wife died. After contracting the virus, she was immediately quarantined by the Air National Guard. A few hours later, her skin melted from her bone, blood pooled in her mouth and her teeth clacked about in frantic fashion. Barry, without hesitation gave them the order to bury a bullet in her forehead before the undead phase swarmed her soul.

Dash nodded. "Yes." He signed 'mommy sleeping' and read the list again. He adjusted his weighty stature in the seat. His short fingers adjusted the seat belt that cut across his white and green Incredible Hulk T-shirt.

"I don't want to bother you with facts and all that shit," his father said. "It's a horrible virus that recycles the living to the dead. This new species feast on the living and tear every layer of flesh from your bones. They will gorge on your blood and snap your muscles between their rotting teeth."

Dash grimaced and signed 'disgusting', a clawed hand that circled the stomach. "Disgusting," he said once again signing the word.

His father continued after a brief laugh. "Sorry, it is disgusting." He repeated the sign. "Son, in every dark storm, there is a lighthouse, a beacon of white light. And this place," he motioned for his son to turn over the piece of paper. On the back of the list was a hand drawn map with the words 'Beaver's Claw' scribbled beneath. His wrinkled fingers tapped the location. "It is by far the only safe haven 'round here for hundreds of miles. The undead cannot enter. They can growl, spit, claw, and run in damn circles." He snorted. "There's no entrance for their kind at these compounds." He itched his beard. The hair's length had become a disheveled contortion of black and grey. The beard lifted a few inches off his cheeks simulating a grizzled hunter living alone in the woods for months without a razor. He continued, "The virus that is eating everyone alive," he sighs, "it won't harm you in the compound. It simply can't. The doctors and scientists there, they will find a cure for this based on all research." His father kept the accelerator firm against the floorboard. "Through these last few weeks, I've encountered random stories about Beaver's Claw being a formidable castle, built high and proud to fight back the enemy."

Dash smiled. His fingers signed 'friends'.

"Yes, friends are there for you to interact and survive with." His father activated the windshield wipers. They scraped across the glass. Months bled away from the calendar since he had last replaced them. A sprawling storm overtook the desolate stretch of road. The endless miles of rock hard pavement, coated in baked blood and strewn with dead maggot eaten corpses reflected a dire scope of hope for the two travelers. "Beaver's Claw is the next town over, about fifty miles or so." The hardened rain pounded the hood of the 2016 ivory white Jeep Wrangler Unlimited. "It's raining like a son-of-a-bitch." A loud crash tore open the dark skies. A flash of lightning blasted the road.

The ash colored man appeared before the jeep. The gaunt figure refused to move. The hollowed, silky residue shifted inside the emptied eye sockets. Skin tainted in reddened oatmeal hue displayed against the lightning's flash. The undead jerked its mouth wide, spilling fresh blood from its cavity. A fresh kill from moments earlier, splattered to the pavement below. A singular growling hum echoed in antagonistic manner toward the approaching vehicle.

Barry's usually sturdy hands lost control of the wheel and swerved with violence. A slew of obscenities ensured as the jeep vaulted through the green and white road sign. The body of the jeep absorbed the deafening impact. The windshield imploded, the front axle cracked in half, and the sign skidded against the muddied earth. The torrential rainfall kept barreling down on the

Pennsylvania landscape mixing with lashes of thunder and whips of lightning.

The weight of Dash's body jolted left, then right. His head obliterated the passenger side window, dragging shards of glass through his scalp. The tearing of skin opened pathways for blood to flow freely down his face. The green collar of his beloved Hulk shirt soon absorbed the blood, before seeping it to the white shirt below. Grunting and hands curled in fists, Dash's body was shuffled across the jeep's cabin once again.

His father endured the brunt of the hectic crash. The jeep's wobbly balance succumbed to the eventual flip. The vehicle crunched hard on the ground, upside down with bulky tires spinning to the stars. A teetering stop against the trunk of oak tree ended the chaos with a hissing of smoke from the engine and spillage of gas from the fractured tank. His body cut in multiple places from the seat belt's taut response. His flesh ripped open, blood coursing all over his trembling body. Gasping for life, he crawled out of the jeep. A whitened beard soaked fresh in warm blood. A violent cough purged internal bleeding.

"Dash," his words lost against the reckless storm. His fingers pushed deeper in the muck, limiting his escape. The jeep's movement ended with a growling, sinister finish. Dash's body was still caught in the wreckage. A low, constant grumbling peaked. The shuffling of decaying feet sloshed through the earth. Their incomplete shadows splintered against the veil of a thin mist refused to give away their locations. "Dash!" His father yelled out. "Dash, get out of the car!" His mouth filled with blood. He gurgled and puked up the residual aftertaste.

The shadows lurked closer. One broken arm burst through the night and clutched Barry's leg. Its nails dug sharp through the jean's denim fabric and pierced the skin.

Barry's voice drowned in a surge of blood. A scream refused to push through the thickened liquid. His Adam's apple bobbed, a cork stuck in his throat, unable to swallow.

Dash stirred awake. His forehead caked in blood, a nasty scratch stretched the length of his head. "Dad?" His voice kept calling for his father. His scraped fingers unlatched the seat belt and he found his way out of the jeep. His right hand removed the shards of glass from his scalp and the bleeding started once again. His eyes blinked away the blood, yet vision still blurry as Dash attempted his escape. The shopping list still tucked with a stubborn tightness inside his left hand. "Dad, where are you?"

His instincts followed the curious footprints pressed in the mud. Dash counted them. He was always good at math. "One, two, three, four," his voice whispered. He counted over forty tracks. The growling intensified. Dash stared at the ground, a deep groove appeared against the wet earth. His eyes followed the groove, all the way to a motionless body, contorted and curled in a fetal position.

Dash looked over the man's torn body. The white beard collected jagged fingernails from the attack. The neck slashed and gnawed on with broken teeth. "Dad," his voice went soft. Tears swelled his eyes. A surge of blood pumped through his father's throat, the quivering soon ceased.

The growling drew closer.

In absolute pain, Dash willed himself to stand up and look around. "Not friends," he whispered.

A disfigured man lurched from the shadows.

Dash sidestepped the attacker. He threw up his hands and delivered a clean shot the man's face. His mind erupted with all the knowledge of how his dad had taught him karate and self-defense. It was a way to strengthen his low muscle tone and coordination. Dash learned structure and social skills. He stuffed the list into his pocket. It was precious and he didn't want it ruined. It was the last thing he had of his mother.

The man countered with a fierce lounge.

Dash swept the man's legs out from underneath. "Breathe, yoga breath". He reminded himself to take a few deep breaths to eliminate the hysteria of the situation. At certain times, the action prevailed. Tonight would not be one of those times. He felt his anxiety and impatience start to catapult to dangerous levels.

A loud bang separated the man's head from its body. A splash of blood sprayed Dash on the right cheekbone.

Dash stared off in the distance. Red and blue lights flashed on the road. He began to reset himself.

Another boom silenced the threat of the incoming horde.

Dash backtracked to the jeep.

The man followed him and kept the gun at shoulder's length. His voice kept a consistent hollering through the storm, "You okay!"

Dash shivered with the rainfall and strained to comprehend the man's dialogue. The blood still fresh from the accident. Dash limped past the jeep and the broken side mirrors. His cracked reflection showed streaks of tears inked in red vertical lines down his cheeks. He stammered, "No."

The man appeared from the dark. He lowered his gun. The rain slipped off the gun's metal with slick ease. "Holy shit." He sized up the young man.

"Dad," Dash said. He raised his arm and pointed. "Daddy's sleeping now."

"Sleeping?" The man seemed confused to the young man's rhetoric.

"Yes." Dash sniffed back the tears. "Mommy too."

"Jesus, kid." The man went to reach for the young man's elbow.

Dash refused the gesture. He signed 'friend'.

The man was confused. "I don't understand."

"Are you friend?"

The man thought about it for a minute. He reached to his belt and retrieved the black flashlight. He placed it underneath his face. The illumination of the man's features revealed an aged face, worn hard against time. Scars and scrapes embedded in the man's flesh. "I'm a cop. Cops are friends, right?" His smile was weird and disturbing, an uncomfortable emotion in a time of uncertain reality.

"Friend?" Dash signed the word one more time.

"Yes, friend. The name is Colton Dobbs." He brought the light to his badge and tapped it. The golden badge covered in blood. "It's been a hell of a fight back there. The undead keep pressing on, and we are running out of options."

Dash just stared. His mind began the process of resetting the scene. When anxiety flooded him, he shut down and reset everything. His eyes blank, body motionless, his breathing cycle even retracted a few breaths.

"We need to go," Colton urged. "Now, hmm?"

Dash reluctantly followed. His parents always said police and firemen were friends.

"Where are you headed friend?" He stepped over a minefield of dead bodies littered in the brush and high grass of the meadows. The crimson blades of the meadow were broken from the fighting. Both men with quiet steps, retreated back to the police car.

Dash reached for the list in his pocket. He reached the car and stared at the white paint covered in cranberry red. The rear taillights were busted, the trunk's odd indentation prodded Dash's imagination to get the best of him. A contorted body lay twisted beneath front axels.

Both men entered the vehicle. The passenger side window was splintered, and fragments of glass protruded from the frame.

"That's my partner. Poor fucker. They got him right through the window. We pulled up after witnessing your crash. The rain masked a lot of the shit that went down. A grey head smashed through the passenger window and began to gnaw at Esteban's face. The right cheek devoured and sliced open with a matter of minutes." He shook his head. "His skin came off in strands, pulling against the muscle, then the ripping from the bone. It made this annoying snapping sound. I couldn't take it anymore." Colton turned the gun sideways and pressed it against Dash's temple, mimicking the motion. "I pressed the gun to his temple and killed him before they could devour him further," his voice was cool and collected. "I've seen a lot of clown shit crazy stuff. But, this takes the fucking cake, the candles, the whole damn thing man." Withdrawing the weapon, he scratched the back of his head with his right hand and the nozzle of the gun.

Dash noticed all of Colton's fingers were either swollen, scratched, or had black fingernails. "Excuse me, sir. Do you have a pencil?" He signed 'pencil.'

Colton sighed and turned around. "You say something?"

"Yes."

"Fucking A, you talk," he said with a snicker.

Dash held up the shopping list. The rainstorm left the paper's durability in question. The pencil's clarity now faded slightly from the wetness. He signed 'write', 'word', and 'pencil'.

Colton stared with confusion. "Wait, wait, is that sign language?"

Dash nodded.

"You want to write something on that piece of paper? That piece of fucking paper right there?" He shook his finger.

Dash nodded. Again he repeated the signing. His patience was running thin. He thought he had already explained himself quite clearly to Colton.

Colton waved his right hand at Dash. "Can I see the paper?"

Dash was reluctant.

"Come on kid," he said. "I'm only going to read it."

Dash handed it over. He felt it pop from his fingers.

Colton's firm grip almost tore the list in half. "You fucking people and your goddamn sign language shit." His eyes scanned the paper. "It's a damn shopping list. Milk, water, juice, and love?" He laughed with a hard snort. "What the fuck does that mean?" He went to hand it back when it he saw the map on the back. "Now, wait a goddamn minute." His eyes widened.

Dash knew he was in trouble. His father has taught him to recognize the personality traits of people, especially strangers. Colton did not appear to be a responsible police officer. Dash's mind at times questioned Colton's true motives.

A voice cackled over the radio. "Officer Esteban, where are you located? We have reports of crash in the meadows off the main road. We have multiple sightings of the rogue group The Hood ransacking motorists and…"

Colton's swollen, bruised fingers snapped off the CB radio. His black fingernails tapped the radio with impatient fury. A short cluck of his tongue. He knew it was too late. Too much information was given for him to spin another yarn of lies.

Dash's mind pieced together the puzzle. "Police? You are not."

Colton smacked Dash hard. "You stay fucking silent. I needed a ride and well, he wasn't too accommodating to me."

Dash sat upright. His hand rubbed the left side of his face. It felt bruised. "Danger."

"Yes, danger." Colton flicked the safety off his Glock and pressed it against Dash's cheek. The sweat rolled down the skin and caressed the gun's metal. "Shut the fuck up. I can't think when you talk." His eyes surveyed the back of the shopping list. "Ah, is this is the location of your safe house? Where all of your people reside in comfort and luxury, while the rest of us rot to shit!" Colton crumpled up the list and threw it at Dash's feet. "I know where this compound is. My team has already obliterated many across the eastern seaboard."

Dash signed, "Why are you doing this?"

Colton smirked. "Why?" He sped up and recklessly dispersed the loose pavement beneath his tires. "Seven months ago, I was rotting in jail cell for a grand larceny. I lost my job at the construction site and my little girl, no more than four years old needed a heart operation. With no money to save her, I robbed a bank with a few other fellas, and it all went south."

"I'm sorry," Dash said. His own mind still lost in the traumatic death of his father. His brain began to misfire, resulting in a heightened sensitivity and stubbornness to adhere to a one-track thought. "I'm sorry." His hands lurched in front of him, fists pounding the dashboard of the police car. Words eroded to grunts and rambling broken syllables. His lower lip pressed outward and covered his upper lip. His body rocked hard in the seat.

"Shut up and calm down!" Colton demanded. He kept the gun firmly in control of Dash. "My girl died while I was in prison. The doctors wouldn't prepare her for the operation because they were too busy with you and your people. It seems that when this virus hit the population, the Down syndrome community was unaffected. A gift from God. Now, these doctors say they have the cure and are creating immunity to the virus. The Down syndrome population was their top priority. My entire family died, and I BLAME you." His mouth curled, and he spit in Dash's face. "So fuck you all." Colton smacked him against the temple with the gun.

Dash rocked back and forth in the car, fresh blood oozing from his wound. Angry, unsettled. His arms flailed horizontally, then vertically, until his motions unleashed a jolt that dislodged the gun from Colton's sweaty grasp. Dash's smacks were unrelenting. Colton's lip pierced open, blood trickling down his chin. Dash caught him underneath the chin with a vicious flail. Colton's fingers reached for the Glock. Grunting and still pinned inside his own world, Dash again hit him with everything he had. Colton's fingers felt the trigger.

Pop. Pop. Pop.

The first two shots shattered the windshield and skimmed off the hood's surface.

The third catapulted Dash against the passenger side door. The pieces of glass from Esteban's attack gouged his neck. The bullet was a clean shot. The hot ammunition grazed Dash's cheek and sailed out the window.

"Next time, I blow your fucking head off those stubborn shoulders." Colton warned. "We have a little road trip to endure together. Stay quiet!"

Dash's eyes welled as he reached down to the floor and picked up the list. His hands covered in blood irreversibly stained the paper. He neatly folded it and placed it with careful caution in his pocket. He then buckled in the seat belt and waited.

Colton's burner cell vibrated in the cup holders.

Dash was asleep, slouched over in the seat. His wound had stopped surging blood. His hands were now stained in red, his clothes spotted in blood, but the list was safe in his pocket from further harm. His snoring didn't help ease the tension of the situation, it only accelerated it.

"Yeah, I completed the next phase," Colton's voice dipped to a low tone. "I killed the cop a few days ago and took his car. It's an older model, worth all those weeks of scouting him and the make and model of the car. Yeah, yeah, I stocked up the trunk with C4 and plastique. I even have some dynamite sticks ready for sparking a nice welcome at the Claw." He gazed over at Dash. "I did stumble on one of 'them', yeah, yeah, the fucking people that are ruining everyone's chances at survival. What? They are providing us the cure for the virus? Bullshit. These doctors can find a cure elsewhere," he paused and swallowed hard. "These people are the domino that knocked society off its perch. They stole our best doctors, military, and scientists. Holed them all up in all these compounds around the country. Albany, Boston, South Carolina, Nashville, Miami, Cleveland, and Gettysburg." Colton sucked in a hard breath. "They took over fucking Graceland! The

King's house! Sacrilege! A transformation into a hospital and scientific laboratory. It's a fucking nightmare."

The car danced over bent, scattered limbs along the highway. The tires rumbled low before regaining traction. Dash bounced around for a moment. His eyes flickered open. A few deep breaths followed and another snoring onslaught. His eyelids grew heavier.

Colton kept the conversation flowing. "How many have you exploded to bits? Albany and South Carolina are remnants of their former selves. Boston remains intact however. They have managed to overtake Boston Children's Hospital and fortified it against our infantry. I am currently a few hours out from Gettysburg and harboring my very own hostage. I will use him as my mule to enter the compound and then I'll blast them all to fucking Hell." Colton turned his eyes back on the road. "I have the radio rigged to the explosives in the trunk. All I have to do is turn it on. I have infected the system to explode using a five minute delay. It's long enough for me to either drive in and leave the car inside, or crash through and burn it all down. Either way, it's a sacrificial mission to save our great country. I will soon be with my family in heaven."

Dash stirred. His snoring interrupted from the ride's jostling. His head pivoted against the seat. Another round of snoring filtered the car.

"I know blowing up the compound erases the possibility of achieving a cure. I've heard rumors that the virus hasn't reached the western coastline. It's still a safe harbor for our people. Once we knockout their compounds, we can reclaim our country by any means necessary." Colton spotted the road sign for Gettysburg. "Batteries dead. Good luck and I'll see you on the other side." He tossed the phone in the backseat.

Dash was still asleep.

Colton leaned across Dash and opened the glove compartment. He kept a watchful eye on the dark road while his fingers fished for the beef jerky he had stuffed in there earlier. His teeth ripped open the package, uncorking a small piece of bond on his front tooth. "Fuck." He slammed down on the horn in anger.

The noise startled Dash awake. His eyes flickered open, his hands rubbing his face in weary motion. "Where are we?" His words were clear and phonetically brilliant. Dash was in the midst of a clarity wheel. The phrase was coined by his mother when everything aligned in his mind, if only briefly, Dash's intelligence was unmatched in those moments.

"On our way to blowing up your fucking friends," Colton said, snapping off a piece of Cajun pepper jerky. "So sit back."

"My clarity wheel," he whispered. "No sir." Dash shook his head. His hands reached for the door handle. His short fingers clasped the metal latch. "Dash is hurt. Hurt by you. Bad man. Dash needs to go home." His hands rattled the door. It wouldn't budge.

Colton laughed. The beef jerky hung loose in the corner of his dry mouth. His foot pressed hard on the accelerator. "Let's open up this baby." The car zoomed down the desolate patch of black road. The tires churned up either twigs or body limbs, spinning them out to the side of the road. The car rocked for a few brief instances, but soon regained its gruesome path.

Dash's face reddened in anger. "Outside!" His fingers rattled the latch. The door inched open. A blast of cool air seeped in the hot cabin of the cruiser.

Colton jammed the pedal down hard. The car trickled up the speedometer. Seventy, seventy-five, eighty. Colton jerked the car hard right, off the pavement and split open the blades of grass underneath.

Dash launched his shoulder on the door's frame. He felt the door's release and the bitter smack of the air from outside. His left hand grappled with the stubborn seat belt. "Outside!"

Colton's eyes widened. "Get back in the car asshole."

Ninety. Ninety-five.

The needle vibrated at the century mark.

Dash's clarity wheel had collapsed, and he began to spiral out of control emotionally. His lungs screamed loud and pure.

The gust of wind deterred the thought of any realistic optic of escape.

The road sign approached without warning and with a clean snap severed the door from its hinges.

In that split second, Dash read the words on the sign from the escaping side mirror.

Gettysburg, 1 mile ahead.

Dash released the seat belt. His thoughts drifted to his parents. His body lurched for the opening. His hair flapping about. His skin pulling taut from the slapping winds. "It's okay. It's okay."

Dash felt Colton grab him hard by the nape of the neck and yank him back inside the car.

"Are you fucking stupid? Or just suicidal?" He seethed. "You are my ticket inside the compound if all else fails. So, wise up and learn the game son," he said. He released his grip. "Buckle up." He snapped Dash back in while steering the car with his left hand.

Colton spit out the opening not caring if the wind smacked it back at Dash. "You want some?" He waved the jerky about.

Dash remained quiet. He signed 'share' and 'hungry.'

Colton tossed the beef jerky out of out the car. "You don't get to eat. You can suffer just like your friends will." He snickered and kept the pedal pressed to the floor. The cruiser returned back to the main road and with a daredevil's pinch, Colton took the exit for Gettysburg. The tires squealed, and the body of the car rattled.

Dash closed his eyes tight and covered his ears. He never liked loud noises.

Colton flicked Dash on the left cheek. "Wake up! We are a few minutes away from the end of your people."

Dash stirred awake. The sky was still pitch black. The radio time indicated it was nearing a new day.

11:50 p.m.

Colton kept the consistent speed on the road. The front of the cruiser clipped the legs of the approaching undead. Their bodies exploding ooze all over the car upon impact. The driver's side window sprayed in black blood. The windshield wipers removed the excess remains with stubborn ease.

Dash signed 'disgusting' and made a sick face.

Colton kept pressing on. Five more miles.

Dash looked at Colton. He then stared at the radio.

The black knob.

Four minutes.

"Music," he said.

Colton twisted his head and saw Dash's fingers twist the knob. The radio ignited to life.

Johnny Cash's 'Folsom Prison Blues' played loud over the conversation.

"What are you doing?" Colton seethed.

"Hero." Dash smiled. "Play the game." His mind was embracing another clarity wheel. He smiled once more. He took out the list and clutched it in his right hand.

Colton's right arm released from the wheel clenched in a fist.

"My friends, not yours." His left hand caught Colton's fist inside his small hand. "No." His voice was stern and direct.

Three minutes.

Dash applied direct pressure. The bones in Colton's hand began crackling like tinder. He twisted the hand backwards, bending the elbow past the point of flexibility. The deafening scream of hurt drowned out by the song.

Colton snapped off the remaining bonding of his teeth in brute force. The humerus fracture was a distinctive clean break through the skin. A shower of blood splattered against the radio's dials.

The compound stood off in the distance. The watchtower lights flooded on the approaching vehicle.

Two minutes.

Dash grabbed Colton by the outstretched humerus and yanked it further in a taut, defensive action. "All done." Colton's left hand smashed the driver's side window in anger. Glass embedded in his knuckles and opened wide to the red river. Dash reached for the steering wheel and wrestled it from Colton's whimpering hold. He counted down five minutes in his head from the time he clicked on the radio.

"You dumb fuck," Colton screamed. "How?"

"All done. It's okay," Dash assured him. His left hand jerked the wheel, altering the car's path. "I wasn't sleeping. I was playing the clarity wheel. Game over."

Dash slammed his foot down heavy on Colton's pushing the car to its absolute limit.

The lights followed the car as it turned away from the compound's entrance and headed for the woods and the barn.

The cruiser crashed through an abandoned barn, pulverizing the doors at over a hundred miles an hour.

The eruption was quick and brutal, separating metal from the car instantaneously.

Billows of debris shot upward to the night sky.

The barn engulfed in the swirling inferno of heroism. A shower of wood and metal debris plummeted back to earth with a harsh thunderous impact.

The vehicle's lights were melting in blue and red, as the dying flickers of light illuminated the wilderness.

Colton's dismembered body landed in several places, ablaze and burnt to a blackened crisp. His head tethered to his neck as the muscles continued to burn and disintegrate. His eyes, once vibrant with the color of pure evil, now a soupy substance, oozing from their sockets with rampant escape.

The doors of the compound revealed a small military army. They immediately secured the area and quarantined off the crash site.

The sticks of dynamite ignited from the crash and began to explode every few minutes and limited further investigation.

"That's the driver," the older man said. "I could see him through my binoculars from the watchtower. That's where he broke his arm." He pointed to the burnt humerus sticking out from the melting arm. "Look, over there," his eyes sighted a small round object. He walked over and looked down on the weird object. "It's the driver. This is his head." The man took out his pistol and buried the entire chamber in the melting head. Pop. Pop.

A soft explosion pelted the earth with the liquefied remains of Colton Dobbs.

"Where's the other passenger?"

The older man surveyed the area. "The Down syndrome man? I don't know. I'm unable to locate the body. It will be quite some time before we can enter the barn and inspect the full scope of damage." His feet unable to maneuver around Colton's remains, the heels pressed against the slushy residue and tracked parts of Colton all around the field.

"This was another attempt at destroying our research, wasn't it?"

"Yes. They have been destroying a lot of our sites. But, this young man," the older man said. His eyes welled up. "He fucking did it. He saved our entire colony. This kid's a damn hero."

"What's this?" The younger solider picked up a charred piece of paper.

The older man took the item and looked it over. "It's in pretty decent shape, all things considered." He read the contents. "Milk, juice, this word looks like love," he said. "I bet you this belonged to our hero." He stared out across the field. The barn continued to collapse beneath the fire's dying strength. "We can search for his body in the morning, once the fire dies down."

The two men entered the compound and approached the leader. "We found the man responsible for the attack."

The young man nodded.

"He's dead."

The young man nodded again. He looked at the two men. He signed, "All done?"

"Not quite Sir," the older man said. "We found this." He handed over the shopping list.

The young leader read it over. He walked over to the message wall located near the entrance of the compound. His stubby fingers removed a white thumbtack from the corkboard and pressed it through the top of the burnt paper. "Write." He signed.

The older man handed him a pen.

Beneath the word love on Dash's shopping list, the leader added one more word.

In larger scrawling letters, he revealed the addition to the list.

"Hero."

J.N. Cameron's Shopping List

1) Bottled water
2) Red wine
3) Orange and grapefruit juice
4) Milk - 2 percent
5) Diet Orange Crush
6) Raisin Bran Cereal
7) Apples, mangoes, bananas, and oranges

A Night Ride through the Desert
J.N. Cameron

Under the twilight sky, the sepia-stained flatland diminishes on one side into black mountains of paper-torn ridges. In opposite, it expands over a circular horizon to the ocean. The highway snaking through it is a cicatrix of ebony with yellow stripes pulsing down its curves. Along its back, it carries so many thousands of parasites a day toward their destinations.

One of those parasites is a tan, nondescript ten-wheel rig. On its driver-side door is the faint smear of a corporate symbol. The eight-wheel refrigerated trailer behind emits puffs of white from the motor casing on the fore wall. The passenger side window of the rig is open. Out from it, a tassel of ginger hair flutters in the cool wind.

Her name is Maria. She keeps the window down because the driver's stink is even more pungent than the sativa she smokes. She leans her head out of the window, and her knees are pulled up against her chest. The rush of air in her face is a good excuse to ignore anything the driver might say.

Something somewhere in the back of Maria's mind had told her not to accept the ride. But she did anyway. She wanted to get to L.A. by the end of the week at least.

She tries to ignore the creep, but it is difficult. The charcoal beads of his deep-set eyes seem vapid and indifferent. His odd-shaped face often turns to glance out his window at the passing land of cacti and cracked earth. It is a face so comically oblong as to hint of missing chromosomes and perhaps an incestuous secret in the roots of the family tree.

And then there is the itching. The driver holds onto the wheel with one hand, but the other hand keeps darting down under the hangover of fat above his crotch. He scratches madly for about thirty-seconds and then stops for a few minutes. Sometimes he smells his fingers afterwards. He has been doing this for the past hour.

Now she wants out.

Maria wants to get as far away as possible, but she is trying to remain nonchalant. She asks him to stop the truck. He ignores her.

They pass two service stations at a steady 80 mph. When the sign for another exit flashes by, she realizes that he doesn't plan on stopping. She sits back in her seat and rolls the window halfway up. A tension hangs palpable in the air.

Maria takes the last pull from her cherry-paper joint and then flicks the roach out. It streams like a tracer sparkling into the dark behind and bounces off the road. The sun has vanished now, and a starry sea blankets most of the sky. But far to the north, a mass of black clouds is forming.

The driver is still silent, and now he seems angry. His face has flushed, and he has a white-knuckled grip on the steering wheel. She decides to try to get him to speak. When he first picked her up outside of Flagstaff, she asked him if he had a cell phone she could borrow. He had said no.

She must convince him to stop the vehicle somehow. At least, she should try to plant the seed in his mind.

"Do you ever sleep?" she asks. He still has not introduced himself, so she has no name to call him.

The driver is quiet for a moment. She doesn't think he is going to reply, but then he does.

"Why? You getting tired?" His southern accent is unusually high-pitched, almost falsetto. Odd for such a large man. He reaches to his side for a two-liter plastic bottle and spits a stream of brown into it. A dribble runs down his mouth into his brown-grey beard. After returning the spittoon to its place, he again scratches his crotch.

"I have an extra blanket in the cabin back there if you're tired," he offers.

"Maybe later. I could use a nap," she tries her best to hide the disgust in her voice. "What about you? When do you sleep?"

That is when Maria happens to look down and notice something pink sticking out from under her seat.

Girls' socks.

They could be large enough to be a teen's and have a frill of lace sewn around the tube openings. It is beyond unsettling…it is unnerving. Goosebumps rise on her skin, and the blonde hair on her forearms stands straight. A chill passes through the cabin.

She wonders if the driver would notice her picking the socks up. She waits for the right moment.

"I don't need any sleep," he finally replies. They hurtle past another highway rest stop. He nods in its direction as the neon lights blur by. "Sodomites abound at them places."

"Well, I could use something to eat," she tries to look casual as she reaches down and scratches her shin. Her heart thumps loud enough that she is sure he can hear it. His head does not turn to watch what she is doing, so she reaches down further and grabs the socks. She pulls them back up to her right side. They are between her and the door and out of his view.

Maria turns the socks over in her hand. She rolls the tube down a little. A female name is marked on the inside. Annie Hayes.

Keep it together…keep it together, she tells herself. If she can just get him to stop, then she can escape somehow.

"Any possibility you might buy me a burger?" her request is bolder this time.

"Hmph! You're hungry?"

"I'm starving! I would sleep so much better after a bite to eat."

He thinks about it. After another good scratch, he answers.

"Well, I guess we could pull into a place I know near Braxton. After that, it's a long ways through the rest of the desert. I won't be stopping again 'til Needles."

The place he chooses is a small diner in the middle of nowhere. He turns off the highway and drives several miles straight into a bare pan of land between a mesa on one side and mesquite-covered hills on the other. The moon has shrunk into a small marble that is bright and bluish and gives rise to wavering shadows from the sporadic boulders and cacti.

Desert Rose Café, the sign on the diner blinks off and on in neon red.

When the diesel engine coughs to a stop, Maria can still hear the high whirring of the refrigeration unit on the trailer. The driver opens his door and steps out. She is taken back by how tall he is. His long head is almost above the top of the big rig window.

"I have to change, if you don't mind," she says to him.

He grunts something and walks towards the diner. She looks around. There are no other vehicles, just one motorbike. A lone figure, a man, is behind the counter inside.

She watches as the driver walks across the lot and into the front door, and then she leans forward and reaches back up under her seat. A small box. She pulls it out and opens it.

More socks.

There are women's socks and girls' socks, but no men's socks. They are all sizes and colors. There are yellow socks, green socks, socks with flowers, socks with hearts, silky white socks, socks with frills, and socks with stripes. There is a pair of dirty softball-uniform socks, and a pair of soccer socks.

She tries not to think about how he obtained the socks or why he keeps them. Instead, she stuffs the box back under the seat, and then pulls a faded blue hoodie out from her backpack and puts it on. This is her chance to escape, but he would see her make a run for it.

She decides to convince the other man in the diner to help her.

She formulates a quick plan in her head, and then grabs her backpack and jumps out of the rig. While crossing the parking lot, she notices the approaching storm. The cobalt starlight in the east fades as layers of rolling cumulus spill over the night. Blasts of sheet lightning quietly spread in the clouds' wake, and vertical lines of precipitation pour from beneath.

The diner is a small, prefabricated unit from the mid-fifties. The metallic outer walls have gone to rust, but the windows are clean. When she opens the door and steps inside, the doorbell jingles.

No one greets her.

No one is in the booths or at the bar. A display of pies rotates in the glass covering on the bar top. A cherry pie sits next to rhubarb next to key lime, and above is apple topped with a slice of cheddar.

A pot of black coffee is steaming, and the air smells like fresh donuts. The jukebox is on, and Elvis croons "Love Me Tender."

At the far end of the diner, the driver suddenly steps through the swinging doors from the kitchen.

He walks to the middle of the bar and sits down.

"Where were you just now?" she asks him, staying near the door.

"I was talking to Eddie in the kitchen. I ordered us both bacon and eggs. Don't worry, it's on me."

Outside, the air first turns to dust and flying debris as the gale rushes in. Tumbleweeds roll and bounce across the parking lot. A peal of thunder trumpets from above.

The floodgates open.

The torrent completely obscures the motorbike and truck and leaves only a few feet of visibility. The sound of the rain against the small building is like the din of a steam train bearing down over rickety tracks. The noise drowns out the jukebox. The lights flicker but stay on.

The truck driver sits on a barstool facing the kitchen and sips from his coffee. Maria considers grabbing a plate and hitting him in the back of the head. She wonders what damage she could do with a table knife or fork. She wonders if she should scream for the cook.

But then her luck changes. He stands up from the bar and announces, "I have to drop a load. Be back in a few."

He walks to the end of the diner, near the swinging doors to the kitchen. Before the swinging doors are two side doors. He opens the one that has Gentlemen stenciled on it and closes it behind him after stepping inside.

She doesn't hesitate. She leaves her backpack on the counter and walks toward the kitchen. She looks over the cook's counter, but it is too dark. She can hear and smell something frying. Bacon?

The lights flicker again. This time they go off and stay off.

She stops in the darkness and grabs the counter top. A boom of thunder shakes the entire building. Two small, red emergency lights blink on above the bathroom doors. The darkness is lessened with an eerie glow.

She continues between the booths and stools toward the back. By the gentlemen's bathroom, she stops to listen. The driver is grunting, straining, and mumbling to himself. She quickly steps past to the kitchen double doors.

She pushes the doors open and steps inside.

The crimson hue spills through the counter and doors and washes over the body on the floor. A steak knife has been pushed to the hilt through one of his eyes. A slick syrup spills from the wound and feeds the growing pool around the body.

She wants to scream, but she holds it.

She looks around and a blade glints on the counter. It is a meat-cleaver. She picks it up and turns back to the doors. She notices the phone hanging on the inside wall by the sink. The line is cut.

When she opens the doors again, she expects him to burst out of the bathroom. She slowly moves forward, step by step.

She holds the butcher knife up, ready to chop down. The wide, flat blade is shaking.

Now she is in front of the bathroom door. She does not hear anything.

Maria makes it past the bathrooms and down the diner to her backpack. It is still pouring outside, and the visibility is now even worse. She throws her backpack on and pulls her hoodie over her frazzled, red hair. He is still in the bathroom, so she steps outside.

After four or five steps of fighting the wind to walk in a straight line, she stops. The rain has not let up, and she is completely soaked. She hopes that the driver will not be able to find her in the downpour. If she can push forward, she might find a place to hide in the desert.

She continues with her arms outstretched and searching. If she looks down, she can barely make out her black tennis shoes sloshing through inches of the ochre, alluvial runoff. She fights the current, foot after foot.

She bumps into the rig.

She feels alongside of the truck to the trailer and follows the side to the back. At the back, double doors are held in place by a vertical bolt and padlock.

But the padlock is open.

She now has a choice other than wandering out into the deluge. She could sneak into the back of the trailer. If she could stowaway to Needles, then she could jump out in the city.

At least I should look inside, she tells herself.

Still gripping the cleaver, she pulls the padlock off and then slides open the bolt. She cracks one door open and throws her backpack up. She sets the knife down and then climbs inside. She pulls the door shut behind her. She feels along the bottom ledge and finds a ring for the padlock to fit through. The door is bolted from the inside, and now he cannot surprise her.

A new chill that makes outside seem warm overtakes her. She takes out a towel from her backpack, but it is soaked through. She wrings it out and shakes it. Then she pulls off her hoodie and shirt, revealing a bare torso. Her hands are shaking, and she dries off the best she can.

Through the barrage of the storm on the trailer, she can still hear the whirring of the refrigeration motor. There is a freezer somewhere nearby. Maria leaves her clothes spread over the floor and feels forward in the darkness. She moves toward the sound of the motor, toward the back of the trailer.

She comes to a metallic wall and a door.

It is easy to push open. The doors fold inward, and a fluorescent tube flickers on.

She exhales a cloud of billowing condensation, and then she gasps.

The greenish-blue light reveals a meat locker. Chains and hooks line each side of the freezer. A nude woman or girl dangles from each hook.

The bodies are of all races and ages. Some are thin and some corpulent. All have ice-sparkling skin. Their moments of death are frozen in the hideous grimaces they bear. Some of their screams open around a protruding hook end, and some are hooked through the neck or eyes.

Nearest to her, a teen girl hangs with the hook through her mouth and out the back of her skull. Maria wonders if she is looking at Annie Hayes, the name marked inside the pink socks. She reaches a trembling hand up to brush away a strand of grimy hair from the corpse's face. The strand breaks and falls to the round and shatters.

This can't be real. I'm dreaming. I have to be dreaming.

She is not surprised when the lock snaps and the trailer doors burst open. The driver stands there. She does not move.

He climbs inside, and the structure creaks with his added weight.

Still, she does not move. She traces her fingertips over the dead girl's cheek as he steps closer and closer.

"That's right," he whispers to her. "Don't you move. I need your socks."

The driver puts a hand on Maria's shoulder.

He turns her around.

To her, his face is like an elongated skeleton. Eye sockets open into a blackness colder and deeper than death.

He raises a small, ball-point hammer and brings it down on her forehead.

Her vision disappears, and a flower explodes through her mind. A lotus unfolds into blossoms of neon colors and hues that swallow every synapse.

And then nothing.

Nick Swain's Shopping List

...... The World......

...... And Everything in It......

Recess for Billy
Nick Swain

> Is *all* that we see or seem
> But a dream within a dream?
> -Edgar Allen Poe

Billy sat on one of three benches by the playground fence, writing every curse word he knew in the sand with the broken tree limb he'd found. Kenny Topper came sprinting over from the jungle gym. "Hey, Billy boy!" he said, "you watch *Happy Days* last night?"

"No," Billy scoffed. "I watched *The Twilight Zone*."

"No kidding? Which episode?"

"The one with the greedy relatives who get their faces transformed into monsters by those hip Mardi Gras masks."

"OH WOW!" Kenny's face lit up like a jack o' lantern when Billy finished telling him about it. "God, I wish my mom would let me watch it."

"Don't be such 'a square, Topper. You got a set up in your room, don't you?"

"Well yea, but…" His sentence fell short, and Billy knew then that Kenny had never even entertained the idea of watching the show without his square mother's permission. "Well hey, I got to run. See you 'round!"

Kenny ran off towards the soccer field and Billy went back to writing profanity in the sand, looking up every few seconds to get a load of what his classmates were up to. He saw Ron Ferrell and Seth Brunkowitz at the picnic tables by the courts. They were using rubber bands to shoot folded bits of notebook paper pellets (which they lined with paperclips to make all the more vicious) they called "hornets" at the new kid, Leeson, who was trying to study something in his notebook that was a good four-inches thick with papers. "…Stop it…Stop it…" Leeson would say indirectly to his tormenters, brushing off his shoulder every time he was pelted with a hornet. Billy knew that Ron and Seth wouldn't let up, and he wondered how long it would take Leeson to grow tired of their shit and hit one of them over the head with that impressive binder of his; that's what Billy would do if Mike & Ike over there tried that on him.

He saw Becky Gontra with the rest of the congregation, who had pompously titled themselves the Cool Girls Club, hanging out by the tic tac toe spinning board. Billy thought that Becky was kind of cute. You know, when she wore her hair down…and smiled at him… and for a stupid girl. Not that he'd ever tell her any of that. Or anyone else; Billy didn't socialize much with the other kids. From where he sat, they were another species.

He looked down the right side of the fence and saw Mike Connors throwing the pigskin back and forth from a short distance with the Daughtry brothers. Billy hated Mike. Mostly because Mike was a turkey. A regular stiff. But also, because he knew that it was Mike who told the teachers on him whenever he'd swipe an extra milk or when he'd take a box of the chocolate and peanut butter bars that the teacher brought for the whole class home with him.

One-day Mikey, Billy thought.

He eyed over the rest of his fifth-grade class, most of whom were busy painting some sort of banner for the science fair next Thursday. Billy decided it was more fun scribbling swear words in the ground. And if Mike Connors saw him and felt loose lips syndrome coming back on, at least he'd have time to kick it out of the sand. Because for the third day in a row, Ms. Shepard and Mr. Smith, the teachers who were supposed to be watching the class full of eleven-year old's, were off somewhere in the gym making out. Billy had seen this for himself the first day when he snuck back inside to get some water from the fountain, and he was sure that they'd seen him from the supply closest they were in. If they had, it didn't do anything to keep them from bailing out on their chaperone duty to go off and indulge in their strange grown-up urges. He wondered if Becky had ever kissed anyone like that.

Billy finished his obscene list with the word *pussy* and tossed the stick over the fence and into the woods; his Pops had taught him this word when he'd tell Billy to take a gulp out of the funny tasting cans he always drank from; when Billy would cough the stuff back up he'd say "Don't be such a pussy, Bill. That's what men drink. You wanna be a man, don't ya? Well drink some more then!" He couldn't tell his old man, but he hated the stuff; it always made him feel sick after he drank it. He didn't get how the old man could take down so much of it.

He held his chin up and watched as a flock of geese flew overhead. A few of them honked as they made their way past the tree line and glided over the playground. The birds were in their determined arrow formation and Billy just hoped that none of them would shit on his head. A few hundred feet above, amid billowing white clouds, a jetliner plane flew in the same direction. Billy looked down just in time to watch Mike Connors miss the football thrown to him by the oldest Daughtry brother, and chase after it as it sprung closer and closer to the fence with each bounce. Billy hoped that a bear would reach out from the woods and take Mike for lunch. He also really wished he had some bubble gum. Or a Lucky. He closed his eyes.

***

Billy looked back to the sky and the plane exploded.

There was a fierce, earth rocking explosion and flames momentarily engulfed the sky. Just before the explosion the plane seemed to stop in the air. Not slow down, just froze for a second. Then, **KA-BOOM!**

The migrating geese froze, too, hovered in place below the plane. The sound of the blast became muffled and then all at once muted. The flames seemed to be smothering themselves, and the fiery scraps of plane that should have rained down on the playground seemed only to float around the smoke. Billy wondered what the other kids would think of this.

The demolished jetliner imploded into itself, and the line of geese fell from the sky. They came crashing down all over the playground and the soccer field, and now Billy knew what the others thought because they were screaming. The smoke and metal in the sky seemed to vanish as a black orb took its place. Billy could see that it was a black hole, and it was eating up the puffy white clouds around it along with the plane. He could see Kenny Topper and some of the others gathered around one of the geese that had crashed by the soccer goal. It seemed dead, they all seemed dead. Billy stayed put, with his eyes moving sporadically from the bird corpses back to the hole in the sky. He could see Becky and the other girls jogging over to the soccer field where most of the birds had landed. Mike Connors and the Daughtry brothers were following suit. One of the geese had landed on Ron Ferrell's shoulder and he was running around the court with his shirt off, yelling for his buddy Seth to "Get 'em off 'a me! Get em' off!" But Brunkowitz was more interested in kicking at the unresponsive bird with one of his Keds.

Then Billy could see that one of the birds wasn't dead. The one by the slide that had landed closest to him started to twitch in disturbing, spasmodic convulsions before it flopped on its side and staggered to its feet, then fell back on its stomach. Then its beak began to protrude from its skull, ripping the flesh in odd places around its face, producing the revolting sounds of meat tearing apart. Its wings expanded. They became enormous, veiny and bat-like. Its black, beady animal eyes now had glowing red dots in the centers of them. As its predatory wings began to flap, Billy could see that it wasn't only this bird. It was all of them. There were terrible trans mutating birds all over the place. And Billy thought they looked really cool.

Some children ran, most stayed and watched. Becky and her friends were among the party that was fleeing towards the school gymnasium. Mike Connors and his dingbat pals stood around the bird that seemed to be finishing its transformation most rapidly. Billy smiled, and watched as the creature opened its newly improved beak and showed off its brand-new set of chompers (the kind a Great White Shark would envy). It sank its new teeth into Mike Connor's ankle and whipped him upside down (the pretentious clip on bow-tie Mike wore everyday shot off his collar when this happened) as it took flight and struggled back up to the sky. Billy couldn't help but laugh.

The bird that'd landed on Ron Ferrell's shoulder bit down into Brunkowitz's foot (the same one he'd been kicking it with) and dragged him into the air, hanging from its mouth. Billy could see the mutant bird that had taken Mike away was the closest to the black hole in the sky—which was of course where it was taking him— while he thrashed his arms around wildly, like he might be trying to fly himself. It flew straight into the black eye and disappeared with Mike Connors. His ululating cries of terror that could still be heard from below were immediately stifled. Then the one carrying Brunkowitz's vanished with him.

Billy thought about maybe just sitting on the paint chipped bench and watching the rest of his classmates get picked off and carried into the hole in the sky. But he could still see the beast by the slide that seemed to be having a hard time taking off with its new flight gear. Or at least, so far... It was using its new wings to crawl through the sand towards him at a tremendously unnerving pace, and Billy considered making a run for the gym with the others. But he could see that the mutated birds of prey scanning for victims from the sky were closing in on them, and he knew most of them would never make it. And if he tried for it neither would he.

And then Billy remembered the thicket of bramble bushes in the woods on the other side of the break in the fence. Mr. Smith had once sent him into the spur patch to retrieve a Frisbee during P.E. It had been awfully thick, and he'd cut himself pretty bad collecting the Frisbee. But he thought that if he was careful crawling under the spurs and into the bush he might be safe. A kind of barbed-wire shelter.

He went for it. A twenty-yard dash to the thorn thicket, and hopeful salvation. As he darted from the sand and the crawling creature in it that was gaining momentum, he heard the oldest of the Daughtry brothers crying out as one of those things carried him away by his shirt collar. He could hear girls shrieking from a short distance and he wondered if one of them was Becky. Above, the black hole was making an ominous vacuum sort of sound. The sound of suction.

Billy was less than ten feet away from the tree line, and he was sure that he could feel one of those birds on his trail. He loosened his fist and flattened his hands like he might karate chop something, lowered his head, and ran like hell for the thicket. Knowing that if he tripped up on as much as a loose shoe lace, he'd be a goner. He made it to where the fence splits in two and dove into the bottom of the thicket like he would a swimming pool. There was no time for caution. He felt the talons of the bird that had been close enough to almost reach out and grab him, shred through the back of his shirt as it missed and crashed into the worst of the spurs. It thrashed violently as it tried to free itself from its spiked prison, and Billy crawled safely below it towards the patch of dirt where there were no thorns. The monster above him was bleeding, and he could feel some of its blood trickle down on the nape of his neck. He got to where he could sit up and saw that the thing had torn its way out and flew from the woods. It didn't come back for another go at Billy, instead it soared over to the courts and snatched up a sobbing Ron Ferrell, who had taken cover under the picnic tables before being dragged out by his pants leg. Billy could see through the briar as Ron vanished into the sky. One of his sneakers came toppling down and crashed onto the monkey bars, producing a temporary metallic ringing.

Billy looked to the school and saw the last of the Cool Girl Club being grabbed by their hair and taken into the sky. He didn't see Becky anywhere, which meant she either didn't make it inside, or she did. Billy sort of hoped it was the latter. But he *could* see Kenny Topper, who was being carried away by his stomach in the mouth of one of those things. He was crying.

Poor Topper, Billy thought. He'll never get to watch The Twilight Zone.

Billy saw one of the mutated geese circling above the playground like a vulture does to a dying animal. He knew it was preparing for an attack, and so far, as he could see, he was the only one left. And even in middle of the bramble bushes he wasn't invisible. That was part of reality.

It came plummeting down from the sky like a kamikaze and crashed into the briar patch purposefully. Right in the blood riddled spot of thorns the first bird had been caught in. It snapped it monstrous jaw ravenously at Billy, who was inching backwards, deeper into the thorns and away from the safe patch of dirt that the flying beast was fighting its way into.

He could feel the spurs digging themselves into his bare back where his shirt had been torn, but that had to be better than being snatched up by a monster and taken into a black hole in the sky and into who knows what dimension. As he pushed farther back, he felt a jab at his back. It was a rock, and he didn't think much of it until one of that thing's wings had gotten past the thorns and actually *touched* his foot. Then he used his brain and dug the rock out of the earth quickly. He raised it (as high as he could, given the sharp ceiling above), brought it down, and struck the dumb animal on the head with it. The bird shook it off and went back to snapping its alien jaw. Billy brought the rock down on its head a second time, and it must have realized he was going to keep on doing it. It pulled its wing out of the bush, and retreated into the sky with the rest of its flock and into the orb. There were no more children to snatch up.

And then the black hole just ate itself. That was the only way Billy could process the image of it disappearing. It ate itself, along with the undead mutant geese and all his classmates. It was just gone; like nothing had ever happened. The soft blue sky with the sun shining cheerfully high above gave the impression of innocence. There was nothing left to give any kind of hint as to what had just happened. Aside from a few mismatching shoes that had fallen from the sky and some geese blood in the briar patch.

Billy crawled out of the thicket and saw that neither Ms. Shepard, nor Mr. Smith were back yet. Maybe they'd been outside. Maybe…

Billy gazed around and decided that there was nothing for him do here. He cut across the playground and onto the soccer field that would lead him to the school's back exit. Something in the grass caught his eye—something shiny. He went closer to inspect and could see that it was a quarter. He could also see that there was more change, scattered all over the field. At first, this only seemed curious. And then Billy realized it was the change from his classmate's pockets that had slipped out as they were being dragged through the sky and into the void.

Billy picked up all the change that he could find and added it to his own. He'd have $1.67. Billy smiled, stuck his hands in the pockets of his Levi's, and strutted from the playground. He'd stop by the arcade on his way to Zappy's convenience store to see if they had any new issues of Weird Tales.

***

From the P.E. storage room, a man with a crew-cut and a whistle dangling from his neck peeked out of a cracked door. Narrow eyes examined the grounds from a surreptitious angle.

"See anything?" asked Ms. Shepard from inside the closet, retying the strings of her blouse. "I was sure I heard something."

At the end of the soccer field, the man did notice something. A young boy ambling away from the playground, his collar yanked up around his neck, his hands stuffed into the pockets of his cuffed jeans. The coach thought he looked like a tiny-hoodlum.

"Yea. It's just Junior James Dean. Looks like he's skipping out, again."

"Well pretend like you didn't see him and come back in here. Now that there's some light I can see my watch. We've got another seven minutes."

"That kid's crazy," Mr. Smith went on. "A nut. Just like his old man."

"Are you going to come back in here with me or you going to go blow your whistle?"

He closed the door and went to her.

"What about the other kids? Everything else ok, out there?" she panted as his hands worked about her. His mouth buried in her neck.

"Yea, sure I guess. Didn't see anything. Only…"

"What?"

"Well, it did seem a little… quiet."

Nick Manzolillo's Shopping List

A barrel of pennystick pretzels

2 bottles of Buffalo sauce

A Milky Way

2 boxes of taco shells

8 packets of taco Seasoning

3 pounds of ground turkey

6 pack of Sweetwater 420

A bag of gummy sharks

Saltwater Fish Tank
Nick Manzolillo

"I want it," Billy Tanner said, his face lit up by the blue glow of the aquarium tank. The creature within was without label. It was loose limbed like an octopus and more crimson than fire coral. It was long, like a barracuda, yet there was a thickness to it, with three fins that would flow and glide through the water like a piece of ribbon. Its eyes were composed of black little dots along an indented face that lacked the crease of a mouth or beak. Despite its long body, its three fins brought to mind the triangular upper half of a starfish. The thing in the tank was a Frankenstein mess that could easily have been doodled in a fourth-grade art class. Billy pressed his face against the glass and, a little louder this time, said, "I want it."

Billy's father, Mr. Benjamin Tanner, looked up from his phone. "Oh yeah?" he grinned, even though he heard the kid the first time. He admired his son for not asking.

Leaders tell you what they want, plain and simple. "How do you plan on earning it?" Mr. Tanner asked. The art of bargaining, he figured even an eight-year-old could learn that.

"I'll help the maid work."

"How about you don't get in the maid's way, like the big stink you made on Sunday, and we'll call it a deal?"

"Deal," Billy said, his breath fogging across the glass. They were no longer in the official exhibition hall of *Fins and Friends: Marine Aquarium* but Mr. Tanner had never been one for staying behind the lines, especially in his later years. There comes a certain point where everybody in Chicago knows your family name, your associates and your net worth, and, they don't just hold the door open for you, they tear down the walls. When Mr. Tanner was with his son, they could go anywhere the little guy pleased.

"Backstage" at *Fins and Friends* was a little like exploring the unused props section in the basement of a Broadway production. Empty tanks and heaving bags of fish food were scattered aimlessly beside banners and cardboard cutouts of dolphins and penguins standing upright in bathing suits and sunglasses. Backstage, biologists conducted their experiments and tended to all the sick animals in rehabilitation. It was also where the beasts that hadn't been found a place among the public displays were kept.

Mr. Tanner knew Mark Bridgett, the director of programs, because Mr. Tanner was one of the original investors. Shedd Aquarium was a popular tourist destination in the Chicago area, but *Fins and Friends* eventually become a steady enough competitor that featured live concerts, carnivals and other monthly promotional events that turned an easy profit. Mr.

Tanner also knew of some "shifty" things that Mark Bridgett allowed to go on behind closed doors. To sum it up, you wouldn't believe the amount of hoops young, eager-to-learn marine biologists have to jump through. At *Fins and Friends,* if you were rich and smart enough, then during after-hours, your research knew no limits short of your own potential. Mr. Tanner was a gentleman enough that he didn't have to make any threats. While Billy stared at his newfound pet, Mr. Tanner waved Mark over from where he was talking to a fish-goo covered employee. He asked Mark for a number and then smiled at the lack of zeroes he was told in response.

***

It was a day and a half before Billy's new pet, which he was planning on calling Slinko, was set to arrive. He could hardly stand to sit and wait in front of his videogame consoles or do laps in his child sized castle fort that took up half his playroom. It was summertime, but with his parent's often working and his "play nurse" only being available during the weekends, he could find little to entertain himself. The several bags of generic fish food (in the form of protein pellets) that Mr. Bridgett sent Billy's dad arrived within hours after they left the aquarium, but apparently there were certain "procedures" that needed to be put in check before Slinko could arrive. Slinko was apparently so special and unique that Mr. Bridgett cautioned Billy and his dad to "monitor" the creature's feeding habits because he wasn't entirely sure of any dietary restrictions or necessities it might have needed.

That first night between picking out his pet and waiting for its arrival, Billy dreamed of picking Slinko up out of his tank and bringing the strange, slippery creature to the top of his play castle. Billy sang to Slinko about having to defend the castle from "bad guys, zombies, and Orcs!" In his dream, Billy decided that Slinko looked a little like a dragon, as well as a great many other things, so he placed Slinko on the edge of the flagpole at the play castle's highest peak. Deciding he wanted to snap a picture with his Xbox Kinect camera, Billy bounced down the castle's slide but when he got to the bottom and gazed up at Slinko, he saw something strange. Slinko was gone and there was another boy, sitting at the play castle's highest peak. A boy with blood red hair and black little dots scattered like bizarre freckles across his face.

"Who are you?" Billy asked the other boy, who opened his mouth and let loose a long *gurgle* that ended with him drooling out a cup's worth of yellowish liquid all over the side of the castle.

"Hey! Why are you sick?" Billy asked, but the other boy only gurgled louder. The bloody red hair turned golden blonde, just like Billy's. The black freckles faded like anti-scars as the other boy's skin became fairer, just like Billy's. Finally, the boy's face seemed to droop and sag as the cheekbones rearranged themselves and…he became a mirror. A mirror that continued to drool yellow slime and gurgle like a frog with a hook in its belly without an ounce of air in its lungs to even make a hearty croak.

"That's gross! You're weird! Get off my castle!" Billy woke up screaming in his sports car framed bed. Of course, his parents didn't hear him. Before his beating heart could steady enough for him to fall back asleep, he was overcome by the inexplicable stench of low tide.

***

Not even four hours after Slinko arrived, Billy was bored, playing the first-person shooter *Destiny* on one of his PS4s. His fingers rotated over the joystick lazily as he blasted aliens while Slinko, ignored, floated silently. The tank was a rectangular display case on top of a marble column that could just as easily hold a statue or some other inanimate object. Billy thought Slinko was cool and all, if only because of how weird he looked. Billy knew that he couldn't actually play with him in his castle like he did in his dream, or for that matter do much of anything with Slinko, but none of Billy's friends had a pet like Slinko, so that counted for something.

Billy began remembering the weirdness of his dream when he glanced at Mr. Slinko's cage and noticed that something was wrong. Slinko's eyes had changed and Billy's stomach started to feel weird when he realized those eyes totally looked like a person's or that of some kind of land creature. Each eyeball was composed of a silvery blue iris encircled by white. The pupil was still a petty little inkblot. Slinko had no eyelids and seemed incapable of blinking, as Billy held a staring contest with it until his eyes began to water. Slinko's eyes lacked any kind of intelligence or even life, it was almost as if they were painted on. If it weren't for how those eyes seemed to shine with the same slimy texture as the rest of its body, Billy would have been sure of that. When Billy opened his eyes there was a silence that he could almost feel, and then Slinko blinked, mimicking him as its eyes sunk and disappeared into the hidden folds of its head.

"Holy crap!" Billy yelled, and his first instinct was to run out of the room to find his dad, or his mom, if she was home yet. Slinko stopped Billy in his tracks by humming.

A metallic echo, like a quarter spinning and circling down a drain began to warble from the thing that was beginning to seem less and less like a fish. It was as if the glass and water weren't even there as the humming grew louder and drowned out the music from Billy's still active videogame session. The creature's eyes seemed to grow wider as its body begins to tremble and pull itself together, tighter, like an orb. A black slit appeared below its humanoid eyes...a smile, the semblance of lips, and then white squares of bone began to pry that mouth apart. Teeth, the fish was growing teeth, just like Billy's.

Crawling on his hands and knees, Billy pressed his face to the glass. He'd heard somewhere that octopi can change their color and of course he'd heard of puffer fish that contract and expand their belly's full of venomous spines when they feel threatened. Billy's nose touched the glass as the creature squirmed away. One of its fins began to stretch to the aquariums lid, the appendage growing longer and narrower, like a tentacle without suction cups. Curious, Billy sprang up and removed the lid, wondering just how smart Slinko really was. He'd never heard of a sea creature escaping its cage before. Billy leaned the tank's lid against the side of the marble column. When he glanced back to the water, a toddler's red, sinewy hand extended from Slinko and grabbed him by the jaw. He managed to let loose a gurgled scream when his face touched the water. The sound of his voice barely rose above the tune of Slinko's humming.

***

When Mr. Tanner fetched the leftover steak out of the fridge, he realized Billy had stopped talking to the fish. "Slinko," he called it, like he never evolved from being a toddler. Still, Mr. Tanner wondered what his wife would think of the thing. It was beautiful in some ways, yes, sort of like a lava lamp or better yet, one of those jellyfish lava lamps he saw an intern prop on her desk one time. Mark was adamant that the new "fish" couldn't quite be classified, thought it seemed to like eating the generic fish food well enough. There was no guaranteeing how long the thing will live, but Mr. Tanner figured that if the worst were to happen then it'd be another educational lesson for Billy.

Still chewing his steak, Mr. Tanner walked over to Billy's closed playroom door. He could hear Billy playing his damn games again. Tanner had never touched those ridiculous TV toys, but he still knew there was no way Billy was *learning* anything from them. They're books and movies without the lesson, the intellectual message. They were simulated sports that harm Billy's body more than they nurture it.

Mr. Tanner pressed his ear to the door. He could hear something else, a low rumble, almost like an amplified version of when you press your palm to your ear.

"What are you up to..." Mr. Tanner barged into the playroom and nearly gagged from the overwhelming stench. The meat went sour in his mouth, and he couldn't help himself as he vomited all over the carpet. The carpet that was already damp in the first place.... Mr. Tanner heard the bathtub turn on upstairs and that damn Billy, what did he do? The room, and the fish tank, were both empty, the water still clear and tinged blue by the decorative rocks along its bottom. Why the hell would Billy take Slinko out of its cage?

Something began to rustle from within Billy's play castle. "Hey, you in there?" Mr. Tanner called to Billy. Someone was in the bathroom and Mr. Tanner wondered if his wife, Gwen, had snuck in. She'd been a moody thing for the past couple of months.

"Billy, come on out. What the hell did you do with your Slinko?" Mr. Tanner asked and got nothing back in response, only more rustling just beyond the main entrance to the play castle. The inside of the thing was no bigger than a teepee. "Do you hear me? Come on." Maybe Billy had his headphones in. Mr. Tanner knew that Billy was still too big for that damn castle and that if he didn't eventually get rid of it then it'd be the place where Billy fingered his first girl and cracked open stolen beers. Men do shit out in the open, and dare to be judged, Mr. Tanner thought.

Leaning forward with a back that got tighter every year, Mr. Tanner slid open the plastic door panel. Inside was a pale boy. His body was crooked, as if all of his bones were jagged. His arms, legs and fingers were squiggles, and his bloody red hair seemed to ripple with the life of a sea anemone. The stench nestled away in the play castle was again overwhelming to the point that Mr. Tanner was forced to dry heave as a sharp bludgeon of pain hit him square in the stomach. Mr. Tanner had smelled plenty of rotting food in his time (his uncle was a butcher) but this was something else. There was an awkward sweetness to it that almost smelled good, like the hot sauce Mr. Tanner dumped into his burritos. The contradictions began to form a headache that threatened to claw through Mr. Tanner's skull. Half mad and writhing on the floor, Mr. Tanner could hardly raise a hand to ward off the crooked boy, as the squiggly creature from the sea descended upon him. Those crooked fingers weren't forged by crooked bones after

266

all. They were of damp rubber that sifted into Mr. Tanner's nostrils and open throat like the all-seeing eyes of an endoscopy.

***

When Gwen got home from her impromptu trip to the doctor's office, she wasn't in the mood for anybody's problems except her own. Doctor Vinny saw her immediately because he still remembered what her parents did for his mother six years ago when the poor old lady had no place to live while Doctor Vinny was drowning in med school debt. Gwen's life is one built on power and the idea that, when you share just enough of it, you get friends that can make you accomplish anything. Friends that will give you *everything*. With that all being a fact, you'd think it'd have been easier for Gwen to re-up on Vicodin.

Doctor Vinny would have had to file her as a new patient and apparently "they", as in government people Gwen had no ties to, checked for doctors that pull that kind of scam with their friends. She figured, if only her husband would run for office and quit just taking the mayor out for drinks.

Stepping through the front door, Gwen barely had a chance to set down her purse before a low tide stink grated across her sinuses. At her family's beach house, she would often take one of the rowboats out from their private dock and on days after the full moon low tide, Gwen would dread stepping with her bare feet through the rotted, flopping creatures along the beach. Gwen dimly recalled hearing about Billy getting a special new fish that Ben described to her as "weird, but kind of fascinating, like the most mesmerizing parts of an octopus and seahorse."

There used to be a time when Gwen would wish her husband would spend more time with the family, especially when Billy was a nightmare of a baby and she had to hire not one but two nurses to look after him. After Ben began working part time and spending more days at home, Gwen found that she could barely function. If Ben started coming home at night and during his lunch breaks expecting to share a meal and spend "quality" time together, then that would mean Gwen would have to give up all of the little pleasures she'd become fond of. Her painting had to get put aside because she couldn't find any inspiration when that man was airing his thoughts out to her every twenty minutes. Coming home to that fishy stench without the mercy of opiates, she immediately began to make plans to go back to smoking weed like a teenager.

"What the hell's going on in my house?" Gwen asked as she slipped out of her jacket. Moving beyond the front hallway and into the living room, there was a squishing sound as her heel sunk into the carpet. "What the hell, Ben!" There was no keeping it in. The smell was neutral, coming from every corner of the apartment. How could one fish even do that? Gwen decided that if her bedroom smelled just as bad as the living room, she'd get a suite at the closest Marriot. Either way, that began to seem like not such a bad idea.

A banging sound began coming from the bathroom upstairs. Gwen could hear Billy's videogames in his playroom but Ben, he had some answering to do. She figured that he was probably cleaning the fish tank or something in the bathroom. A clear narrative began to form in Gwen's head. Someone was moving the fish tank around, probably to the kitchen and the sink, and it spilled all over the living room carpet. Gwen figured that maybe the new pet was in the bathtub, which didn't matter much to her considering it was the guest bathroom. Ben should've just hired somebody to do all the fish related crap, but whatever happened was probably a part of his new bonding time with Billy. The man Gwen married used to be practical, and efficient. He would've been the kind of father that lead by example, that held an aura of tingling mystic that would've inspired Billy to fall in line and look up to him like some kind of legendary idol. If only Ben could see how his change of heart was messing up their family's internal balance.

With an arsenal of sharp words prepared to shame the two prominent members of the opposite sex in her life, Gwen burst into the guest bathroom. She didn't puke from the smell, but it pushed her back against a wall and forced her to squeeze her nose with two well-manicured fingertips. In the tub there was a boy, floating face down. Billy…Some primitive maternal instinct infected Gwen's mind like a parasite, as she ran and then nearly fell as she slid across damp bathroom tiles to the edge of the tub. On his own, Billy rolled over and sat up. He was in only his underwear and the water he'd been laying in was more mucus than H2O. It dripped off him in oozing trails of slime, but Gwen quickly forgot the subtle grossness, as she got a good look at what had become of Billy's face. His eyes and nose were gone, and there was only a slack jawed mouth beneath a visor of beady black eyes. The back of Billy's skull was still covered in hair, but it sagged, like the squishy pouched head of an octopus. A metallic hum began to emit from Billy's throat, as Gwen realized some of his teeth had fallen out. Her son or not, Gwen screamed and ran back downstairs.

She slipped again, on the soggy staircase, her clogs finding a stray trail of what may be the same mucus that the thing that used to be Billy was swimming in. Gwen's screams became short little yelps as she brushed through the living room and stopped cold when she heard sounds in the playroom. It was like the guttural choking of a man.

"Ben!" Gwen yelled and barged into Billy's former room. Atop a marble pillar there was a fish tank. Crammed inside was Mr. Tanner, his bones cracked, folded and bunched together like a pretzel. His skin was pale and peeling, his eyes blank, and white. A spindly, webbed hand grabbed the half-ajar side of Billy's play castle door and began to slide it open. The sudden rush of a strange, stomach stabbing odor brought Gwen to her knees as she sobbed and puked, the dizziness immediate and pulsing through her veins. The stench of rot did nothing to describe the sheer wretchedness that filled Gwen's sense of smell. Her mind began threatening to tear itself in half.

What used to be Mr. Tanner crawled on all fours from the play castle. His hair was blood red and his body was jagged and resembling a half-cooked ramen noodle. "Tummy," the caricature of Gwen's husband gurgled before letting loose the same soft humming Billy echoed upstairs. Gwen curled up on the soggy playroom carpet and stared at the dead thing in the fish tank. The name Slinko was emblazed on a golden nameplate slapped across the pillar. "In your tummy," the thing that wanted to be a person said, as the bastardization of Mr. Tanner crouched over Gwen and pressed both pairs of those rubbery appendages to Gwen's stomach. The fingers stretched, and spread, and Gwen could only tip her head back to shout as something crept down her throat. She glanced at the open playroom doorway and the last thing she saw was Billy, standing there, soggy yet solid, the back of his octopus head pulling itself together as his visor of little black eyes began to form a pair of almost human pupils. Gwen tried to laugh, as something else became one with her.

***

Mark Bridgett was the kind of guy that was always looking for a deal and when his good—if not sometimes distant—buddy, Benjamin Tanner, offered him a bargain to buy out his aquarium, he took it. Transferring a business was always a pain in the ass, especially when *Fins and Friends* was meticulously set up to walk the fine line between a legal and illegal establishment. Benjamin cut him the check before even asking if Mark would part ways with the place. When Mark saw just how big the number was, he went along with the whole thing like the strange little blessing it was. With a pregnant wife ready to plop out another blond, spoiled child, Mark figured Mr. Tanner was rethinking all of his business decisions. All of that thinking must have started to wear away at the guy, because right before the deal he looked like he'd been cramped into a washing machine set on high spin.

Mark got all of his affairs in order in less than a month and then the Tanner family became the proud owners of a new aquarium. Mark could have cared less about why Mr. Tanner chose the aquarium of all places. If Mark were honest with himself, getting new animals had been proving to be sort of difficult. Forget whales, just maintaining the three dolphins the place had pushed him dangerously close to the over budget mark.

A week after officially selling the place, Mark found out that Mr. Tanner fired every single employee. He even fired the marine biologists that were using the place as a researcher's paradise and this, suddenly, began to seem like a big problem to Mark. If the wrong researcher started feeling burned, then Mark could still find himself in legal trouble. Hell, Mr. Tanner would, too. This is how Mark came to find himself standing outside the *Fins and Friends* management office, late one Tuesday afternoon, because some people, no matter how rich and powerful they were, just didn't get it.

Mr. Tanner didn't pick up his phone, but the lights were on and Mark could swear he heard someone moving around right before he rang the buzzer. The management offices connected to the back of the aquarium. The whole place resembled a stadium because it actually used to be one for a city college before they got the budget to build a bigger facility elsewhere. Mark used one of the keys he kept to sneak inside, because at that point, both Mr. Tanner and him were in the same kind of shit and so formalities could be cast aside for the moment.

The main offices were empty. As Mark headed across the main floor, he noticed that, while all the tanks and lights were on, all of the fish were missing…the big main tank that featured a spiraling observation deck that stretches three stories tall was completely empty, full of only foggy blue water. It had everything from sea turtles to moray eels, rays and even nurse sharks. Mark heard footsteps and rustling, and the aquarium, as big as it could seem on a Saturday afternoon when it was full of screaming kids and frantic parents, was mostly a hollow place. After closing, you could literally hear all the fish bumping around the edges of their tanks. It was haunting, yet not unlike the pattering of rainfall on a bedroom window.

One of the backstage doors was cracked open, which was good because Mark had only kept a key to the main entrance. "Mr. Tanner?" Mark called and walked in on a feast.

Dolphins and seals were sprawled about with their guts strewn across the floor and dangling from Billy's little pale hands. Mr. Tanner sat on a bloody, hollow turtle shell that resembled a throne, holding an angelfish to his face as he bit through scales and cold meat. Gwen was hunched over in the corner, surrounded by half eaten sea creatures. Both Billy and Tanner were shirtless, with strange pot-bellies that, if Mark didn't know better, he would swear were full of babies. Gwen herself was bone thin and it seemed like she was starving, drained, despite all the half eaten and still somewhat flopping beasts surrounding her.

"Mr. Bridgett!" Mr. Tanner dropped the angelfish and stood up on wobbly legs. It was as if he was made out of rubber, he stretched and lurched wildly out of proportion. "Welcome to the spawning!" A metallic humming began to emit from Mr. Tanner's slowly elongating jaw as Billy began to mimic the sound. Gwen moaned and shouted about "making it all stop!" Mark had seen all he had to by that point and running away seemed like one hell of a great idea.

Of course, Mr. Tanner's long arms wrapped around the back of Mark's neck like twin eels the moment he came to a stop in front of the massive three-story tank. It's not that Mark forgot the horrors of that terrible feast, but rather, he stopped in his tracks because of the creatures fluttering through the murky tank's blue. Of the same breed as Billy's pet, there were at least two-dozen more Slinkos fluttering through the tank. When Mr. Tanner grabbed him, Mark was only able to pee his pants and regret ever accepting that weird, unclassifiable fish as payment from a fledgling researcher who was short on funds. That bargain Mark got really did turn out to be something else.

Dhinoj Dings' Shopping List

I pack fried cashew nuts

Evan Williams whiskey- IL

A shovel

The Body Parts Gang
Dhinoj Dings

It was Alexa who proposed the name "The body parts gang."

"But don't you think that's sort of a blunt name for our…gang?" said Ashok, unable to find any better word for their ragtag group.

Arching an eye brow, Alexa said, "How's that? I think it's a cool name. Got a nice ring to it."

"That may be true, but then again, don't you think it's too obvious a name, related to what we do?" Ashok scratched the back of his head.

"So, what if it is?" Alexa took a couple of steps towards Ahok, as though saying, 'You wanna mess with me?'

"No, I am just saying," Ashok said in a placating tone, throwing his arms up in the air.

Hearing his mellow tone, Alexa simpered. She even smiled—which was something of a rarity, as anyone even casually acquainted with her would tell you.

"The name is not meant as a direct reference to what we do. At least not completely," she said. "It's a name that shows our solidarity as a group."

When the other four members of the group frowned in confusion, Alexa sighed.

Like explaining the basic principles of quantum physics to a three year old, she said in a patient tone, "If our gang is the body, each of us is a body part. Are we agreed on that?" The rest of them nodded. "Yes, and if we—the body part—stay and function together, the body would perform well. That's what the name means."

Everyone nodded again.

Only, Gladys spoke. "Well, in that case you could have suggested 'Many-parts-but-one-body-gang!'"

For a second Alexa thought that Gladys was pulling her leg.

But when she looked up at her (Gladys was two heads taller than her—the two heads perched one over the other), she saw an earnest smile on her face (On the top face, that is. The bottom one always remained inert, expression-wise).

It occurred to Alexa that Gladys's statement was an honest opinion.

Following this realization, she didn't know whether she should punch her in the face or pat her on the back sympathetically for having such a terrible IQ.

But before she could say anything, Ravi said, "No, that can't be a name! That's very uncool. Not to mention, hard to say. Imagine if we have to create a cool chant for the gang, like something that we say as a group before we go on a mission or something, we would have to say something like 'Many-parts-but-one-body-gang-Go-Go-Go!' How silly would that sound? Ha,ha,ha!"

Though no one else in the gang thought much of Ravi's joke—indeed, judging from many a blank faces, it didn't even look as though they got the fact that it was a joke—everyone agreed that the name Gladys suggested was uncool and so totally unsuited for their gang.

"I was just saying…" Gladys said timidly. Faced with this group animosity towards her name suggestion, she cowered against one corner of the room.

***

They were inside one of the many cashew nut processing factories in Thazhuthala.

The village, though small, had a few such factories, even though the volume of land in which cashew nut trees grew were getting lesser by the day, more farmland being converted for putting up hotels and resorts. The proximity to backwaters and the laidback calmness that pervaded the village was only recently beginning to get noticed by land developers.

It was night and the factory had but a lone security guard posted at the gate—an elderly man, an ex-policeman who was at the moment sitting at his station—watching a porn video on his smartphone.

He had done a round of the premises about an hour ago and had seen nothing amiss then.

And, about half an hour back, when the group which would possibly come to be known as "The Bodyparts Gang" broke into the factory, he didn't hear anything either.

"So, what do you think, Shambu?" Alexa turned to the only member of the gang who had remained silent so far.

Shambu seemed to have been lost in thought—introspection was part of his nature—so this wasn't really a surprise to the others.

For a second, Alexa thought he might not have heard the discussion that'd been going on, let alone the question she just asked. But then, Shambu looked up, and staring at her with his jaded, yellow eyes, said, "Yes, I too think the name Gladys suggested is total rubbish."

Looking at Gladys, he added, "Sorry, Gladys."

Gladys wrapped her arms around herself as though she was suddenly overcome by cold and cowered even more towards the corner.

The room where they stood was some thousand square feet in size. It wasn't cavernous like many of the other spaces in the factory. A single naked bulb hung from the low ceiling.

This space was used for storing what could be called as "secondary cashew." The nuts that didn't make the cut as "Export quality."

There were two other rooms like this, in which were kept the nuts that would be sold in the domestic market, for lesser price, as opposed to the export variant that was sold at a higher price point.

There were more than a dozen wooden crates in the room, each filled to the hilt with the secondary nuts.

Ravi presently snickered seeing the crates.

"Why, what's funny?" said Alexa.

Shaking his head, Ravi said, "I just thought how wonderful it would be if the crates were filled with severed body parts of humans!"

For a second, there was silence, before all of them burst simultaneously into laughter.

Alexa clapped her hands as she laughed. Shambu slapped his thigh with glee.

Even Gladys, who had been cowering, stretched to her full height and laughed.

The collective noise that they made echoed wildly inside the room.

It was only when they heard the whistle of the security guard that they realized that they must be making more than acceptable levels of noise.

"Hush, guys!" said Alexa, gesturing to everyone with her hand.

In the ensuing silence, they heard footsteps approaching the door to the room.

***

Dogs. It must be dogs yelping. So thought the security guard.

Stray dogs were often seen in the area and many times in the past, some of them had found their way into the factory premise—the barbed wire fence that ran around the compound was no deterrent to dogs blessed with a body flexibility that's the envy of many a professional dancer.

Usually, when he would whistle, the dogs would come to him and he could raise the iron baton in his hand to scare them away.

But this time, even though he had whistled repeatedly, no dogs came out.

In fact, he couldn't even hear any dogs howling in the distance, which was almost a guarantee in such situations—dogs having a keen ear to hear whistles from far away.

The factory was inside a small lane off the main road that connected the two small towns of Kottiyam and Kannanallore.

The winding lane led one to the small shrine of St. Antony where the lane diverged to the left and the right.

The path to the left led to the St. Mary's Church in Kannnanllore while the one on the right joined at the national highway to Trivandrum—the capital of Kerala, that was just over sixty kilometers away.

And between the factory and the shrine was a stretch of almost a kilometer that was devoid of houses or any other establishment—commercial or domestic.

As the security guard stood in front of the store room from which he had heard the cackling noises, he felt an overwhelming silence floating towards him from all the empty spaces that surrounded the factory.

It was as though a mist rose from the ground and flowed to him in waves, encircling and then covering him in a misty lather.

It wasn't the silence of the night, the guard realized. It was an unnatural silence.

He realized that he couldn't even hear the crickets anymore.

It was as though nothing dared disrupt this silence.

During his time in the police force, the elderly man has seen some bad shit. Things terrible enough to make him lose faith in humanity more than once, and also made him want to quit the job more than once—only the thought of marrying off his two daughters kept him from quitting.

Now, both the daughters were married off and were living happily with their husbands.

And even though he lived in a modest house with two small bedrooms and a well in the backyard, he was happy enough about it and so was his wife. He had no intention of making any more significant addition to his wealth.

Not now that he was past the age of sixty.

He had taken up the job at this factory only because the pay would be a nice supplement to the humble pension that he got from the government. And also because it wasn't that far from home—his place was very near the St. Antony's shrine at the end of the lane.

In other words, he didn't really need this job. Not enough to suffer this unnatural fear that had suddenly come upon him.

He hesitated opening the door to the store-room, sure that there was something inside.

Not someone, but something.

Unlike the atrocities perpetrated by humans that he had witnessed during his years as a cop, whatever awaited inside the room held in its bosom the potential for atrocities the kind of which humans—or any other beasts of the earth for that matter—were incapable of.

He felt oddly sure of this.

"Get a grip on yourself," he muttered to himself. "Don't get superstitious like a little girl."

Steeling himself, muttering a prayer, reminding himself that he was hired to do a job—the job of seeing that the factory remained secure and safe during the nights—he pushed opened the door.

***

Gladys was the first one who pounced on the elderly man.

She was driven by the small harassment that she suffered from her gang mates for the name of the gang that she suggested.

She now wanted to divert her mind from that little episode and found the security guard as an apt object for that.

Soon as she landed on his chest, the elderly man fell back on the floor, the gleaming black baton falling from his hand and rolling out past the open door.

At first he thought that his assailant was wearing a mask.

But when he realized that the twin heads in place of a single head—the one above with wrinkles all over its skin and the one below with its eyelids closed and a twig-like protrusion sticking out of its mouth—was real, he opened his mouth to scream.

But no scream escaped him as before that, Gladys stuck her hand—the one with the crab hand like ending—inside his mouth, stifling any sound.

With her other hand, she took hold of his left leg, and with just one swift pull, pulled out the leg from its socket, as if he were a doll.

Pain, unimaginable pain shot up the man's body even as he watched the grinning Gladys beating his detached limb repeatedly on the side of one of the wooden crates that contained the secondary cashew nuts.

It was as though she was keeping rhythm to a song that was playing inside her mind. A discordant song that only she could hear.

Every time she beat his leg against the crate, the security guard winced in pain, as though the leg were still attached to his body.

It was a phantom pain which nonetheless felt real to him.

As real as the burning pain of a missing leg, the gaping wound at his socket bleeding profusely, fast painting the floor read.

He saw one of the fiends that stood behind Gladys crouching on all fours and lapping up the blood delightedly, lashing a foot long tongue forked at its edge like that of a snake's.

Sensing the eyes of the security guard on him, Shambhu raised his head and looked at the old man with his yellow eyes—the pupils two thin vertical slits—before going back to drinking the blood.

It wasn't that he was particularly hungry or thirsty—he has fed on a human not more than two hours ago—a sumptuous supper.

It was just that the sight of blood, and more importantly the intoxicating smell of the precious life fluid that bled from the old man's body, a smell that rose above that of all the cashew nuts in the room, made him salivate, made him crave for it.

Shambhu the introspective couldn't help it. It was just the way he was.

Delighted by the taste of blood, he even gave a short yelp of joy, raising his head and smiling to himself.

Gladys, meanwhile had stopped beating on the crate with the security guard's detached limb, and now used the man's leg on his own face. She repeatedly slapped him across the cheek with it, so hard that on the third time, everyone heard the bones on the man's cheek break.

The security guard moaned with pain, though the sound was soon stifled by the pressure of the crab-like hand that was still pressed inside his mouth.

Excited by all the fun that Gladys was having, Alexa now came forward and spat right on the lying man's chest.

Of all the five demons in the Body Parts Gang, Alexa looked the most like a human.

In fact, except for the red tail that rose from behind her and tilted inwards to the back of her head, she looked like any other twenty five or twenty six year old Malayali woman—maybe a little more beautiful than most.

But the projectile of spit that left her mouth was not something that could be produced by an ordinary human.

For one thing, the thick globule of spit was green in colour—as though it was coagulated slimy water.

For another, no sooner than the globule of spit hit the man's chest than it burned through the cotton shirt he was wearing—a grey shirt which was part of the security guard's uniform—and through his skin.

Before you knew it, there was a gaping wound at the centre of his body, curled up folds of exposed flesh exuding a charred smell as though the flesh was burned with acid.

The man moaned even more but Gladys saw to it that the bulk of that painful sound remained inside his own throat. Searing hot tears spilled from his eyes as he began to pray for unconsciousness or death, whichever came first.

As Gladys was about to raise his leg over his head and bring it down on his face once again—perhaps for the last time—Alexa suddenly grabbed her hand, preventing her from carrying out her intention.

To Gladys' querulous look, Alexa said, "You could detach his neck if you beat him on the face once more!"

Smiling wickedly, Gladys said, "That's the idea."

"But the Lord would like it more if we come up with something more interesting, don't you think?"

Gladys frowned.

Giving her an I-will-show-you-how-its-done look, Alexa took the man's detached leg from her hand and pushed the leg, stump first into the open wound in the man's chest.

The pressure with which she did this ruptured more than a few things inside the old man's body.

The hole widened on his chest.

Whereas it was fist-sized before, it was big enough for someone to insert her head in now.

And as Alexa continued screwing the stump of leg deeper into the wound, out popped his heart along the side of the open wound.

The heart came coiled around a piece of intestine.

Blood spluttered from the old man's mouth. His last breath came out through his nostrils along with small bubbles of blood.

Waving a hand over the corpse, which lay with the torn leg jutting out from its chest like a broad hockey stick, Alexa said, "Now, doesn't this look like a sculpture?"

In response, the rest of the gang clapped their hands.

"Yes, it does!" Ravi said enthusiastically. "I am sure the Lord will be pleased with it."

He was referring to the lord of hell—the one, who has sent gangs like the Body Parts Gang to earth—so that they could bring him "human body parts re-arranged so that they would look like an abhorrent sculpture."

The reason? Why, it was just the latest of the Dark One's fancies for art.

A connoisseur that he was, he wanted to fill up hell with "modern human art" as he termed it. "The more macabre the better!"

The gang hadn't expected to make any human sculptures when they came into the cashew nut processing factory this night.

In fact, they had just grouped together to share notes of their progress. The village of Thazhuthala has been exceptionally good for them—in a sleepy village like this, it was always easy to find prey in the night.

The old security guard was just a surprise bonus. But the kill—everyone agreed—turned out to be more artistic than most of their kills so far.

Chanting together levitation verses over the dead body, they watched as the corpse floated up from the floor and exited the door and the factory itself.

The lifeless body lifted up in to the air before plunging down into the bare earth, where it began its descent into the depths of hell where the Dark One could admire their latest offering.

No sooner had the corpse broke through the ground than any sign of the ground ever having disturbed too vanished.

Satisfied with their latest handiwork, Alexa—the self-appointed leader of the gang—gave directions to each member on where to go and who to kill and in which manner the corpse should appear.

They had just two more days left before they needed to return to hell.

The gangs with the least impressive sculptures, the Devil has promised, would form part of the Dark One's next art project—a collection of "dilapidated demon sculptures."

"And none of us wants to become part of that collection, do we?"

Everyone nodded, saying "We don't," to Alexa's question.

Clapping her hands, she said, "Then let's go!"

The members of the Body Parts Gang spread out into the cold Thazhuthala night.

Richard Raven's Shopping List

Loaf of bread
roll of clear plastic
Mayo
Heavy tape or snap ties
Black Forest Ham
Mop
Lettuce
plastic bucket
Tomato
Shovel
Smoked Cheddar cheese
Latex gloves

The Butcher's Return
Richard Raven

"*That damn camera's going to be the death of you one of these days.*"

Ronald Holmes couldn't help but grin as the words of his wife cycled through his head. Deidre had been saying things like that to him almost every day of their four years of marriage. What she meant, what he had always understood her to mean, was that she believed he took a few too many chances when on the prowl for that perfect photo. That he would one day fall through the rotted floor of some old abandoned house and break his fool neck. Perhaps, step on a snake as he pawed his way through brush and trash piles to get the perfect angle of the shot he wanted and die of the resulting bite. Or, worse still, that someone craving their next hit of meth would simply blow his head off or slit his throat for the money in his pockets.

But Ronald, for the most part, had always shrugged aside his wife's well-meaning words of warning. For one thing, he was always careful. Always. In fact, he believed there was no such thing as too careful. If he happened upon a snake or a meth-head—and he had encountered a few of each—he never hung around that place very long. For another, he simply couldn't help himself; he had always found the power of the camera addictive. Very addictive. More so, he believed, than any drug or alcohol. Even more than a motorcycle, an addiction he had experienced and survived back in his younger days. But that was a long time ago; these days his addictions ran toward old home sites, deserted buildings, all manner of things and places viewed by most as eyesores, but he found it all fascinating. He had always seen more in deserted and forgotten places and things than most; the camera saw even more than he did. It often amazed him to see what the camera had captured that had escaped his naked eye.

Ronald, dismissing what Deidre had said to him as he left the house a few hours before, concentrated as he positioned the shot in his Nikon's view screen. It was an old bench that had grabbed his interest, one of many in what had once been a park. He stood near one end of the bench, sunlight washing over that end of it, the other end deep in the shadows created by the trees that were reclaiming the old park property. The bench had no seat, what remained of its wooden sides and armrests hardly more than rotted pulp. A narrow strip of metal, what had once formed the top of the backrest and now tarnished almost black, was all that held the two ends upright.

He finally found the angle he wanted and hit the shutter button.

When he checked the image, he loved the mix of sun and shadows, the dark trunk of a tree in the background, and the way the thicket of untended grass and weeds further heightened the forlorn sense about the bench that hinted at better days long in the past.

Damn, what a great shot! The best, by far, of the many he had snapped of that bench and the others scattered about the grounds. He was still admiring the shot when…

"Don't see many people out here anymore," a voice said from behind him, the words spoken in a whispered monotone.

Ronald jerked, sucked in a breath and wheeled around. Behind him stood a woman, rather disheveled in dress and appearance. *Meth-head.* The first thought that occurred to him. She was staring, not at him, but at the bench and with dulled, faraway eyes. Ronald swallowed dryly, his heart still racing.

"Sorry," the woman murmured. "Didn't mean to give you such a start."

"No problem," he said, his voice a bit raw. "I just had no idea anyone else was even here." There was, in fact, no one else there when he arrived. He was sure of that. So how had she slipped up on him so quietly through the bone-dry grass and leaves?

True, as Deidre always told him, he often lost himself when busy with his camera, but he was never *that* lost!

"Like I said," the woman murmured, stepping past him toward the bench, "few ever come out here anymore." She ran her fingers along one of the armrests; it amazed Ronald that the wood didn't simply crumble under her touch. "I used to bring my little girl here, and I'd sit at this very bench and watch her playing on the swings."

What? Frowning, Ronald glanced over his shoulder, eyeing the old and rusted swing a short distance away. There wasn't much of it left. All the seats and chains were gone; what remained of the frame looked as if it could collapse at the slightest push. Still frowning, now more puzzled than ever, Ronald looked back at the woman.

He understood that the city had closed the park some fifteen years before; that the city council had finally decided to bulldoze the entire plot and to put the property to some future use. Despite her rumpled clothes and ratty appearance, Ronald judged the woman no older than early- to mid-twenties. He based this judgement on the fact the woman's face was without a single line of age, and there was even a bit of a youthful shine in her otherwise blank and lost eyes.

No older than she looked, how could she have brought her daughter to that park? He wondered if she even had a daughter or if it was all in her head. A delusion, perhaps, induced by the habit he believed—now more than ever—that she had?

Likely. So likely that Ronald decided it was time to leave, and started walking away. He couldn't help but feel pity for the woman and other such unfortunate souls, but he knew their situations were often of their own making, and that most had little to no desire to improve their circumstances. The last thing he wanted was to witness a ranting meltdown over the way life had treated the woman so unfairly.

Besides, he had come to that abandoned park with his camera that Saturday afternoon mostly to avoid the potential and often-caustic ravings of a brooding female. It wasn't his wife he wished to avoid—never Deidre…but her daughter, Nina.

Well, not her real daughter. Deidre had never been able to have kids of her own. It was her brother and his wife, a woman also unable to conceive, who had adopted Nina when she was very young. Less than a year after the adoption, when her brother and sister-in-law died in a tragic car crash, Deidre assumed custody of the child and finished raising the girl as her own. Deidre was the only mother the girl had ever known.

Ronald and Nina had an emphatic understanding: she didn't like him, and he had little use for her, though he went through the motions for Deidre's sake.

In truth, Ronald had no serious issue with the girl beyond her lousy attitude, both toward him and things in general. An intelligent and very pretty girl of nineteen, she just had a dark, even foreboding view of things that Ronald found intolerable. She seemed to see every person as a potential enemy and treated them accordingly. It also grated on his nerves how the girl, when in one of her fouler and darker moods, would brutally speak her mind, and to hell with those whose toes she might tread upon or whose feelings she would crush. She even did it to Deidre, often embarrassing her. *"A character flaw she undoubtedly inherited from one of her biological parents,"* Deidre had once said with a hopeless and resigned shrug. A flaw that she, Deidre, had never been able to correct, and finally gave up trying when the girl hit her teens. Nina was the only real sore spot that existed in his marriage to Deidre.

The trouble now was that Nina was home from college for the weekend. She and Deidre had made various plans for the duration of Nina's brief stay. None of which—at Nina's insistence, Ronald was reasonably sure—included him.

Fine by him. He loved Deidre, who was his second wife, and he had no desire to argue over the girl she loved as fiercely as she would her own flesh and blood. Nor did he wish to deprive them of the chance to spend time together. From the day Nina first went away to college, Deidre had struggled with the "Empty Nest" syndrome.

Ronald was only a few steps away from the bench, already wondering where next to go with his camera, when the woman he had encountered spoke again, stopping him.

"Mister? Why would you want to take pictures here? Why would you even want to come to this place? You know what happened here, don't you?"

Ronald had turned to face the woman. "No," he admitted. He had only lived in the city since he married Deidre; he was still learning the place and its history. Despite himself, now genuinely curious, he asked, "What happened here?"

"This is where he found all those young women," was the whispered reply. The woman still had her back to him, the fingers of one hand still stroking the wood of the bench's armrest. "This was his hunting ground."

"Whose hunting ground?" Ronald asked, his forehead furrowed.

"Melvin," the woman replied, her voice now laced with an unmistakable note of fear. "Melvin Ragsdale."

* * *

Melvin Ragsdale? Jesus Christ…
The name hit Ronald with a jolt, the face of the man he had seen on the news suddenly vivid in his mind. The man that a few of the more imaginative and morbid members of the local media had dubbed The Butcher. The man had killed—hacked to pieces was closer to the mark—eight young women. To that point in Melvin Ragsdale's murderous spree, having been careful and meticulous, police had very little to go on and no idea who they were dealing with. Then Ragsdale slipped with

his ninth victim; she lived just long enough to put the police on her attacker's trail. They tracked him to an old duplex apartment in one of the seedier parts of town, and they found him at home, alone. There had never been a chance for a peaceful resolution; during the ensuing standoff and subsequent shootout, Ragsdale killed one of the uniformed officers, a young female rookie, before dying himself in a hail of bullets.

All this Ronald remembered from the news coverage he had seen fifteen years ago. As he stared at the woman's back, he recalled that police believed that Ragsdale had, in fact, abducted his victims from one of the city's parks—the one thing that police claimed that all the victims had in common. What the police couldn't establish with any certainty was Ragsdale's motive. The man had no friends; the few that claimed to even know him had all expressed fear and animosity toward the man and could shed no light on his thinking or actions.

Ronald looked around, his eyes taking in a few of the stark and bare light poles that still stood along cracked and stained concrete paths. "So this is really the place?" he murmured. More of a rhetorical statement, rather than a question that sought further confirmation. It was just as well; he neither got an additional answer or even a simple reply. The woman, he noticed, was no longer staring down at the bench. She now appeared to be gazing straight ahead at something between her and the encroaching trees, her hands at her sides. Her body looked rigid.

Ronald had no idea what she was staring at as if mesmerized; he could see nothing at all in the shadows created by the trees. The only thing he could tell for certain was that whatever she was looking at had seemed to upset her.

"Are you okay?" Ronald asked, not sure he really wanted to know. For several long seconds, a moment that seemed frozen in time, the woman didn't move or offer a reply. Then, finally, she turned to face him. Her face bore a pained expression; in her eyes was what he could only describe as fear. Stark and raw fear.

"Leave," she whispered. "Leave here now…please, I beg you."

That sounded like a wonderful idea to Ronald. He turned and walked away, again stopping after only a few steps.

The impulse came out of nowhere, seizing him suddenly, and one he couldn't resist. Without a second thought, he turned slightly toward the woman, raised his camera with one hand, and snapped a picture of her.

Then he left the park, wondering, *Why the hell did I do that?*

When he reached his car parked on the street, he looked back toward the park. He could see no sign of the woman. Nor could he see the bench he had photographed or any of the others. Could see nothing beyond the light poles and the rusting relic of the swing. Stark and silent sentinels in an overgrown plot of ground.

Damn, what a spooky place this turned out to be. He got behind the wheel of his car, started the engine, and drove away…glad to be away from there.

* * *

It was late in the day when he made it back home. Deidre's car wasn't in the driveway, she and Nina, if he remembered correctly, not due back until later in the evening. Ronald made himself a sandwich in the kitchen, then took it and a glass of iced-tea into the small bedroom at the back of the house that Deidre referred to as his "Man Cave." There was a desk in the center of the room, upon which sat his laptop, an ink-jet printer, and several stacks of magazines all devoted to photography. Deidre considered his camera merely a hobby, but one she really didn't mind, despite what she often said. *"There's things a lot worse that you could be doing with your spare time,"* she had once said, a wry smile on her face. *"Lucky for you it isn't women or booze."*

While Ronald took her good-natured ribbing in stride, he didn't think of his camera as a hobby. There were several writers in the Indie Community who often came to him for photos they could use for book covers, so he was making a little money. Not much, but a little, and the best part was that word of his abilities with a camera was beginning to spread, more and more writers reaching out to him.

He found that he couldn't take his eyes away from his laptop all the time he was finishing his sandwich and iced-tea. Anxious though he was to download the photos he had taken and see just what he had, he was more consumed with a burning curiosity to go online and learn more about Melvin Ragsdale. Ronald had been able to think of little else since leaving that park.

He decided the photos could wait a little while longer.

A search of Google revealed numerous sites and articles either devoted to Melvin Ragsdale or that contained information about him. At first, it was mostly general info, most of which Ronald already knew or had remembered about The Butcher. As he worked down the page, though, the articles became more detailed. Details that formed a bloody and chilling view inside the twisted mind of an obvious madman. Ronald found several photos of the man: dark hair and dark, glaring eyes, a weak chin and thin lips always pressed tightly together as if he was angry; a hawk-like nose set in a gaunt face that seemed incapable of showing emotion or even assuming a smile.

One evil-looking son-of-a-bitch, that's for sure…

One link took Ronald to a website devoted to *"Murderers and Other Monsters."* It was there that he found not only another picture of Ragsdale, but portrait shots of all nine of his female victims.

And it was then that Ronald got one of the worst shocks of his life.

For there, among the victims, was a photo of the woman he had seen at the park. Number nine, the one who had lived long enough to finger Ragsdale. He would just be damned if he could understand or explain it, but Ronald had no doubts that it was the same woman. Same oval face and heart shaped mouth; a small and pointed pixie-like nose and the same long and straight dark hair.

"Susan Marling," Ronald breathed, reading from the screen. According to the bio, a twenty-three-year-old unmarried mother of a daughter, aged four. *She said she had a little girl…and I doubted it.*

Of course, he had doubted it! The time factor and her apparent age didn't add up. What was he supposed to do? Sit there and think—*believe*, for Christ's sake! — that he had seen and talked to a dead woman? He had never believed that such things really happened. It was just too…crazy and impossible! He had always felt that people who did believe in that kind of bullshit needed professional help.

A shrink, rehab, AA—whatever!

Yet his gaze had drifted to his camera sitting next to the printer, and there his eyes remained, fixed and unblinking. The camera often saw more than he did…and he had snapped a picture of that woman. And without really knowing why he did it, either. He hadn't checked the image, though. It was about the only one he had taken that day that he hadn't checked…

…and now it was like the damn camera was daring him to pull that image up and have a look at it.

Like he had a choice about it? That he could simply erase all the images on the chip and conveniently forget about the crazy notion bouncing around in his head?

Slowly, reluctantly, he reached for the camera.

And it was then, having lost all sense of time and awareness while online, that he jerked in surprise when the door to the room opened. A gasp burst from his lips as a figure stepped into the room.

"Hey there, sweetie," greeted a soft and pleasant voice, the words accompanied by a pair of bright and smiling blue eyes.

Jesus Christ. Ronald blew out a breath and slumped in his chair. "Deidre," he breathed. How long had she and Nina been home?

"My God, Ronnie, are you okay?" she asked, her step faltering as she padded on bare feet toward him. "If I didn't know better, I'd swear that you've seen a ghost."

Either that, or I'm well on my way to losing my goddamn mind. "N-No," he stammered, waving a hand at his laptop. "Just got busy with something and didn't realize you'd made it home."

"Been home for a little while now, but I knew you were probably busy and I didn't want to bother you." Deidre leaned down, kissed his cheek, then glanced at the laptop's screen. He heard her sharp intake of breath; she quickly looked away, a look of horrified revulsion on her face. "God Lord, Ronnie," she spluttered, moving away from him, "The Butcher? Why in the name of Jesus are you looking up anything to do with that fucking creep?"

One of only a few times he had ever heard *that* word come from her mouth, and never said with such vehemence. Her reaction took Ronald completely by surprise and left him unsure how to respond. It was as if she had taken what she saw on his laptop as an affront to her personally.

But could he really blame her for reacting the way she was? Considering the kind of monster Melvin Ragsdale had been and the level of vicious depravity he had visited upon his victims? Before his death, the murdering bastard had most of the women in the city afraid to leave their homes, be it day or night.

"Oh, I get it," Deidre went on, hands on her hips and glaring at him. "Doing a little research for one of your writer friends?"

"No," Ronald said, shaking his head and carefully considering the rest of his reply. "I happened to find my way today out to the park where he, supposedly, hung out and abducted his victims. I ran into someone there and they told me it was the place. This person called it his *'hunting ground'*, and—"

"And that stirred your insatiable curiosity to find out for sure, I know," Deidre interrupted, her voice now soft as a sigh and without even a hint of anger or criticism. She placed one hand gently on his shoulder and reached with the other and closed his laptop. "Judging by the way you almost came out of that chair when I walked in, I'd say you've more than satisfied your curiosity."

She would get no argument from him. He wished now that he had never bothered with it…and not only because it had clearly upset Deidre. He was still puzzled by her reaction, but he was thinking more of the photo of that woman on his camera. Despite Deidre's return to calm and the reassuring hand on his shoulder, Ronald still felt like his head was going to spin right off his neck. *That couldn't have been his ninth victim! No way in hell can that be possible!*

"Anyway," Deidre said, changing the subject, "Nina and I had something to eat earlier and she's already in bed and I'm on my way there now. Are you coming soon?"

Damn, is it **that** *late? How long have I been sitting here?* Ronald nodded. "In a little while. I first want to download the photos I took today. I won't be long."

Deidre leaned down for another kiss, then started for the door. There she stopped and looked back at him, her brow knitted thoughtfully.

Ronald knew her and the look now on her face well enough to know that there was something on her mind. Something troubling her that she wanted to tell him about but wasn't sure how to say it. For several more seconds she struggled with it.

"What?" he finally prompted.

Deidre sighed and moved back into the room. "I'm sorry I almost bit your head off," she said. "It's just that..." Her voice failed her, and she again seemed locked in a struggle for the right words.

"What is it, sweetheart?" Ronald said, frowning. "Tell me."

Another sigh and Deidre appeared to make up her mind. "I should've told you about this long before now, but I kept silent about it for Nina's sake. Ronnie, you know she's adopted, but what you don't know is how she became a ward of the state."

Ronald didn't know that—knew little of Nina, in fact, beyond the time after he met Deidre. He remained silent, eyes on Deidre and waiting for her to go on.

"The truth is that her birth mother died…she was murdered. The woman was the last of Melvin Ragsdale's victims. That's why it shook me so badly when I saw that on your PC about him."

Ronald had gone cold inside, his thoughts again focused entirely on the photo of the woman stored in his camera. *She said she used to bring her little girl to play at that park. My God…can it really be true?* It was several seconds later, though the silence in that room seemed much longer to Ronald, before he could bring his mind back on track and find his voice again.

"I take it Nina knows this about her real mother?"

"Oh, yes," Deidre said, her voice heavy with resignation. "My brother and his wife never said a word to her about her mother or what happened to her, and I resolved to keep the secret from her after they died to spare her further grief and to, perhaps, save her from that burden to carry the rest of her life. But as she got older, she got curious and, somehow, found out on her own. When she confronted me about it, I had no choice but to tell her the truth. This was a little more than a year before we met. She was such a sweet child growing up…but finally finding out the truth changed her. It turned her into the dark and brooding, the mistrustful and cynical young woman she is today."

Ronald couldn't think of anything to say, the feeling of cold sinking even deeper in him. While this revelation answered many of the questions he had regarding Nina, it left him even more bewildered. The camera on his desk held his gaze, and he couldn't stop the thoughts that ran rampant, one after another, through his mind.

"Anyway," Diedre sighed, "that's my way of saying I'm sorry."

"It's okay, sweetheart," Ronald murmured, then added, "I understand," though, in truth, he didn't understand a thing. The truth about Nina…the woman he had seen and talked to at the park…more than he could get his mind wrapped around.

Deidre had crossed the room to where he sat, leaned down and pulled him into a hug. "Hurry to bed, hon, if you can," she whispered in his ear. "Gets kind of lonely in that big bed at night when you're busy in here."

He assured her that he wouldn't be long, then watched her leave the room.

Long after she was gone, he remained in his seat behind the desk, aware of nothing beyond the camera in front of him. An uneasy feeling lay like a chunk of rotten meat in his stomach. Finally, he told himself to quit stalling around and get on with it.

It took only a couple of minutes to download the fifty or so photos he had made. He began scrolling through them, one at a time, in no hurry, finally arriving at the one he had made of the woman…

…and there she was. The same woman whose picture he had seen online. The very same woman, no doubt about it…and yet different. Decidedly different.

The young woman he had seen and talked to had looked like any normal living and breathing person. But the one in his photo, to his shock and horror, looked like the ghost she undoubtedly was. There was enough of her essence to recognize her—to even see the fear in her eyes…but he could see right through her, the old bench clearly visible behind her.

Yet that wasn't the most frightening thing about the photo. Not even close. The camera, as always, had seen more than he had.

For standing behind her and to one side of the old bench, was a second figure. A taller figure that towered over the woman, the dark eyes staring straight at the camera. On the gaunt and clearly ethereal face was the most insidious smile Ronald had ever seen. A face he had thought incapable of a smile.

My God...that's him. Ragsdale . . .

Then, right before Ronald's wide and horrified eyes, the figure of the dead killer blurred as if rushing toward him from the laptop's screen. A blinding burst of white from the screen; a sudden sense of heat like a blast of sunlight, then Ronald felt as if something had slammed into him, rocking him in his chair. After that . . .

* * *

. . . he waits a long time, until the house is still and silent, before he finally leaves the room, closing the door softly behind him. The rest of the house is dark. His eyes quickly adjust; he moves like a shadow down the hallway and to the kitchen. There he quickly locates what he's looking for. He selects the one he wants, the biggest of those ensconced in the block of wood sitting on the counter near the sink. He runs his hands over, first one side of the long blade, then the other, his fingers moving ever so lightly over the finely-honed and razor-sharp edge.

The feel of the edge makes his fingers tingle with anticipation, the pound of his heart and the rush of blood through his veins forming a low thrum in his ears. A smile has appeared on his face in the darkness. The old feeling is back in him again, the gnawing need now fully awakened from its long slumber; he savors the feeling like an exquisite taste dancing on his tongue.

He slips first to the master bedroom and pushes open the door. From out of the murk of shadows he hears slow and steady breathing. He creeps forward, pausing at the side of the bed, staring down at the sleeping woman. Little more than a lump under the pale sheets, but he can see enough of her to know she's lying on her back, one arm bent at the elbow and her hand near her face. He can smell just a hint of her perfume. A smell he hates—always has. His face twists into a grimace.

"Eleven," he whispers. No one other than himself has ever counted the rookie cop among his kills, but she was number ten. Realizing his imminent death, he had deliberately targeted the young woman, carefully aiming the rifle in his hands and slowly squeezing the trigger. The bullet took her just under the nose; he had the pleasure of seeing her face blown apart, the back of the bitch's head exploding in a spray of blood and brains and hair.

No more than she fucking deserved. No more than any of them deserved.

The image of the cop slumping to the ground fills his mind's eye as he clamps his free hand over the mouth of the woman lying in the bed.

She comes awake at the instant of contact; begins to struggle frantically as he quickly and deftly draws the butcher's knife across her throat. A deep and vicious slash, he feels more than sees the blood that geysers from her ruptured flesh. As her body bucks with surprising force, her head immobile by the hand still covering her mouth, he thrusts the knife through the sheet and her thin night clothes—the point of the blade piercing her heaving belly just below the navel—and slices up to her sternum.

Incredibly, even as her entrails boil through the gaping wound in both flesh and cloth, she continues to struggle, but that doesn't last long. He keeps on slashing and stabbing, pulling and ripping; hurling pieces of her about the room. He is in a complete frenzy—more so than with any of the others. It is long after she has gone silent and still, only when there isn't much of her left, that he stops, finally satisfied.

No chance this one will blab to the cops...not that it really matters.

Still...

His breathing gradually slowing, he remains there beside the bed for a time, eyes closed, relishing the warmth and the stickiness of the blood that covers his hands and arms and that he can feel running down his face and neck. The rush is incredible, almost sexual in its intensity. Then, as the feeling begins to recede, like the fading spasms of an orgasm, he leaves the gory mess he has made of her and moves into the hallway and slips silently to the quest bedroom.

This one...number twelve...he has been waiting for, and for so long; he takes even more time with her. More time than he ever spent with any of the others. Several times he must stop and wipe the blood from his face and eyes.

When he finally leaves the house, he still holds the bloody knife in one hand, and something else equally bloody in his other. The keys to the car belonging to the asshole who set him free he finds in a pocket of the blood-splattered jeans he's now wearing; he drives away into the night. When he arrives at the park . . .

* * *

. . . he found the bitch that got him killed waiting where he had left her beside the bench. She was crying when he abruptly left her, and she was still at it now. The sound of her sobs—and a beautiful sound it was— made him smile.

"I knew it was a mistake for him to come here and take those pictures," she said, her voice thick and hitching. "My God…I should've warned him sooner."

"Wouldn't have done any good," The Butcher drawled. "I knew who he was and what he was here for, and I had his ass the second he took the first picture."

"Why, Melvin? Why, for God's sake?"

"I told you, the night I left your ass for dead—three for every bitch that wronged me…especially the two-timing whore that left me and took my kid away from me."

"And now you've killed my kid. My beautiful daughter—as if you hadn't already wrecked her life, you stinking piece of scum."

"Then I guess you can call it a mercy," he laughed, and hurled the severed head he had brought with him from the guest bedroom at the crying bitch. The head rolled to within a few inches of her feet.

"Nina," she sobbed, turning her face away, unable to look at her daughter's head.

The Butcher stood there watching the crying and moaning bitch, the knife still gripped in his hand, until she finally turned away from him and headed toward the trees behind the bench.

And there, formed into a broken line, stood all his victims, including the last two. They were all staring at him with burning, hate-filled eyes.

"Hey!" he called out, suddenly inspired. He stepped toward the head on the ground and kicked it after the retreating bitch. "Don't forget your darling daughter! I mean, fuck, it's been so long and all."

"Fuck you, Melvin," she said softly from the darkness as, one by one, the others turned and melted into the trees. As Number Nine faded from sight, trailing after the others, she said, "You've took everything I had…now you can't hurt me anymore."

True enough, and he didn't have time to screw around with her or any of the others. Done with them, and he had things to do, business to finish. Business interrupted for too long as it was, and not a lot of time left to him in which to do it in his new and borrowed body. As soon as some asshole discovered what he had left at that house, the cops would be all over him. Fuck, they would find him eventually—he had no illusions about that…but he would just be damned if they would get another chance to kill him. Nor would he ever spend a day in jail, a vow he made with his first kill. Before he had to endure either of those options, he would, himself, kill the fucker whose body he inhabited and, hopefully, in a place where no one would ever find the rotting corpse.

So he would use the hours of darkness he had left and take down as many bitches as he could. If he didn't make his goal, the goal he had set fifteen long years ago…well, he would just have to wait a while longer until his next chance came along.

The only thing he hated about it was that he had never been able to get at the one bitch that deserved it most. The one he had knocked up, who had done nothing but fuck with him and took from him the only thing he had ever cherished.

Then again, he wasn't all that tore up about it. After all, a bitch was a bitch and they were all the same.

And here comes number thirteen. From the sidewalk near the street he heard what he knew to be the click of high-heels. That time of night it had to be a hooker. Probably some skank strung out on crack and probably not even sure what world she inhabited.

Good enough. He might even drag her ass back to the trees and have a little fun with her before getting down to business.

Why the hell not? It had been a long time, and what difference did it make? He only wished now that he had thought of it back at the house. The fun he could have had with those two…the young one, Nina, especially.

Before he had, yet again, lived up to his nickname and left them both carved up like a pair of butchered cows.

Wait a minute…that's not one, but two bitches coming this way. They were close enough now that he could hear them talking and laughing, their heels rattling along the sidewalk. *Goddamn, this was always the best place to hunt…*

Megan E Morales' Shopping List

Steak
Asparagus
Red Potatoes
Garlic
French bread
Mushrooms
Heavy cream

The Dead Boys
Megan E. Morales

Chapter One

1986.

Matt Reeves was, without a doubt one unlucky gal.

For starters there was the boy's name she'd been lumbered with; just who in God's name called their beautiful, brand new and shiny pink baby daughter *Matt*? A mother who was too busy tripping acid to know—or care—what the registrar wrote on the birth certificate, that's who. And from that ignominious start to life, Matt had seemed cursed with one run of bad luck after another—a mother permanently high on some illicit substance or other, a father who'd run screaming before they'd even cleaned the blood and shit off of Matt's baby brother, one abusive 'uncle' after another, a string of shitty boyfriends who only wanted Matt for one thing—two if you counted money—and a handful of schools who'd asked that Matt Reeves not return following a whole host of suspensions.

All of which added up to how come Matt was none too surprised to find herself mid air in the pitch darkness, falling downwards to Christ only knew where, the ground having given way beneath her feet what seemed like a lifetime ago.

She'd only gone to the carnival to get herself and her kid brother out of the house awhile. Mom was off her saggy old tits on bath salts and fucking some random guy who stank like rotted meat she'd met out in the street and the two of them were upstairs fucking like some bad porno with the sound cranked up to eleven. Matt figured her little brother really didn't need to be hearing any of that and had dragged him away from the TV for a night of fun and thrills on the rides and sideshows down at the pier.

She remembered the sound of a guitar filtering its way through the sounds of excited voices and fifty's music that filled the carnival, and the deep, resounding voice accompanying it with one of Rush's lesser known songs—something buried in the nether regions of their second album, unless Matt was otherwise mistaken. She'd homed in on that voice, pulling her whining brat of a brother along by his arm, her hand gripping it so tightly that she felt the thin bones in his wrist crackling against one another.

He'd probably be wondering where she was by now, although not in the slightest part concerned for his sister—he was used to Matt taking off with some boy or other and leaving him to his own devices, and he was independent enough to find his own way home from the pier. Plus Matt had seen him hooking up with that nerdy Johnson kid he often hung around with—just moments after she'd bumped into the mysterious and decidedly gorgeous Bryne. Freddy Johnson was there with his folks and the Johnsons were good people—they'd most likely feed the boy before they gave him a ride home.

As she fell through the blackness, Matt Reeves had a little time to lament that no one would miss her until well after breakfast time tomorrow, and that made her feel just a little more lonely.

Matt landed hard on the ground. A thin dust flew up around her in the darkness and she coughed loudly before straining to adjust her eyes in the absolute lightlessness of her surroundings. Her arms and chin felt scraped and she groaned as her right knee and hip joints twinged and crackled, sending shards of pain the length and breadth of her leg. She could feel that most of her body was beginning to bruise up from the fall and she knew full well that if she didn't get out of the trap Bryne had so callously pushed her into, she'd most likely die down there.

She scrabbled to her feet, feeling decidedly sore yet thankful when she was actually able to get up from the cold, dry floor—at least nothing seemed to be broken, and that was a good thing. Add to that the fact that the enigmatic Bryne hadn't put her in a coffin or a ditch somewhere—she chastised herself at being such a dumbass for ignoring her gut feeling that there was something about the handsome young man that felt inherently *strange*—and Matt allowed herself to feel a tad better about her predicament.

Reaching out her arms either side in the blackness, Matt felt around with her hands. Her fingertips located a rough, damp wall and she rapped her knuckles on it, hoping against hope that she would find a hollow section, or maybe even a secret passageway like they did in the movies—there was *always* a secret passageway! And when she didn't find one, Matt huffed.

She wanted nothing more than to stomp her foot like a disgruntled toddler, angry and frustrated that she wasn't getting her own way. But she didn't. Matt was lucky insomuch that she was a good five-ten in stockinged feet—the perfect model height, thank fuck for genetics, the one thing her nightmare of a mother had managed to get right—and so when she raised her hands upwards, her fingers rapped against a low part of the ceiling. Encouraged, Matt ran her fingers across the cool stone, desperately feeling for a latch, a lock, *something*.

Finally, Matt's scrabbling fingers located the latch she had been praying was there. She slid it free, thankful that there was no padlock holding it in place and gave the thick wooden panel that it secured a hearty shove upwards with a brute force that she didn't realise she had in her. She squinted against the harsh light that flooded in and split the darkness like a bright burst of flame.

"Holy shit," Matt growled as she rubbed at her aching eyes as they fought to adjust from the darkness.

A rope ladder was thrown down and Matt grabbed at the thing with both hands. Screwing her eyes up against the unforgiving light that assaulted her from above and fighting the fear of what fate may be awaiting her at the top of the shaft, Matt slowly, steadily began to climb.

After what seemed an age of climbing one wobble step at a time—just like in the good ol' days of high school gym—Matt reached the top of the shaft. She stepped out and away from the cool, dusty air of the darkness below.

"Well, Hi –"

Matt threw a well-aimed fist at Byrne's pretty-boy face, her nostrils flared in anger.

Bryne staggered back from the blow, almost losing his footing as his nose broke with an audible *crack*.

Matt braced herself for the boy's retaliation, more than ready to reduce his good looks to little more than a bloodied pulp.

But no, Bryne simply regained his composure and smiled at her with a scarlet trail of blood oozing from one nostril and his left eye dark and swelling. It was a smile, yes, but to Matt it was a smile that would make a lesser person run screaming with piss staining the front of their pants. Undeterred, Matt stood her ground and stared right back at the boy with that well-practiced *screw you* expression on her dust-grimed face.

The two boys who up until now had stood quietly behind Bryne—Matt recognised them as his stooges from the carnival—began to laugh, one of them staring at Matt with a stupid, awe-struck expression on his face.

"That was for leading me into—whatever this bullshit is!" Matt snarled at Bryne. She windmilled her arms to indicate the hole she'd just climbed up out of and this new place before giving Bryne the finger. She took a step or two backwards, hoping to get some distance between herself and Bryne so that she could make a run for it. She knew better then to turn around though, presenting your back to people like that was usually the last move the dumb blondes in the movies ever made.

A hand clamped down on Matt's shoulder. Hard, firm, and with long, strong fingers that dug painfully into her bruised clavicle. Matt yelped and froze on the spot. Of course there was one of them behind her—Bryne and his cohorts didn't look like they were quite *that* stupid. She sighed, knowing all too well that she was trapped. She turned her head and again recognized the huge frame of the man who blocked her escape—

he'd been lurking in the background at the carnival too. The big guy had a disconcerting blank look on his face, and Matt guessed that she was pretty much screwed, and not in a pleasant way.

"Now Matt, light of my life," Bryne said in a quiet, mocking tone. "We can either do this the hard way, or the easy way—entirely up to you, my darling," he teased. He took a step or two towards her, the blood from his nose slowed to a thick, congealed trickle.

"Do what?" Matt spat at the boy, her eyes fixed firmly on his and blazing with fear and hate.

Matt knew in her gut that this was not meant to end well, that she would most likely end up dead or initiated into something far worse, she'd seen enough exploitation movies on the top-loading VHS player to know at least that much. Matt also knew that she had a fair chance of fighting her way out of this. Having said that, the big guy gripping her shoulder was unnaturally strong, and she figured she'd tire out pretty quickly, her body fatigued from the bruising and sheer panic from falling into the hole; any attack would have to be swift and effective. Matt curled her fingers, making them into rigid claws; all ready to claw out Bryne's eyes should it be necessary.

"Become one of us, of course," Bryne replied. As he spoke, he nonchalantly cracked his nose back into place with two of his fingers.

The sound it made reminded Matt of a sodden stick snapping and it made her feel sick to her stomach. "And what is that, exactly?" she asked, not really wanting to know the answer. She kind of had a sinking feeling that this was some kind a sex cult—she was all free love and easy screwing, and Bryne was especially fuckable, but she really didn't swing that way—and wondered what had drawn them to her if that were the case. Was there something about her that screamed *slut*?

"A Black Eyed Kid," one of the guys replied.

Matt stared at him.

"A Black Eyed Kid…?" Matt repeated the words slowly, deliberately, as if they were strangely alien in her mouth.

"Yeah," another of the guys—Carter—said. "That's what Harry said, you stupid or something?"

"Is that supposed to mean something to me?" Matt asked, confused and more than a tad insulted that they saw her as any kind of kid—she was seventeen for Christ's sakes! Truth was, she'd never heard of Black Eyed Kids before, much less met one; and if she was supposed to be impressed by their whole hot, mysterious gang thing, they were looking at the wrong girl.

"You want to fill her in, Ward?" Bryne said with a sly grin to the big guy who still had his fat, stubby fingers digging into the soft flesh Matt's shoulder.

Ward snorted his derision, as if Matt were something he just stepped in on the sidewalk. "Kid, we've been around before you've been born," he said, his voice deadpan as if this was a well-rehearsed speech. "We've also been out of people's sights for a long, long time— humans have a ridiculously short memory span, and even the few that do have a long memory, well—they really can't do anything about us in the long run." He let go of Matt's shoulder and leaned against the wall—stick a cigarette in his mouth and he'd look like some fat parody of James Dean.

"And you just happened to choose me?" Matt asked. She looked across at Bryne who was running a pale white hand through his short, bleached blonde hair.

"I saw something in you Matt, something dark. Haven't you always wondered why you couldn't stand being with your human family, having those vaguely suicidal thoughts? Sometimes having to put on sunglasses during the night?" He pulled out a switch knife with a keen, glinting blade that was adorned with peculiar markings and took a purposeful look towards Matt.

Matt eyed the knife with a sick knot in her guts.

Matt shrugged. "Sometimes. I just figured it had something to do with me being resentful," she said, her mind dwelling on the fact that she'd pretty much taken sole care of her family since her mother was not there emotionally or mentally to take care of them anymore.

Bryne hummed but didn't answer.

Frozen in fear, Matt tried to back away from the switchblade, but by the time Bryne was standing directly in front of her, it was too late.

With a lightning swift motion, Bryne jabbed the knife into Matt's stomach. Winded by the force of the blow, shocked by the feel of the cold steel slipping through her insides, Matt clutched at her bleeding midriff and gasped loudly. "What the f—?" She groaned as instinctively she pressed her hands to the jagged rip in her belly, exerting what pressure she could onto the wound so that she wouldn't bleed out and die on the chilly, filthy floor she sank down onto.

"Welcome to the new nightlife, Matt Reeves," Bryne said with his sharp teeth glistening in the half-light. And Matt didn't have the time to question how the boy knew her last name before her head slammed hard to the ground and her world went completely black.

"Dude," Carter said as he looked down at Matt, his eyes transfixed to the bloodied hole in her bare midriff; it was already beginning to heal at a rapid pace, along with the ribs she'd cracked when she'd fallen through the trap—he could hear the sound the bones made as they shifted and knitted back together in her still chest.

"Yeah," Harry agreed.

"Dude," Carter said.

"Dude!" Harry joined in,

"We get the point," Ward snapped, annoyed at the clowning. He'd have thought that having lived with Harry and Carter for so long that he'd be used to it, but no, he never had and they still irritated the crap out of him, goddammit.

"When is she supposed to wake up?" Harry asked. Ward shrugged and then bent down to take a better look at Matt. He pried open her eyelids and saw that they were completely black, the transformation was all but complete. He studied the girl's beautiful face and grinned for the first time in a very long time.

"Look, he *can* smile!" Matt said, her words groggy and slurred, her mouth grave dirt dry. Ward helped her up off of the ground with one hefty yank on her blood slicked arms and a sharp crackling noise echoed in the cavernous room.

Carter winced at the noise and whistled between his teeth as he studied the newly metamorphosed girl. Matt's arms were almost entirely black, and from where parts of her jeans ripped, it appeared that most of her legs were similarly colored. Her nails looked to be a tad bit sharper too, and in stark contrast to her darkened limbs, Matt's face was a ghostly, chalky white—Carter thought that Matt looked like a wilder, angrier and decidedly female version of Jim Morrison.

Matt struggled to gain control of her raging emotions, which in her new state was proving somewhat problematic; instead, she found herself growing angrier and angrier, a thick red mist clouding her enhanced vision. Matt stepped forward towards the gang, her elongated finger nails clicking against each other as she stared each and every one of the boys down as the full realization of what had happened to her hit home. Slowly, deliberately, Matt stalked up to Bryne, air in the room filled with icy tension.

But, before Matt had time to act upon the boiling rage that churned deep down like a living, malevolent thing in the pit of her stomach, Bryne split the eerie silence between them. "I think that it's time to go hunting, boys," he said with a wicked smile.

Matt stopped dead in her tracks, all of her evil intent dissipating like dew on a summer's morning. She wasn't entirely sure she liked the sound of that. What exactly was Bryne's version of hunting? Luring yet more hapless people down into his trap until he had a whole coven of black eyed people to do his bidding?

Ward pressed a long finger to his lips as Matt opened her mouth, her question silenced. She sensed that if she was going to survive whatever this was, she was going to have to follow *some* guidelines, no matter how much they may rankle.

Bryne led her outside, the others close behind. Matt's skin tingled in the outside air, nails shrinking back to their more usual form and she let out an involuntary hiss at this new and unknown sensation. Matt patted her face, hoping that nothing untoward had grown there and was relieved to find that her skin was as smooth as it had ever been. She walked over to her motorcycle and slid her right leg over the coolness of the seat. And there she perched, no thoughts of gunning the engine and tearing off along the highway away from Bryne and the others—she simply sat patiently and waited for the others to mount their rides.

"This is going to be fun!" Harry laughed.

"Just follow us," Bryne said to Matt, choosing to ignore Harry's idiocy. He climbed onto his awaiting bike and it soon roared to life between his powerful thighs. Bryne sped off along the tired old street that had certainly seen better days.

Matt popped a wheelie as she followed Bryne, the wind battering against her face as the sea salt greeted her lips in a friendly kiss. She smiled to herself, most likely she'd get windburn for this, but she honestly didn't care.

The billboards declaring the ongoing Pepsi VS Coca Cola war (*which one would* you *choose?*) appeared to be practically omnipresent the farther they traveled from the hellhole she'd awoken to less than an hour previous, and Matt grinned at the beautiful, swimsuit-clad people rollerblading on the hot cement. She heard a scream from somewhere ahead and Matt's hackles rose, her heart racing. She sped by the movie theatre—they were re-showing the *Nightmare on Elm Street* movie for some stupid reason and the scream was from a young blonde chick who'd been scared witless by some idiot dressed as Krueger who was playing the line.

Quickly distracted from that, Matt felt something itching beneath her skin; almost as if something was clawing to get out, to be free. It felt to her like myriad ants crawling the length and breadth of her body, and she didn't like it, not one bit. Matt rubbed at her arms as she rode—one at a time—hoping that the friction of her leather jacket rubbing against her skin would make the itching stop. If anything, the harsh caress of the leather made it worse. She realized, too, that her teeth were also beginning to hurt, and wondered if that was because she'd been grinding them so hard back in the room where she had arisen like some present-day Lazarus, or from something altogether more sinister. Matt hoped to dear God it was because of the grinding; she really didn't think she could handle becoming a motherfucking vampire right now.

Matt grasped the bars on her motorcycle as a sudden burst of suicidal thoughts thumped through her mind with full force as she caught sight of Luna Cliff. Through the rush of wind whistling through her ears, she heard the seductive sounds of the waves that crashed so relentlessly against the sharp rocks upon which dozens of people had impaled themselves across the years, lives ended, bodies pounded to little more than rotting fish food.

Soon, Bryne, Matt and the others stopped in a quiet, run-down neighborhood. There were a bunch of sorry-looking houses built closely together, each one with an absurdly spacious front lawn. Some of the lawns were in pristine condition, but most contained only a handful of straggly flowers and large, dusty dead spots created by dog pee and lack of water.

"What are we here for?" Matt asked, although she had a sinking feeling that she already knew the answer. She looked around, nervous, and saw that there was absolutely no one around and that the windows of every home were firmly closed. And through the curtainless windows of the nearest house, Matt could see that the occupants were watching *Miami Vice*.

"You'll see," Bryne said, and as Matt stared at the boy, the handsome features of his face shifted and changed to make him appear much, much younger. With great, confident strides, Bryne walked along the path and up to the front door of the house.

Matt's mouth opened wide in shock upon witnessing Bryne's remarkable transformation

"Is that an invitation?" Carter asked with a lascivious grin and gestured towards Matt's mouth.

"Shut up, asshole," Ward growled and slapped his compatriot upside the head.

They all watched as Bryne knocked on the door of the house. A woman in her mid 30's opened the door with a smile on her face as she looked out at what appeared to be a fourteen year old kid on her stoop. Bryne offered a pitiful smile and stared at the woman with a pleading look in his eyes.

"Can I use your phone, lady? I'm lost," He sniffled.

Matt watched as the woman froze, as if she'd caught the feeling from the off that this was not all it seemed to be; something perhaps to do with the unearthly vibe Bryne was giving out, Matt knew that some people were more sensitive to the otherworldly than others.

Smart lady.

"I—I don't think that's a good idea," the woman said and backed away from Bryne. She appeared to reach for something secreted behind the door and Matt figured it was most likely a baseball bat—the lady didn't look much like the gun type. And in a dark corner of Matt's mind, she kind of hoped she'd get to see the woman use whatever it was on Bryne.

"Please, lady, I just need your phone," Bryne whimpered, although a little of his pleasant composure slipped at the woman's hostility.

"I'm sorry," she said and slammed the door in Bryne's face.

Bryne leaned against the peeling paint of the thin door. "I know you're still there, lady, I can see your shadow," he taunted.

No answer.

Bryne waited awhile in silence and when eventually he did walk away from the house, Matt noted that it was with a jaunty pep and a look in his eye that made the boy appear incredibly *refreshed*. As if he'd just eaten a hearty meal. And as he walked, his features aged and in two shakes of a lamb's tail, he was back to his normal self.

"So, this is how you eat—?" Matt asked as Bryne climbed back onto his bike.

"You certainly catch on quick," Bryne's voice dripped sarcasm. He gave her a broad, wicked smile and added, "And Matt? It's the way *you* eat now, too."

Fuck.

"No." Matt gulped audibly, her mouth bone dry and aching. "You have to reverse what you did to me, you bastard." She snarled and gestured towards her body which still tickled and crawled, making Matt feel like some dirty junkie desperate for her next fix.

"Can't be done, babe," Bryne replied cheerfully.

"So—what—?"

"It was back in the 1400's, you know?" Bryne offered by means of an explanation. "I was young and stupid back then, laying down with any piece of tail I could because I had the money—and what do you know, I caught me a disease that killed me in the end, there were plenty of those around back then." He let out a thin, strained chuckle. "Fun times, huh?"

Matt's eyebrows furrowed as she tried to read the boy's deadpan countenance.

"Anyways—I found out a neat way to cheat death." he continued. "All I had to do was find a crossroads demon and to sell my eternal soul to the devil," he sounded quite matter of fact about this, as if discussing how best to fix a motorcycle problem. "The deal is that I must collect souls at the crossroads—those who are stupid enough to wish themselves to me—it's quite easy once you get into it." He offered Matt a wry smile and a shrug of his shoulders. "I was actually supposed to go back to the crossroads and surrender my own soul a long time ago, but I never did—I guess the demons are happy to let things lie as long as I'm providing them with souls. The boys and I chose to stay here, and we picked *you*."

"Thanks—I feel so fucking special," Matt growled.

"And so you should," Bryne told her, his tone without humor. He ran his lithe fingers through his spiked, blonde hair that glowed in the moonlight and Matt thought that he looked a little like Billy Idol. "You're the first one that I've ever turned," Bryne said with a glance at the left-hand side of Matt's face, which was blackening like the flesh of some long-dead corpse.

"So I'm just some kind of lab experiment to you?" Matt scoffed. She wanted nothing more than to lash out at Bryne, but she had a gut feeling that she would seriously regret that; plus there was the simple fact that Bryne had, in effect, created her, and didn't that go against biology?

"Pretty much," Bryne laughed.

Matt glowered at the boy's handsome features and muttered underneath her breath.

Chapter Two

"I'm not doing it," Matt said with firm resolution in her voice. She stared at the dark wood of the door through which she could hear the muted sound of David Bowie ordering his goblins to laugh.

"Aha, why not, *Matthew*?" Carter said with that shit-eating grin of his, he knew full-well that Matt hated her unabbreviated name. "Children are such tasty little things."

Ward shrugged his agreement, for once choosing to remain silent.

Bryne groaned—loudly—this was going to be much harder than he thought. Snorting his frustration, he dragged Matt away from the door by the nape of her neck, an idea forming in his mind; was it not close to Halloween—that most *delicious* holiday of all?

Bryne's trench coat billowed out beh2ind him as he walked along the sidewalk and towards the carnival, eying the children who passed beside him with tooth-rotting candy bulging in their gaily decorated bags. He smiled as they quickened their step when they looked up and saw who he was, some practically sprinting as they held on tightly to their dearly earned prizes.

Ward bared his slightly uneven teeth at the children, pleased with the nourishing fear that his rictus grin elicited and making it pretty clear as to what may happen should they get too close to him or his gang. He, Bryne and his cohorts walked through the sparsely populated carnival, up to a ride that was only there for a short time—it made an appearance each year and was a definite crowd puller. They waited until the blue cart started to move before they made their way into the ride, Matt in tow.

They sat in the backmost cart, watching with intent as one of the carts ahead of them, one that held a group of older kids and three small children, each one squirming in the all too small seats. One of the youths held a young child that looked to be around five— maybe six years old—who held to her mouth a large, blue cotton candy stick that was larger than her head. Beside the girl, her brother—possibly only two years older held her hand so that she wouldn't attempt to get off the ride. The other child was much older and somehow didn't seem to belong to their little group, and he looked around at the spooky attraction, eyes wide with awe.

The attraction itself contained myriad fake spider webs that draped pretty much everywhere and harbored fairly convincing plastic spiders with menacing red eyes. There were Draculas, too, that popped out of their caskets whenever a cart neared, to elicit those delicious, shrill screams of fearful delight. All in all, the whole thing was really quite tacky, and Matt couldn't help but wonder how she had ever been afraid of such things when she was younger.

"Ready to make your move, Matt?" Bryne asked her, amusement dancing in his eyes as the cart trundled along on its rickety tracks.

"Sure," Matt said quietly.

In perfect synch, everyone—with the exception of Matt—jumped out of the cart and waited in their prearranged places. When the string of carts neared the dim exit sign, they all jumped out of the inky shadows shrieking and hollering to scare the living shit out of the little kids. Not wishing to face Bryne's wrath, Matt jumped on the cart and joined in with terrifying the children; giving it her full on demon, even going so far as to slit open a wrist with the switchblade Carter had given her.

The blood from the jagged tear in Matt's wrist—not much more than a shallow slice and nowhere close to a vein—dripped out on the little girl's cotton candy and the all of children screamed bloody murder.

"Matt?"

Matt glanced to her side, and her eyes widened. There, her little brother stared at her with sheer terror and disbelief in his eyes at the sight of his sister who was clearly no longer human. Horrified that in her new state she had not recognized her own sibling, Matt opened her mouth to say something to the poor, traumatized boy, *anything;* but there was an insistent yank on the collar of her shirt and with a fleeting apology in her eyes, she was gone.

"Did you have to do that? He's family!" Matt hissed. She slapped Bryne's hand away and glared at him.

"Family? Let's get real here, Matt—you've never considered your family *your family* in the first place." Bryne growled. "*We're* your family now," he added with a soupcon of menace.

"You still didn't have to do that," Matt grumbled.

"Of course I did—you were going to go further with them, weren't you?" One sharply defined eyebrow raised.

Matt hated to admit it, but Bryne was right. Matt *was* going to take her gruesome show a step further, just to make the taste of the kid's fear a tad bit sharper; she had quickly acquired the taste for it and found that children's terror filled her up in all the right places. To Matt, it felt akin to when in the summer she'd just had the right amount of sun on her skin without getting sunburned, or to being fresh out of the shower with hot, tingling flesh—that crawling ant sensation on her skin feeling was finally gone. She wanted *more* because she was already getting greedy, and wasn't that a frightening thought all by itself?

She looked down and saw that the skin on her bare arms was no longer black, and she let out a long, drawn out sigh of relief. Even in the garish glow of the carnival lights she could see that her skin was a far more healthy looking chalky white with just a hint of a blue tinge to it—looked a little weird, but hey, you lose you win some.

Matt flexed her gloved hands and looked up at Bryne but didn't answer his question; there really was no need, because he *knew*. Bryne smirked at her and opened the doors to the bunker to where Matt's life had so quickly become a shitshow, and Matt sighed as she followed him down the stairs, wishing once more that she wasn't such a dumbass.

"Where are we supposed to sleep?" She asked as the boys kicked off their shoes, her eyes beginning to droop with fatigue.

Ward pointed at the poles that were installed into the ceiling and Matt stared in disbelief. Ward laughed loudly, and Matt realized that it was the first time she'd heard anything close to mirth coming from the boy's mouth since they'd met and oddly, that unsettled her more than anything else that had happened to her that day.

"I'm just screwing with ya—your room is down that way," Ward said and jerked a thumb towards the hallway that she'd not noticed before. Matt flipped Ward off as she set off towards the hallway, yanking open the heavy, creaking door with a weary tug that had the tired muscles in her arm complaining.

Her designated room was painted a dull, lifeless gray, and at the dead center there sat an oversized bed with a thick, metal frame that looked like something straight from medieval times. She stroked the cold steel with tentative fingers, as if expecting the bed frame to burn her, and when it didn't, she felt strangely disappointed; Matt craved the sensation, like she deserved it.

She clambered beneath the crisp, white covers that were tight-stretched over the sumptuously thick mattress and sighed at their cool, gentle caress upon her tender skin. And in the instant her exhausted head hit the firm duck down pillow; Matt fell into a deep, troubled sleep and dreamt of her new life.

After a short while, Bryne peered into Matt's bed chamber, studying with pride—his brand new creation.

He watched her sleep awhile, studied the roll and twitch of her eyes beneath their sealed lids, her chest rising and falling with mechanical regularity, the moon's chilly light glowing upon her delectably pale skin, and he felt immensely satisfied with what he had done.

All in all, Matt Reeves looked like she was meant for the new life he had gifted her. Quietly, Byrne closed the door behind him and left Matt alone to her vivid dreams.

That following morning, refreshed from a heavy night's sleep, and shaking off much of the shock of what had happened to her the day before at the hands of Byrne and his motley crew, Matt crawled her ass out of the way too comfortable bed, pushed back her hair and looked for a mirror, to fix her appearance up to face her brand new day.

There was one in the corner of the dingy room, a grimy square of cracked, slivered glass, precariously hanging onto the gray painted, bare brick wall by a tattered piece of string and an old, rusted nail. She squinted at her reflection in the struggling light and staggered back at what stared back out at her.

She looked like some grim spectre, as if the mirror itself no longer recognized her as human or anything close to that. Scared, Matt pressed a hand against the mirror and felt a cold, clammy panic coursing through her trembling body. Put quite simply, she just didn't look like herself anymore; the Matt Reeves that she'd thought she'd known was completely gone.

And in her place, she saw a girl with dark brown hair covering her forehead, and whose eyes were the darkest shade of black; gone was the iridescent blue that would startle people whenever she looked at them, in its place, the hue of a whole new kind of frightening; no wonder her kid brother had looked at her the way he did.

Her arms were black once more, the skin on her forearms smooth and dark, yet it was with some relief that Matt saw that her upper arms were not; they had remained that pale—almost translucent—white that she so loved. Absently, Matt rubbed at them, hoping perhaps that they would turn a healthy human pink color, but that turned out to be little more than wishful thinking.

Still, she told herself, at least she wasn't a shitsucker.

Matt pulled the mirror from the wall, the tiny nail pinging off and clattering somewhere in the gloom behind her. She hurled the glass at the floor, smashing the thing into myriad tinkling shards that returned her gaze with her own black, accusing eyes. Heart sinking, a low, grumbling ache in the pit of her belly, Matt walked away from them, and out of the grim confines of the room, closing the door behind her with a resounding bang.

The gang were sitting around reading magazines, a couple of them idly cleaning their keen claws with their switchblades.

Matt wrinkled her nose at the odious gunk they gouged out from their nail beds, her guts churning as they flicked the stuff on to the floor.

"Don't knock it until you try it, Mattie, only way to get the dirt out," Harry told her with a dumb grin, not even bothering to glance her way as he pocketed his blade.

"If you say so," she replied with a grimace.

A beat up boom box sat in one corner of the room, perched precariously upon a wobbly old camping table. The unmistakable sound of Bon Jovi wafted quietly from the music machine, and Matt couldn't help but tap her foot to the beat of *Bad Medicine* as she eagerly awaited the bad ass guitar riff she knew was on its way;

and a part of her cried out inside, as memories of a life left behind flooded her mind.

"You guys wanna hit up the pier tonight?" Bryne said, leaning back in his chair like some big shot. "Teenagers with heartache always end up at the crossroads at this time of the year."

"Sounds fun," everyone agreed.

Everyone, that is, except Matt. She remained quiet.

Bryne sighed.

He knew was going to have to fix this—everyone had trouble accepting their new selves in the beginning—but Matt really was taking this to a whole new level, with her petulant display of regret. He would have to show her that she was *meant* to be part of their elite pack, and that it was a true honor to have been selected. Plus, she was going to have to suck it up, accept what she had become, and understand once and for all that there was no going back.

And, if for some reason the stupid girl decided to go home, which was always a danger, despite his warnings, Bryne was fully prepared to have to take care of the problem—should it arise.

***

Night came soon enough, and Bryne led his gang out into the enveloping cloak of the darkness beyond their lair. Through habit, they gravitated towards the Ferris Wheel, attracted like moths to a porch light to its gaudy covering of glittering bright lights. They blended into the crowd and watched as the plethora of aimless teenagers passed by them, not one of them caring to pay any attention to the bikers that leaned against the wall and studied everyone with dark, hungry eyes.

"I think that one's going to do something stupid," Matt said. He pointed to one spotty faced teen who was talking in an exaggerated, animated fashion to a younger girl who was busy ignoring him in favor of an older, bigger jock who was making no bones about checking out the impressive twin mounds that pushed out her tight sweater.

"A good eye, my friend," Bryne said with an approving sneer, "a *very* good eye."

Without warning, Matt clasped a hand to her chest. Gasping, she fell to the ground on her knees, groaning in agony. "What's happening to me?" She stuttered as her chest let out an eerie orange glow that shone through the thin material of her shirt, illuminating her breasts from behind. Matt clutched at her chest, as if attempting to stifle the glow, her newly sprouting claws tearing minute slices in the flimsy cotton.

"You're getting your first call!" Bryne informed her, as matter of fact as if this was a dull, everyday occurrence. "Congratulations, Matt!"

"Fuck—" Matt cursed before she disappeared.

It felt to Matt like her body was being tugged every which way, and her eye sockets burned from the inside out with the dazzling array of psychedelic colors that ensnared *all* of her senses. She closed her eyes tight, fighting the irrepressible urge to gag—although precisely what she had to throw up, she had no idea because she no longer ate. Still, the nauseating sensation rode through her guts and sent the acid tang of bile to sting the back of her throat.

The ground crunched underneath Matt's shoes, and she allowed herself a sigh of relief as once more she felt the solidity of *terra firma* beneath her feet. Mercifully, too, her stomach no longer felt like it was going to turn itself spectacularly inside out; and when she dared open her eyes, her only companion was the same young man she'd seen before, standing at the particularly well groomed crossroad with a shovel clutched tightly in his hands.

Byrne and the boys caught up with Matt at the crossroad. They, too, recognized the young man, and as they approached, they heard all too clearly the exchange between him and the girl.

"I've seen you before!" He said, backing away from Matt, clinging on to his shovel as if his very life depended upon the thing. "I never thought that the rumors were true!"

"Seriously?" Matt scoffed at the young man. "You didn't think the black eyes were a dead giveaway?"

"Good point." The young man all but smiled.

"What is your business here?" Matt asked, leaning towards the guy, as if trying to catch his scent. She wasn't quite sure precisely how this worked, but she figured she'd got the gist from Bryne; somehow she would take a person's soul because they wanted something so badly that they were prepared to sell it to the Devil himself. At this, Matt felt a nagging sliver of unease for the young man and couldn't help but wonder if he really knew what he was doing.

"I want her to love me," the young man told Matt.

"Is that it?" Matt asked him in disbelief. He was prepared to sell his immortal soul for one stupid girl who barely knew he existed? Oh, she felt so sorry for the poor guy.

"Yes," the guy replied, his eyes cast downwards, "that's it."

"It's your choice," Matt said with a resigned sigh, "I'll be back in ten years." She held out her hand out for the guy to shake. Timidly, the guy relinquished one hand's hold on the shovel and shook Matt's hand, his own clammy with nervous sweat.

As they touched, Matt felt her body jolt as the young man's soul entered her body. She closed her eyes and revelled in the unexpected burst of pleasure that swept across her senses, delighted at just how sensually *warm* it felt.

As the delectable sensations ebbed, Matt opened her eyes to look at the young man who appeared pale and drawn, as if during the act of handing over his very soul, the enormity of what he had done had finally dawned.

"A pleasure doing business with you," she said to the young man, and disappeared in the same manner in which she had arrived.

Matt reappeared at the pier and threw up behind the Ferris Wheel, her hand clutching the cool, graffitied metal railing to steady herself as little more than a dribble of hot, yellow slime ejected from her tormented stomach. Done, Matt rested her head against the cold steel, enjoying its soothing touch upon her fevered brow.

"What have I done?"

Chapter Three

"She did better than you did your first time!" Bryne said to Harry with a hearty laugh at the guy's expense.

Harry scowled. "At least I wasn't a fuck up like Carter—he went back the same year and killed *his* guy off in a car accident. People are still talking about that one!" He pointed accusingly at Carter, who launched himself at Harry with a growl and tackled him to the ground, pushing his face to the sand and demanded he say *uncle*.

Matt was still pale and shaky on her feet when Byrne and his gang caught up with her back by the pier. She looked up to find Byrne standing by her side. She wiped her face with the back of her wrist and grimaced at him.

"See what I mean, Matt?" Byrne smiled. "You are *totally* meant for this life!" He wrapped a protective arm around her shoulders and led her back towards the bright lights of the pier, where Matt could taste the salty tang of people's fear.

As they walked, Byrne's fingernail nicked the soft skin of Matt's neck. She gasped at the sharpness of the pain and grasped at herself, feeling a thin trickle of blood making its way down her neck. She side-eyed Bryne, who looked as if he didn't realize what he had done. Or didn't care. The blood on her neck made her skin feel tacky, dirty, and she scowled.

Matt still felt wobbly from what she'd done to the young man at the crossroad, and to her chagrin, she could feel the itchiness creeping beneath her skin again, that unwelcome, decidedly unpleasant sensation. And, along with it, there came the familiar, deep hunger that clawed at her stomach, and she moaned inwardly; for it meant only one thing to her.

A gaggle of young men walked by, jostling each other and being loud in the way of juvenile drinkers. They stared at her, eyes undressing her, crawling the length and breadth of her body. Matt smiled at them.

"Hey baby!" one of the guys called over, and his friends accompanied him with ribald wolf whistles and obscene gestures.

Matt had an overwhelming urge to tear into them, rip their stupid throats out and claw open their soft, warm bodies and watch as their viscera slopped out onto the pier in one big, steaming, stinking mess. This was a new development for Matt, she could all but *taste* the coppery aftertaste of their blood on her tongue and was distressed to realize that it made her feel hungry.

Quickly, Matt pushed the feelings down; she wasn't a murderer, and she certainly had no intention of becoming one.

Her throat throbbed uncomfortably.

Desperately, Matt tried to avoid looking at the guys; they were a ways down the pier now and had moved on to the next unfortunate girl who caught their inebriated attention. But still that gnawing hunger for bloodshed ate at Matt's insides, like some malignant parasite demanding its next feed.

She saw her little brother—he was sitting on a bench pretending to read a newspaper—peering over the thing like he'd seen in the comedy movies he enjoyed so much, trying his level best not to appear to be spying on his big sister, but failing miserably.

Matt groaned quietly to herself and made her way over to the boy—Byrne and the others had split up to look for their own meals so no one noticed her leaving their side—and so without further ado, Matt sat herself down next to her brother, wincing as she saw his breath hitch and a shadow of fear cross his angelic little face.

"Matt?" he whispered.

"Do you know how dangerous this is?" Matt hissed at the boy. "Showing up here and spying on me?" She pushed her legs out, trying to appear casual just in case Bryne came looking for her—she had yet to fathom his fascination with her, beyond the obvious, of course.

"What happened to you, Matt? You just upped and disappeared." The kid sounded genuinely worried. As he spoke, he looked at Matt from the corner of his eye, keeping his face forward so as not to garner attention, and looking extremely dorky while doing so.

Matt snorted. "Yeah—it wasn't my choice. I thought I was just going out with some new friends, but it turned out that it wasn't like that," she explained with a shake of her head, "as you saw for yourself last night."

"Mom's worried," her brother offered.

"Don't bullshit me," Matt scoffed at the kid, "that bitch hasn't worried about me since I was eight years old." She looked at her little brother and saw the sadness in his bright blue eyes. "I'm sorry that I was never around for you—and that I was a crappy big sister. But what's done now is done." She said, her eyes tracing the fat, loud headline of the newspaper that sat crumpled on the kid's lap:

CHALLENGER SPACE SHUTTLE DISASTER!

A shiver ran down Matt's spine, and when she looked up from the grainy monochrome picture of the fiery plume that spelled out the deaths of seven astronauts—one of them a teacher, for Christ's sakes— she saw that Bryne was looking for her.

Matt shuddered inwardly; she was never going to be able to have a moment for herself. Her little brother peeped up from his newspaper, following his sister's pained gaze. Matt shoved the newspaper back over the kid's face. "Don't look," she hissed.

Calmly, Matt got up and made her way over to Bryne and the others, desperate to put some distance between the freaks and her brother.

"Don't worry, Matt, I won't forget about you," the kid said to her back. "I'll find a way to help you— promise."

Matt ignored him.

"Found a pretty blonde to take out tonight?" Ward asked wryly as Matt strode up to them with a smirk fixed on her face that she didn't quite feel.

"You could say that," Matt said. She stretched out her arms and popped her knuckles with a satisfying crunch that echoed loudly through her gloved fingers.

Matt's complexion was turning back to the sickly, chalk-white once more, and the guys stared at her. They knew that she either had to feed quite a bit more, or that they had to take her home before she got out of hand.

"I'll be right back," Ward said, with a strange half wink that distorted his face.

"What was that about?" Matt asked Byrne, her thin eyebrows furrowing as she watched Ward turn a corner and disappear. She breathed in heavily to steady her nerves, inhaling the delectable aroma of churros and corn dogs.

A perfectly wonderful combination.

"You didn't feed enough, did you?" Bryne asked Matt, pinching her chin with two of his fingers as he stared into her eyes. Although disappointed at her lack of sustenance, he was pleased to see that her eyes were taking on their permanent black color.

Matt's lips pursed as she tore her face away from Bryne's tight grasp. She glared at her maker. Said nothing.

"That's what I thought," Bryne said. He let go of Matt's chin to acknowledge Ward's return. Bryne gave the guy a nod of satisfaction at the sight of the two jocks he'd brought with him. They both looked as dumb as a box of rocks, one sporting a bright green Mohawk, the other completely bald.

"I'm sorry! I didn't know that those were your bikes! We would've brought your bikes back!" Mohawk wailed, fear etched all over his spotty face.

"You don't have to apologize to these fuckers!" the bald one growled. He hawked and spat at Ward's foot, his eyes flashing defiance.

Without warning, Ward stomped on the guy's foot—hard—and Bald Guy's eyes widened and his mouth fell open in a silent yowl.

From where she was standing, Matt heard the guy's toes crunch—one by agonized one. Matt felt the jock's fear bleed into her body, and she sighed in relief—as much as the sudden flash of violence had sickened her, the nourishment it had provided felt so incredibly good. The gnawing hunger in her stomach was gone, but the feeling of wanting to tear into one of the jocks was still there—something innately primitive and irrefutably savage; something that Matt knew she had no chance of suppressing.

Coldly, calmly, Matt stalked towards Mohawk and tore into his body with her razor sharp claws. And for as much as the jock screamed and struggled, Matt overpowered him with ease, the need to fill her body with fear was too strong for her to contain.

Blood splashed everywhere, soaking the ground, the wall, the jock's bald headed friend, and Matt. She cracked open Mohawk's skull with her foot as he crumpled to the cold, hard dirt and the pinky-gray of his brain matter splattered against the bars of the Ferris wheel. And still Matt savaged the body, although it no longer resembled anything even remotely human, its parts no longer connected, its innards spilled out and soaking into the dirt.

Drenched head to toe in blood, gore and the slippery mucus of viscera, Matt looked like something ghoulish straight out of a horror film; she looked up at Byrne, licking her lips as she crouched over the bloodied mess she had made.

The bald guy stood frozen to the spot, sheer terror overriding any natural urge to fight or flee; his mouth gaped wide with a strained, wheezing sound coming from it, as if he were screaming with cut vocal. With a weary sigh and roll of the eyes, Bryne snapped the guy's neck before the scream found its voice, and the jock slumped to the ground next to the mutilated corpse of his friend.

"And that is exactly what happens when you don't feed," Bryne chastised Mast. He glanced dawn with disdain at the mess she'd made of the jock, and then he winced at the state of the girl's clothes; they were ripped to shreds and drenched in the dark crimson which glinted wetly in the gaudy lights of the Ferris Wheel.

Matt was completely out of it, the fear that came along with killing gave her more strength and she felt like she was flying; her chest heaved with exertion, her eyes black and demonic, glaring out from her gore-soaked face. This was one hell of a high, her racing mind told her, *even better* than the time twelve year old Matt had gotten into her mother's mushroom stash, secreted in a small, white cookie jar in the laundry room.

"The first kill is always the hardest," Carter told Matt as he stooped to pick up the jock's strewn body parts that were scattered across the ground, seeping the last of their blood into the dirt. Looking up, he grinned at the Ferris Wheel as it turned, its garish, multicoloured lights reflecting in the blackness of his eyes. "Are you thinking what I'm thinking?" He asked Harry. Harry nodded, his face cracked in a broad grin. Carter dropped the jock's arm he'd retrieved from the dirt and cackling, he followed Harry towards the wheel, all but skipping like a pair of naughty school children.

***

The last thing Matt remembered was staring blankly at the ocean's rolling waves as they smashed against the rocks and into Bryne's dark, fathomless eyes.

She awoke sitting upright in a decidedly uncomfortable chair, her head leaning forward at an awkward angle. She groaned loudly at the crick in her neck. She rubbed at it, grimacing at the dull throb in her vertebrae and glared at Bryne who was staring at her with some amusement.

Bryne laughed at the expression on Matt's face. "Look who's *finally* awake!" he said, grinning. He clapped his hands in delight and looked proudly at his new protégé.

Matt cast her mind back to the night before, her thoughts still nebulous.

She gasped.

The thoughts came flooding back to her; of refusing to feed and then the overwhelming urge to rip into the warm, living flesh of some stranger. Of tearing apart the jock with the Mohawk like he was nothing, and relishing the high that she never wanted to end, and of staring into Bryne's eyes. Blood had sprayed everywhere, which she remembered vividly, Matt stared down at her clothes.

She grimaced.

To her chagrin, Matt was barely wearing any clothes at all, the rips and tears in what remained of them exposed pretty much all of her pale skin beneath. Absently, she fingered the very obvious tears that were staring at everyone in the face, shivering against the cool air that caressed her near-naked body.

"Don't worry about it, Matt," Harry said with a soupcon of sincerity, "I don't think anyone noticed that those were *real* body parts at the attraction, probably think they're leftovers from Halloween." Harry cackled, bumping fists with Carter.

"For now," Ward said dryly.

Bryne's short, bleached blonde hair shone iridescent in the moonlight. Matt tried not to stare at it, instead, she shook her head and grumbled, "What am I supposed to do with *this*?" She tugged at the remains of her shirt, further exposing her breasts. "I can't walk around in broad daylight with ripped clothes! I'll get arrested!"

"That's no problem," Bryne told her. "You can scare someone into giving you clothes." He shook his head at Matt and gave her a patronising smile.

Matt sucked on her teeth at his dismissive tone, determined not to get into it with Bryne. At least not just now. "Right," she said.

"Do you still feel hungry, Matt? After the way you tore into that guy—" Carter stopped dead as Bryne glared at him.

"I *could* eat," Matt shrugged.

"That does it then! Let's go find some people to scare!" Ward declared, and to a man—and woman— they climbed onto their motorcycles, gunned engines and roaring back out into the night.

***

"Now, Matt, *concentrate*. All you have to do is to imagine how you looked like when you were younger," Bryne said, leaning so close that Matt could feel his cold breath on the back of her neck.

She closed her eyes and thought hard, recalling how she didn't really have friends back then, and how she was always too small for her age because her mother spent all of their cash on drugs and junk food. Matt remembered the constant feeling of hunger back then, and the resentment she felt when her mother brought home her little brother, practically throwing him at her to bring up.

And with this, Matt's body shrank down into that of a small, pitiful child with shiny brown locks that cascaded all the way down to her waist, and large, bright blue eyes that rivalled Bryne's.

Bryne smiled at his creation, his white teeth gleaming in the sliver moonlight. "Perfect."

Matt approached the door of the house. Knocked timidly upon it with her little girl knuckles and cleared her throat.

The door eased open and Matt smiled brightly up at the woman within. She was, Matt guessed, early 30's, and was all gussied up, ready to go somewhere—her shoes looked expensive and her hair was tied up in a neat, tight bun. The woman's eyes widened as she took in the frightful sight of Matt in her torn up clothes.

"Where are your parents?" the lady asked Matt, bending over to eye level.

"I don't know," Matt replied, her voice small. She stared up at the woman with those big, baby blues. "Can I come in?" Matt said, "*please*?"

"I'm sorry," the woman gasped. She straightened up; her nostrils flared as if she'd caught scent of Matt's nefarious intent. Quickly, she slammed the door.

Matt closed her eyes at the sensation of the woman's fear entering her veins. Bryne came out from his hiding place in the bushes and took Matt's hand like she was actually a small child and led her quietly away.

She tore her hand from Bryne's when they were out of sight of the house and willed herself back to her regular size, ripped, bloodied clothes and all. As she grew, Matt felt the flimsy material ripping even more, and she didn't have to look down to know that her breasts were entirely exposed. She heard the sound of

Carter laughing, and she even managed a wan smile when she saw him holding up a selection of clothing.

"Thanks," she grumbled at him when he threw the clothes at her. She glanced at the offering and shrugged before stripping naked right there on the street, in front of Bryne and his gang. What did she care anyways? They'd seen just about everything she had to offer already—may as well cop an eyeful of all the goodies.

Carter had chosen well, the guy had quite the eye for fashion; a silky leather jacket—most likely calf hide—a red shirt to go beneath it, a pair of denim shorts that were practically indecent they were so brief, although they did show off Matt's legs to perfection. She slapped them on, and then slipped on her own-well worn boots that covered almost to her bare knees.

"That looks nice," Carter whistled.

"Yeah—at least my ass won't stick to my bike," Matt *harrumphed*. That was a sensation she hated, the hot leather clinging to her bare skin. "I'm just gonna head out for a ride," Matt declared, her eyes flashing towards Bryne, as if daring him to say otherwise.

"No worries—as long as know who you're coming home to," Bryne replied with an air of superiority.

Matt bit her tongue; Bryne could make a permission sound like a threat and grated on her already raw nerves.

"Alright—*mom*," Matt sassed the guy, taking great pleasure in the displeasure that crept across his face. And with that, Matt swung a leg over the seat of his motorcycle, revved the engine and tore off like the Devil himself was on her ass.

The wind bit into her face as she rode, the sharp tang of salt in the air made her lick her lips, and she smiled. She had no plan as to where she'd ride to, and it didn't really matter to her, because she knew her pack brothers could find her whenever they chose to do so. Still, a little time to herself was nice, you know?

Matt was surprised at herself for so readily embracing the new *her*, and the bizarre role that Matt had had thrust upon her; although she still resented having had no choice in the matter. What also surprised her was the stirring of mixed feelings she had for Bryne, all she wanted to do was run her fingers through that stark, blonde hair of his and caress his naked skin and find out if it really was as smooth as it looked...

"Oh, I'm so screwed." Matt muttered beneath her breath, the words lost to the wind. And in an instant, she felt the irrepressible urge to turn around—a *tugging* sensation—and she sighed. Bryne was impatient for her to return, that much she knew for certain. She looked down at her watch.

Shit.

She had been gone for two hours, no wonder Bryne was getting antsy.

Matt turned the bike around and headed back to the bunker, making the return trip in far less time than the outward. She parked Byrne's bike up along with the others and returned to her chair in the confines of her new home, pausing only to brush away a fat, black spider that was crawling across it.

"That was a long trip," Bryne growled, clearly not amused.

"Sorry," Matt mumbled, but not really sorry at all. She was, however, beginning to feel lethargic, the weariness in her bones spreading up to fog her brain. She looked around and saw that they were all showing signs of fatigue, and so when Carter arose from his chair with a loud, exaggerated yawn and headed off to his bedroom, she followed suit. Matt shuffled her weary way into her room, and pulled the door behind her, the lock clicking just as she collapsed upon the welcoming softness of her bed.

For as tired as she was, sleep evaded Matt, her mind whirring like a troublesome insect.

Maybe she wasn't so screwed after all?

If it were only that easy.

Chapter Four

Bryne was staring at her.

"What? Do I have something on me?" Matt asked. She looked down at her arms, her mouth flapping open with shock, and everyone burst into laughter. Although Matt's upper arms remained snowy white, her forearms were dark as ever, the smooth skin a rich, dark gray color that reminded her of death. And yet, Matt no longer cared that she had become *the* freak amongst the group of freaks.

Nonchalantly, she leaned back in her chair. She crossed her long, lithe legs and gave the gang a thoughtful glance. "So—do we ever get to eat regular food?" she asked, placing her hand underneath her chin.

"We *can*, but it doesn't taste as good as fear," Bryne told her, boredom in his tone.

"So let's go eat!" Matt jumped from her seat; she had no intention of being stuck down there in the dark, dank bunker for any longer than was necessary. She pulled on her jacket, enjoying the caress of the velvet soft leather on her discoloured arms.

Carter shrugged. "We haven't had human food in a while..." he mused, before following Matt out of the bunker.

Ward yelled after him, "You're not allowed outside without adult supervision, Carter! Not since the last time!" And, getting no response from his friend, he, too, followed Matt from the bunker.

Harry winked and fell in line, making his way outside into the night.

"Goddamnit, Carter, you'll be the death of me," Ward grumbled as he and Ward mounted their cycles and followed Matt and Carter, tearing recklessly through the darkened streets, pushing the limits of their machines and breaking every speed limit there was.

Matt's heart raced as her motorcycle purred beneath her body, the vibrations of the road coursing through her hands, and the wind whipped and screamed about her ears. She howled out loud with the joy of her newfound life, sounding akin to the lone coyotes that made their way into town in search of an easy trashcan dinner. The rest of the gang joined her, their high voices striking an odd resonance in the warm night air.

Matt swung her bike onto a small, rough road, her bike bumping along and sending sensual vibrations through her bare legs and shorts-clad ass; she felt a new rush swash through her veins.

This fresh feel of recklessness was electrifying, and Matt never wanted it to stop, deep down she felt *immortal*, and she wondered how come she'd not asked that question—*was she*?

Looking behind, Matt saw that they were all tagging along. She grinned at them and revved her engine. Bryne had been right, she *was* meant for this life; this is what she always imagined for herself—living totally free and having nothing to ever hold her back again. After so many years of being trapped beneath her mother's drug-addled thumb, bringing up her kid brother like she'd given birth to him, of having grown-up responsibility thrust upon her way too young—Matt Reeves was finally free!

They pulled up to the busy pier and parked their bikes.

Bryne nodded his head at Carter as they neared a fast food stand that reeked of hot fat and cheese. "Go get pizza," he ordered.

"Sure thing, boss!" Carter chirped with a skip in his voice.

The rest of them picked a spot at an uncomfortable bench, their knees knocking together in the confined space beneath the hard plastic. Matt leaned her head back and closed her eyes behind her sunglasses. And even with her eyes shut tight, she could sense someone staring at her; Bryne.

Again.

"Fuck off, Bryne," Matt growled at him. She flipped him the middle finger, her golden, jewel encrusted ring—a vestige of her human life—twinkled in the lights of the pier. The ring didn't hold any sentimental value, but it was pretty.

Bryne laughed at her, the sound grated on Matt's nerves like fingernails on a chalkboard.

It wasn't as if Matt didn't have feelings for the guy—she just didn't want to admit it to his smug, self-absorbed face. If she was going to be his, Matt was going to damn well make him work for it. After all, *he'd* turned her into some kind of freakish monster, so a little grovelling on his part was the very least she expected.

They dug into their pizza with a ferocious gusto similar to Matt's at the shredded corpse of the jock the night before. The feel of the hot mozzarella sticking to her lips and the sticky grease between her fingers was simply divine, and Matt couldn't help but crack a grin. It was the perfect antidote to the blood and terror that surrounded her now, a little slice of normality. She finished up in record time, and then polished off two more before folding her arms across her chest and declaring herself well and truly stuffed.

Bryne wrapped his arms around Matt's shoulders and smiled as she leaned her head against him without realizing, or at least, without acknowledging her actions.

"Did you make up with mommy yet?" Carter mouthed to Bryne, and Bryne rolled his eyes at him, before resting his cheek against Matt's dark, thick hair.

"I think they look hot," Carter said, catching Matt studying her arms in the fading daylight.

Matt laughed at the guy and play-punched his arm. She looked at her—*boyfriend?*—who she thought looked so much like Billy Idol as to be spooky. She fought a smile as she stood up, stepping over a discarded beer bottle that was near her chair, inhaling the fresh air that was bristling with dark intentions.

In the distance, the wind howled, and to Matt it sounded as if it were *screaming*. Bryne and the others heard it, too, and each had a look of eager anticipation upon their youthful faces. It became clear to Matt that the screaming of the wind was no coincidence, and she wondered if she would ever get used to the surprises that her new form kept on throwing at her; she felt itchy again, and hungry, despite the three fat, greasy slices of pizza she'd downed.

Matt needed another fix.

And at that point she knew that she was actually *grateful* Byrne had found her—*chosen* her—because it meant that she could never return to her old life, even if right now she was struggling to cope with what she had done, and the fact that she knew she would kill again and again.

Matt, Byrne and the others left the pier, driving out on thrumming motorcycles into the darkening night, with evil intent upon their faces—out onto the streets of Luna Bay.

Residents closed their windows and gazed fearfully out through twitching curtains as the sinister gang of eternal teenagers drove by, remembered stories passed along the generations, dark, twisted tales of the Black Eyed Children who feasted upon fear and stole away the soles of the sad and lonely.

D. W. Jones' Shopping List

Canada Dry Ginger Ale,
Starbucks Frappuccinos,
Parliament Lights and meat.
I'm not picky with the meat. As long as it is warm and does
not attempt to bite me back, it will land in my shopping cart.

The Vape Shop
D.W. Jones

The glass case creaked, as if in pain, protesting against C.C.'s massive weight as he continued to wipe the same spot with a paper towel. His stomach growled with an impatient reply. As long as he kept busy, time would shuffle along on its own. No need to stare at the clock. It always had a way of spitefully freezing when it felt it was being watched. Nope. He'd finish the rest of the glass cabinet, for the fourth time that day, look back at the clock to find that the waiting period had passed, and it was time to eat.

He didn't like this one bit, but he learned over the last few months that there wasn't much room for argument when it came to Their decisions. He either obeyed, or his world would simply cease to exist. They would consume him just as quick as he would his next snack.

Snaaaaacckkk. His mouth watered as the word stretched out before his eyes; a warm length of taffy pulling away from his greedy fingers. He tried averting his gaze when the dreaded clock came into view. He closed his eyes with a determination only matched by that of a child watching the shadows beckon for its flesh from the dark corners of the room in the middle of the night. He was sure he hadn't seen its face clearly enough to tell the time, so he walked around and began wiping down the front of the cabinet, peepers clamped shut.

He took a breath and opened his eyes to a clear reflection of his wide face staring back from the glass. His head, a bloated basketball pierced with two tiny blue orbs, appeared small atop a pair of shoulders spanning almost four feet across. Beads of anticipation bled down his smooth, round face as his stomach protested the wait with a cry of its own.

He smiled, recalling his father's teasing about his girth. How one Halloween, the old man threatened to paint his face orange and enter him in the local giant pumpkin contest. At the time, C.C. cried his way through a handful of candy bars, hidden away amongst the silent trees behind the house. He grinned, knowing the old bastard got his in the end. His little friends had made sure of that.

The bell hanging above the front door chimed, alerting him to new customers, but as he turned around, the door closed and empty of a body. False alarm. Happened a lot in those days, with Spring Breakers running amok in the streets. Probably some kid lost from his buddies and trying to find them, one store at a time.

His stomach rumbled for a moment, paused and then growled so loud that he could feel it ripple in waves across his massive belly. With a hesitant hand, he squeezed a fold of flesh on his side so hard, it made his vision quiver. He hadn't had to use pain to mask his hunger in years. It made his 950-pound mass feel small and insignificant. He was not made to feel small and hadn't felt insignificant since They vanquished the world of the evil that was his father. No, this latest change to Their deal was not working out.

He let out a sigh as he slowly looked up to the clock, sure that enough time had passed. "Shit on my face," He said, staring at the minute hand that had only moved three notches towards victory. Taking a few lumbering steps forward, he growled, "Three fucking minutes?" His stomach seconded; bubbling with disappointment of its own.

C.C. turned around, slumping his weight into an imposing 6'8" moping slouch. The frown tugging his meaty jowls towards the floor spoiled, rotting away to a sneer of anger. He balled the heavy hands hanging at his sides into cinder blocks of bone and gristle, shaking with fury. Taking a deep breath, he tried to calm the rage.

Moving back to his spot behind the lengthy counter, grinding his teeth, he wondered why. Well, They'd told him why, in no uncertain terms, the night before, but it amounted to nothing more than simple torture. They certainly knew that, with Their supposed eons of knowledge.

He inhaled a quick snort of air and blinked twice. *Knowing.* He let the word marinate before swallowing it whole. Didn't really need to waste all that time on questioning why. If They didn't know, it wouldn't matter. And how would They discover his disobedience, if not for his own admission? They never came out during the day, and it was only 3:32 pm. *Stupid clock.*

Kneeling behind the counter, he pulled a white cardboard box marked *King-Sized Snickers* from beneath the bottom shelf.

C.C. was no stranger to hiding his habit. He was the Nougat Ninja. The Sumo Stampeder of Sweets. Years under the watchful eyes of his parents, always looking for a way to one up the other when catching him shoveling his face. Father at the ready, belt in hand and a demonic tongue slashing with hate and shame. But this wasn't the thatch of woods behind his father's house. His punishment would be so much more severe than a few welts.

His stomach growled, painfully twisting the image of Them from his immediate attention. It really didn't matter what the threat was. Being eaten by those...Things, couldn't compete with his stomach in the long run. It always won and always would. Anyone with a pair of working eyes could see the truth in that.

He looked up at the clock, who'd given up only one more of its precious minutes. Sliding his hand across the lid of the box, he said, "It's between you," patting the box, "me and that fuckin' clock on the wall." He pointed a thick finger and an angry glance at the quiet time keeper, daring it to tell.

Content the clock understood the threat, he turned back to the box and lifted the lid. 12 out of 50 King-Sized Snickers lay in wait. He couldn't close shop until the day's quota was met so 12 would have to do. He let his weight drop back, slapping to the ground. He snatched two bars as he folded his giant trunks beneath him, resting into an Indian style crossing. Dropping one of the two bars to his lap, he ripped into the other, broke it in half and shoved the whole thing into his mouth at once. Eyes closed, he chewed that bar into oblivion, swallowing the entire mouthful three seconds later. Saliva seeped from the corners of his mouth, dripping chocolate drool down his chin. Nostrils flaring as he breathed deeply.

C.C. lifted the second bar, ready to strip it down, when the bell rang again from the door. It was Them. It had to be. His eyelids exploded wide as his fist closed tightly around the defenseless candy bar. Jaw clenched, his butt cheeks took the cue and followed suit. They were here to exact his punishment. He could barely taste the disobedience on his tongue and somehow, They knew. Dropping the crushed bar, he pushed himself forward, burning his knees across the carpet, and pressed his face against the open slit in the back of the cabinet.

"I'm just saying, if you wear that stupid thing again tonight, I'm gonna punch you in the throat," The young man threatened, pointing to the fanny pack the other kid wore around his waist.

"Why do ya have to be such an asshole?"

"'Cause I can be," he replied, threatening to throw a punch and laughing wildly when he made the other boy flinch in fear.

C.C. let loose a raspy sigh. His ass relaxed and sighed as well. He hadn't been discovered after all. Just a couple of college students out for a good time. "Got a mess back here I'm cleaning, gentlemen. I'll be right with ya." He picked up the roll of towels from the floor and wiped the chocolate from his face.

He popped up from behind the counter, kicking the box of candy back under, and announced with a wide grin, "Welcome to C.C.'s Smoke Shop." He spread his arms, displaying his tiny shop like any worthy salesman would do. It seemed the quota was about to be met.

"What the..." The Bully yelped, jumping back away from the display case. His dollar store flip flops twisted, nearly sending him to the floor. He stumbled about, to regain his balance, his gaze never once left the goliath stretching the width of the room. The man was huge. He

358

couldn't tear his eyes away from the confusion of the behemoth towering over them. It made no sense. Sure, he'd seen plenty of pics of obese people, most of which were bed ridden because they could no longer move about, but this? This man was easily 1000 pounds. He had to be 7 feet tall at least. By simple law of physics, this man should barely be alive, much less on his own two feet, popping up like a bloated Jack who had just eaten the box.

Fanny Pack nudged the Bully, trying to get him to break his rude stare. The last thing he wanted was a confrontation with this juggernaut. The Bully continued to stare, mouth slowly gaping in shock.

"Hey, C.C.," Fanny Pack asked, taking a cautious step toward the counter. "I'm Chris and this is Charlie. How ya doin' today?"

"I couldn't be better," C.C. answered, lowering his arms to the counter. "What can I do you boys for?" His stomach growled, begging for the second candy bar. The counters frame groaned, begging for mercy.

"Hey, C.C.," Charlie asked, "be honest..." The look on his face went from curious to deviant. He stood in front of a giant steel fan, cocked and ready to throw a massive handful of shit into its spinning mouth.

Chris inhaled a snatch of air as he nervously glanced over his shoulder. The door was maybe six feet away. When the shit hit the fan, he'd have no problem getting the Hell out of there before this behemoth could waddle on after, if he could walk at all.

"You were back there eating, weren't ya," Charlie stated, leaning into the counter a bit, keeping his eyes glued to the fat man. He smiled, almost daring him to sling the shit back.

Reflex hooked his face, twisting it into a painful looking snarl as he eyed Charlie. The knuckles in his right hand popped as it flexed against the counter. Like a magnet, his death grip was being pulled toward this little shit's throat before something else occurred to him. Why was this little punk asking him about eating? Was he really trying to piss him off... Unless?

He eyed the smaller one with the fanny pack, who merely smiled in return before ogling the door again and looked back at the inquisitor. He had never met one before, but it was obvious that these two worked for Them. They were spying on him. That was how They'd kept watch over him. Other humans, working for Them, just as he had for so many months. Made sense. Those two were probably standing right outside the door when he decided to disobey Them.

He bowed his head, eyes watering as his tongue fished around his 2massive mouth for some excuse. No, They didn't care for excuses. An apology would be better. Maybe a bit of begging would be called for as well. He squirmed behind those beady blue eyes and felt a cold trickle of sweat slide down his back. He was about to become the days quota.

No sooner had he decided what to say, his reflection staring back at him from the glass countertop offered up another theory for the little jerks' observation; a dribble of chocolate clinging to his chin. His visage in the glass split as a swelling grin spread his mouth wide open, displaying a row of enlarged teeth. Their size was well proportioned with the rest of his too-big-to-be-true frame. These little pissants in his shop were just that; a couple of little pissants.

C.C. whipped his head back, letting loose a howl of laughter as he thanked the stars above. "Can't hide anything from you kids these days, can I?" His laughter turned to giggles as he licked a paper towel and wiped his chin.

Charlie scoffed and stated, "Dude, you couldn't hide behind a tank!"

"Jesus, Charlie," Chris said shaking his head as he took a single step toward the door. This monster was a bite Charlie couldn't possibly swallow, no matter how many shots of bottled courage they'd already downed that day.

"It's okay, kid," C.C. said, and in fact, that was the truth. He was so elated at the fact that he hadn't been discovered, nothing else at that moment really mattered. "A guy my size has to have thick skin...you know," He began, grabbing his belly with both hands, "to keep all this fat in." He shook his handfuls as he laughed heartily.

So much of this man was now in motion; Ripples colliding with one another, creating smaller waves zig-zagging across his mighty torso. Chris felt a shift in the room, as the frenzied air began to brush past his face. This guy was so big that he created his own personal gusts of wind simply by moving.

Charlie just watched, like a stoned hippy caught in the molten dance of a lava lamp.

As happy as C.C. was at that moment, Charlie's stare was beginning to needle him. Best get this transaction completed before he was forced to snap the pissant. "So, what can I do for ya?" He leaned forward, hands on the counter top, allowing just enough of his weight to make the glass creak in pain, as he stared back at Charlie.

Chris cleared his throat loudly, hoping his friend would catch on, which he didn't. "Well, sir, we're looking for a couple of electronic cigarettes."

"Oh," C.C. said, feigning interest, "As you can see, I carry a wide variety of e-cigs and juices," waving his hands across the counter. He'd rather have waved his hand across Charlie's face. He glanced over to find the rude stare unbroken. "Anything in particular that you're looking for?" He said, meeting Charlie's eyes. Something close to a healthy ass kicking was what C.C. wanted to suggest, but the transaction had to take place. The boy would get his, no doubt.

Chris shrugged, even though no one was looking at him.

"Let me help ya out," C.C. said, as he knelt behind the counter. He opened the cabinet, moving a few boxes around in search of something and stated, "You boys are on Spring Break so you probably don't have much money." He found the box he was searching for, pulled it out of the cabinet and stood back up. "I'd also have to offer a guess that neither of you boys are smokers and if you are, you haven't been smoking for long."

He kept a hand on the wooden box as he eyed both the boys for an answer. Charlie's eyes weren't speaking, but Chris replied, "I can't stand the smell myself, but Charlie smokes."

C.C. turned to Chris and said, "And would I be correct by assuming that you probably wanted to look cool...maybe catch a fine piece of pelt at the night club?"

The smaller boy blushed as he smiled, nodding his head in admission.

C.C. smiled as he opened the box. "I believe I have something that'll work for ya," He said, pulling a small metal cylinder from the box. He stepped from around the counter, quicker than he should have been able, and disappeared through the curtain closing off the back of the shop to customers. He reappeared even quicker, holding a second box. "What kind of candy do you like?" He asked Chris, opening the lid to the second box.

"I guess I like mints?"

C.C. nodded, retrieving a particular vial from the box with a green liquid inside. He unscrewed the metal cylinder and poured a few drops of the liquid inside. "Try this if you'd please," he said, handing the e-cig to the kid.

He took a couple of drags from the contraption, with a confused look framing his face.

"Ya gotta press that button right there and then take a pull," C.C. instructed.

"Dumb ass," Charlie said under his breath, but loud enough for everyone to hear. If they did hear him, they ignored the insult.

Chris pressed the button and pulled deeply on the cig, almost immediately coughing out a plume of mint scented vapor.

"Just gotta go easy the first couple of times," C.C. stated with a chuckle.

"I don't know," Chris said disappointed, "I really wanted one with the light on the end, you know, so it looks like a real cigarette."

"Oh my God...you're so dense," Charlie said, snatching the device from his friends' hand. He pushed the button and turned it around, so he could see the little red light on the tip begin to glow. Chris smiled, took the device back and pulled another drag.

Charlie leaned into the counter, eyeing the contents of the second box. "Do you have one in there that tastes like pussy?" He was the only one laughing at his stupid joke.

C.C. eyed the little cretin and said, "No, but I believe I might have something in here just for you." He pulled out another e-cig from the first box, but this time, filled it with a yellowish liquid. He handed it to an apprehensive Charlie.

"Let me guess, this is the cat piss flavor," Charlie said with a sneer and a few quick sniffs of the mouthpiece. He was sure this freak did something to what he was being offered. Maybe the fat man kept an e-cig tucked between his giant butt cheeks, just waiting for an asshole like him to come in. Probably added a bit of his own urine to the cat piss mix he was being asked to suck on. Nope. No way in Hell he was gonna fall for that one.

"That's actually one of my own creations," C.C. said proudly, "I call it Lemon Bliss"

"I'm sorry, did you say Women Piss," Charlie chuckled, lost in his own amusement. He just couldn't shut up, even knowing he had already crossed a line with this monstrosity. He handed the e-cig back to C.C. and said, "I think I've changed my mind."

Chris looked over at Charlie and said, "What are talking about? This was your idea."

"Dude! Will you just look at this guy," Charlie stated, pointing a finger at C.C. "Do you really want to buy something that he's had those sausage fingers on?"

"I think your just being an asshole," Chris stated, taking another drag.

"Whatcha call me," Charlie demanded as he balled his fists.

C.C.'s stomach let loose a howl. It had waited long enough for the second candy bar and would wait no more. He felt like it took a bite out of his patience instead as he leapt over the counter like an Olympic hurdler and landed with a thud in between the boys. They both looked at him with eyes wide, shocked into surprise. There was just no way possible that this guy could have jumped like that. "No, Charlie," He said, stretching the boy's name out like a length of already chewed bubble gum, "The question is, what did you," poking a thick finger into the boys' chest, "call me?"

If Charlie had eaten that morning, he probably would have come close to shitting himself, as his world became eclipsed by this angry giant. A warm squirt moistened his crotch.

Chris acted quickly, trying desperately to end the massacre before it began. The giant's back faced him, and he couldn't see Charlie at all. A part of him hoped the fat man had swallowed the other. "C.C., as you can see, Charlie's an asshole." He said, accentuating the last word. "And do you know what happens when you punch an asshole?"

C.C. snickered. He knew the answer to the question and decided he liked the boy even more for asking it. It was too bad though that reality dictated that he was guilty by association.

Maybe he'd have a little fun instead. He balled up his right fist, held it up to Charlie's face and laughed as the boy's face completely vanished. "I believe I'd come away smelling like shit!"

Chris coughed out his next hit, making room for a wild laugh he hadn't had in years. C.C. smiled at the shaking boy behind his fist and laughed as well. Charlie's machismo tapered into a tiny whimper of fear as C.C. slowly pounded off to his spot behind the counter.

Picking up the yellow vial from the counter, he asked, "Are you sure you don't want to suck on this cat piss for a bit?" A new roll of laughter split the room in half, leaving Charlie in the middle, being picked on. And he didn't like it. Not one bit.

"You know what…" Charlie said as he backed off towards the door, "you two chuckle fucks can suck it." He grabbed the door with one hand and his crotch with the other.

C.C. flicked his shoulders forward, as if he were going to give chase. Charlie's eyes exploded wide as he flew out the door.

Chris started laughing even harder. He knew he was going to get an ass kicking when he got back to the hotel room, but in his mind, it was well worth seeing the look of mortal fear on Charlie's face as he ran for safety. He made a mental note to hold onto that image for the rest of his days.

C.C. looked at the boy, tears of laughter blurring his crowded eyes. This kid was all right in his book. Too bad he partnered himself up with such a jerk. Guilty by association. And as much as he wanted to tell the kid to run for the hills that night, he knew there was no escape. There were no hills, or mountains tall enough to hide away from Them. Once the stuff was ingested, there was no way back. They would come for him that very night, no matter how far they ran. The boy took another drag from the e-cig as C.C. sighed.

"So, how much do I owe you," The kid asked, retrieving his wallet from his fanny pack.

"For you kid, not a thing," C.C. replied with a wave of his hand. His foot toed under the counter, pushing the box of chocolate.

Intent on paying C.C. something, he slapped a twenty onto the counter and said, "In that case, this is payment for services rendered." The fat man cocked a brow and squinted an eye. "For the show, I mean. I've never seen fear on Charlie's face like that before. If those cameras actually worked," pointing to one of the two video cameras in the shop, "I'd pay you every dime I've got for a copy."

C.C. glanced up at the camera above the counter. It was so long ago that he'd found those in the trash. Not only did they not work, he'd almost forgotten entirely that they were even there. Smart kid. Too bad. He tossed the bottle of green liquid at the boy and said, "Now get lost, kid. I'm gettin' hungry."

366

Chris let a tiny yip break his smile as he turned around for the door. At the last moment, before stepping through to the daylight, he turned back and said, "Thanks C.C."

The moment the door closed, he heard Chris yell, "Hey, give that back." He knew Charlie would take the boys prize away and there was nothing he could do about it. More so, nothing he wanted to do. Chris was dead the moment he took his first hit. Now he felt happy in that he knew Charlie would share the same painful fate.

The fat man pulled the candy box out again, snapping another bar in half and shoved it in. As he chewed, he thought about the days designated feeders; The Creeping Shadow. He kind of wished the kid had come in the next day. Friday's feeders were The Jungto; They were fast and quite efficient. The boy wouldn't have suffered, much.

The Creeping Shadow on the other hand gave C.C. the willies. They'd take Their time, not because They were lazy, but incredibly small. About the size of a melted gumdrop, They worked in tandem with one another. As one, from a distance, They appeared as a living shadow, slowly creeping towards Their dinner. But at closer glance, one could see their tiny claws intertwined, creating a blanket of teeth and terror, all eyes trained on their meal. It usually took them a few hours to consume the victims' bones, always saving the teeth for last. Once They finished, all that remained was a bean bag of human flesh and organs for the young ones to play with.

With the order filled for the day, C.C. decided to close shop early and head on home. He stopped at a restaurant on his way and shoveled a whole meal down his throat before the waiter could ask if it came out to his liking. The sun was beginning to tire by the time his apartment complex came into view.

He opened the front gate to the courtyard when something moved in the blurry edge of his vision. He turned to the right and almost missed a slender shadow scoot behind a parked car. Was that a tail following the shadow? Couldn't be, the sun was still up. C.C. jerked his eyes to the horizon with disappointment. The sun had in fact disappeared, leaving behind a dull orange haze ushering in twilight.

He took a breath and turned back to the car. The shadows the car sat in were inanimate. Nothing moved. Slowly squatting, he tried looking under the car as he rolled through the mental images he had of the many different species of creatures under his care. He couldn't recall any of Them having tails, except...

C.C. stood up so fast, his feet left the ground for a quick second, causing him to lose his balance. He squeezed through the open gate and ran to the front door to the complex. Not hobbling or walking fast. Full out sprinting. His arms flew out in front him, one of his hands fumbling with the keys, before he slammed into the door. His left arm blew through the glass, as his attention remained on getting to the right key.

By now, he was certain it was a tail, and that was not a good thing to see. The only creatures he recalled with tails were The K'syph. They were the only species that he did not cater dinner for, and for good reason. It was explained that The K'syph were cleaners of a sort. They always lagged whichever creature fed that night and dined on the leftovers. Out of all the creatures he was introduced to that long-ago night, The K'syph, were nowhere to be seen. The Old One, who seemed to play the leader of the group, warned of the ones with tails.

Something about them not being seen and a warning if they ever were.

He slid the key into the door, pulled his left arm out of the broken frame cursing as he kicked the door open. The sting of fresh urine pinched at his eyes. He charged the elevator, one horn short of a rhino stampeding through the lobby. The little fuckers that pissed in his foyer would have to be dealt with later. Left arm stretched out with candles of glass biting his skin, flickering red and yellow; the sweet icing of stained fluorescents and running blood. His fist crushed the call panel as he rolled to the right, back swallowing any evidence there was a door behind him.

C.C. shook his left arm, creating an odd chorus between his quick shallow breaths and the shards of glass falling away to the tiles below. Trained on the door, his eyes didn't move. The rest of him shuddered. Rippling images of various creatures riding waves of terror across his massive being crashing into his face. He slammed his right hand into the call box once more with a sweaty thud.

The world beyond the door slept in a pale orange haze, soundly and snug. Nothing moved. The front door, on a pressure hinge, finally decided to close, sounding the alarm for all to wake as loose pieces of glass broke against the bricks. Still, nothing moved. No wispy trails of animate shadows or mysterious tails attached to unseen malice. Nothing.

Suddenly, something moved across his back. The surprise sent him reeling forward for safety, but his feet panicked, shuffling around as if they couldn't agree which way to go. His left hand grabbed the extinguisher on the wall as the other flailed about blindly. Neither kept him from crashing into the floor. Sprawled out, his left arm twisted behind him in defiance of the fall, still holding the extinguisher that landed on his back. Somehow, the image of tiny things, sharp and hungry, scampering across the floor, aiming for his ear holes, faded before the pool of piss not four feet in front of his face.

"Do you plan on keeping me prisoner here?" A voice asked from behind him.

C.C. pushed himself up as he turned around. Trying to exit the elevator was an old man, pointing a cane at him. He recognized the man as a tenant in the complex but didn't know his name. In fact, he didn't know any of their names and that was how he liked it.

With no reply on the horizon, the old man scooted forth, and began poking C.C.s legs with the tennis balled end of the cane. "Come on now," he said, jabbing the fat man. "Get up, come on."

"Give me a second, Grandpa," C.C. commanded, swatting the cane away. He popped up from the floor quickly, crunching glass beneath his feet. He immediately turned back to the broken front door, eyes wide.

"I'm not your grandpa, you little..." The old man began, pausing to correct his words, "You big piece of shit!" At that, C.C. turned around and slapped the old man with a scowl that looked almost painful to display.

"What did you call me?" He took one, long step, towards the old man.

The old guy gasped, pulling the cane close to his chest. He scampered around C.C. and didn't say a word until he reached the broken door. He turned around, pointing to the puddle of piss on the floor, "And you couldn't wait until you got upstairs?"

The door to the elevator was closing as C.C. shot the old man a middle finger. He would've warned the old coot about going outside but fuck it. The old man would get his just desserts. His stomach growled at the word.

The small lift groaned and shuddered as it pulled the great C.C. to the third floor. He loved torturing the machine. As the door opened, Nirvana's *Come as You Are* blasted down the hall. Last week, it was gangster rap. He thanked the ceiling for a different group of renters with better taste in music. Next week, it would probably be country music and in that case, he would leave the floor to the spring breakers and find a hotel room for himself.

He nodded his head to the music as he made his way down the hall. As he passed the second door on the right, it became apparent by the shaking door frame where the music was coming from.

"Shit," he mumbled. He didn't mind the music, from down the hall, but these kids were right next door. It was going to be a long night. Just as his door came into view, he stopped walking and shoved himself against the adjoining wall; the door was wide open. He still took up just as much space in that hallway. He couldn't hide if he wanted to. The wall rumbled with the bass line from the song, keeping him from hearing anything from within his apartment.

His stomach grumbled, holding onto the word dessert and not letting him forget. *Quiet down, you!* He inched his feet closer to the door, as he slid along the wall. It wouldn't have been the first time some degenerate had broken into his apartment, but he didn't want to take the chance.

Taking a deep breath, he turned around and slid sideways through the doorframe and stopped short of taking a second step in. He kept his fists clenched tight as he scanned the dark living room for any movement. "Hey, you," he shouted into the room, as he flipped the light switch up on the wall. Still, nothing moved. Keeping his eyes on the living room, he shuffled sideways into the tiny kitchen. Left hand reached out blindly for the block of knives on the counter. He snatched the first handle he touched and quickly sidestepped back the living room.

Satisfied the room was empty, he turned his attention toward the closed door of the bedroom. He steadied himself, knowing that something waited beyond that door. He reached up with a slow, shaky hand, for the door knob when a noise pulled his attention away.

He turned around, looking back at the open front door. Whatever it was sounded distant. He contemplated the bedroom door again when the sound grew louder. Tightening his grip on the knife, he drew closer to the wall behind the sunken couch.

C.C. leaned an ear into the plaster as the scratching grew loud enough to drown out the music from next door. Soundgarden belted out a live version of *Black Hole Sun* as something broke through the ceiling and snatched a thatch of hair from the top of his head.

"Son of a ..." C.C. cursed, backing away from the small hole above him. He reached up, touching the now wet, bald spot on the top of his head. Whatever it was took a piece of his scalp with the handful of hair it yanked out. Stretching upwards, he jabbed the knife into the hole, stabbing at different angles, trying to skewer the culprit.

Suddenly, the wall behind him exploded in teeth and hunger as three creatures burst through, clawing Their way through the air to his back. C.C. birthed a scream he could never imagine producing as the little bastards anchored themselves to his flesh. Two of them clung to his lower back, while the Other climbed, using the giant's spine as a ladder, each step becoming painfully clear that C.C. was in serious trouble.

He spun around and rammed the other wall with his back, screaming again as one of them dug deeper in. He pressed his weight into the wall, doing all he could to ignore the pain. One of the creatures wheezed loudly before it popped. The other felt as though it was burrowing into his kidneys. Pushing himself off the wall, he threw his feet out in front of him and landed on his back. From his left side came a splattering sound, followed quickly by a viscous liquid spraying across the floor that smelled like burning rubber.

The hole in the ceiling came alive, baring a set of teeth that glowed against the darkness. A small pair of red eyes peered down at him as the teeth parted with a screech. Two small arms ending in three sharp, hooked claws sprouted out as the creature dropped down on his face. It growled, raking its claws across his face. C.C. reached up and grabbed the Thing by its head. It thrashed around, tearing into his knuckles with its claw. As it bit down on his forefinger, he brought his other hand up and squashed It, spraying his face with that black blood. Its teeth continued to glow with life as he wiped its carcass from his palms.

He turned his head and spit as much of the stuff out of his mouth as he tried to get back up. He froze when something scuttled across the floor. He squinted against the sweat stinging his eyes when the last creature launched its final attack. The Thing jumped onto his face, grabbed his left eyeball and pulled, holding on as the other clawed hand sliced into his neck.

C.C. rolled over onto his stomach, as the creature tugged on his optic nerve, continuing to search for an artery in the fat man's neck by scraping away the excess. He kept the right eye closed, more out of pain than protection, but the horror of his situation was still all too clear. He reached up to grab the Thing, but it protested with its claws.

He felt a pop as the room went black. A wave of nausea crashed over him. A spear of hot steal thrust into his brain. The pain was too much. He didn't need to open his only eye to know the Thing had yanked out the other. He cursed loudly, trying to get a grip on this Thing, when it reached out and grabbed his tongue. Panic took the reins. He began smashing his fist into his face, trying to connect before it ripped out another vital organ. He bit down as hard as he could, hoping to taste It instead of his own tongue.

The Thing screeched as C.C.s chompers found their mark, biting into its invading claw. It kicked, puncturing his double chin in several places before pulling away from his closed mouth, minus a hand. He found his opening and exploited it, slamming his face into the floor, refusing to stop until the clawing ceased. C.C. pushed bits of the creatures' hand from his mouth with his tongue. It tasted like it smelled; melting rubber. He laid for just a moment, before jumping to his feet. The K'Syph. Once They smelled blood, They'd come. And if he didn't do something about it, They would continue to come until he was just fat to be rendered.

He stood, cupping his hand over the bleeding hole and eyed the puddles of gore and teeth littered around his feet. He scraped the roof of his mouth with his tongue that felt swollen and rough. C.C. stumbled to the fridge, looking for something to wash that acrid taste away. Grabbing the two liter of flat cola, he downed it, spit it out in the sink and took another swig. The last mouthful he swallowed and nearly choked it back up, making his one eye blur with a tear. It felt like there was something stuck in the back of his throat. He forcefully swallowed several times, but the lump remained. The acidic flavor coating his mouth began to burn, as his tongue tingled, like it just awoke from a cramped nap.

He scraped his fingernails across his tongue, trying desperately to get it out, whatever it was. He took another long pull from the bottle and swallowed as hard as he could; one giant mouthful to flush the tank.

The light bleeding in from the window flashed as something crossed its path. Time to go, and he knew exactly where he was headed. He picked up the knife and stopped short of shoving his way through the door. His head vibrated from the internal screams of his mind demanding that he look, so he did. He stood there, staring at the four bodies, mashed and spread out against the carpet. *Look!!!!* He looked, from one pile of flesh to the other. *Do you see it? Look again!!!*

Out of the four piles of flesh, only one still had some semblance of what it looked like before C.C. liquefied it with a swift pounding; it was the last one with the missing claw. Well, not missing, just no longer connected to its host. He poked it with the knife, almost hoping it would pop up for a rematch. He looked around and grunted when he found the little claw.

A hissing sound came from the window, reminding him that he needed to go. Now. He stabbed the amputated claw with the blade, just enough to skewer it to the end as he glanced up to the window. A purple mist, swirling with yellow stars that seemed to swim against itself, seeped through the window panes.

Curiosity had him rooted to the spot. Even with his own life in danger, he could not move, caught in the hypnotic twirling of the smoke, that wasn't smoke at all. The mist, heavy with hunger slid down the wall slowly. Once it connected with the floor, the twinkling stars within began to dance, faster and faster until they became a blur of flesh and bone. Its frame, weak and smudged stood, solidifying as it curled into itself. The last thing he saw were the teeth, adorning a mouth that was quickly inhaling the left-over bits of mist clinging to its back and tail. *Go now!* C.C. slid through the door frame and slammed the door shut.

Something tickled his lips. He ran his tongue across and tasted blood. Bringing his hand up to his face, he felt a warm stream, running down his face from the eyeless socket. C.C. had all but forgotten the wound. Must be in shock or something.

He touched the drooping lids cautiously, waiting for a stab of pain to call his hand away, but none came. Pushing in, the eyeless lids parted and curled, as his finger went in. Still, nothing. He could feel his finger probing, just absent of any pain or discomfort. He decided he had gone far enough when his last knuckle pushed against his brow. He wondered for a moment what his brain would feel like.

Another wet crunch from behind the door pulled him from his stupor. *Time to go, one-eyed Willie.* The curiosity of the lack of pain was quickly eaten away by anger. Anger at the fact that he'd been betrayed. Betrayed and mutilated. Left for scraps. *They took your eye, man, your fucking eye!*

His knuckles popped as he squeezed the handle of the knife. "I believe it is time to go," he growled as he made his way down the hall. Waiting for the doors to open, he ripped one of the sleeves from his t-shirt and stuffed it into the weeping socket. Pain may have become a stranger, but he didn't want to risk bleeding to death before he had his revenge.

C.C. raised the blade, bringing the claw before his one good eye. Was that right? Did that denote the other eye was bad? *It's fucking gone.* That's more like it. Call it what it was.

He studied the skin, an overlapping of leathery scales, blending into a tuft of fur that began at the wrist. Three long, curly fingers hung limp, multiple knuckles running down their length. And at the other end, three yellow talons, curling in an arc under the first knuckle...

Three talons...

He turned the knife around, in turn, spinning the claw. There were three fingers, but only two talons...*It's gone!* He looked around the floor, thinking it might have fallen off.

His stomach cramped, bubbled and then let loose a moan. He swallowed, thinking about that missing talon. Swallowed again when he realized what it was stuck in his throat a moment ago. *Not gone. Relocated.* The elevator doors opened.

C.C. spent the fifteen-minute cab ride trying to come up with a different plan that didn't end with his giblets being gnawed on, but none came. He could ignore the assault, run like Hell and set up camp in a different state. Maybe a different country all together, but that wasn't a solution. It merely delayed a painful death in a strange town. It would hang over his head like a halo with a hook, dangling a hotdog in his face. Always reminding him that it was near. Wasn't that why he took Their deal to begin with? Being morbidly obese kept death close, but what They gave him promised to keep it away. A denial to gravity and an afront to the laws of physics. Death came in many forms. When They came for him again, making up for Their mistake, there would be no pinky swears keeping Them at bay.

Pluck your heart and hope to die, stick a talon in your eye.

"You sure I can't take you to a hospital, man," the Cabbie asked, hoping to stretch the measly $42 fare out a bit more.

For the umpteenth time that evening, C.C. had forgotten about his missing eye. He stepped out of the cab and snickered as the shocks pushed the car back up to a normal height. He gently touched the piece of cloth sticking out from his socket, expecting a flash of pain.

He pulled a crumpled fifty-dollar bill from his shorts pocket and handed it to the Cabbie. "Keep it."

"Hey, thanks, man," the driver smiled, tucking it into his bill fold he kept hidden between the front seats. "Want me to wait for ya?"

"Nah," C.C. answered, shaking his head as he eyed the landfill over the cab. "I'm gonna be a bit."

"Your funeral, boss," the Cabbie replied, but spoke up just as he began to pull away. "By the way, you really shouldn't eat those glow sticks, man. They'll kill ya." His tail lights vanished as he rounded the corner, leaving C.C. standing in the middle of the street wondering what he was referring too. Didn't really matter though did it?

He crossed the street and pushed his way through the neighboring woods. Three minutes into the journey, he would come across a section of fence that had been cut open, granting him access to the landfill, but he thought he was being followed. Every few steps, he caught a glimpse of light, faint and blue surrounding him. Figuring it for a flashlight, he crouched down behind a sable palm and waited. Whoever it was would give themselves away the next time they flashed that light in his direction and he would smash them. No time to ask why. The K'Syph would have figured out by now that Their dinner was denied and scurry back home. If They made it back before him, his element of surprise would be blown. He was sure that would be the only way for him to make it all the way through to the inner chamber.

"Come on," he said quietly. There it was. A haze of blue light and then it was gone. "What the..." and there it appeared again. What did the Cabbie say? Something about eating a glow stick? He slowly opened his mouth and watched as a sliver of blue light shot out from between his lips. He gasped as he brought his hand up to his mouth, like he was checking his breath before a good night kiss. "Christ on my crotch..." He moaned, staring at his blue hand. The thought of swallowing a handful of Smurfs tickled his mind. All of them, sitting around a campfire in his stomach, using their combined magic to light their new domain.

Time to go, Smurf Smoker. C.C. stood back up and trudged along to the opening, trying his hardest to ignore the flashlight that replaced his mouth. The side of the Mt. Trashmore hill was a few steps ahead. He'd have to worry about himself later. For now, revenge would have to do.

He stopped at the hillside, scanning the woods he'd just come through for any followers. Satisfied he was alone, he turned back to the hillside and unzipped his pants. He began to urinate as he directed his stream in a specific design against the grassy hillside. Slashing it upwards, across to the right and back down through the first stream, he spoke the words of entry, "Nuthb, Trinuyg, Wasgth."

He took a cautious step backward as the ground began to tremble. The side of the hill yawned open, like the mouth a waking giant, revealing a darkness he couldn't peer through. A fetid stench pushed against his face reminding him there were more pleasant places to be at that moment. He took a deep breath, squeezed the handle of the knife tightly and stormed into the pitch.

Two steps in, he stopped, turned around to find the hole closed as if it weren't ever there. *No going back now.* Turning back to the tunnel, he wished he'd brought a flashlight. He raised his hand and said, "Can't even see my own..." but he could. The blue light seeping from his mouth was enough to send the shadows reeling away, slithering back down to Those who waited at the other end.

C.C. looked around briefly, before his internal voice piped in and nudged him along. The tunnel stood about a foot over his head and twice as wide as he was. He grinned, keeping his mouth opened slightly, as he made his way through, steak knife leading the way. A few steps further and a soft sound tickled his ears. It was coming from up ahead, there was no doubting that, for where else could it have come? He stopped as the ground beneath his feet began to shake slightly. It was Them, he was sure. They must have known he was there and they were trying to escape. Making a run for it before he could exact his revenge. A growl escaped his lit mouth as he pushed forward.

The soft sound quickly became louder as he ventured deeper into the hill. It sounded like an alarm, something warning the Others that he was coming. He pushed forward, doubling his speed until a yellow tinge of light appeared up ahead. C.C. closed his mouth, swallowed what little fear he still harbored and rushed forward into the glow.

The tunnel gave way to a chamber, lit by dozens of small torches poking out from the garbage encrusted walls. He hadn't noticed the silence until a swooshing sound pulled his eyes to the right. He caught a shadow shimming into one of the smaller tunnels leading off to the right. The opening was half the size as the one he just came through. There was just no way he was going to fit in there. Looking around, he found all six of the new tunnels were too small for him.

He could venture back, but where did that leave him? Waiting for death to come a knockin'. He could try to squeeze through one of the smaller tunnels, but he'd surely get stuck. The only thing he had left was the very ground he stood on. He looked around once more, this time taking note of the distance between the first tunnel and the six others leading into who-knows-where. He backed off towards the first tunnel, keeping an eye on the other holes of blackness, and a tight grip on the blades handle.

Here we go. He took a breath and yelled, "Ding ding goes the mother fucking dinner bell." His eyes danced, shifting from one tunnel to the next, waiting for a reply of teeth and talons to come spewing forth. He turned around to check behind him and found silence waiting there as well. Had They all really vacated? If They had left, there would be no revenge. At least not on his part. He cleared his throat, and yelled, "I'm here..."

"We know why you're here," a voice hissed from the gloomy depths of one of the holes.

He turned quickly, sure the voice came from one of the two tunnels to his left, but there was no movement to confirm. Sweat rolled down his face as he stared into the gloom, unblinking.

"I need to speak to The Master," he demanded of the darkness, hoping he was the only one to catch the stuttering fear in his voice.

The chamber erupted in a cacophony of chatter. Unknown syllables followed by clicks and chirps flooded his ears. He turned, cocking an ear to each side of the chamber only to discover that the sound was coming from all the tunnels, including the large entrance he used to get in. Out of one of the tunnels, came a more familiar sound; laughter. They were all laughing at him, most in their own tongues. They hadn't escaped after all. They fortified and prepared for his arrival.

"How will you speak with your tongue flopping at your feet, Chubby Crowder?"

That was it. They had no intention in allowing him an audience with The Master. He had walked himself into his own death. He took a step backwards toward the first tunnel when his stomach growled, sending a wave of nausea upwards towards his throat. It was an alien sensation as he couldn't recall ever throwing up before. His mighty legs began to tremble against his weight, losing whatever magic They granted him. He dropped to his knees and gagged, his stomach wrenching with each false alarm, sending the blue light splashing against the wall between each breath.

He dropped the knife, beginning to panic from the lack of air. He could still breathe but couldn't get enough air to fill his massive lungs. It felt as though someone parked their car on top of him, unable to expand his chest completely. C.C. didn't notice the lack of laughter. Suddenly, the gagging stopped just as quickly as it had begun. Beads of sweat poured over his face, but he no longer had the strength to wipe them away. His arms shook beneath him, weak and threatening to give. He stayed on all fours, panting like a black dog beneath the summer heat. He shuddered as something touched his back. He reached for the knife but fell face first into the dirt. With barely the strength, he turned his head to the side, trying to get his mouth out of the dirt.

"Oh, C.C. You have made it home, haven't you?" The voice was slurred, like a drunk with a swollen tongue.

Lying on his belly, it became almost impossible to breathe, but he no longer possessed the ability to move his giant limbs. That forgotten fear had once again come home to rest, standing tall atop his massive frame, holding him down. He found himself immobile with the magic They bestowed upon him repossessed.

He gasped like a fish out of water as hands began touching him, grasping at flesh for a firm hold. The voice shouted something unintelligible before those hands lifted him and rolled him over onto his back. The Thing speaking leaned into view, caressing his massive stomach with what appeared to be a melted hand. He recognized the voice and tried desperately to keep his eyes closed to the horrific sight as it spoke. His stomach wrenched again causing him to cry out.

"You have brought Our new edition home," the Master announced.

"This is not my home," C.C. growled through the pain.

His eye lids parted and shook at the site hovering above him. He'd seen the tumor infested face of The Master before, but never so close. Those growths on its face pulsed with a life of their own, like eggs about to burst a new life into this dank world beneath the trash. The overpowering aroma of festering garbage and other refuse that lent this chamber life stood no chance against the rotting odor dripping down from Its misshapen mouth.

The Master raised its head and laughed. "You...you...you are nothing. Nothing more than meat!" It continued to cackle and laugh as it took a step backwards. "A brief reprieve from the boredom that haunts us all in this place of abandonment."

C.C. screamed as his stomach wrenched one last time before his rib cage split apart, cracking open in two down the middle like a gory bear trap waiting to be tripped. He'd finally lost the battle with his true nemesis.

The Master knelt, taking C.C.s lifeless left hand and moved it tauntingly towards the gaping hole. "Come now, little one, I know you're hungry."

A single eye appeared in the gaping hole, blinked twice and disappeared. Suddenly, C.C.s oversized stomach exploded from the gore and latched onto the hand the Master waved back and forth, with a set of teeth that glowed an eerie blue. With one gulp, It swallowed the hand whole. It blinked Its single eye as It turned around and began to dine on what was once Its own master.

"Come, my Children, while the meat is still warm," The Master instructed, inviting the denizens of the dark to come out and play as he leaned down and took a bite out of the dead man's cheek.

Jeff Stevenson's Shopping List

Ice cream
Coffee
Sprite
Bananas
Soup

The Video Nasty
Jeff C. Stevenson

There were four of them and they had no clever name to call themselves. Not the Four Musketeers or the Fantastic Four or the Fearsome Foursome. Just four twelve-year-old boys: Jeremy, Wes, Sticks and Rory. Best friends and, while not related, they all shared birthdays that occurred within the same month.

It was the summer of 1983. Jeremy and Wes had known each other since third grade, Sticks—so named because he was obsessed with Rush's drummer, Neil Peart—had moved to the neighborhood a couple years earlier, and Rory had transferred to the boy's school the previous Christmas.

In addition to their birthdays being so close together, they also shared a love of all things horror. They read everything by Lumley, McCammon, Koontz, Saul,

Straub, Farris and King. They went to every movie: *An American Werewolf in London, The Evil Dead, The Howling, The Fog, Creepshow*, as well as all the *Friday the 13th* sequels.

But like all boys, they wanted a taste of the forbidden fruit, the item that was hidden away, out of reach on the top shelf. They didn't just want the gun, they wanted the bullets that fit the chambers.

They wanted to watch the video nasties.

The UK coined the term and it was a phrase unfamiliar to most in the small town where the boys lived. These forbidden and disgraced VHS cassettes—criticized for their violent content by the press, social commentators and various religious organizations—had a way of slyly creeping across the world and eventually being stocked in the dusty back shelves of most every video store in the US. They were in extremely high demand with wait lists that made the boys learn patience at a very young age since it would take weeks before the title they wanted was available. Between the four of them and their separate accounts, they were careful to choose and coordinate their selections, so it was rare when they didn't have a Friday night video nasty to watch.

There were more than seventy titles deemed inappropriate and Wes, Sticks, Rory and Jeremy were determined to see them all. No one at *Incredible Sights Video Sales and Rental* cared that the boys weren't technically old enough to view them; as long as they had three bucks in cash and their family's active credit card membership, they could check-out whichever videotape they wanted for three days.

The ones they were eager to see were usually badly dubbed films made in Italy or Spain or somewhere in Hollywood and they were distributed by *Go Video, Rank*

Video, Intercity Video and *Vestron Video*. The most sought after titles included *Cannibal Holocaust, Axe, Don't Go in the Woods, Toxic Zombies*, and *Nightmares in a Damaged Brain*. The cover designs were similar: Women screaming, the title in bloody lettering, usually a "Banned in 17 countries!" statement.

Most of the movies were 90 minutes long so the evening was easy to plan, very regimented. The boys plotted their weekend around the video since it would require a sleepover, privacy, and plenty of pizza and ice cream. Jeremy's house was best since he had a finished basement. They'd start watching at 10 p.m. and by 11:30, the pizza and ice cream would be gone and at midnight, right on time, his dad would open the door to the basement and good-naturedly yell down to turn that shit off and go to sleep.

Everything ran like clockwork until the weekend that Jeremy rented a tape none of them had ever heard of.

***

Jeremy was the only one to actually see the videocassette cover for the movie called *The Video Nasty*. When the videos were checked out, they were placed in thick plastic shell cases with no information or poster art about the film. That particular weekend, none of the boys had received the call that their wait-listed choice had arrived, which meant the host for that evening got to choose which videotape to rent.

It was Friday afternoon and Jeremy was at the very back of the store near the restrooms. That's where the horror movies were kept; it was as if *Incredible Sights Video Sales and Rental* was ashamed of the very lucrative genre they stocked. The covers were all displayed like mini-posters. Jeremy walked back and

388

forth, eyeing the titles. They had already seen most of them and, in desperation, he was just veering over to the sci-fi section, which would have been a compromise unless he found something incredibly brutal.

A sharp shuffling noise, like something sliding into place, pulled him back to the horror section. The store was pretty empty, so it was quiet; just a couple customers in the comedy row, a few looking over the new release titles, and the guy at checkout. Jeremy went back to where the noise had originated. One of the videotapes—*Splatter Farm*—had fallen to its side, exposing a film behind it. Curious what film *Splatter Farm* had been covering, he picked up the cardboard slipcase, then almost dropped it in surprise. It was cold—really cold—to the touch. Like it had just been removed from the freezer. It wasn't damp, just felt like a block of ice covered in paper.

It was titled *The Video Nasty* but there was no lurid art, just the words printed in a basic, non-scary font. There was lettering below the title, some credits maybe, but they were small and blurry. Obviously, the wraparound art that housed the video had been photocopied several times over and other than the title, the words were illegible. Even on the back, which was usually a description of the plot with some screen shots, the sentences were too small, impossible to read. There were four images but they, too, were indistinct.

The videotape had quickly warmed in his hands as Jeremy turned it around, examining it for clues as to its content. He was only able to decipher the letters KCD and the words *Kalem Club Distributors* on the edge of the box. He wasn't familiar with that company but figured it was worth renting based on the title alone, and the guys would get a kick out of the lack of information.

"Not just a video nasty but a video *mystery*!" he imagined himself telling them.

At checkout, he handed the cardboard slipcase to Matthew. The process was that Matthew would check off the information in the thick inventory book, put the sleeve on the shelf behind him, and then place the rental into a plastic shell.

Matthew flipped back and forth through the notebook a bit, glanced at the title, then back at the book. "Where'd you get this? Horror, right?" He knew his regular customers. Jeremy nodded.

Again, he moved pages around in the book. "Weird, it's not in here, and it's not new."

Behind Jeremy, some people were growing impatient, so Matthew just wrote the title of the video into the book. "We'll figure it out later. I never heard of this, so let me know if it's any good, okay? It's due back Tuesday."

***

Friday night.

Jeremy had explained about the tape to the guys and at first, they thought he was only kidding. After all, they knew their horror films and none of them had ever heard of a movie so perfectly titled: *The Video Nasty*.

"Maybe it's porn?" Wes suggested hopefully.

Jeremy shook his head. "You know they don't have any porn there."

Sticks asked, "And Matthew hadn't heard of it?"

"Nope. It wasn't in the book, either." Jeremy realized he had forgotten to tell them how he had discovered it, the rustling of the tape, how it was hidden behind *Splatter Farm*, how cold it was. Spooky stuff that they would love, but he felt an urgency to view the movie so he didn't tell them.

A little after ten p.m., he pushed in the tape of *The Video Nasty*. They all settled in for the mayhem to begin. The TV static gave way to simple white lettering on a black background: *Kalem Club Distributors*. There were usually coming attractions, but the screen went black. No opening credits, no title appeared.

It just started.

It was terrifying. The initial image was horrific but the boys didn't look away or couldn't. Jeremy tried, but he was paralyzed, locked in a vice. The images held all four boys like a magnet. They couldn't process what they were seeing; it was beyond anything any of them had witnessed before in a horror movie. Usually, they'd make derogatory comments as they watched or scoffed at the bad acting or dialogue or warned the women not to go into that house, that room, that bathtub or shower.

But the boys said nothing. They only watched; it was all they could do. There was a clock on the wall over the TV set. Jeremy was able to glance at it for an instant—11:05 p.m.—then his eyes crashed back to the film, compelled to view it, but he wanted nothing more than to look away, escape from the basement. He took some relief that since it was after eleven, they were already an hour into the movie and so it had only another thirty minutes until it was over.

He didn't know how the guys were doing; were they as mesmerized and repulsed as he was by what they were seeing? With focused effort, he managed a sidelong gaze at Rory, Wes and Sticks; he couldn't even fully turn his heard. What he was able to see astonished him; he didn't recognize his friends. They looked like three little old men, hunched over on their knees, their pale faces reflecting the garish colors on the TV screen.

Their eyes were misshapen black orbs, their mouths were open and slack, stroke-like, as if they were gasping in disbelief at what was on the television before them.

Jeremy's eyes burned as he stared at his friends. He wanted to call out to them, but his tongue was pressed to the back of his throat; he could barely breathe. Then he felt a pressure on both sides of his head, like gnarly, large old hands, thick with callouses, knobby and misshapen with arthritis. Ancient hands, but strong ones that firmly turned his head back until he was facing the screen again.

Impossibly, it was almost midnight. Why was the movie still playing? He had to pee but there was no way he was able to move. Jeremy strained to hear the thud of his dad as he walked across the kitchen floor to pull open the basement door and yell at the boys to turn that shit off. Jeremy wondered: Would his father's voice break the spell?

12:20 a.m.

1 a.m.

The video had been playing for three hours. *Where's my dad?* Jeremy cried to himself, his teeth clenched. *Why isn't the movie over? When would it end?*

2 a.m.

2:40 a.m.

3 a.m.

Five hours. Jeremy realized then that the film must have been duplicated on the slowest speed possible, giving the video six hours of footage to display.

The boys had another hour to endure.

***

It was just after 4 a.m. when the visuals and sounds abruptly ceased. The screen turned to static, a gray mass of chaotic energy the flickered relentlessly across the monitor. Then it went black. Jeremy saw the reflection of the four of them for an instant on the TV, then the video started to automatically slowly rewind as the machine whirred and groaned. The four of them remained motionless, kneeling.

Sometime before 4:30 a.m. the tape returned to its starting point. The machine ejected it.

To Jeremy, it felt like waking up too suddenly. He was disoriented. There was a sour, acidic smell. One of the guys had wet his pants. He heard whimpering, didn't know if it was from himself or someone else. The boys didn't speak; either they couldn't or had no words to express what they had just spent six hours watching.

Within minutes, Jeremy was alone in the basement. He didn't remember the guys clumping up the stairs. It was after 8 a.m. Had he dozed off? Dizzy, his legs still half-asleep after not moving for so many hours, he reached out and grabbed the videotape, pulled it free of the machine. It was chilly to the touch; not cold, but there was an icy feel to it. And just for a second, he thought he heard a muffled, low-pitched growl, or maybe it was just the gears of the player.

He placed the tape back into its thick clamshell case, snapped it closed. He felt like he had put it in a cage; now all he wanted was to take it out of the basement, get it out of his house. Jeremy started up the steps to the kitchen. It was silent; everyone was still asleep. It was Saturday morning, a sunny day. He opened the door, the shades banged against the glass pane in their familiar way. Outside, the air was cool and fresh. He felt as if he was waking from a long, dark fever dream, like he had been terribly sick with something, but now he was well. Whatever images he had seen, surely they were just part of some nightmare. No movie could ever contain such sights or sounds…

Jeremy eased his leg over his Huffy bike, pushed off, heading toward *Incredible Sights*, a twenty-minute ride. Two police cars rushed passed, followed by an ambulance, but he barely noticed.

He knew he was too early, the store was closed but there was the deposit slot. His hands were shaking a bit as he tried to push it through, the plastic rattling loudly in the still morning air. It didn't fit; either the opening was warped or the video case was too big. This had never happened before. Jeremy panicked as he shoved, twisted and pushed the plastic case against the slot, tried to force it. It finally dropped through. Maybe he heard a faint, low-pitched snarl right after the tape hit the bin inside the store. If he did, if there was something unnatural about the video, it was someone else's problem now.

With the videotape no longer in his possession, the anxiety and horrific images that had clung to him seemed to loosen and then drifted away as he pedaled away from the store. Now it really was like a dream, so stark and overwhelming when you're in it, but so quickly forgotten when you're on the other side of sleep.

When he got home, he felt the need to shower. He realized that he was the one who had peed his pants. *Maybe the other guys had, too*, he hoped, embarrassed. He knew he needed to be clean and cleansed from whatever he had exposed himself to Friday night. After the shower, he started to chow down on *Cap'n Crunch*. It felt good and right and normal to just shovel it into his mouth like he always did Saturday mornings. Usually the guys were with him, each eating from his favorite cereal box.

Jeremy had no idea how long he went through the motions of pouring cereal into the bowl, adding milk, eating and repeating the movements. At one point, he realized he was eating *Honey-Comb*s, the empty box of *Cap'n Crunch* discarded at the end of the table. The sugar rush was peaking just as he heard his mom call out from the basement.

"Jeremy? You up there?"

What was she doing down there, how long had she been there? he wondered, startled.

"Yeah?"

"Get down here right now and fix this television!"

He clumped down the stairs. His mom and Kate, his sister, were kneeling in front of the TV console. There was something about their position—one of worship or deference to the large black monitor—that bothered Jeremy. He recalled seeing Wes, Sticks and Rory last night in the same postures, like withered old men, watching the movie in terrified awe.

"What's wrong?" he asked as he approached them.

"Why'd you tape over *Mary Poppins*?" Kate demanded, almost in tears.

"Huh?"

"Look at this," his mom said. She pushed a video into the player. Immediately the simple white lettering on a black background appeared for *Kalem Club Distributors*. Jeremy stumbled forward, pushed the eject button. The silence that followed was a strangled one, cut off and tense. The tape in his hand had the cheerful and familiar Disney logo, was labeled *Mary Poppins*. Confused, he pushed the tape back in. Pressed play. After a second, the gears pulled at the tape and the *Kalem Club Distributors* logo reappeared. Jeremy immediately punched the tape out before the film could begin. His mom and Kate watched him, not speaking.

He reached for his sister's copy of *Alice in Wonderland*, pushed it in.

Kalem Club Distributors.

His hands trembling, he fumbled with three other video tapes. The same result. Helpless, he turned to his mother. She looked at her son, pulled Kate protectively closer.

Jeremy said, "I don't know what's going on. I didn't record over your movies. I don't know what happened."

His mom stood, switched off the VCR, turned a network channel on. "Just watch some cartoons, Katie."

They all looked at the screen. It was a news bulletin, a female reporter standing in front of a home. A familiar one.

"—never seen such carnage before," she was saying. "This police officer told me that he and his partner responded to a call at approximately 8:30 a.m., less than an hour ago. A young man had called to report he had just murdered his entire family. When police arrived, the boy—not yet publicly identified due to his age—was waiting on the front porch. Upon further investigation, police located the mutilated bodies of two younger children—a 4-year-old and a 6-year-old—along with the parents."

"Wes," Jeremy said, the word pushed suddenly out of him. "That's Wes's house!"

"What?" his mom said as he ran up the stairs. "Jeremy! What's going on? Where are you going?"

In the living room, Jeremy's dad was wildly twisting the dial on the TV set. The same image on each channel: *Kalem Club Distributors*.

His father caught his eye. "What the hell is wrong with this TV?"

A news bulletin, different from the one in the basement, appeared on the screen.

"A young man is in police custody after authorities said he hacked to death his mother and father earlier this morning. This is the second of three homicides we are currently covering."

"Sticks," Jeremy mumbled, dumbfounded. His dad turned from the TV to his son.

"What?"

"Rory," Jeremy said as a new image on the television revealed the front of his friend's house.

"What are you talking about?"

From downstairs, the sounds of *The Video Nasty* started up. The floor reverberated with the vibrations of the bedlam depicted in the movie. Jeremy could hear his mother and sister screaming, something growling. It all came back to him; he recalled all he had seen.

His dad called out to his wife and daughter as he rushed past his son, down the stairs.

A moment later, Jeremy followed, closing the basement door behind him.

Sergio Palumbo's Shopping List

Old-fashioned paper wrap
Caribou dry meat
Salted fish
Proper firewood
Add icing at will...

Unk-unk

Sergio 'ente per ente' Palumbo
edited by Michele Dutcher

Warwick Kaehler climbed aboard the TTC subway car he had been waiting for. The air coming from an open window reached his hair and started, or at least tried, to mess up his very short chestnut curls, but his haircut—that he called a 'conservative hairstyle'—heroically resisted, as the man observed while briefly staring at his reflection. His blue eyes, positioned over high cheekbones, gave him a sort of deep, wise look, which was in accordance with a man in his 50s. He wore a formal gray jacket, close-fitting around the waist, or so he liked to think. He had a rather down-turned, closed sad-looking mouth, or this was how his friends and colleagues thought of his usual expression. A thin neck, if compared to his overall build and average height, completed the picture of how he looked.

He sat down and immediately went for his tablet, then he started reading the Toronto Sun using the user-friendly navigation. It didn't take him long before he saw something that alerted his attention and he enlarged the text for easier reading.

Yesterday a woman had been found dead in downtown Toronto. Then the report went on to say that the local health officers believed that an unusual illness, possibly an unknown fatal virus might be involved. This was the second possible case…a man had been found dead, the same way, two days ago. He was at first believed to be an average drunk sitting outside a corner store, with nothing to do and nowhere to go. The details were unclear…Though Warwick could enjoy unlimited access to the Toronto Sun online and other digital tools that newspaper provided, there was not much data known about the unusual deaths so far.

This immediately made him think of a horrendous event he had undergone at the time of the spreading of SARS in 2003 in Toronto, and the terrible ghettoization for the doctors who worked in hospitals, along with the many deaths that had occurred. Since the day when, upon returning home to Toronto on the 23rd of February, a woman had started to develop symptoms, and on March 5th, 2003 she had died of unrecognized SARS…after which things had quickly worsened. Transmission to a family member who was later admitted to a community hospital in downtown also started leading to a large nosocomial outbreak.

Those sad days, 44 people in Canada had eventually died from SARS, approximately 400 became ill, and 25,000 Toronto residents were placed in quarantine. As the only city outside of Asia that was affected significantly, the town received intense media coverage. He didn't want to have such bad recollections of those terrible times encroaching on his mind now, but this couldn't be helped...It happened every time he read about a virus in some newspaper, and this produced even more worries because he happened to know about these things that had taken place somewhere in Canada, more so because they occurred within the boundaries of his hometown, of course...

Warwick slowly had to use all the self-discipline he could muster to regain his composure. But he was well aware of the fact that such news alone had already made that morning look bleak, dark and dreary gray. 'Maybe fresh air will help...', the man thought, as he got off the TTC subway car and walked for a while along the underground "PATH" Walkway System before approaching an escalator and reaching the surface. Downtown always offered a good mix of office buildings, leafy residential streets, and shopping areas full of cafés, restaurants and stores. And then there was Lake Ontario, in the near distance of the lively harbor front. Sailing out into that expanse and around the three Toronto Islands always provided fine views of the city. Small sailboats, motorboats, and tours were always available from the moment the icy winter loosened her grip on the region.

Looking at the few trees he saw along the way and the color of the blue sky, he squinted into the sun, his hand protecting his eyes. The sun felt delightful after three days of rain, undoubtedly. Warwick considered that Toronto was certainly delightful during Spring, but he had always loved summer even more and they would be entering that season in a few weeks.

A very strange diversification of nearly five million residents drawn from more than one hundred ethnic groups, was how many people thought about Toronto. Others reputed it to be the true financial and commercial center of Canada, indeed. The city was also full of some important fine art museums, world-renowned art collections in fact and many modern galleries–and this was precisely the way Warwick preferred to think about this area. There were many famous people that had made this city great throughout history, in many fields of knowledge, science, industries and entertainment. And one of them, a friend of his named Antoine Laurier, had just passed away after a very long illness two days ago.

Having worked for about 10 years as the manager of the Toronto Dominion Centre, the well-known site consisting of five jet-black skyscrapers—whose southern tower displayed a strong collection of Inuit Art on two levels—he had eventually died, much to the overwhelming grief of his only daughter. His young wife, too, had passed away three years before, due to a road accident, an unexpected loss that the man had never truly recovered from over the course of time. During his lifetime of studies and travels due to his job, the never-tired Antoine had collected a lot of books, old tomes, and several documents coming from different historical periods. He also had been proud of his few sculptures of mythological beasts and strange beings as well as scenes from everyday life, not dissimilar from those on display at Toronto Dominion Centre he worked for. He had, in fact, installed an entire wing on his house where four walls had been completely turned into a sort of library full of wooden cabinets and dusty shelves all around. This was the reason why the daughter of his dead friend had thought of Warwick and had called him to her father's home. There were so many wonderful things in that part of the house that deserved a better destiny and she had reputed him to be the right person, given their friendship, to have a first look at it all—so they could decide about the best destination possible before most of them went to the public libraries where some manuscripts and papers were going to be sent soon—in accordance with Antoine's last will. And so Warwick had reached his dead friend's home again, where he had last visited one month before his death.

The house was in Lawrence Avenue West, near TTC Subway's Lawrence West Station, not far from Forest Hill Memorial Arena. You could easily take the Number 1 Line to get there without using your car, which was exactly the same as he did every weekday when he went downtown. As the man approached he noticed something he always did whenever he got to that two-story building: it needed painting, as least as far as he could see. Of course, Antoine had never cared a lot about how things appeared externally, although you could really say that the inside of his house was full of several well-preserved, richly-decorated and valuable objects from ancient times.

It was his dead friend's daughter, Francesca, who welcomed him in. Tall and slender, the same as her father, she was also blonde and brilliant, just like her dad. When the man looked into her dark eyes, he found at once the sadness of the recent loss although well concealed behind the young woman's good manners. She was 22 and she immediately asked him to join her for tea in the sitting room. Most of the house looked tidy, as usual, except those overcrowded shelves indeed.

"You never change…" a sympathetic Warwick told her.

"And you always have the same hairstyle that seems sculpted, you know, like something on my father's ancient statues…" the woman said, making fun of him with a smile.

Soon they started talking about traditional Eastern European traditions, occasionally straying into something more exotic. This had become the usual subject of their choice, since during the last months they had all started meeting together in that house for dinner, at least once every week, to discuss history, travels and research around the world. It was Francesca, anyway, who got back to the point and to the reason he was here today.

Warwick stood up and followed her to the wing of the house that he knew was completely full of books. He was being allowed to look through the tomes to pick out the ones he preferred most, for his personal library. "I'd like you have some of those, your choice of course, before the rest is allocated elsewhere—in accordance to my father's last will. Take your time, I'm at home for the whole day, select what you think might be the most valuable to you. Given your great friendship and everything you did for us, I am sure it's the best thing…"

"I see, and appreciate your gesture. I took the whole day off exactly for this purpose," the man nodded in a knowing look.

As she left him alone in the wide room that looked like a small museum, the man started looking around. Not that he didn't know yet most of the sculptures and the titles that were present inside, as he had been there many times before. If you paid attention to the cover of the books, you would immediately be aware that there were some high-priced and unusual tomes, of course, provided that you were already well-experienced in that field of knowledge.

At a certain point, among all the hundreds of texts, what attracted his interest was a well-worn book his eyes stumbled into by chance: it looked like an old travelogue, or a diary of some sort, undoubtedly. That book was a recent addition, surely, because he had never seen it in the library before. As he was curious about it, he went for that and put it on the wooden desk that was once the favorite of his deceased friend. The cover appeared to be in poor condition, and it seemed that it had gone through many troubles and adverse circumstances over the course of the time. How old was that manuscript? The answer came to him easily as he opened it and started reading inside. And he remained truly speechless: the author was Rear Admiral Sir William Edward Parry and it dated back to 1823.

What the hell!

All that made the man immediately think of earlier recounts of the explorations of the Arctic. As far as everyone knew, it was Frobisher and Davis—the first explorers who came from Britain in the 1570s and 1580s—to sail throughout the Arctic looking for a Northwest Passage to Alaska by boat. The hope was that Europeans could ship things from Europe to China without being forced to travel all the way around Africa. By 1600, the Inuit people began to meet French and English traders occasionally, though they caught many diseases from these first French and English visitors, which proved fatal to many people. Several European and Central Asian migrants came later to visit Inuit villages or settled there to show that the Canadians or the United States government ruled the Arctic. Of course this led to the Inuit people to begin to trade furs to European traders in exchange for steel knives and other tools, and for food.

Warwick sat at the wide wooden desk with both eyes studying the first pages of the text. Frobisher and Davis' explorations aside, there was also that famous English man that went to the Arctic: Rear Admiral Sir William Edward Parry. In 1827 he attempted one of the earliest expeditions to the North Pole, setting the record for human exploration farthest north that stood for decades, before being surpassed by Albert Hastings Markham in 1870s. The man was surprised to find in that collection of valuable documents an old travelogue like this one pertaining to such explorations which seemed to cover a portion of the expedition of the famous West side of Foxe Basin in 1821–23. What he found much more surprising was that, judging from the pages he had immediately read over, there were some details and descriptions of facts that had never been made available to the general public, at least apparently…

According to the old text, in April 1821 the Admiral had again left for the Arctic. Others with him were George Fisher, scientist, William Hooper, diarist, Lieutenants Crozier, James Clark Ross and Henry Parkyns Hoppner, then a Midshipman. The reader had, in fact, studied something before about Lieutenant Hoppner, in some history book. Experience from the previous voyage made many improvements possible. The two vessels under the Rear Admiral's command were nearly identical, and all the crewmen were issued better clothing than before.

The goal of the expedition was to find a passage near the northwest end of Hudson Bay. After working slowly through the ice of Hudson Strait the exploration headed directly west. Then the Admiral found himself in Repulse Bay, Nunavut, and when he re-checked he discovered that he was land-locked. He then mapped part of the coast and stopped at Winter Island at its southeast corner. From the first Inuit he met there he learned that further north the coast turned west.

In March and May two sledging expeditions were sent inland. Freed from the icy expanse in July he then went north where they waited for it to clear, but the covered sea did not clear. The ship was not finally freed until 8 August. Since it was late in the season, the Admiral sailed for home which he reached in mid-October 1823.

Warwick remembered he had read something, long ago, about the Journal of a Second Voyage by Sir William Edward Parry that appeared in 1824. He also knew that the Admiral had gotten a post rank shortly after returning. However, that didn't matter at the moment, as it seemed that there were some interesting, and never heard before, recounts of those two sledging expeditions that were sent inland across the iced surface in March and May 1823. *And what was written in those pages was really interesting, and valuable, by all means*!

As the man completely forgot about the time and kept reading those recounts that had provided the first-ever well-informed and well-documented account of the economic, social and religious life of the Inuit, his mind was really taken, eager to study Parry's writings, with pen and ink illustrations of Inuit everyday life. There were some things detailed here, and many peculiarities that seemed to have never been made publicly available before, or so Warwick thought anyway.

It was a short step from opening the book to immersing himself in having a deep read of most of the pages. What he found very interesting, and unheard of so far, was the description of the first journey some men sent from the ship of William Edward Parry had made using dog-sledging for transportation. Also a second journey was mentioned, though Warwick only found a few details about it. Anyway, those men had been sent ashore, following the order of the Rear Admiral himself, once the main vessel had been stopped by the icy sea that didn't allow a safe passage anymore. Certainly, further exploration by land was their purpose, as it appeared indicated at the start of the report handwritten as a diary.

The leader of the four men was Midshipman Frank Ackert and these were his words.

This region at the end of the Earth is certainly among the coldest, windiest, and most secluded places on the planet. Freezing has built the ice into thicker and thicker layers; wind and waves have certainly worked to break it up but for the moment and for the rest of this season that long unending expanse extends into the sea. There is no water from the warmer Pacific and Atlantic oceans that flows into this Arctic area, warming the deeps and air, or clearing ice from the coasts. A sort of silent, prolonged and, at times, worrying sleep wraps it all in its whitish cold hug. Also the animals, at least the very few we have spotted, seem to move and act more slowly. Starvation and death by exposure are constant threats. Certainly, to survive the contrasting seasons of these extreme areas, animals have to deeply change...

Wooden narrow runners like the four we make use of are best for hard ice, they 'float' easily over the surface of the ground without sinking in too far. All of the sleds are loaded with equipment, food, and a few other supplies, and have dogs to make them move, of course, working in a strict hierarchy under their leader in the sled team. They are strong and intelligent, but compulsive fighters, at times. Such animals can survive freezing temperatures as the snow surrounding them acts as an insulating blanket as they sleep, helping to keep them warm at night.

When you look at those lands and the wild or unpredictable climates that rule here, you might easily think that such regions will be never completely conquered by humans like us. However, we were very surprised when we arrived at a large outpost made up of typical small shelters where more than 40 locals seemed to live. With all that icy snow, it was difficult to imagine this was possible. On second thought, some Native peoples like this were known to have survived in the inhospitable Arctic regions for thousands of years.

Once we approached and got off our sleds, we were almost unable to keep standing up because of the intense cold and fierce winter winds. After introducing ourselves and trying to make ourselves understood, although it was really not easy, we explained what we were doing and why we were there. An exchange of gifts took place and we could easily tell that the valuable furs we received were of great value and of high quality. That society was organized in family groups, with each member having a specific job according to sex and age. They let us join them for lunch and gave us some traditional dishes that included sundried caribou sweetened with berry sauces or smoked and dried local fish. You couldn't imagine how you end up appreciating these offers, as food is scarce for most of the year in this area.

When we left that outpost, we headed for the westernmost part of the zone, and it didn't take us longer than one week before reaching another outpost manned by the locals. However, on this occasion things went very differently and we understood at once that we were not particularly welcomed here. At first, it was the old **angakoq**, *the man who was the repository of ancient* *traditions, that wore a very unusual fur headdress paired with the coat of quelled un-smoked leather, who displayed aggressive behavior and didn't smile at us not even one single time. Important individuals like that man fulfilled many roles, from doctor and meteorologist to performer of miracles. He, too, in the end offered us some food, as it was customary among such peoples, though it immediately seemed to us that he didn't like to have us around. And, in fact, something happened that soon changed everything.*

At that moment Warwick Kaehler briefly paused to scratch at his face, though he quickly started reading the remaining pages, as the manuscript looked really interesting.

We hadn't stopped there for long, just taking time to rest and eat something. Anyway, when we already were back to the open expanse on our sleds the bad luck fell upon us. Master-at-arms Kaur was the first to drop dead, all at once and unexpectedly, the same as a person might throw an old object of no use or a damaged pot on the ground, as he was still on sled going at full speed when he simply fell. I ordered the others to stop but it was just too late for him. As we looked at his corpse in surprise and examined his body, we found no evidences of the cause of his death, except a sort of whitish exanthema on his face. It was with great terror that we found, anyway, hidden inside his clothes, a bony object of abstract shapes, that seemed to have been carved by the local peoples. I didn't remember anyone giving him that and the other fellows couldn't recall anyone handing the object to the dead man as well.

*So, how had it gotten there? Was it possible that the strange **angakoq** had put it in the clothes of Kaur unseen? But why?*

Soon the hearsay of some sort of sorcery of the Natives of the Ice began spreading from mouth to mouth in the group. They were all obviously afraid, believing they may have all been cursed in some way and I didn't know how to calm them down. It was when the second man died, one day later, after a sudden fever, followed by the same very pale exanthema, that I knew I was losing control. It became hard to regain hold of the situation at that moment. From that day on, our exploration turned into a desperate race to go back to our vessel as soon as possible... a camp that lay somewhere lost on that presumably unending icy expanse. There we hoped we would find medicines, and a possible treatment for whatever this strange disease might be. We had to find something or we felt we would all die!

At that moment Warwick suddenly stopped reading. He thought again of the description of the exanthema reported in the diary as found on the body of the dead. He was an epidemiologist and a man of science, but that old report truly and deeply attracted his interest. *A sudden fever followed by deep exanthema…*That might be the symptoms of some known diseases of children like Roseola, for example, though it didn't cause death that way, certainly. And then there were those whitish manifestations that were not connected to Roseola at all.

Was the leader of that group speaking about an unknown deadly virus that had never been reported afterwards? He didn't remember ever having to read anything like that in the many volumes he had previously studied in university—and he thought of himself as a well experienced epidemiologist, for sure. *Some small infectious agents that could kill a man just after one day's duration?* He certainly wanted to know much more, so he kept reading until the end of that diary of Midshipman Frank Ackert.

As it was revealed in the next few pages, it seemed that another two men died before the sleds eventually returned to the vessel stuck on the icy plain. The handwriting was hard to read at times and became darker and more complicated in some parts.

Once they eventually arrived, all the tools, instrumentation, supplies and personal objects that those remaining men had had with them and that had come back from the exploration by land, along with their clothes, were put into two huge wooden shipping crates being in the cargo hold of the vessel, only meant to be opened and studied with the utmost care once back home. But they were never opened again; at least there was no report about it in the last pages of the book. Probably, no one dared to do so, or the academicians warned the British officers not to act so foolishly because of the great dangers involved in such an investigation, anyway. Anything was possible…*So, what became of those crates?*

For a moment he was caught in his ponderings. Then his mind came back to what he had previously read that same day, the newspaper article on his tablet…*what sort of exanthema had been reported on the body of the man, and the poor woman found dead, supposedly because of a virus?* He had to check the details more deeply. And that was exactly what he did once he opened his device again and got back to that electronic page.

And then he saw it. It was written as follows: 'Given the very pale exanthema found on the corpses, the local health officers suspected that an unusual illness, possibly an unknown deadly virus might be involved.' He had forgotten he had read that part, and now it all made him worry more and more. *Was it just a coincidence?* Actually, he didn't believe in coincidences…Maybe something else was in action, and it was better to have a look at that matter, much better earlier than late, finally he told himself.

"Do you know anything about this text?" he inquired of his dead friend's daughter once he reached her in the kitchen. "I don't remember seeing it before among the tomes of your father…"

"That text? Let me have a look.." she replied, eyeing the cover of the old travelogue. After she was handed the object, she immediately seemed to call something to her mind. "Now that I see it, I remember what it is. My father was really very excited when he first read it. That comes from the Toronto Dominion Gallery of Inuit and, if I correctly remember, it popped out or was discovered during the refurbishing of the lower level of the museum where some very old objects are held, waiting to be properly studied and catalogued. There was an acquaintance of his working there—someone who found the document and gave it to him so he could read it and evaluate its contents before any formal announcement was made...But my father died before completing what he was doing…"

Warwick exited the kitchen and then headed for the sitting room where he sat on the antique davenport that stood in the middle of the room. You could tell by the look on his face that he was clearly worried.

At that moment, Francesca approached him. "So, what's the matter? If you have questions about the book, you should probably go find that employee who originally brought that old book here. I remember that my father invited that man to our house and talked to him a few times before he began to study the text…Later on, father's acquaintance also thought that he had found some old wooden crates that were on a

British vessel in the 1800s that explored the Arctic. If I remember correctly, he maintained that those were sent to Canada from Great Britain in the 1960s, and just by chance happened to be in Toronto now…"

"What?" Warwick immediately asked, and then had the immediate thought, 'Did Antoine tell anyone else who worked at the museum about what he had read in the report written in the diary?'…the expression on his face immediately turned wild. *"What employee are you talking about?"*

***

It was already 2:00 PM when he left the house and took leave of Francesca. Before going to the museum, Warwick thought he had better go and have a look in person at the corpse of the woman that, according to the newspaper, was found dead yesterday. As an epidemiologist who was widely known in Ontario, he was sure that there would be no problem gaining access, if he just asked to study the body for the purpose connected to his job, of course. The truth was that he really wanted to see that for himself. If there was any sign of what the old diary he had read reported, maybe it was better to know as soon as possible…

He found someone that he had never seen before at the entrance of the edifice situated near the hospital itself. After giving him his credentials and explaining why he was there, he was asked a few questions about why he had interest in all that, and if he knew the dead person. Eventually, the epidemiologist talked the person at the door into letting him in.

The two men went into together and got to where the corpse was being prepared for burial. Warwick also found another man there whose dark clothes made it obvious that he was not a member of the medical team of the hospital. The tall Native-looking man glanced at him in silence, with an expression of interest on his face. His hair was jet black while his eyes appeared to be hazel, with both irises surrounded with a narrow but clearly marked ring. The size of his nose appeared slightly shorter at the base and wider than common among whites.

"Isn't it too quick to prepare the corpse for burial?" the epidemiologist asked the others in the room.

"There is no next of kin who could claim the body, we made the appropriate inquires." It was the Native fellow who answered his question, speaking in a low voice. Then he tried to cut the conversation short. "No need to wait any longer…"

"Well, if a virus was supposedly involved in the death of the woman, as it was reported on the newspapers, shouldn't the body be kept in an appropriate wing of the hospital for a deeper investigation?" Warwick stared at the other and said in a doubtful tone.

"We already did everything that was called for by protocol," was the reply he got.

The epidemiologist's heart began to beat faster. He didn't like that. He needed to keep very calm.

"If we can be of any help…" added the man who had let him in.

"I'd like to have a look at the documents you have here at the hospital with all the details about the dead woman," Warwick inquired of him. He only had to wait for a moment before he was handed what he had requested.

He thoroughly read the papers and found that the news he had seen on the Toronto Sun was correct. That sort of whitish exanthema on her face was unknown, but it was reputed to be irrelevant: it was her heart stopping unexpectedly that had caused the death.

It seemed to him that these people had hurriedly jumped to that conclusion. As there was nothing else he could discover or do about the situation, the man thought it would be better if he just left. He still had to get to the museum and talk to that employee Francesca had told him about.

He felt the deep silent eyes of the Native following him to the exit of the room.

***

It was already 4:00 PM when Warwick got past the general admittance door of the Toronto Dominion Gallery of Inuit Art on Wellington Street West. He still felt ill at ease about what had taken place while studying the corpse, and those two individuals that he had met there didn't dissipate his doubts; on the contrary, they had made the situation even more upsetting…

At the reception desk he sent for Mr. Balaguer Lanco, while introducing himself as a friend of Antoine Laurier, the former manager of the Toronto Dominion Centre itself. As he was waiting for him to come, something really unexpected happened.

There was a young dark-haired employee who was attending to his duties at the main entrance, as he probably did every day. Then, a moment later, the man seemed to stumble into something, though there was nothing on the floor that might impede his walk, and felt strange, weak. The epidemiologist just had the time to turn his eyes to him that the young employee simply dropped dead in front of him.

Screams started erupting in the hall as the few tourists present looked at the scene, and it was at that point that Warwick spotted another slender long-haired man not far from the corpse, who was exiting the area, trying to get to the entrance. The epidemiologist didn't know how, but - regardless of all that was happening inside the lobby—he was able to have a look at the name on his plastic pass with the credentials dangling from his neck. He read Balaguer Lanco which indicated that he was probably the employee he had come to interview. Without thinking, Warwick shouted out his name. "Hey. Mr. Balaguer Lanco, would you please come here? I have some questions for you…"

What the other did really surprised him. The man started running away, as if he had seen a monster or a policeman. His actions really worried the epidemiologist more and more. Not less, actually, than the voices he heard coming from the place where the corpse was, as people started saying: "Look at his face! He looks like the dead woman they talked about in the newspaper!"

This fact prevented the man from keeping his eyes on the running employee who was already at the exit door. And so he heard, though he didn't see, the shot that was fired outside, which made Balaguer Lanco immediately stop before disappearing into the streets nearby.

What followed next was another great surprise to poor Warwick. That was becoming a day full of unexpected situations, as he figured out as soon as some agents in dark suit surrounded the employee, with the same tall Native man from earlier that day walking behind them.

***

Over the course of the interrogation, the Native agent and another blonde-haired man from his team listened to what Warwick had to tell them. They took notice of every single word the epidemiologist said, even the more improbable or strange ones they heard. So, the two found out about the old travelogue discovered in Antoine Laurier's house and the diary about the Arctic exploration in 1800s, and what Warwick thought about it all.

The news the TV channels and the internet sites said that it seemed that the death of the employee at the museum had been caused by Balaguer Lanco himself. It was reported Balaguer held a resentment because the other man had stolen his lover—and this fact had started worrying him, driving him to distraction, making him crazy, both at work and off duty. Until he had made his move.

It was not clear, nor was revealed, how Lanco had committed the murder, and not many details were given about that part of what had happened. But there was no one else who was apprehended and brought to the police for further interrogation that day. So, many doubts still remained. But the epidemiologist was sure enough about what had happened there. "I know what it is…" Warwick told himself, although he doubted that anyone would ever believe him.

The tall Native agent named Eohane looked at the middle-aged epidemiologist as he left the room and moved away from the security office. They had been after him since the moment he had left them, once the epidemiologist had seen the corpse, obviously.

Eohane thought it would be better to talk to Warwick later, in secret. If what Warwick had said was true, maybe they would finally find the whereabouts of other documents pertaining to this case, that important book they had been searching for all these years. And he wanted to secure that book—the sooner the better.

Indeed, the Native man knew something else that the epidemiologist certainly could not imagine. After that first expedition by sleds over the icy expanse at the time of Rear Admiral Perry, there had been a second expedition, following the return of the few surviving crewmembers who had come back to the vessel. But that part was not in the travelogue nor in the lost diary that Warwick Kaehler had found and read.

The other part of the report about the second dog-sledging expedition, with a prolog that summed up what had occurred before, had long been kept, in secret, by the CSIS (Canadian Security Intelligence Service). The second diary recounted the events that took place during the retaliatory action ordered by Rear Admiral Perry. He had ordered them to return to the place where the suspicious **angakoq**—who was in reality a practitioner of dark arts, an **Ilisitsoq**, calling down misfortune on his enemies—lived so they could discover what he had done, by all means.

Actually, those men had reacted brutally, making the Native confess by force. It was revealed in the report that it was the Inuit himself who had set all that into motion so that the Westerners would become ill and die. Actually, it seemed that the tribe of that angakoq had always held a deep resentment against foreign invaders who, since the previous centuries, had started reaching the icy plains where they lived, causing many deaths and disasters due to the unknown illnesses they brought, willingly or unwillingly. The diseases that the Europeans brought with them had spread, killing thousands of their people...A ruin to their tribe, undoubtedly.

So, that old man had conceived a weapon created using sorcery, to get rid of them and send a clear message, *don't come back here again!* There was an indication of everything that had happened in the second diary—and the Canadians had kept that book at the headquarters to study further. But no one on earth would have ever known of it here, which was the same about so many other ancient objects of power that were kept under surveillance, or held in safe places nowadays.

Their special team had been activated as soon as his superiors had been told about the discovery of the first dead body in downtown Toronto, the homeless man, and of the second corpse of the woman. Within his team, they called such circumstances as **unk-unk**, that meant a problem that had not been and could not have been imagined or anticipated, or a series of inexplicable events. The strange symptoms visible on both of them made them realize this was something very different from a commonly known virus. This, along with the news they had received about two very old wooden crates dating back to the 1800s that seemed to have been inadvertently damaged during the refurbishing while on the way to Toronto Dominion Gallery of Inuit Art, releasing part of their contents outside... This unfortunate accident had made everything else go into motion. Someone might have taken something or put it in a non-secure location.

At that point, other worries wrapped the mind of the Native agent sent to the place. He had studied the bodies and had concluded there was evidence that the cause of death of the victims was connected to the old sorcery of the Peoples of the Ices. However, what had surprised him even more was that, contrary to what he thought, there was nothing like a bony object of abstract shapes carved long ago, found in the clothes of the first corpse. Such was the traditional means that was once used to call to our reality **tupilaq**, the souls of the underworld, **Adlivum**, the usual home of the wicked dead, and cause illness and diseases. Therefore, whoever had found that thing somewhere and had been able to play on its deadly use, after he had completed what he wanted, eventually had removed the object. *Was the first victim's death just a test to prove the old curse was still truly effective? Might that individual make use of such thing again in the near future?*

Then, the case had turned to another direction. Probably, the first victim, the homeless man, had just been a first try, and the woman, the second victim, was the true target. But it had not ended there, because after causing that death by putting the curse on her the delinquent had removed the bony object from her clothes. *So, the bad news was not yet over...*

Maybe another victim like those had to be expected soon...

By luck, they had put all the details together and had finally acted on time. At least, *almost on time...*

Once the CSIS had discovered who that dead woman was, and what her connection was with both Lanco, a previous lover of hers, and her last partner - who was the museum employee who had lastly died so unnaturally - they had come in a hurry. Unfortunately it had not been quick enough to prevent the revenge seeking Lanco from putting the same curse on his last ill-fated victim...But they had arrested him, once and for all, stopping that man before he could continue making use of that object which had caused such bloody deaths.

Eohane found himself thinking about what might have happened, long ago, if his ancient people would have turned to using such a terrible thing over and over; possibly they would have been able to force the strangers that came to explore and settle their icy lands to stop their conquest of the North. In any case, now that object was in the secure hands of the CSIS, as duty required. One day that magical artifact might prove useful for their government, as a weapon, the Native agent, considered. *One day or another…*

It was now time to bring back that old thing, along with the other equipment of those forgotten expeditions, to the wooden crates they had come out from. Waiting for a better moment in the future…maybe, or maybe not, who knows, he concluded with a smile.

Only time would tell…

David M. Simon's Shopping List

1 lb. ground sirloin
1 lb. spicy Italian sausage
Onions and garlic
4 cans stewed tomatoes
1 can tomato sauce
1 can kidney beans
1 loaf crusty sourdough bread
Six-pack, Great Lakes Brewing Co. 73 Kolsch beer
—Yes, I'm making chili

Your Heart Shall Hunger
David M. Simon

Owen Wilton was having a dandy Valentine's Day.

Owen and his current hot-and-heavy, a sweet young redhead named Serena, were on the way back to his place after lobster and champagne with all the trimmings at the swankiest place in town. Owen was past thirty, but his youthful, choirboy-with-a-killer's-smile good looks were fully intact. He was a serial dater who fell in love with alarming regularity. Serena, though, maybe she was the one. They had been together for nearly three months, and Owen had felt no urge to stray. They were taking a shortcut along the valley parkway, the trees still bare, a full moon shining overhead. Owen was enjoying the happy haze of a champagne buzz, Serena cozied up to his shoulder, eyes closed, one hand tracing lazy figure eights on his thigh.

When that same hand casually grazed his crotch, Owen jumped and hit his head on the car ceiling. That's when it happened.

The heavy thud was unmistakable; they had hit something. Owen stomped the breaks harder than he should have, fishtailing the back tires. When the car shuddered to a stop, Owen was close to sober and scared half to death. *Please*, he silently prayed, *let it be a deer or a dog. Anything but a person.*

Owen patted his own chest, making sure that he was still in one piece, then glanced over at Serena. She had gone paste white. Serena scooted across the seat and wrapped herself around him. Owen pried her hands from his neck and kissed her forehead. "Stay here, baby, I'll go check it out," he said, with more confidence that he felt. He left the headlights on and exited the car.

There was something in the brush by the side of the road, ten feet from the car. It was right in the path of the halogens, but he was still having trouble making it out. Heaped there in its own murky pool of shadow, it seemed to repel light. Owen shook his head, desperately trying to clear the remaining fog, and approached.

"Serena, come here! You gotta see this!" he yelled from where he kneeled next to whatever it was. She made her way on legs that would barely support her, avoiding even a peek at whatever it was until she was securely behind Owen. Then she glanced down and stifled a scream; it came out more like a high-pitched squeak.

The thing was shaped like a large human baby, with an oversized head and short, chubby limbs. It was bald and naked, skin a smooth, dark walnut brown, the facial features soft and unformed. There was nothing baby-like about its genitals. Even soft, its penis was a foot long. Two leathery wings sprouted from knots of muscle at its shoulder blades. They were more like bat than bird wings, covered in coarse, bristly feathers; in any event they did not look big enough to support the creature in flight.

"Shit, what is it?" Serena managed to get out. "Is it dead? What the fuck is it?"

"I have no idea," Owen said in answer to both questions. He reached out and poked it in the arm. When nothing happened he lifted up one arm a few inches and let it drop. The skin was curiously soft, almost velvety. Owen felt a surprising urge to touch it again. He realized with embarrassment that he had gotten an erection. "I think it's de—"

The creature's other hand shot out with shocking speed and wrapped pudgy fingers around Owens's wrist. He yelped in pain, and Serena screamed. Its eyes opened wide, showing milky white orbs with no pupils. As Owen struggled to free himself, it spoke in a dry, feathery voice, like sandpaper on metal. "Your heart shall hunger for that which you hold dear." The fingers clamped down even tighter, then released. Owen crab-walked blindly away as fast as he could. He hit Serena's legs, and they went down in a tangle of limbs.

Owen and Serena got shakily to their feet and moved even further away from it. "I think it's really dead now," Owen said. "Let's get the hell out of here." They ran back to the car, giving the creature a wide berth. Owen did a hard U-turn, spitting gravel, and headed back the way they had come.

***

Owen crawled into bed next to Serena, leaving the lights on as she had requested. Serena had been nearly hysterical at the time of the incident. Now, after a couple of hours, it all seemed like a bad dream. Owen, on the other hand, was weirdly jazzed by the whole experience. "Man, that was something else," he said as Serena snuggled against him. "What a way to spend Valentine's Day!" He smiled at her until he received a small smile in return. "I have a confession to make," he said. "When I touched that...whatever it was, I got a hard-on like you wouldn't believe. And it wasn't some kind of gay thing, either. There was this, I don't know, a sex vibe. It was amazing."

Serena looked at Owen with a playful pout. "So," she said, "some monster with a big dick gets you more excited than me. We'll see about that." She reached down and found him already hard. "Mmm, I hope this is because of me..."

Owen answered her with a deep, lingering kiss. "Happy Valentine's Day, Serena," he whispered into her mouth as he pulled her on top of him. "What was that he said? 'Your heart shall hunger for that which you hold dear.' Baby, he was right. You're the only thing my heart hungers for." Owen cupped her ass with his hands and maneuvered her into position, then gently slid her down onto his cock. Serena gasped and arched her back, grinding, pushing him into her as deep as possible.

"I hope your heart can handle this," she said with a wicked grin. Serena braced her hands on his chest, rolling and snapping her hips, riding him hard. Owen closed his eyes and lost himself in the rhythm of flesh slapping on flesh, matching her thrust for thrust.

Serena shrieked. Owens's first thought was, *she never came like this before. I'm the man!* In the second it took him to realize that the keening wail he was hearing had nothing to do with pleasure, a burning pain sunk into his chest.

Owen opened his eyes and thought he had gone insane. His chest had ripped apart down the middle, skin and meat flapped open like he was on an autopsy table. As he watched, his ribcage split with a sharp crack and spread wide. Inside Owens's chest, his beating heart tore almost in two, and several rows of sharp, crooked teeth appeared in the gaping red hole.

Serena had reared back, still impaled on his cock. As she tried to push off, Owen found himself grasping her wrists tightly, pulling her toward him. Serena sobbed and begged him to stop, but he could no longer hear her. All that mattered was the hunger. When her fingers were in reach of Owens's heart, it clamped down, the teeth biting deep.

As his heart worked its way up her arms, crunching bone, pulping tissue, Owen continued to fuck Serena, steady as a piston. Blood splashed the walls, saturated the bedding. Owen fed the hunger, drawing Serena down, pulling her toward his ravenous heartmouth.

Serena's arms were gone. Owen knitted his fingers behind her head and angled her face into his yawning chest cavity. Her incoherent babbling abruptly stopped as her face was eaten, the skin stripped away, the bones splintered. Serena's skull cracked with a sound like breaking porcelain.

Owen pulled more of her body to him and his cock popped out. It didn't matter; Owen fucked air, his hips bucking. Serena's midsection took a long time to consume, but Owen was patient, folding down ribs, scooping in wayward entrails. As Serena's heart passed through, an intense wave of love washed over him and he came hard, spurting into the air. After that it was more workmanlike, first one leg, then the other. When Serena was completely gone, Owen curled up in the pool of blood and gore that his bed had become and he went to sleep.

***

Owen woke up a little before noon, feeling surprisingly rested. His chest had knitted itself back together, leaving behind a dull ache but no visible sign. Owen cleaned up, scrubbing down the walls and headboard, tossing the bedding into a garbage bag. He gave up on the bed itself, settling for flipping the mattress over. He took a long, hot shower.

The dull ache in his chest intensified, began to throb insistently, and Owen made peace with the reality of his situation. He dug around at the back of his sock drawer and came up with a small black leather address book. He paged through thoughtfully, then dialed the phone.

"Maria? Hi, it's Owen. Yeah. I've been thinking about you. Can we get together? Maybe coffee? Or even better, how about a bite to eat?"

Angela Thornton's Shopping List

Wet rock 'for the sharpening of the Scythe.'
New skin suit for the congregation of humans
Bauble 'to store the human element'
Witches dying breath
Icor of hell toad
Virgins first blood 'better than the last.'
A sip of the ethereal 'for the dying time.'
Mandrake
Salt
Red brick dust
Web cask from a widow of black
Chalk
Wax
Heart of rooster
Eldritch eye of a prince
Rope

Apportens Mortis Inc.
Alizure Indigo

The summer night zephyr blows outside sending the sweet scent of the nocturnal flora through the air. The soft amber glow of candles meant to keep spirits at bay, emanates from the windows of the houses as the occupants slumber, sets a peaceful ambiance. This ritual of theirs, serves only to stroke my curiosity. With no distractions, I can go about my business as I wish. This is *my* time.

Imagination is much more prevalent in the darkness. The witching hour as it is coined, allows spirits the time to play with the dreamers mind. And, in the recesses of the human conscious, the darkness casts its own illusions.

This night is sublime. I can shift and strew things about, even wail and lament without a single stir, although I find myself somewhat a voyeur. I must admit, it is a curiosity of mine. Just why is it that humans sleep so sound? Is it a preparation for death? It would seem that all the noise I make, would wake them. But no, they sleep as though they were lifeless. Never arising to see me or hear me. The soft rhythm of breath and heartbeat never changes. It is all very perplexing sometimes.

Some homes I visit, there are so called sensitives that can *sense* me, but never unless *I* wish it. However, since you sought me out, I thought I would oblige, seeing as you *feel* this is your domain.

Be that as it may, the sooner you realize this is a mistake, the better you shall be. After all, did I not enter your home unsuspected? The candles meant for protection did nothing to hinder my entrance. I watched as you prepared yourself before I allowed you to see me. You were fearful to see me, yet your curiosity got the better of you. Thus, here I sit before you, allowing you to see me, hear me, all to satisfy your yearning for knowledge of things best left alone. You are like the others, fearful of things you do not understand, yet you *think* you are the master of your own reality.

You know, people float along in their lives as if they are the center of the universe. Little do they know they are but fleas on the dog's back, until the time comes that they must vacate their temporary occupancy.

Ah, but sometimes I do get lonely, wishing for some kind of interaction. Some kind of acknowledgement, something, anything at all. I suppose this is why I converse with you now. So, how do I choose who to take and who to pass over you ask? Simple enough I suppose, I have a list, yes; I said list. An order from my employers, *they* choose who leaves this plane, who lingers, also when and how. It is my job nothing more, nothing less, and I do it without *emotion*. For to have emotion is to falter. Humanity is weak, sick and in my opinion, could use a complete do over. I loathe, did you hear me?! Pay attention! Why are you looking away? I *said*, I loathe what you humans have become. And believe me, I have seen a lot of things in my years doing this job. Most human beings are manipulative, sarcastic, disillusioned creatures that feel only for themselves and nothing more.

Nothing is an issue unless it happens to them on a personal level, then and only then is it important. They take and give nothing back. They demand to be taken care of as if it's their right and nothing else in the universe matters. Well, I prove that sentiment *wrong*, every *minute*, every *hour* of every *day*.

Oh yes, I almost forgot. I do have a partner of sorts. He, I say he, however *he* is neither male nor female. He just...*Is*. If that makes any sense to you at all. You must understand we are in everything, and everything is in us, yes we are all connected. My partner carries the taken ones to whichever plane to wait for the next step. Good Lord, I've rambled on enough. I do get long winded, however you wanted to know some about myself and what I do, so I obliged your curiosity.

Hm? What was that? I am sorry; I missed the question. Ah, you want to know about specifics and such. Well for example, if they chose you, I would come to collect you. Then my partner would check your essence to see how you matched with his orders. Then off you go, it is all very simple. What do we look like you ask? Well, it's all relative to the person. We can be a gentle image or a terrifying creature, like some horror movie so many of you like to watch. However, most of the time I choose a more docile form, something from a fond memory, or a loved one. It's more soothing for those that will not have to sit in purgatory, so to speak.

My partner chooses something more ominous, perhaps a black figure, with a long coat and boots with eyes of fire. Sometimes he dons a hat, sometimes not, he is a touch more wicked than I. He takes great pleasure in putting horrors into the minds and hearts, of those that are not worthy of a peaceful departure. It is simple; we are just as you see here; we are Apportens Mortis Incorporated.

I can see you have many questions. I suppose that I should have conveyed my point in a more articulate manner. You see, you are about to embark on an incredible journey. One that many have traveled. May you return? No. I am sorry but you may never return to this plane as you are now, I suppose your spirit may after a time.

Sigh. Oh, don't do that. Don't try to stall, or bargain with me. Would I allow you to get your affairs in order? No, the warning signs were evident for some time. *You* chose not to heed them, those concealed blood filled phlegm coughs into your pillow at night, the garbled labored breath. All the signs, even confirmation from your physician. However, I do enjoy this game, I will let you run for a while, then we must be on our way. Remember, I am always behind, in front, and beside you. There is no hiding, no place on earth you can travel to get away from your fate. It is your time. It says so right here on your chart, there is no mistake. We. Do not. Make. Mistakes. Simple as that.

Groan, oh good Lord, you're going to try to run. Oh well, go ahead, entertain the idea that you can escape, I'll wait.

While I enjoy the present game watching my quarry scamper about, the voice of my employer filled my being, like an ominous symphony of damnation. The form filled the corner of the room blocking out what little light was there, enveloping me in the murky shadow. I could not move, all I could do was listen to its voice.

"Why do you falter, Anaiel? We are weary of these games you play with the human elements. Do you have possession of the life essence? Time is fleeting, the fabric for new life will be set out of kilter. So, lest you wish for your own to be extinguished, you will gather the human element posthaste. There are many who would gladly take your place." Zuriel said.

"Yes, right away. I will correct my aberration, forgive my negligence." I reply.

The perilous essence lifted releasing its foreboding weight from my form, and I could move once again. Yet, the visceral voice echoed around me.

"See that you do, Anaiel, else I will have to *personally*, get involved. The essence void must be filled. Either by the human you are to collect, or by your own." Zuriels' voice echos as his spirit departs from my presence.

I scour the house for my quarry, detecting each place where they had hidden then moved. It was as if looking at an iridescent inkblot along the places they had been. Their thoughts like eidolons scream at me, filling my mind with their horrors. Being accustomed to this, I felt nothing, after all many multitudes of people succumbed after various attempts to fend me off yet they failed.

You may as well show yourself. End this with some dignity, you are just prolonging the inevitable.

Time is of the essence, I grow tired of this game we play, I do have other clients, and my patience grows short. The reflection in a mirror hanging on the wall catches my attention. It hung crooked adjacent to a closet which seemed to be a perfect hiding place for the human.

Encroaching closer, I walk through the closet door to find my quarry. The human huddled upon the floor quivering, crying, trying to conceal hacking blood filled coughs and sobs. Reaching down to grasp the glowing essence of their soul, I see their eye-shine. Curious, I take a step backward. Inspecting my prize, I failed to notice they had taken hold of my vestments, with an iron grip it entwines us. It is futile for me to escape. As it twists and turns tightening its grip, its voice envelops me.

"*You* hunted me after I pleaded for a reprieve, you offered me none. Now, here you are as a fly in the spider's web. *You* chose to toy with me. *You* ignored the signs, the swiftness of my movements, the absence of a human element. *You* chose to impart upon me your secrets which were not yours to tell. And so, you the hunter hath become the *hunted*. Your employers have found your essence past its usefulness, therefore sent you to me. How else could you explain your partner's absence?" The creature says. Its eyes bright in the darkness as its obsidian form seeps more through the human husk.

More tendrils of shadowy tentacles stretched forward from its back, seeking an anchor to holdfast upon. Its breathless laughter emanating from its human shell. I find myself floating in the midst of its obsidian void. It spoke to me as it twisted itself around my being, filling every inch of my core, toying with me in its iron grip as a cat toys with a mouse.

"What is the meaning of this? Do you not know who I am? How dare your insolence!" I exclaim. I swirl in the depths of its blackness, tumbling in a spiral until I find myself with the creature once more in the closet.

"It is simple enough, Zuriel cast me into the humans' husk. It seems your folly to toy with the human elements has finally caught up with you, Anaiel, and now, your penance is due. You shall take my place beneath Apportens Mortis, and I shall walk reborn among the ethereal agents. It is *my* time for rebirth, you have chosen to waste your gift. I shall not be so foolish." The creature said. Its voice fell upon me, like an ominous storm cloud. Within the creature's dead gaze, I struggle with all my being to free myself of this fate.

"There is no need to struggle, your essence string has been severed. You tempted the weavers one-to-many times. Zuriel has deemed you terminated, effective *immediately*." The creature said. Its words echoed throughout my being, like a thick mire devouring everything in its path with lethal precision.

I am unable to reply, as my essence is drained from me, I can no longer resist the creatures' death grip upon me. The creature entwines itself around me tighter. I used to collect the human element for the ages. Now, I am a mere memory, a thought upon the cosmic zephyr. The essence restored in the web weave of the ether, I now reside in purgatory. I await my rebirth, waiting for the mishap of another associate so I may exchange places. I had been foolish, next time I will not falter. The creature lives reborn in my stead as I wait in its dark abode beneath Apportens Mortis Incorporated.

Other HellBound Books Titles
Available at: www.hellboundbookspublishing.com

Made in Britain

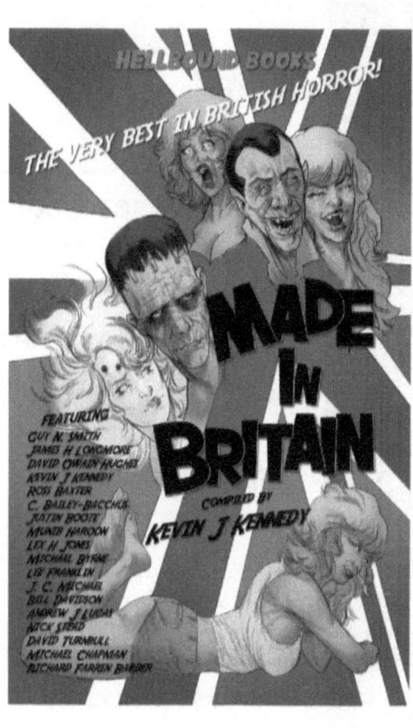

There is something quite special about this fine collection of tales of terror from the Sceptered Isle, each and every one crafted in the dead of the night by twisted, fevered minds, who have brought crawling and slithering to life the darkest denizens of the blackest shadows to terrify those brave souls amongst you who are brave enough to read...

For your delectation, Dear Reader, we have assembled together between these illustrious covers an array of the finest British authors writing today:

Guy N. Smith, James H Longmore, David Owain Hughes, Kevin J Kennedy, Ross Baxter, C. Bailey-Bacchus, Justin Boote, Munib Haroon, Lex H Jones, Michael Byrne, Lee Franklin, J. C. Michael, Bill Davidson, Andrew J Lucas, Nick Stead, David Turnbull, Michael Chapman, Richard Farren Barber

ROAD KILL: TEXAS HORROR BY TEXAS WRITERS - VOL 3

Everything is bigger in Texas - including the horror!

A Piney woods meth dealer clones Adolph Hitler. A nightmare exorcist meets an inexorable fined. An eyeball collector gets collected. The apparition of a lynching victim tracks down his executioners. A Texas lawman is undone by shades of his past. A Baphomet recruits converts as a local summer camp.

The tales of the baker's dozen who appear in this anthology demonstrate why everything is scarier in Texas…

Including tales of terror from

Jeremy Hepler

Madison Estes

Bret McCormick

James H Longmore

ER Bills

Shawna Borman

And many more...

I'll Come Back to Get You

In the midst of a Manhattan heat wave, Adel Daniels' husband doesn't return home from work. A few days later, she receives a Polaroid of him; on the bottom of the photograph are the words I'll Come Back to Get You, on the back is written their six-year-old son's name - is he the ransom, or the kidnapper's next target?

Assistant Chief Detective Steve Willards heads up the task force assigned to the case, along with FBI Profiler Gail Skillman. They quickly learn that every person involved has a secret, and the truth is only as reliable as memory.

A week later, Penny Spencer's husband Graham, doesn't return from work and she receives a Polaroid of her husband - on the bottom of the photo is written, One, Two, Don't Be Blue, I'll Come Back to Get You; their son's name is written on the back.

Before Willards and Skillman can unravel the motivation of the twisted kidnapper, one person is murdered, a third adult is taken, and one of the children is abducted.

But, it isn't until an assault is made on the FBI profiler that the final pieces fall into place; but even then it may be too late for those who have read the words - I'll Come Back to Get You.

Mother Legs

A giant, telepathic spider befriends a small boy, seeing the world through his eyes, with murderous intent... When Blake Turner's addict mother disappears in rural Canada, he assumes she's simply relapsed. But, when his search for her uncovers evidence of a terrifying monster and the sinister conspiracy to hide its existence, he must decide just how far he is willing to go to protect his loved ones. With only a depressed park ranger and a local reporter to aid him, Blake delves deeper into the mystery to discover what the creature is, and why it wants to start a family.

Schlock! Horror!

An anthology of short stories based upon/inspired by

and in loving homage to all of those great gorefest movies and books of the 1980's (not necessarily base in that era, although some do ride that wave of nostalgia!), the golden age when horror well and truly came kicking, screaming and spraying blood, gore & body parts out from the shadows... This exemplary 80's themed/inspired tales of terror has been adjudicated and compiled by one Mr Bret McCormick, himself a writer, producer and director of many a schlock classic, including *Bio-Tech Warrior*, *Time Tracers*, *The Abomination*, *Ozone: The Attack of the Redneck Mutants* and the inimitable *Repligator*.

Featuring stories from: Todd Sullivan, Timothy C Hobbs, Mark Thomas, Andrew Post, James B. Pepe, Thomas Vaughn, Edward Karpp, Jaap Boekestein, Lisa Alfano, L. C. Holt, John Adam Gosham, Brandon Cracraft, M. Earl Smith, Sarah Cannavo, James Gardner, Bret McCormick, and James H. Longmore.

An Unholy Trinity
**3 TERRIFYING NOVELLAS, 3 SUPERLATIVE
AUTHORS, 1 BIG, FAT, JUICY BOOK!**

ENÛMA ELIŠ (When on High) – Terry Grimwood.
The Babylonian Creation story is a tale of monsters and cataclysmic wars. An epic saga dominated by the gods Tiamat and Mardak, bitter rivals who battle for supremacy over
the unformed universe. It is a story replete with Minotaurs and scorpion men, dragons and monstrous blood-sucking demons.
A myth, a fantasy...
But when a traumatized ex-soldier rescues a young woman, washed up and barely alive on the shore of a sleepy English seaside town, the fragile borders between myth and reality begin to crumble and gods and their legions wake from their long-slumber.

THE REMNANT - C. Bailey-Bacchus
When fifteen-year-old Bianca Baker is blinded by rage and hatred, her inner demons take control and turn an ordinary school trip into a horrific tragedy. Witnesses to

her violent act, succumb to Bianca's aggression and agree to say events were a terrible accident. Sixteen years later, those involved find the past clawing its way from the shadows to haunt them, and this time there is no way it will stay buried.

ALICE IN HORRORLAND - Vanessa Hawkins
Alice is an 11 year old orphan living within the veins of industrial England. When she meets a mysterious gentleman with the power to turn into a white rabbit, she finds herself tumbling down a manhole into Horrorland. Here the creatures are strange and uncanny, lost in a revolution of madness. Drug addicted Caterpillars, grinning cats and homicidal Mad Hatters gambol around Alice like blood-drunk mosquitoes. However, at the center of it all is the Queen of Hearts: said to have given up her own a long time ago…
Horrorland used to be so wonderful… Can Alice make it so again?

HellBound Books Publishing

**A HellBound Books LLC
Publication**

http://www.hellboundbookspublishing.com

Printed in the United States of America